Absolute Zero

Books by Chuck Logan

Hunter's Moon
The Price of Blood
The Big Law

Chuck Logan

Absolute Zero

HarperCollins*Publishers*

HarperCollins books may be purchased for educational, business, or sales promotional use. For information, please write: Special Markets Department, HarperCollins Publishers Inc., 10 East 53rd Street, New York, NY 10022.

FIRST EDITION

Designed by Nancy B. Field

Library of Congress Cataloging-in-Publication Data

Logan, Chuck.
  Absolute zero / Chuck Logan.—1st ed.
    p. cm.
  ISBN 0-06-018572-4
    1. Triangles (Interpersonal relations)—Fiction. 2. Ex–police officers—Fiction. 3. Minnesota—Fiction. I. Title.

PS3562.O4453 A64   2001
813'.54—dc21
                                                  2001024962

01 02 03 04 05 10 9 8 7 6 5 4 3 2 1

For Aunt Betty and Aunt Louise, the Siegrist twins

absolute zero: *Physics.* The temperature at which substances possess minimal energy, equal to –273.15 degrees C or –459.67 degrees F.

—*The American Heritage Dictionary of the English Language*

Absolute Zero

Prologue

The beep-beep-beep *was a reassuring sound that brought him back like the sing-along bouncing ball; if he were safe at home the sound might be the soft cricket in the clothes dryer downstairs signaling that the load was through. If only life had not speeded up . . .*

But it had, and now they'd put the pain on mute, along with everything else—the up, the down, the light—and they'd set him adrift in the dark with nothing but the beep. So he tried to scan along but the rhythm kept slipping away. Which figured, because he'd been thrown out of high school band—alto sax—on account of he couldn't keep the beat.

Then he coughed and sparks lit up a corner of his mind, enough to get him oriented and he knew that he was waking up, and he understood that the dogged beep was the pulse of his heart hooked to a machine.

Which meant he was still here.

He was alive and laid out flat on his back with his eyes shut tight and he didn't have the strength to open them, so he'd just lay back for now, all alone in the dark, waiting for the lights to come up.

Surfacing, he flashed on chemical nondreams and artificial sleep. His lips were gummed together, and when he parted them a parched numbness puffed his mouth and his throat and it felt like he'd been French-kissed by the creature in Sigourney Weaver's

Alien. *Then a sharp electric pincer prodded his right wrist four times—*jit-jit-jit-jit—*and made his fingers jump.*

Now he was being moved because he felt the stale hospital air slide over his face, and he heard splashes of sound like underwater voices that became clearer until distinct words spilled down and trickled on his face.

"Train of four," *the first female voice said.*

"Doesn't that hurt now that he's coming around?" *a second female voice asked.*

"This guy, with his neck; I want to make sure he's back before we medicate for pain."

Then they splashed away and there was more motion and then they came back.

"He's breathing well, sats are good, rhythm is good."

"Okay, let's rouse him, get him to raise his head, squeeze a finger, swallow. And wait for the eyelids; the littlest muscles are always the last to come back. Who's got the Narc keys?"

"Got them right here. I've got everything today."

"Sign out twenty-five milligrams of Demerol and give it IV."

The voices faded, the shapes acquired edges, then fluttered away, and tile-lined the walls and was dotted with stainless steel, and it all shimmered in and out of focus. Latex fingers carried a slender plastic syringe with green markings across his vision. A fluorescent light hovered overhead, and from its center materialized the face of a blue-gowned young woman with white-blond hair. She had serious gray eyes and copper freckles on her cheeks and she smiled.

He enjoyed the colors of her face and her hair. He found them vital, feline. He thought: a happy lynx.

"Hello there," *said the happy lynx.* "Can you squeeze my finger?"

He squeezed the cool finger in his hand.

"Good," *she said.* "Now can you raise your head?"

A stiff sensation laced tight up his middle and warned him not to move, but he made the effort and got his head up a little. Which was a mistake. Oh, wow.

"Take it easy." *The nurse patted his forearm with long, cool fingers.* "You've got a few stitches in your belly."

Pain jogged his memory and he tried to talk but no spit came. All he managed to get out was a single cotton word: " 'peration."

"That's right. You've had an emergency operation that went just fine and now you're in the recovery room," she said.

"High," he said slowly, finding some spit.

"Hello, yourself."

"No. Stone . . ." He took a breath, wheezed, "Grog . . ."

"Yep, we gave you something. We're about to give you some more of the good stuff."

"Hi," he said.

"Right. Stoned, huh?" she said.

"No. Hel . . . lo. You're . . . pret . . . pretty." His eyes probed around on the front of her blue tunic and focused on the laminated picture ID alligator-clipped to her pocket, and he read the printed title: Amy Skoda CRNA. "You're pret . . . ty, Amy," he said.

"Thank you, and you're lucky to be alive."

He blinked at the blue shapes circling around him. "Where?"

"It's all right now. You're in a hospital."

He nodded and the beep speeded up and he caught a panic flash of jagged black sky coming down, and frigid gray water rising up in ranks of whitecaps. He swallowed and muttered, "Storm."

Amy nodded. "Mister, you've had quite an adventure."

"Others?"

But she disappeared and the question hung unanswered. He waited and waited as it all slowed and went dim. Then the blue shapes above him startled and retreated. He heard shouts.

"Heads up, gang! We got another one!"

"C'mon, they need help."

The blue commotion surged away.

Then someone.

A hand appeared and held up a syringe. This syringe was thicker, a dull gray plastic, not skinny like the other. It moved up and out of sight.

"There you go," *a voice said—a different voice.* "It should be better now."

Jesus God. No. Ow. Not better. They'd jacked him back into the storm. Black waves flooded from his arm, into his chest, drowning him on the inside. His lungs . . .

"Oh, fuck, oh, no," said the voice, backing away.
Hey, come back . . .

. . .

He felt his thoughts seep away like the last bubbles of oxygen escaping his brain. And the commotion in the hall faded off and all he heard was the bleat of the heart monitor until it slipped off key:
Beep beep . . . boop.
Boop.
Boooop.
Boop.
And he lost the goddamn beat . . .

And his eyes took one last picture of muscles undulating down his arms, and just like he thought, the relentless waves from the storm had followed him right into this hospital room and were rolling under his skin.

Then he just—stopped. Nothing. Nothing erasing him line by line.

        . . . .
        . . . .
        . . . .

"Oh shit! Call a code. He's arrested in here."

Chapter One

Broker was used to sleeping alone because his wife was in the army and, except for her pregnancy and a short maternity leave, she had been absent on deployments to Bosnia during most of their marriage. And he was used to waking up in a freezing sleeping bag because he'd grown up in Northern Minnesota. What he was having trouble adjusting to was waking up alone in the cold bag and seeing the pale stripe on the third finger of his left hand where his wedding band had been.

So he coughed and rubbed his eyes, and the absent ring cued up the agnostic rosary in the back of his mind: *You just never know . . . never know . . . never know . . .* and it was, *yeah, yeah,* and he was talking to himself and his lips moved to dismiss the thought, but he had to appreciate the irony. *Mister Serious Student of the Unexpected.*

Didn't see it coming, did you, dummy?

She'd left two weeks ago and took their three-year-old daughter, Kit, off to army day care somewhere in Europe.

She said he could come along and take care of Kit. He said she could quit the army and stay home. So it stuck there between them. Their daughter watched nervously as Mom and Dad agreed to take an informal time-out, removing their rings and storing them in the top drawer of the bedroom dresser.

His reaction to the standoff was to exile himself from people he knew and retreat into the North woods. He'd purge himself with fresh air and hard work. Specifically, Broker volunteered to close down his uncle Billie's outfitting lodge at the end of the canoeing season.

And now, as he greeted the ice-water dawn, the subject was still fragile as glass. Carefully, he held it by the stem and tucked it away.

So.

Uncle Billie and his golf clubs had hopped a Northwest Airlines flight to Broker's parents' condo in Arizona. Broker had hung a CLOSED sign across the driveway of the small resort he owned in Devil's Rock, north of Grand Marais, on the Lake Superior shore. Then he'd driven down Highway 61 to Illgen City, turned on Highway 1 northwest to Ely, in the Minnesota Iron Range. Arriving at Billie's Lodge, he found a list of instructions next to the telephone. The canoe trip was at the top.

Broker had looked over the permits and perused the clients' backgrounds. He'd be playing wilderness guide to Milton Dane, a lawyer; Allen Falken, a surgeon; and Hank Sommer, who called himself a writer. All three were from the Twin Cities area.

Broker told himself guiding was no big thing, that he'd done it lots of times.

But that was more than twenty years ago.

In the intervening time the canoes had been upgraded from aluminum to lighter Kevlar and fiberglass. The freeze-dried food and camping gear were much improved. But otherwise, the drill was the same. He studied the itinerary, selected the proper maps, and packed for a party of four, going in by canoe to shoot a moose among the lakes of the Boundary Water's Canoe Area, BWCA for short.

And now it was the third morning of the trip.

Broker blew on his chilled hands and rubbed them together. He'd gone to bed breathing in damp lake water, lichen, and pine needles moldering on granite bedrock. A mild rain had tapped on the tent walls and eased him off to sleep. Now a loud winter silence replaced the patter of raindrops and his breath clouded in the chill air.

Hank Sommer bumped him as he rolled over in the narrow tent and snored. He lay on his back, half out of his sleeping bag, with his mouth open. He had buckteeth and a receding chin disguised under a short, unruly beard. When Broker reached over and jabbed him in the ribs, Sommer rearranged himself and stopped snoring. His cell phone, which had caused so much debate on the trip, was nestled next to his cheek.

It became clear from the start that Broker had been hired to carry the load for Sommer and to paddle his canoe. "Sorry, I've got this little medical condition," Sommer had admitted at the start.

"What medical condition?" Broker had asked directly, since it could affect their travel.

"This, ah, little hernia thing," Sommer had said, patting his side. So every portage on the way in, Broker had humped the boat and went back twice to haul all the packs while Sommer eased along with just his rifle case and a small shoulder bag.

Allen Falken, the doctor, appeared none too pleased that Sommer had put off elective surgery to go on this trip. But, Allen conceded, it was a routine inguinal hernia, a painless minor bulge. For half the century, men just wore trusses. It should be all right as long as Sommer took it easy.

"How easy?"

"He shouldn't lift over forty pounds."

"So if you get a moose, Sommer will take the picture and I'll carry the meat."

"Something like that," Allen had said.

It meant that Sommer was the weak link, so Broker wanted him in his canoe in case anything went wrong. Besides, he was curious. Sommer was a Minnesota fiction writer and Broker—strictly a nonfiction guy—had the feeling he should have heard of him. But he hadn't. He figured Sommer wanted to shoot a moose so he could write about it.

Broker was doing some hunting himself, but not for a trophy moose. Running from his marriage, he spent the days scouting the treelines and lakes half hoping to catch a younger, more resilient reflection of himself.

And he wasn't alone. By day three it was clear that marital discord paddled with them as Sommer conducted a nasty long-distance feud with his wife on his cell phone.

As they canoed deeper into lake country, Broker overheard enough of the terse conversations to gather that Sommer and his wife were fighting over money.

Onward.

Right now Broker needed a fire and a pot of coffee, so he shivered into trousers, a fleece sweater, and a pair of old tennis shoes. Carrying his stiff boots, he unzipped the tent and hunkered outside.

Well, he'd wanted the rain to stop.

And nothing stops water like ice.

The campsite, and probably all 140,000 square miles of the BWCA, wore bridal white. Brocade, lace, floss, and fluff—the tents, the gear, the hulls of the two canoes, every pine needle, clump of moss, and boulder were gilded with frost.

He watched his breath condense, then tatter off gently in the still air; he estimated the temperature at 34 degrees. He was not distracted by the beautiful fantasy spun in the trees. They were still twenty miles from Ely traveling on water cold enough to kill them.

But Broker had to grin. Even with hypothermia as a risk, Sommer's cell phone became an issue with his buddies because it violated the first rule of the wilderness, which was: You are on your own. Allen and Milt wanted a clean break with the hyperconnected world they'd left behind. Sommer wasn't impressed by such purist conceits. Older, crusty, he'd pointed out that he'd once spent a year sleeping on the ground, and he'd muttered a few profane references to the 101st Airborne and 1969 and a place Allen and Milt had never heard of called the Ashau Valley, and he *would* bring his goddamn cell phone, thank you very much.

So.

Broker toed a hoary clump of grass. Maybe the sun would come out and melt this fairyland. And maybe it wouldn't. If this cold snap continued they'd have to be careful.

He stirred the banked coals in the fire pit, added tinder, and built up the fire. Then he placed his boots near the flame to thaw. He walked a hundred yards into the brush to where he'd hoisted the food packs on the branch of a tall spruce beyond the reach of prowling black bears. He carried the packs back to the campfire and set out utensils and ingredients for breakfast.

You could still drink from the lakes along the Canadian border, so he took the coffeepot to the shore, poked through a wafer of shore ice, and filled it. Then he scooped up a handful and brushed his teeth. A few minutes later he had a blue flame hissing on the small Coleman camp stove.

He stretched, rotated his neck, and gauged the stiffness in his back and shoulders from two days of paddling and portaging. Starting to show streaks of gray in his forty-seventh autumn, Broker still looked like he could knock a man down or pick a man up, and like he wouldn't talk about it either way. His dark, bushy eyebrows met over the bridge of his nose, his eyes were quiet gray-green, and he wore his thick, dark hair trimmed just over his ears. At six feet tall and 190, he was ten pounds over his best weight. A few more days on the trail would pound down the kinks and trim off the flab. But he had to admit, as he scanned the white solitude, that he was starting to feel his age. For the last two years his chief workout had been chasing his daughter around.

He stooped, attended to the fire, and when the coffeepot perked he withdrew a cigar the size of a fat fountain pen from a Ziploc bag and carefully nibbled the plug. When the coffee smelled done, he turned off the camp stove, poured a tin cupful, and wedged the pot in the coals. Then he went down to the shore and found a seat on a granite ledge. There would be no sunrise today to go with his morning coffee. Not even a shiny spot in the overcast.

A match flared and migrant smoke from Spanish Honduras mingled with the steaming Colombian bean. Cigars were a weaning vice—all tease and foreplay—no inhaling. They got him off the cigarettes and now he worried that the thing that would get him off the cigars would be Ben and Jerry's ice cream.

"Good morning, I think," announced a voice that ended in a cough. Turning, Broker saw Milton Danc's short salt-and-pepper hair poke through his tent flap. Milt was nursing a cold, which did nothing to diminish his childish delight as he looked at the forest made over into frosted parsley.

Milt at forty-five stood six foot one in pile underwear and felt boot-liners. Broad shouldered, deep-chested, and deliberate in movement; he collected a cup of coffee and joined Broker on the sloping rock beach. He drew his knuckles across the stubble on his square chin and shivered. "Jesus, it's *cold.*"

"Yeah, and I got a feeling we're going to see some big, cold snowflakes," Broker said.

"Still beats the office." Milt toasted Broker with his coffee cup.

"Agreed. But maybe we should stay put till this front works on through," Broker said.

"No pain, no gain," Milt said with a grin.

"Right. And pneumonia is God's way of telling you to get out of the rain," Broker said.

Milt was unmoved. Being a serious white-water kayaker, he refused to be impressed with the concerns of flat-water paddlers. He pointed to Broker's tent and said, "Heads up."

Across camp, Sommer emerged from Broker's tent robed in his sleeping bag.

"Check it out, we woke up on a wedding cake," Sommer said, blinking at the hushed foliage.

Then he stooped, knelt, felt around for a flat place on the ground, found one, laid out the bag, sat down on it, and folded his legs in a casual lotus position. With the rest of the bag drawn around his shoulders he sat upright and draped his hands on his knees. Just like yesterday.

Broker studied the lanky writer sitting Buddha-fashion against a background of snowy spruce. Sommer had this tattoo on his left wrist, like a colorful bracelet, until you got a good look at it, and then you realized that the color scheme and sequence were the exact reds, greens, and grays of the lethal coral snake.

While Sommer did his morning meditation, Broker and Milt talked weather and drank their coffee. Then Sommer unfolded from his sitting position, bent forward, placed his forearms on the ground, clasped his hands, tucked in his shaggy head, and slowly hoisted himself up perfectly vertical into a headstand.

"Does that every morning, too?" Broker asked.

"Yeah, he's trying to stay mellow." Milt paused and rolled his eyes. "Until Jolene rings him up again."

"We should be out of cell-phone range soon," Broker said.

"Knock on wood," Milt said.

Chapter Two

"So, what do you think?" Broker jerked a thumb at the low clouds.

"I think you're right, it's going to snow," Milt said.

"I heard that," Sommer called out, as he lowered his feet to the ground, sat up, and looked around. "How soon?"

"Can't tell. There's coffee by the fire," Broker said.

Sommer poured a cup, squinted his hazel eyes, ran a hand through his thick blond hair, and lit a Camel straight. Barefoot, wearing just a T-shirt and Jockey shorts with the cell phone tucked into the waistband, he appeared immune to the cold. His size 13 feet ended in long toes and were attached to heavily muscled, slightly varicose legs. His chest seemed narrow because his sinewy arms were so long, and his neck was embedded in wedges of more wrinkled muscle that sloped up from his shoulders. In addition to the poison bracelet on his left wrist, he had five red teardrops tattooed on his right forearm. The tattoos had a crude jailhouse texture and Broker, who had some experience in evaluating jailhouse art, reflected that the raunchy designs might harmonize just fine with a woman named Jolene.

When Sommer took his coffee back into the tent to get dressed, Broker wondered aloud: "Where's a writer get arms like that?"

Milt raised an eyebrow. "Oh, he'll get around to telling you about how he grew up in the factories of Detroit."

As Sommer disappeared into one tent, Dr. Allen Falken emerged from the other. He stretched and stood for a minute, methodically kneading moisturizing cream into his hands, taking extra care with each finger. When he finished, he inspected the overcast sky.

"Well, super," said Allen. A general surgeon, and the youngest at forty, he was racquetball-smooth and wrinkle free. Broker cooked plain trail-fare and Allen proved to be a picky eater. And he fussed with his appearance; fresh from his sleeping bag, every strand of his thick sandy hair was in place like a styled wire hedge. He had wide blue eyes under a broad forehead, wide cheeks, a long narrow nose and tapering chin, strong hands and supple, well-tended fingers.

"I doubt it's going to rain again," Allen said, eyeing the misty sky and forest.

"Probably it'll snow," Broker said.

"Good, easier to see the moose against a white background. What's for breakfast?" Allen asked as he rubbed his hands together to warm them. Three precise rubs, no wasted motion. Broker was forming the impression that Allen never stopped following instructions.

"Oatmeal, Tang, toast and jam," Broker said, getting up and returning to the campfire. He threw his cigar stub into the coals and, as he prepared the porridge, speculated that they wouldn't be out here unless it was a once-in-a-lifetime hunting trip. They had won a state lottery that allowed them to take a moose in the Boundary Waters in the "greatest wilderness, big-game hunt east of the Mississippi."

From their banter Broker had learned that they had climbed Mount Rainier, mountain-biked through Moab, and rafted white-water rapids in Chile. Now they intended to paddle twenty-five miles into rough country and tote out a bull moose to add to their trophy repertoire.

Their destination was a burned-over area on Lake Fraser, a two-hour paddle to the north, where tender green shoots had thrived in the ash and were prime moose-browse. So far, they'd been out for two days in the rain with no sign of anything bigger than a fox.

When they'd eaten and were finishing their coffee, Broker went on record with the prudent option: "I think we should hunker down in camp until this weather blows over."

"Quit, huh?" Sommer snorted.

"Get dry," Broker said. "We're wet and chilled. Milt's getting sick. We should fort up with a good fire."

Sommer scrunched his mobile face in a Gallic shrug, "C'est la fuckin' vie. It's not like we're in Nepal. We're just a few miles from Ely."

Milt seconded Sommer with a curt nod. Allen scoffed, "Ditto. It's Indian summer, right?"

Broker laughed and tossed the dregs of his coffee on the fire. "Okay, sure; let's hit it," he said and thought how Northern Minnesota killed a few zealots like these guys every season. But then, that was part of the lure of this trip. They wanted to push the edge a little.

Dzzzttttttting.

The electric whine from Sommer's cell phone ended the discussion. Broker, Allen, and Milt grimaced with a there-goes-the-neighborhood expression.

"Goddamn shit," Sommer said.

Dzzzttttttting.

"Motherfucker." Sommer furrowed his scruffy brow and flipped open the phone. "What?"

A tiny, forceful female voice delivered a speech inside the slender plastic phone. Sommer stepped on her remarks in a dogged voice: "This is not the time to discuss the subject of trust." Pause. "Oh, for sure. We tried that and the first thing you did was drain the account." Pause. "Okay, your half of the account." Pause. "It's how you did it. Giving money to Earl behind my back."

In a spontaneous display of consensus body language, Broker, Allen, and Milt rose, tiptoed away, and formed an awkward huddle a discreet distance from Hank.

"Earl is the old boyfriend," Allen explained.

"She wrote him a big check, so Hank cut her off, closed the joint checking account," Milt said.

"Put all his money in a trust she can't touch, to teach her a lesson," Allen said.

"Don't call me again when I'm hunting," Sommer growled. He grimaced and held the phone away from his ear, up toward the overcast sky. "I don't need this shit," he hissed. Then, in a sudden fit he threw the phone like a shortstop firing to first base, and the black plastic rectangle skittered off a spruce branch, bounced, then rolled over next to Broker's boot.

A youthful voice rattled distinctly from the phone, "I'm just trying to be responsible, goddammit; and responsible people *pay their debts.*"

Broker picked up the phone and held it at arm's length.

The voice continued. "You have all these bills piled up on your desk going back two months. The power company called. They're going to turn off the lights. Hank? Hank?"

Gingerly, Broker handed it back to Sommer who was now furious and clearly not tracking her conversation. "Not with my money. Not to that pimp!" he shouted into the phone.

"Earl was never a pimp," the voice said. "And it's *our* money because we're married."

Milt shook his head. "I told him he should have made her sign a pre-nup."

Allen worried his lower lip between his teeth and tried to explain, "This is one beautiful woman on the outside but as to the inside Milt and I disagree."

"Bonnie fucking Parker is what I think," Milt said.

"And I think she cleans up well, like Eliza Doolittle, a lotus growing in a field of shit and Hank had the good sense to pluck her," Allen said thoughtfully.

"We'll see who plucks who." Milt glanced at Broker and shrugged. "Allen and I have this bet going. It's a classic nature-nurture debate; she was a stripper and a drunk who hung out with some rough people. Hank met her in an AA group in a church basement. I don't think she can change, Allen thinks she can. Obviously so does Hank."

"Fuck this," Hank exploded. He wound up and threw the phone again, except this time he lobbed it over their heads in a long arc that ended in a splash twenty yards out in the lake.

"And that settles that," Milt said.

Broker watched the circular ripples radiate out from the spot where the phone disappeared. He cleared his throat. "Sure can get quiet up here," he said, deadpan.

After that, they set off in separate directions to practice male solidarity through denial, and to break camp. While Broker did the dishes, Milt and Allen efficiently collapsed the tents, stowed them, and organized the cumbersome Duluth packs next to the canoes. Sommer hung back and brooded with a cup of coffee and a cigarette.

After he finished the dishes Broker packed them and scanned the low clouds as he laced up his boots. Snow didn't bother him. But he felt a draft comb through the pine needles, like someone had eased open the door of a walk-in meat freezer. And in the chill he sensed the charged air marshaling and packing tighter.

They stamped out the campfire and stowed the last of their gear. Sommer clambered gingerly over the mound of packs and took his seat in the bow of Broker's canoe. Milt naturally took the stern position in the other boat. A little after 8:00 A.M., they pushed off from the campsite and entered a maze of narrow channels that threaded toward Lake Fraser.

Paddling side by side, Broker and Milt kibitzed about canoes. Milt had wanted one of the fast, lighter Kevlar models that were currently popular. Broker preferred the old-fashioned aluminum Grummans. The popular Wenonahs, he argued, were great for racing in a straight line on flat water, but he distrusted the square cut of the bow and worried it would dig into a breaking wave, not ride up it.

They'd compromised on fiberglass Bells—a broader craft with more lift in the line of the bow and more stability for heavy loads and bad weather.

Then Milt and Allen pulled ahead and when they were out of easy earshot, Sommer turned in the bow seat and shook his head. He seemed to have been holding his breath since the phone incident. Now he exhaled and grumbled. "Sometimes I feel like a cliché, marrying a younger woman. Thinking I could help her change."

Broker studied the older man for two long paddle strokes. As the cold water swished and the canoe rocked he watched Sommer's expression slip. Suddenly he saw into the dilemma of a physically rugged man who was grappling with aging and was losing the strength he'd always taken for granted.

Broker spoke in a low, soft voice no one on the trip had yet heard: "I married a younger woman and I thought she'd change after she had a baby but she didn't."

And that pretty much dried up the conversation for a while.

Up ahead Milt and Allen put down their paddles, unzipped their gun cases, and loaded their rifles, which they then carefully positioned against the thwarts. Then they picked up their paddles and pulled farther ahead.

Sommer chuckled. "Look at them go. They want to be first."

"First, huh?"

"For the next big thing—which in this case is some poor, lilypad-chewing moose." Sommer chuckled, raised his voice, and hailed the other canoe. "Who gets the first shot? Who will be the Alpha Wolf and hang the antlers?"

"Pipe down," Allen yelled back, "you'll scare everything away."

"Oh, that's good," Sommer exclaimed. "What do you think? Some moose is going to get wheeled down to the shore all prepped and anesthetized on a table for you to carve up?"

Milt and Allen pulled about fifty yards ahead and no one spoke. The white trees enforced quiet, like a hospital ward. There was only the splash of the paddles, puffs of their breath, the occasional knock of wood on the gunwales.

Then Sommer shrugged and wondered out loud, "What do moose do in this weather, anyway?"

Broker said, "Got me."

"Hey, c'mon, you're the guide," Sommer said.

"I'm the cook, I set up camp. I'm not a hunting guide. It's illegal to guide or assist in the state lottery hunt up here if you've already got a moose," Broker said.

"That's what I mean, you've shot a moose, right?" Sommer said.

"It was a long time ago," Broker said.

"So how was it?" Sommer asked.

"Shooting a moose is like shooting a garage door."

Sommer jerked around and laughed. "That's good, I'm going to steal that."

"So you steal stuff, huh?" Broker asked.

"You bet. All writers are thieves."

"I always heard there are two kinds of thieves: the ones too lazy to work and the ones who think they're too smart to get caught. Which kind are you?"

Sommer laughed. "The smart, lazy kind. Actually I'm more like a ball of wax; you know, everything sticks."

"And that's why you want to shoot a moose, to pick up some details?" Broker asked.

"Nah," Sommer raised his paddle and pointed at the canoe up ahead. "I want to see *them* shoot a moose. Especially Allen."

Broker fixed on the blue back of Allen's parka and asked, "How's that?"

"I admit I wouldn't mind seeing a surgeon field-dress a moose," Sommer said.

"I hear you," Broker said, suppressing a smile. Then they stopped talking and looked to the paddles, their arms rising and falling in a crisp morning cadence, working out the kinks, easing into the day. Despite the overcast sky they were happy to be free of the rain and they warmed with the work.

"So what is it you write about, anyway?" Broker asked.

"The Four Great American W's: Women, Whiskey, Work, and War. And of course, sex and death."

Broker was smiling now. He asked, "How's your side feeling?"

"I'm good," Sommer said, appearing to be more relaxed. Unlike Milt and Allen who looked around frequently to find the source of an invisible irritation, Sommer was momentarily at ease with the silence of the north.

"So how old are you, anyway?" Broker asked.

"I was born a week after the Battle of Midway."

Broker rested his paddle. "June, 1942." *He's fifty-seven, ten years older than me.* Looking closer, Broker noticed the faint webbing at his throat and in his cheeks. He saw the dapple of dark pigment on his bare wrist between the cuff of his parka and his glove. *Ten years*, he thought.

"Not bad," Sommer said.

"I read military history to go to sleep, like some people read mysteries," Broker said. He shook his head. "Up until now the only writers I've met were newspaper reporters. They don't sound much like you."

Sommer acted indignant. "Hey, I'm a thief, not a fucking vampire."

Broker grinned at the remark and a few minutes later the frosted woods opened and they squirted from the last tight passage into a long, open stretch of lake.

"Life vest," Broker reminded Sommer who had neglected to put his on. Sommer pulled on the vest and snapped it tight. Their paddles dipped and swished in and out of the glassy, motionless water and, except for the chill air, the distant treelines could have been a blur of steam. They were well into the open water when a feather of breeze drifted down. Long, dark ripples began to gouge Lake Fraser as if an invisible giant was dragging his feet.

"What the hell?" Sommer looked up as the feeble light drained from the sky and left the day in shadow. There was no warning.

The air and water puckered as the wind set its cleats. The tree-tops bent, the forest dulled from white eye candy to dirty ash. The straight-line gale just smashed down through the clouds.

"Get serious, people . . ." Broker rose in his seat and yelled to warn the other canoe. The blast tore the words from his mouth and threw them away.

Chapter Three

"Ahhouuu."

Milt gave a dare-danger howl as he and Allen sculled in place until Broker and Sommer pulled abreast of them. Then Milt brandished his paddle at the storm. This show of bravado rankled Broker who was gauging the power of the onrushing wind in the way the pines were cranking at the north end of the lake.

"Cinch those vests tight," he shouted.

Milt sat up abruptly as the full might of the squall exploded around them and the lake erupted into something like a horizontal rapids. Wide-eyed, chastised, he turned to Broker. Ten yards away across the bucking water, there was no mistaking his sober assessment: *This is some serious shit we're in.*

"No mistakes, no mistakes," Allen shouted.

"Dig it," Sommer yelled. Half turned, with one hazel eye flaring over his shoulder, he raised his paddle to drive it into the gray slope swelling up to his front. The stiff wave—three feet high—crashed over the bow and showered him in ice water. The next wave reared, coiled, and Broker leaned into his paddle and watched it come. It had never been warm. Even in summer. For thousands of years that gray water had cherished a geologic memory of its glacier mama.

"Paddle," Broker yelled. "Stay into the wind."

"No shit," Sommer yelled back, his voice giddy with excitement, and they met the wave head on, riding a choppy boost of adrenalin.

Milt swung in so close the canoes bumped gunwales. His powerful twelve-inch wrists drove his paddle in a foaming sculling motion and, freed from his landlubber plodding, he danced on the water. His face clenched in a diagram of practical fear under taut control and formed a question: *What do you think?* His eyes measured Sommer and Allen, who wore braced but game expressions.

Broker looked from Allen to Sommer, back to Allen: *What about Sommer's guts?*

Allen shrugged: *Have to.*

"Fuck you guys," Sommer snarled, digging in with his paddle.

They sailed on the plume of a wave, dropped into the trough, and the plunge set them all paddling furiously to keep pointed up wind.

They had less than ten inches of freeboard on the heavily loaded canoes. One slipup abeam of these waves and they'd take a boatful of water. If they capsized, the wind would batter them back down the lake. The life jackets would keep them afloat but hypothermia would do them in before they washed up on the far shore.

One look into Milt's eyes confirmed it: dumping a canoe in these conditions, this far out, was a death sentence.

"Can't take a chance on turning back," Broker shouted. He stabbed his finger toward a blur in the distance where a rocky point jutted into the lake, about a quarter mile to the left front. Milt nodded, concurring. He could see the waves peter out on the lee side.

"Tricky. We'll have to quarter . . ."

"What?"

"Quarter. Off the wind," Milt shouted again.

"Understand," Broker nodded vigorously. Then he braced himself and paddled into the freak storm as sleeting rain slashed at his Goretex parka and threatened to freeze, turn white, and blot out his vision.

Jesus. The plunging winds split sideways, sheared off, and scissored slapdash patterns through the water—moguls here, herringbone there. Broker tried to line up Sommer's green parka with the end of the point that appeared, then disappeared, playing peek-a-boo. This practical exercise in dead reckoning did nothing to mitigate the swooping ant-on-a-twig sensation as the tiny canoe rode the big water.

Abruptly the wind shifted and they found themselves in an eerie acoustic shadow. Sommer threw a look over his shoulder and his expression was vital, happy almost; danger had peeled years from his face. "Hey, Broker, tell me . . ." his voice boomed in the lull.

"What?"

"You voted for Ventura?"

"You're fuckin' nuts."

Sommer's wild eyes flashed and his reaction to a world that was determined to kill them was to grin, as they wobbled in the belly of a wave with the next crest coming at eye level. Tons of gray-green lake water slid an arm's length from their faces and they were . . . laughing.

"Stephen Crane. Great line. End of *Red Badge of Courage*," Sommer shouted sentence fragments in the gusty wind.

"Huh?" Broker strained to hear.

"They met the Great Death . . ."

"Hey, fuck your Great Death."

". . . and found that . . ."

"Found?"

". . . was just the great death," Sommer roared.

"Fuck him, the horse he rode in on, and the colonel who sent him," Broker shouted.

"See, it goes easier when you lighten up," Sommer shouted back.

Which was true. They fell into a powerful slot, pulling together, riding rather than fighting the water. The wind shifted back full force, plugging their ears; but a hot fear now greased their muscles and they were gaining distance. Broker saw the point much clearer now. "Hey, we're almost . . ."

Sommer answered with a wild bray of pain. Teeth bared, he braced his arms on his paddle athwart the gunwales and trembled.

Fear flipped in Broker's chest from tonic to paralytic. "You gotta . . ."

"Jesus," Sommer bellowed.

"Paddle . . ." Broker screamed.

Sommer's eyes revolved, immobilized by the pain. The bow started to swing. The next wave . . .

"Don't quit on me, goddammit!" Broker roared.

Sommer gritted his teeth, straightened up, bent stiffly to the work, and powered them into the wave.

Broker hollered, "You okay?"

Teeth clenched, Sommer swore, "Fuck you, paddle."

"We have to . . . quarter. Off the wind," Broker yelled.

Sommer looking over his shoulder at Broker, shook his head. *Can't hear.* Broker stabbed his paddle through the air to give the angle and direction.

"Angle left," Sommer shouted. Broker nodded his head vigorously.

A wave battered them every two seconds, the crest pulsing in one direction, the trough pulling in another. As they teetered on the crest, they were shoved back by the stiff-arm wind. Leaning forward, they muscled a hole in the blast and plunged down. The waves clubbed Broker's arms as he extended his J-stroke, adding a sweep to propel the canoe to the left, to cut an angle across the trough. Then he reversed sides and swept his paddle to straighten up into the wind as they climbed the next roller. He was trying to compensate for Sommer's reduced strength, and the added torque invited tendon and bone to separate.

But they had the technique, and Sommer settled into a jerky but steady paddle as, wave by wave, with total concentration, they crabbed to the left.

They went blind in the drenching needles of spray for whole parts of minutes and could only cling to the direction of the wind. Squinting into the gray shuttles of water and foam, Broker saw Milt's canoe heave up out of a trough with Allen, a resolute figurehead, paddling doggedly in the bow as Milt bent with grim power in the stern.

Reach, dig, pull, recover. Reach, dig, pull, recover. They clawed for the point on a parallel course.

Five minutes of progress. Ten. Then another spasm crippled Sommer and he cringed over in the bow. His paddle absent, they wobbled, broached a wave, and took on water. Broker's arms and shoulders cracked as he redoubled his paddling to plow back into the wind. They were losing forward motion, slipping back into the belly of the wave.

They seesawed in the trough and suddenly it was Broker's turn. For a long, terrible moment he sat frozen, gripped by vertigo and muscle strain, unable to lift his paddle. His forearms were bowling pins, the muscle and tendon fused in spasms. He couldn't feel his hands or his fingers. His arms had gone numb below the elbows.

They were going to swamp on the next wave.

Sommer turned in the tossing canoe and saw Broker struggling to raise his stone arms. Broker would never forget the way Sommer's raging eyes willed themselves calm.

Strict with duty, Sommer faced forward and stretched his long arms to the paddle in a powerful sweep. The canoe nosed up into the onrushing wave. The muscle spasm passed and Broker raised and swung his paddle. But he was mostly on the rudder. Hatless, parka hood cowled at his throat, blond hair streaming, Sommer's powerful arms dug a zigzag trench up and down the waves.

Broker couldn't tell the time and his head was a clutter of migraine splinters. He knew they were soaked and freezing and way past complete collapse. Water sloshed in the canoe up to their shins and made the boat handle like an iron barge. But they were close, within fifty yards of shore, in among geysers of spume breaking off the rocks. Then it was thirty more yards, then twenty. The waves played tricks with Broker's eyes and the rocks heaved up around them like huge pitted molars, salivating foam. But strength was flowing back into his arms. When he heard the keel scrape on granite he knew it was going to be all right.

"Sommer, man; you saved our ass," he shouted in relief.

Sommer had nothing left but a growl of pain. Spent, he pitched forward and crumpled into a ball.

Then he dropped his paddle.

Broker watched the paddle vanish, a streak of yellow in the gunmetal foam. Now the bow rose, swung around without Sommer's paddle to nail it down, and they rolled sideways and took on a gunwale full of water, and the next wave crashed over them. A ton of ice water slammed into Broker and squashed the air from his lungs.

And they went under.

Chapter Four

HOLYJESUSFUCKINCHRIST!

The ice water shattered his blood into red pins and needles. But it was ice water ten yards from shore because Broker felt the reassuring slip-slide of mossy stone under his boots. He pushed up and shot the surface. With his heart and lungs booming too big for his ribs, he bit off chunks of glassy air. Then he hugged his life jacket, checked the snaps to make sure they were tight, and blinked up into streaming snowflakes. Couldn't see where the snow stopped and where the stinging water started.

So he thrashed toward the shore, swung his head around, and located Sommer's straw-colored hair bobbing on a crest closer in, among the rocks. He punched through one wave, two, reached out, and got a grip on the swamped canoe that heaved up, buoyant with built-in floatation. Gotta think. Survival bag.

He grabbed the red waterproof duffel bag bouncing from the thwart in front of the stern seat, popped the pressure clasp, and yanked it free, as the canoe wallowed deeper. Using the bag for a float, he kicked over to Sommer who rolled up in the water, coughing.

"Hurts," Sommer cried out.

"Quit whining." Broker tried for levity through chattering teeth and a voice that rattled like a snare drum. "Not the end of the world. You're on top the water. You got air."

"Hurts," Sommer said again.

Clutching Sommer's life jacket, hugging the bag, pumping his feet, he surged through the thrashing surf until he felt his boots scuff solid stone. Having terra firma under his feet backed off the freezing panic, and he forced a deep, shuddering breath and fixed on the problem of survival.

Hypothermia made simple demands on humans who'd evolved in tropical savannahs. They needed fire to get warm and dry, and shelter from the wind. They had to stabilize the body's core temperature.

Or they would die.

Coughing, puking lake water, he manhandled Sommer's loose body up on the slick granite. He had to get Sommer's brain and vital organs out of the water. Seconds were precious now.

Sommer was injured and in shock. Broker went the other way and was on fire with adrenalin. For now, he did not feel the cold or even Sommer's weight. The wind blazed on his sopping clothing and the snow zinged like white-hot sparks. But it wouldn't last long. So he quickly checked Sommer for broken limbs and bleeding and found nothing. Which meant it was something internal, something far worse.

He dragged Sommer across the granite slabs up to a loose cobble beach, dropped him, and staggered up the shale. He needed a protected nook in the granite bluff, out of the wind. And found one among a jumble of tall boulders. Better, the broken rocky base of the ridge had trapped tangled piles of almost dry driftwood.

He tossed his duffel into a slant of boulders that formed a broad cranny ten feet deep which stopped the wind on three sides and provided some overhang against the snow. He ran back, seized Sommer's life vest, dragged him to cover, peeled off the life vest, opened the duffel, dug out a space blanket, and quickly tucked it around Sommer. The reflective wrap would hold some warmth until . . .

Broker shook his head, getting disoriented.

He should gather wood, start a fire. But he had to look for the other guys. He started shaking. Which meant he was losing his fiery edge to a vast, cheerful fatigue that so loved the shelter. So he forced himself out and ran from the bluff, scanning the wind and snow. Milt wore a red parka, Allen's was blue.

He clambered up the rocks to gain a vantage to overlook the point. If they'd missed the end of the promontory and swamped, they'd be blown back across the open lake.

But he saw Milt almost immediately, a red blur in the surf two hundred yards away on the edge of the point. Knee-deep in the foam, Milt was trying to land the canoe. Allen's blue jacket moved to shore and back, carrying packs. The canoe was hard to haul because it was full of water. Broker ran toward them. They needed that canoe.

A surge of waves pounded the two men out of sight, and when they appeared again the canoe was tipped, draining. Milt staggered, fell, stood up, and Broker realized he had wrenched the canoe on its side and shook it out through sheer force. Broker scrambled to them and saw three paddles stacked safely ashore against a pack. Good.

"Sommer?" Allen gasped, dragging another pack.

"Bad shape. Don't know. He's up the beach, a kind of cave. Need a fire," Broker yelled.

"Fuck!" Allen scowled. "My medical kit with some decent pain killers. Lost it on the way in."

"Your canoe?" Milt grimaced to Broker. His right arm hung at an odd angle.

"Swamped. At the other end of the lake by now. What's wrong with your arm?" Broker asked, getting them moving.

"Can't move it," Milt said, wincing.

Allen started to check the arm.

"Not now." Shivering uncontrollably, out of fire, Broker was naked before the maw of shock. He felt over the packs. They had lost the tents, one of the food packs, and some personal stuff, but they had the sleeping bags and half the food. They'd be all right if they could warm up.

"Get out of the wind. Move." Shouldering the food pack, giving Allen the sleeping bags, he herded them over the slick rocks. In minutes they were in the dry granite pocket, a magical zone of calm compared to full exposure.

Allen bent and stripped off Sommer's parka, yanked up his shirt, and pulled down his trousers. He kneaded the bulge in Sommer's groin.

Sommer screamed.

Broker looked away, spooked. Milt moved close beside him.

"You all right?" Milt asked.

"My arms seized up out there; he busted his gut on account . . ."

Milt cut him off. "You swam him in. Let it go."

Broker nodded, pawed through his survival pack, cast aside a folding saw, grabbed a small axe, and found what he wanted: the fifteen-minute red highway flare that would save their lives.

Broker and Milt tore into the tangle of driftwood rammed into a rock fissure ten feet away and dragged out pieces. Really shaking now, Broker kicked off branches, grabbed his hatchet, hacked slivers, coring down to dry wood, and tossed it into a small pile. Then he peeled back the flare's cover, ripped off the friction cap, and struck it along the tip of the fuse like a match. A spout of incandescent flame erupted in a sulphurous cloud. The wood crackled.

"Aw right," Milt coughed and cheered, seeing the instant blaze. Ignoring his injured arm, he dragged branches, propped them against the rocks, and stomped them into smaller kindling.

The fire was irresistible and Allen joined them. He had the first-aid kit from Broker's bag in one shaking hand, a plastic vial in the other. "This is all we have. Fucking Tylenol," he muttered. He pulled himself away, returned to Sommer, and carefully finished removing his wet clothing.

Sommer was snake-bellied, with zero body fat. The baseball-sized bulge in the left side of his groin was unmistakable.

"What is it?" Broker called out.

"Not good," Allen said as he coaxed Tylenol down Sommer's throat. "He wouldn't listen. Won the lottery and just had to go hunting with a hernia."

Sommer's grimace was bathed in firelight. "How bad?"

Allen composed himself. "You ruptured yourself, Hank. My index of suspicion is a strangulated intestine."

Sommer sought out Broker's eyes with a perverse, painful grimace. "Sit tight," Broker blurted, "I'm going to get you out of here."

"Not going anywhere," Sommer said weakly as his head

dropped back down. The three shivering men locked eyes and moved closer to the fire.

"The cell phone," Allen said in a dull voice.

"Don't go there," Milt said.

Broker looked from Milt to Allen. They had gotten their wish. They were on their own.

Chapter Five

Numb, Milt gawked into the storm. Allen stared at his trembling, useless surgeon's hands. Broker kept seeing Sommer paddling. . . .

Lassitude, the second fuzzy layer of shock, was setting in, so Broker roused and pounded their shoulders—Milt's good one.

"Okay. C'mon. Keep it simple." First they had to get dried off. Gently they dressed Sommer in fresh clothing, easing him into a sleeping bag and moving him close to the fire. Allen made an ice pack from a T-shirt and some shore ice and placed it on Sommer's stomach. Then they built the fire waist-high, stripped, wrung out their clothes, rigged a clothes line, and set out their wet boots.

Milt's biceps was already swollen purple, hot to the touch, so Allen wrapped it in ice and tied a sling from a sweatshirt.

"Fucking rotator cuff, *again*," Milt hissed.

"Take some Tylenol," Allen said.

Milt waved him off. "Save it for Sommer."

Broker took inventory. They'd lost the coffeepot and the propane stove and fuel, but he found a coffee can full of tea bags and instant coffee. He filled the can with water, then put it over the fire and doled out hefty candy bars.

They'd overbuilt the fire and now they began to stumble in the drowsy warmth. To keep them alert, Broker brewed strong, hot tea which they drank from canteen cups as they gobbled chocolate bars. Allen gingerly spooned tea to Sommer.

"Well, how bad is he?" Milt asked.

Allen calculated. "He has to get to an operating room in twenty-four hours."

Their eyes locked in a fast, triage glance.

"And I can't operate in the woods with a hunting knife and aspirin," Allen said.

"And I can't paddle with this arm," Milt said.

"And I can't do it alone," Broker said, careful to control his voice. On a hard paddle out, he'd much prefer Milt.

"So that's it," Milt said. "I stay with Hank, you two paddle for help."

Broker started making his preparations.

"What are our chances?" Allen asked.

Broker glanced over at Sommer in the sleeping bag. "I won't bullshit you. Getting out's the easy part. It's getting back in that's hairy." He yanked his thumb at the storm. "The wind's out of the northwest. That's classic Alberta Clipper. If something really big's coming down from Canada, we'll hit it going out. The Forest Service has a seaplane base in Ely, and the state patrol has a helicopter. That's his only chance."

Their eyes met. Allen said, "But bad weather could keep them from flying."

"There it is," Broker said.

"I don't have to tell you how serious this is," Allen said. "His bowel has popped through a tear in his stomach wall, the muscles have constricted, and I can't reduce it—push it back in. His intestine is incarcerated, it's not getting blood, the tissue is dying. If it perforates, depending on the size of the tear, his stomach cavity could literally flood with his own shit."

"Peritonitis," Broker said.

"Not the way I'd choose for him to die," Allen said tartly, staring out into the whirling snow.

Sommer curled in the sleeping bag with his knees drawn up in a fetal knot of pain. "Jo-lene," he moaned, going in and out of consciousness.

"Is that?" Broker asked.

Milt nodded his head, raised an eyebrow, and drew out the syllables as an afterthought: "Joe-leene."

Sommer repeated his wife's name like a painful metronome, marking time, and it was all about time now. Two hours had passed since they'd fumbled ashore. Hypothermia was behind them, they had retrieved the canoe from the point, but Broker wanted to make sure that he and Allen were thawed and in dry gear before they faced the weather again.

They hunkered over a topographical map on which their itinerary had been traced in yellow Magic Marker. Allen reached over abruptly, turned Broker's wrist, and plucked the cheap canvas strap on his watch. Broker started to react, then saw that the doctor didn't mean to be rude—he was just curious and his curiosity didn't respect normal boundaries.

"Still running. Twelve bucks, United Store," Broker said evenly.

Allen, wearing a Rolex Explorer II, nodded and continued to lace on his boots. Broker cinched up the survival bag. They had food, flashlights, sleeping bags, a change of dry clothes, a sound eighteen-foot canoe, and three paddles. For ballast, Broker wrapped some dry kindling in a poncho liner.

Allen gave his last instructions to Milt about applying ice packs to reduce the swelling. Broker knelt and put his hand on Sommer's shoulder. "Hey."

"Hiya, homeboy," Sommer said through clenched teeth. Briefly their eyes conjured with credentials, then Sommer quipped, "You still here? Go out there and find me a skyhook."

Allen said, "No food and no water after midnight. This time tomorrow he's going to be on an operating table."

"Allen, we've gotta roll," Broker said, getting to his feet.

"Better get ahold of Jo," Sommer said.

"First thing," Allen said.

"Tell her I ain't dead yet," Sommer said, managing the barest grin. He raised one hand weakly in farewell and dropped it.

Broker and Allen left shelter and went to the canoe that Broker had readied on the cobble beach. The storm winds had spiraled away, leaving the fickle lake relatively calm. They shook Milt's left hand and, with snowflakes pelting their faces, they launched into the restless swells.

Chapter Six

The storm left behind gloomy flurries that stuck to their faces, melting and trickling down their cheeks. The breaking waves were gone, now sluggish swells slapped the bow of the canoe.

"If only she wouldn't have called this morning." Allen paddled furiously and stared ahead at the misty spruce crowns. "Can you believe it. He *threw* the cell phone away."

"Nothing like a domestic dispute." The remark rolled easy and world-weary from Broker's tongue; a cliché from his background in law enforcement.

Allen paused to rest on his paddle and shake his head. "Typical. He does things on impulse, then he regrets it later. That's been the story of his life since he met her." Allen looked up and shook his head. "And *how* he met her, Jesus."

"In an AA group, right?" Broker said, to keep the conversation going.

"Right, but the reason they met personally was, she walks in to this group of guys in this church basement—folding chairs, cinder blocks, no windows, the air full of *cigarette smoke* . . ."

Allen said "cigarette smoke" like he'd just raised Satan.

". . . and she's wearing this sweater and she has these perfect tits. So Hank and this other guy start to wager, like, are they for real or are they implants? So Hank is on the case. He takes her out for coffee—at this motel and gets her in bed and, he swears, no scars, they are real." Allen continued to shake his head. "I was married. You know where I met my wife? In Sunday school."

"So Sommer married a sweater girl," Broker mused.

"Milt thinks she's practically a gun moll. But he's reacting more to her old boyfriend, that Earl character. He's definitely a criminal element."

Broker suppressed a grin at Allen's language. He was getting an impression of Allen as a missionary-position Minnesota Normal.

"I guess some women find that attractive," Allen said. "And Hank has a little bit of that in his past, too. You know, rough stuff."

Broker cleared his throat and looked to his paddle. Getting into the locker-room swing of the conversation, he'd been on the verge of asking Allen to describe more of her.

They were silent for a while, just paddles shoving water.

Allen turned out to be surprisingly strong and steady on the paddle, which led Broker to revise his earlier judgment. The doctor, he decided, was used to digital results and was holding nothing but an analog wooden paddle in his hands, so he was more frustrated than fussy. And, far from being annoyed at Allen's carping, Broker welcomed it because it filled the dreary monotony of sky and water.

Talk was good, because they had a lot of time to fill. Broker figured fourteen to sixteen hours of nonstop paddle and portage to the lodge. And they'd have to camp when it got dark. So add six more hours. If Sommer had twenty-four hours, they'd be cutting it close. And they still had to rely on a plane or helicopter to get him out.

The time stretched out in front of them. Old-fashioned, unplugged, slow Real Time with no crowds, no traffic, sirens, TV, telephones, email, or Internet. Just the creak of the canoe, the hiss and slap of the bow cutting the chop, and the dip of the paddles.

"How long have you guys known each other?" Broker asked.

"I met Hank through Milt. I met Milt at a seminar. He was the keynote speaker on malpractice. Milt invited me to a poker game where I met Hank. That was just after he got the movie deal for his book."

"I don't read much . . ." Broker was about to say "fiction."

"But you've been around," Allen said quickly.

"How's that?"

"Back by the fire, when we were stripping out of the wet stuff. Your shoulder, your back, and your right leg. I spent a month in

Bosnia in '94. Doctors without Borders. I've seen shrapnel wounds before."

Broker let the statement hang unanswered. Three years retired from police work, he still retained the dissembling persona of ten years working deep undercover for the Minnesota Bureau of Criminal Apprehension. Before that he'd been a St. Paul cop. Before that, he'd caught some Communist metal during the last two years of that war people didn't like to talk about and couldn't forget.

After a polite interval, Allen asked, "You're from Ely?"

"I'm not a local. I have a little resort over on Superior, north of Grand Marais. I'm just helping out my uncle on this trip."

"So your family's in the resort business?"

"You could say that." It was an accurate if incomplete answer.

"So how are we doing on time?" Allen asked.

"We're doing fine. If we can keep up this steady paddle till sundown."

"Then what?" Allen said.

"We'll have to stop. We can't take a chance on getting turned around in the dark."

"Agreed," Allen said.

They paddled and portaged through the afternoon and, as the clouds sagged lower and the temperature dropped, the lakes sweated a fine late-afternoon mist.

"It's funny," Allen said, talkative again, "Jolene married a guy who had some money and she thought she'd get to go shopping in Paris, maybe see Florence. But Hank bought a big old fixer-upper and their life turned into *This Old House.* Now he wants to fill it up with smelly cats and dogs. And maybe kids."

Allen turned. "I mean, you have to see this woman to believe her. A figure like hers. The thought of stretch marks drives her crazy."

"Sounds like one of those trophy wives," Broker said. He imagined her blond, tanned, and spa-rat skinny in Spandex.

"Absolutely. And like I said," Allen lowered his paddle, turned, and cupped his hands generously to his chest. "You know, they stay aloft on their own."

Broker laughed. "You seem to know a lot about the aerodynamics of Mrs. Sommer's knockers."

"I saw some topless pictures taken when she was an entertainer," Allen said.

"Hmmm."

"An exotic dancer," Allen said. "Hank Sommer is not your normal writer and Jolene isn't your normal writer's wife."

"And not your normal type of friends, either, huh?" ventured Broker.

"Touché. Very good. That's Milt for you, he's famous for collecting characters."

Allen wore no ring on his left hand. "What about you? You said you were married?" Broker asked.

"Sore subject. I married my high school girlfriend. It didn't survive my residency at Mayo. Now I can't afford it," quipped Allen. "Hell, I'm still paying off med school and the Crash of '87. Certainly can't afford it doing hernias and hemorrhoids for a freaking HMO."

Allen took his frustration out on the lake and they fell into a brooding physical rhythm. The paddles rose and fell, filling time. Broker figured it had to be worse for Allen. His friend was slowly dying in a makeshift winter camp while he moved under muscle power at the same pace as French and Ojibwa fur traders three hundred years ago.

At dusk they came ashore and made camp, using the upturned canoe as a shelter. They brewed cocoa over a small fire, ate their energy bars, and, huddled back-to-back in their sleeping bags, fell into an exhausted sleep.

"Jesus, what's . . . ?" Allen jerked upright and banged his head on the canoe.

"Wolves." Broker, thrilling to the howls reverberating through the dark trees, pictured raw meat in the snow. He'd been awake for an hour, warming his hands over a low fire, listening; ten or twelve animals, more than a mile and a lake away.

"They don't attack people, right?" Allen asked.

"Not here, not yet. In India they snatch infants and eat them. Population pressure probably."

"We don't have a gun," Allen said.

Broker allowed a smile. It was the appropriate response. "C'mon. Let's go," he said.

The wolves ended their serenade as the dark leaked away, and by the light of a fuzzy dawn Broker hoped he didn't look as numb with cold as Allen.

They ate a fast breakfast of instant coffee, chocolate, and Pemmican bars as their breath came in dense white jets. It was getting colder and they stamped their feet to get their circulation going. In the canoe, they fell into the same dogged rhythm, just their muscles yanking at the time and distance. Allen was not talkative today and put all his effort into the paddle.

They lasted two hours and had to beach, take a pee, and stomp around to restore the circulation in their hands and feet. The temperature hovered at freezing, and frostbite whiskered the air. They climbed back in the boat.

Lift, reach, dig, pull, recover.

Broker was watching hypnotic whirlpools of dark water spin away from his paddle when the first snowflake wobbled down almost big as a quarter. Broker glanced up hopefully, grabbing at an old Indian saying: Little snow, big snow; big snow, little snow.

"Another hour," he shouted as the flakes plummeted here and there like crumbs from a huge white weight suspended above them. Lift the paddle, dig the water, lift the paddle. A tent peg of pain pounded between his shoulder blades each time he raised his arms and the rowing chant in the back of his mind mocked him.

You just never know never know never know . . .

. . . When the joke will be on you.

Numb with the pain of the paddle, he didn't notice at first. Then, faintly, he smelled the harsh flavor of wood smoke and raised his head and sniffed.

Definitely wood smoke.

He took the fumes like a dry-rope bit between his teeth and his paddle foamed the water and they rounded a point and saw a gay yellow tent pitched next to a green canoe on a storybook island. A man and woman relaxed in front of a fire.

"Phone?" Broker screamed as he flailed his paddle toward the campsite.

"PHONE!"

The man rose in a defensive crouch, alarmed by the manic energy of the two hollow-eyed men paddling toward him and his companion.

Broker's voice sobered him. "We left a critical injury back on Fraser. *Do you have a cell phone?*" The bow of the canoe clunked onto the rock beach.

Galvanized, hearing Broker clearly, the man yelled, "Gotcha." He dashed for his tent, emerged, ran to the shore, and handed over the button-studded black plastic wand.

The St. Louis County 911 operator switched the call through to the county deputy on duty in Ely and deputy sheriff Dave Iker picked up the phone. Broker recognized Iker's voice. They exchanged quick greetings and then Broker described the situation. Iker dispatched his last cruiser not tied up in weather-related traffic accidents to meet Broker and Allen at Uncle Billie's Lodge. Then he called the U.S. Forest Service seaplane base across town on Lake Shagawa.

Iker continued down his checklist. He alerted the northern team of the St. Louis County Rescue Squad, notified the state patrol, and requested the status of their helicopter. Then he called Ely Miner Hospital to put an ambulance on standby. The hospital dispatcher told him that all the medics were on the truck pileup out west on Highway 169. But the dispatcher would call Life Flight in Duluth and request a helicopter to fly to the hospital helipad. Ely Miner was a Band-Aid station that was not equipped to handle major emergency surgery on a critical patient.

When Iker left his office in the Ely courthouse only one Ely town cop remained in the building to cover the radios and Ely itself.

Outside, he saw low clouds skimming over the storefronts and spitting flurries, so he radioed for a weather update from the cops at the accident site to the west.

"We got us another October Surprise. It's snowing like hell here, and Hibbing's socked in," came the reply. Hibbing was sixty miles south and west. "Two feet of snow predicted. Winds already gusting to forty mph. The state patrol is thinking about closing Highways Two and Seventy-one."

"Sam, break out one medic and head back for Ely. We're way understaffed here. There's a critical stranded on Lake Fraser. I'm going in with the seaplane."

"In this?"

"Affirmative. Call the hangar for details." He keyed off the net and put his Ford Crown Vic in gear. Four minutes later he walked into the hangar at the seaplane base. Outside, a stubby red and white Dehaviland Beaver floatplane tossed on its pontoons at the dock. Inside, two pilots stood at the radio and the one with the mike in his hand said to Iker, "Where we're at, Dave, is dispatch recommends no fly. I just talked to the state patrol. They're not turning a prop in this. The Rescue Squad's socked in and so is Life Flight out of St. Mary's in Duluth. The National Weather Service just officially named it a blizzard and it's going to clobber us in half an hour."

"This isn't a sprained ankle. We got a guy who's going to die," Iker said.

"That's what I told them and it's my call." He depressed the send key on the mike. "I'm going up," the pilot said to his dispatcher, clicked the mike twice, and turned to Iker. "Looks like just you and me. The paramedics are on that truck pileup."

Iker nodded and said, "I got a cop and a medic on the way back in but we can't wait." They leaned over a map and Iker said, "One of the guys paddling out is a surgeon; we'll zip him to the hospital just in case. I know the guide. He says the patient will be hard to find from the air with the snow. No tent. It's not a normal campsite. They're hunkered back in a rock hidey-hole on a low bluff. He says he can steer us in."

"Where are they now?" the pilot asked. His eyes darted out the windows where the ground crew was readying the Beaver.

"Paddling in on Lake One. They should be at Billie Broker's Lodge in about ten minutes."

"Okay," the pilot said. He was clear-eyed, clean-shaven, and neat in his Smokey Bear–green jacket, sweater, and trousers. He'd flown Black Hawk helicopters into Iraq and danced with blizzards working the Alaskan bush. He'd bailed out of flying commercial passenger flights because they were too boring.

"We got one shot," he said. "We drop in on Lake One, pick your guy up, then fly to Fraser and find the stranded party." He pulled on a jacket and moved through the hangar toward the pier. Outside, he shouted over the rising wind. "The tricky part is meeting this big bastard storm on the way back."

The hangar chief signaled thumbs up, the preflight checks were complete. They threw a Stokes stretcher and a first-aid bag in the cramped cargo hold behind the cockpit and climbed in. The Beaver was built exceptionally tough to handle the rugged terrain of Northern Canada. With its fuselage slung and strutted under its long, square-tipped wing, it had all the charm of a back-country, three-quarter-ton mud hole truck.

The 450-horse Pratt and Whitney engine coughed a cloud of exhaust and the aluminum pontoons smacked forward over the chop. An orange windsock on a spit of land across from the dock blasted out at a three-o'clock right angle to its mast and pointed the way straight east.

Broker was paddling flat out, heading for the boat dock in front of Uncle Billie's Lodge and the county patrol cruiser idling next to it. Then he heard the motor.

The engine growl came in low and fast, then strings of rivets caught the pewter light as the Beaver cleared the pines. Bottom heavy with big pontoon floats, it lunged down, practically set one wing tip in the lake, turned tightly, and splash-landed a hundred yards away.

Deputy Iker's brown and tan uniform appeared in the open hatch. He commenced to yell and wave but Broker couldn't hear over the roaring prop, so he sculled up to the pontoon.

"You the doctor?" Iker yelled. Allen nodded and Iker pointed to the shore and yelled again. "That cop will take you to the hospital."

"I thought there'd be a helicopter?" Allen shouted.

"Take my word for it, you want this Beaver more than a helicopter." Then Iker rolled his eyes at Broker. They'd had dinner five days ago and they went back a ways, working a county task force together when Broker was undercover with BCA.

"You," Iker yelled at Broker, "are coming with me."

He pulled Broker up on the pontoon, leaned out, waved to the cop in the dock, and pointed to Allen. The cop nodded. Allen pushed off and, facing about in the bow seat, began paddling for shore.

Broker and Iker tumbled into the cargo bay. Iker whirled his forefinger, the pilot leaned into the stick, the plane wheeled, the prop bit the wind, and they vibrated over the speed-bump waves.

"That was fast," Broker yelled.

"Not fast enough. There's a blizzard moving in." Iker smiled thinly.

"But we'll beat it back to Ely?" Broker asked.

Again the thin grin from the deputy as he banged Broker on the shoulder. "Hey, we eat this shit up, right?"

Broker blinked and shook his head. "We *used to* eat this shit up."

"Yeah, well," Iker tossed a thumb at the pilot, "he's young. He definitely still eats this shit up."

Chapter Seven

Allen rode a police cruiser into town from the east as the blizzard moved in from the west. The harried deputy dropped him off promptly and drove away. Chilled and cramped from the canoe, he stiffly dragged Broker's waterproof duffel up the sidewalk as a thirty mph wind knocked him sideways. He made it through the shin-deep drifts and opened a door with a small orange neon EMERGENCY ROOM sign. He dropped the bag in front of the dispatch desk where a woman stood up to confirm his identity. Deputy Iker, she explained, had radioed ahead and now she was monitoring the rescue party which was in flight to "pick up the patient." She motioned down a corridor and a lean, dark-haired woman came forward in a blue cotton smock.

"Nancy, take Dr. Falken to Boris," the dispatcher said.

The nurse regarded Allen with the tired slit eyes of someone who'd been up all night. Then she led him down the hall to a nurse's station where a wiry man dressed in a white medical smock was talking to a woman wearing a sweater and jeans with fresh snow trapped in the cuffs. She held a clipboard in one hand and a telephone in the other.

"This is the doctor who paddled out of the canoe area," said the dark-haired nurse.

Allen removed his gloves and extended a hand shriveled pinkish-white from cold water. "Allen Falken," he offered.

"Hello, Boris Brecht, I'm glad to meet you. They said on the radio that you're a belly guy."

"That's right," Allen said. He blinked and almost lost his balance as the ward swam around him with bright lights and tile, like a large, very clean, very warm bathroom.

"Is your physician's license current?"

"Yes, I . . ."

"May I see it and a picture ID, and I need a contact number where you currently practice?"

Allen cocked his head. "Come again?"

"Dr. Falken—Allen—I'm a family-practice physician. I take out tonsils, maybe. I can't operate on this man they're bringing in."

Allen was furious. "What are you talking about? He's in bad shape, he could perforate. He needs a level-one trauma center . . ." His shaky smile didn't match his voice; his words and parts of his body were evidently thawing at different rates. "There's supposed to be a helicopter to take him to Duluth."

Brecht pointed his finger at the ceiling. "Hear that moan? That's a blizzard. The roads are closed. There is no helicopter. We're it. We have an anesthetist on call and we're trying to reach her, but she could be stuck out there with the whole day shift."

"Jesus." Allen rallied, as he plucked the clipboard from the woman in the snow-cuffed jeans, took her pen, and wrote a number on the top of the work schedule attached to the board. Then he dug in a zippered pocket, removed his wallet from a Ziploc bag, and handed Brecht his physician's license card and his Minnesota driver's license.

"Call Ron Rosenbaum, he's the senior surgeon at Timberry Trails Medical Group where I'm on staff. Now, how are you set up?"

"We have an operating-room suite on the lower level for scheduled elective surgery when a surgeon is available, usually from Virgina, sometimes Duluth or even the Cities."

"Can you do general anesthesia?" Allen asked.

"We've got a Narcomed II."

"What about the anesthetist?"

"What about her? We're paging her."

Allen forked his index finger and thumb, pressing his eyes and reminding himself not to be patronizing. Get focused. "Let's assume the worst and she doesn't show, who does that leave?"

Brecht grimaced, "If nobody makes it in before the patient arrives—it's you, me, and," he pointed to the woman in jeans, "Judy, which leaves Nancy on her own to cover the emergency room and two other wards. But we can't handle the anesthesia machine."

"Your anesthetist should have an adult intubation tray," Allen said.

"We *are* a hospital. We *have* a pharmacy," Judy said.

"Ketamine?"

"It's there." She narrowed her eyes. "Will that hold him if you open his abdomen?"

Allen shrugged; he'd operated with it on worse trauma cases in Bosnia in very hairy conditions. "It'll have to work if there's no alternative." Then he cleared his throat and gestured with his arms, indicating his bedraggled clothing and wet boots. "Look, I need a cup of black coffee, some scrubs, and some comfortable shoes, if that's possible." He took a deep breath, exhaled. "If there's a room where I could be alone a few minutes and use a telephone. Then I need to see the OR."

"Sure," Brecht said. "I have to call the state licensing board and your hospital—just, you know, going through the motions to satisfy our administrator. He's, ah, gone sort of apeshit on the subject of emergency surgical privileges. Judy will fix you up."

Which Judy proceeded to do. Allen took off his wet clothing and cat-washed in the men's lavatory, then changed into a clean smock and trousers and a pair of somebody's worn Nikes. When he came out of the john she was waiting with a cup of hot black coffee and then she showed him to an examining room. He thanked her, smiling stiffly, as she pulled the door behind her; then he turned his back to the door and planted his shoulders against it.

Allen carefully sat the coffee down on the small nurses' table, wrapped both arms across his chest, clasped his shoulders, and hugged himself. The notion of him operating to save Hank's life brought a slight tremor of irony—he recalled Hank's tough-guy pontificating yesterday morning. Well, Hank, it looks like the situation is now slightly reversed.

His eyes fixed on the telephone sitting on the desk, next to the blood pressure monitor and the coffee cup. He took a moment to clearly remember a time when he was totally satisfied with himself . . .

He remembered Jolene Sommer at that party a year ago at Milt's river place. She had playfully mussed his hair and had told him it was too perfect.

Allen, you've got to learn to unwind a little.

Her touch had left him permanently tousled. Like a warm breeze it had carried hints of foreign vacations and easy laughter. After meeting her he'd returned home to his life and discovered it was a colorless shell furnished with brand-name clichés.

There is more, she'd seemed to intimate.

There is me.

But she hadn't said anything remotely like that. It was a wish on his part. It wasn't that he thought Jolene could change. He thought *he* could change and she might be a catalyst.

Change into someone less wooden, more with it . . .

He rolled his eyes up toward the ceiling and reminded himself: *You're too disciplined, too trained, too tidy a man to contemplate such messy human knots.*

As always, there was refuge in his work. So he sat down at the small desk and sipped the strong, familiar, bad hospital coffee from the familiar generic Styrofoam cup. The room's furnishings were also familiar—the whites, grays, and tans of the examining table and the cabinets, the strident biohazard logo on the Sharpes disposal box.

Allen took a deep breath to steady down. He used diaphragmatic breathing as part of his pre-op checklist to enhance visualization. But this deep breath was to prepare him for the phone call to Jolene.

As he exhaled, he visualized the sprawling house tucked on the shadowy pine bluff overlooking the St. Croix River, south of the Hudson Bridge. His watch said 9:18 A.M. He had an idea of how she spent her days. He did not think of her at night when she was with Hank. The idea of her touching his gnarled old body that smelled of cigarettes . . .

At 9:18, depending on the weather, she'd be settling into the Mission oak rocker in the sunny corner of the kitchen with a cup of coffee. She'd be listening to the morning show on public radio. She followed the current events program every day to build her vocabulary and deepen her range of subjects. She'd have a pen and a notebook in her lap. She'd be taking notes.

Hank was proud of the fact that Jolene had never graduated from high school.

She'd be wearing the white chenille robe that complemented her green eyes and brought out the ruby highlights in her dark hair. Her smooth skin had an olive cast and she joked that she'd deliberately ordered it a size too small, like a pair of jeans, so that it would fit snug. That damn gray cat he despised would be curled on her lap.

When Allen shut his eyes he was startled by the abyss of fatigue that met him in the dark behind his eyelids. The sound of the window shuddering in the wind brought him up sharply on task and he oriented himself on the serious fact that five lives were suspended inside a tiny airplane somewhere in that sky. All to bring Hank Sommer back here.

What if the plane crashed? Suddenly he saw himself comforting Jolene, winning her over. He'd take her to Florence.

Allen killed the fantasy with a stab of concentration. He was gifted with the highest utilitarian virtues; he was meticulous, he was thorough, he'd memorized a Latinized medical library with almost total recall. His steady hands were capable of tying almost invisible knots in synthetic, absorbable Vicryl sutures.

He could not afford an overactive imagination.

So it bothered him when he couldn't control the adolescent excitement that speeded up his heart as he dialed the area code and the number and counted one ring, two, three . . .

"Hello," the voice came on smooth and tight and to the point.

"Jo?"

"Allen, well, that was quick; who got the big Bambi?"

"Where are you?"

"I'm in the kitchen looking at the Weather Channel, you guys must be really catching it."

"I want you to sit down and listen carefully; something happened." He spoke in the available, but guarded, professional tone he used with the families of critical patients. He was not a hand-holder but he didn't stand in doorways with his own hands in his pockets, either.

"Oh Christ, Hank didn't fall off the wagon, did he? The way he was yelling on the phone . . ." She paused. When she resumed talking, first fear stiffened her voice. "Allen? Is everything all right?"

"Jo, it's Hank. He ruptured himself. Bad."

"Oh, Christ. I told him to have that taken care of."

It sounded like she did sit down from the rush of concern in her voice. Succinctly, he explained the storm, the rupture, leaving Milt and Hank in the winter camp, the paddle out, how the guide and the cops were going back with a floatplane, and how he was now stranded in this one-horse hospital with a skeleton staff in a blizzard, anticipating operating under less than ideal conditions.

"Just be prepared," he told her in his best level tone.

The velvet wore thin in her voice as she showed some bare knuckle. "Just what's that supposed to mean? I'm not some fucking Boy Scout—you'd better give me more than that. You'd better tell me he's going to be all right."

"I'm just saying it's bad up here, there's a blizzard. Christ, he's in this little airplane with some cowboy pilot."

"Promise me, Allen. You've got to pull him through."

"Don't worry, Jo." He pressed the cool plastic of the receiver against his forehead and blamed the fatigue, because he found himself looking at all the possible outcomes on this bad morning, and in one of them the plane simply disappeared into the storm and was never seen again. An Act of God.

She broke his glide. "Give me the phone number for the hospital, there must be an airstrip up there. I'll watch the weather. I'll get Earl to find a quick charter . . ."

"I don't think Earl is a good idea under the circumstances," Allen said tightly.

"He's handy, he knows how to get things done. Like hire a plane on a short notice. I'm just being practical."

"Hank hates him," Allen said.

"Let me worry about that. You tuck your head into your surgeon's cap and take care of business. I'm counting on you."

"Yes," Allen said simply, suddenly helpless before the inadequacy of language; so he gave her the hospital phone number, hung up the phone, and tried to wipe the sweat from his forehead with the sweat on his palms. Enough of this bullshit. It was time to get serious.

And finally the traction of his willpower engaged and he jetti-soned the distractions—his personal life, the exhausting canoe trip out of the park, even Jolene. They became irrelevant as he narrowed in focus until his triangular face seemed to winnow to a point.

Then he raised his raw, blistered hands and inspected them. As always, he felt contempt for people who never touched anything except keyboards and telephones and money, who talked their way through life.

He took pride in making his living with his hands. During his surgical residency at the Mayo Clinic he had worn a red-and-white-striped regimental tie under his staff coat. The pattern and the col-ors invoked the bloody bandages of the barber pole that had served as the original shingle surgeons hung out to advertise their profes-sion. The surgeons had followed European armies out of the Middle Ages through the Renaissance and into the modern era. They'd cut hair and they'd amputated arms and legs.

Allen smiled. Then, with the help of Mother Church, they'd rooted out the village midwives and the herbalist "witches" and consolidated their hold on medicine.

He was not without history. He was not without wit.

A surgeon of his generation couldn't wear a tattoo on his arm like the new kids coming up—or like Hank Sommer could, and Allen envied Hank the cryptic messages dyed into his skin. And if Allen could have a secret tattoo it would be a Bard/Parker number-ten scalpel blade and it would say: HEAL WITH STEEL.

Now he mentally stripped himself until he saw himself as nude as a Michelangelo anatomy study. Then he dressed himself in suc-cessive layers of knowledge, confidence, and control. Only when he was fully mentally garbed did he visualize the entire operation, starting from the first incision.

He absolutely believed that anything he could visualize he could make happen in the controlled environment of an operating room.

When Allen stood up, his brow and his palms were dry. The guide, Broker, did not look like he was intimidated by Acts of God; he would persist. He would bring Hank back and lay him on an operating table and, true to the oath he had taken, Allen would insert a blade of the sharpest stainless steel just above Hank Som-mer's pubic bone and slice him open, lift out his guts with his two hands, repair them, and save his life.

. . .

The pilot leaned back, grabbed Iker's arm, and rapped a knuckle on the map. Broker climbed forward and put his finger on the point in Fraser Lake.

"The rocks are real bad. You're gonna have to land in this bay where the point joins the shore, and we'll carry him out to you," Broker said.

The pilot shook his head. "No time. Lots of bad bush in there. We'll take our chances with the rocks. The guy with the bad arm— can he walk?" he asked.

"Sure," Broker said. "He can make it on his own."

The pilot nodded. "Okay. Listen up. You two are going to strap him on the Stokes and haul him through the rocks and load him. We do it the first time or we'll have to ride out this storm on the lake. Which will not be good for the patient."

"Eh, Pat?" called a deadpan voice on the radio. "Be advised. I'm looking out the hangar window and I can't see the wind sock on the point."

"Outstanding," the pilot replied.

At one thousand feet the clouds were clotting fast, and down below the snow rippled like cheesecloth over the pine crowns and water. What had taken Broker and Allen a day of paddling and portaging to travel now buffeted past in minutes and they came up on Fraser. The pilot knew the lake, fixed the point, and flew straight for the spot that Broker had indicated on the map.

Gray smoke smudged the snow and Broker figured Milt had dumped pine boughs on the fire. Then they saw Milt's red parka jerking among the white turtles of rock, waving his good arm.

Iker grabbed the stretcher as the Beaver hugged a tight turn and bumped down into the waves. Iker and Broker edged through the open hatch and balanced on the pontoon as the plane maneuvered toward shore.

"Go. Go," the pilot yelled, pumping his arm.

They tried to step onto a rock but it wasn't going to happen, so they jumped at the most solid-looking footing they could see, and both of them splashed up to their waists in the ice-cold water.

"Jesus H. Christ," gasped Iker, scrambling for shore.

They sloshed through the waves and stumbled up the cobble beach. Milt, unshaven, gray with pain, walked stiffly out to them.

"No water or food since midnight. He's unconscious," Milt yelled in the wind. "Thing is, the swelling went down an hour ago and the pain went away and he was feeling great—then he started screaming. Now he's delirious, burning up."

"Aw God, it perforated," Iker said.

"C'mon," Broker shouted. "He's dying on us."

They stamped into the rocky cul-de-sac, swatting at the smoke and, grabbing Sommer, roughly shoved the stiff stretcher under the sleeping bag and buckled him down. Sommer woke up screaming.

Ignoring the screams, they staggered back toward the plane with their clumsy load. Milt lurched ahead, tripping and falling in the surf until he made it to the aircraft and, using his strong good arm, pulled himself aboard.

Knee-deep in the rocky wash, Broker's legs buckled and Iker, on the back end, tripped. The sleeping bag took a wave, and now their load was heavier, soaked with water.

They dropped him and barely managed to keep his head from going under but the screaming stopped. Sommer had passed out again. Broker and Iker locked eyes and were amazed that the brief exertion had sapped their energy, that they didn't have the strength to lift the stretcher.

But they had to.

Desperate, they wrenched the weight through the rocks and waves and banged it on the pontoon. With Milt pulling one-handed, they managed to get the front of the stretcher into the tiny cargo bay.

"Fucker's too big," Iker yelled, frantic. Sommer's feet, swaddled in the soaked sleeping bag, dangled over the stretcher and bumped against the cockpit seats.

"Wedge him any way you can, shut that hatch, we're *going*," the pilot ordered.

Milt, Broker, and Iker worked in a frenzy with the stretcher, as the pilot banked into the wind and grabbed some sky with an impromptu aerodynamic magic trick. For a few minutes they bounced through turbulence, catching their breath, and then the calm voice on the radio said, "Pat, be advised, they're getting heavy snow and ice—I say again—heavy snow and ice and sixty-plus wind gusts east of Lake Vermilion."

"Roger," the pilot said. Then he yelled, "Map." Iker held it at the ready.

As the Beaver lurched at two thousand feet, Broker looked forward, between the tangled arms and legs, over the jittering dials and gauges on the console, out the window.

God had been busy.

God had built a solid, grayish-white churning wall all across the sky, and that wall was coming straight at them. Broker could see lakes and woods being vacuumed into its base.

One eye on the forest disappearing in front of the oncoming blizzard and one eye on the map, the pilot shouted in the radio, "Closest place to land with road access is . . . ah, Snowbank. So. Okay. I'm going to drop into Snowbank ahead of this thing. Get a vehicle to the boat ramp. You got that?"

"You're diverting to Snowbank boat ramp. Lay on ground transport," the radio voice said.

"Right." The pilot dropped the mike and yelled, "Hang on."

Everybody groaned as the Beaver pitched over into a steep dive and the pilot bent forward, very intent on the churning white wall.

Broker was thrown nose to nose with Sommer's corpselike face and Sommer's eyes popped open as Iker, in the front, climbed his seat while Milt slowly moved his lips: "Holy Mary, Mother of God . . ."

Their eyes were clamped shut and they were braced in the forty-five-degree dive, so they didn't see the seething white wall break over the trees and chew inexorably into the western end of Snowbank Lake, as the Beaver leveled out and swooped down five, four, three feet off the waves, then skimmed the white caps, then bounced, rivets rattling, as it careened toward the boat ramp which was fast disappearing into the tempest, and they never saw the pilot smile as he cut the prop and coasted herky-jerky into the white churn.

It sure beat flying those commercial cattle cars.

Chapter Eight

"Next stop's the dock," the pilot yelled. "I put her down upwind to try and drift into the sucker, so be ready to jump out and tie us off."

But Broker couldn't see anything because the windscreen was plastered with snow as they bucked, blind, on the waves, and he was definitely swearing off small planes forever.

And Iker was yelling into his police radio, "Sam, where the hell are you?"

The radio shouted back, "Dave, I got you visual. We're on the dock but it's like looking through oatmeal."

"This guy's looking real bad here."

"Hey, we're lucky to get wheels turning. The Suburban broke down and I had to commandeer a vehicle. We got out fast as we could."

Milt lay curled in a ball with his face pasty as chalk, and was gripping his injured arm. Sommer hung from the stretcher straps. The pilot pointed to Milt. "There's blankets in that aft compartment. Looks like we got some delayed shock there. And get the ropes."

Broker lifted the stretcher to open the compartment door and Sommer screamed and they all gritted their teeth because there was too much scream and not enough cabin. But Broker kept moving and got the blankets, covered Milt, and went back for the coils of rope. Then he turned to Sommer.

"Hurts Jesus hurts," Sommer said, rocking in his straps as the sweat popped and streaked his scalded face.

"You're going to be all right," Broker said, and suddenly Sommer's hand groped up and clutched Broker's arm.

"Tell Cliff . . ." Sommer muttered through clenched teeth and his eyes were wide-open yellow jets. Not seeing.

"We gotta do something quick. He's out of his head," Broker yelled as he pried off Sommer's fingers. Then, getting his voice under control, he tried to calm Sommer. "Okay, tell Cliff."

"Tell Cliff to move the money. Don't let them . . ." Sommer reared on a needle of pain, licked his cracked lips, and blinked away sweat. "Gotta tell Cliff . . ."

"What? Cliff who?"

"Cliff Stovall." Sommer collapsed back on his restraints.

Broker rested his wrist on Sommer's forehead and came away jolted by the clammy hot flesh. "C'mon. C'mon," he shouted to Iker.

"Working on it," Iker yelled back. Then—"Oh shit!"

They collided with something hard and as the rivets holding the plane together groaned, Broker flashed on the claustrophobic but also indignant vision of scuttling and *drowning* in a blizzard. Another violent crash shook Sommer awake, screaming. What? Had they lost a pontoon?

"Bingo," the pilot yelled triumphantly. "Quick, help me with the rope." He clambered over the seat, tunneled through the crowded bodies, and grabbed the coils of rope. "Think fast. Move. Open the hatch."

They struggled with the door, pushed it open, and squinted into the blowing snow and saw that one of the pontoons had snagged on the deck and pilings of a boat dock.

The pilot yelled, "C'mon, we gotta tie her down before we float away."

Two bundled figures waiting on the dock turned out to be a county deputy and a paramedic, a woman. They helped Broker, Iker, and the pilot struggle up onto the slippery planks, and they all commenced to fasten ropes to secure the plane.

Broker concentrated and tied a bowline. He squinted at lights that hurt his eyes and realized he was staring into powerful low beams that showcased the churning snow. A huge maroon Chevy Tahoe with tire chains idled at the end of the dock.

When the plane was anchored, they hauled Sommer and Milt up to the dock. The robust brunette paramedic took one look at Sommer and yelled, "C'mon, let's get him in the truck."

The pilot accepted a thermos of coffee and, armed with a Louis L'Amour paperback, stayed with his plane. Everybody else piled in the Tahoe. As they plowed back toward Ely, Sommer screamed and writhed and drew his knees up to his chest at every bump and shift. After three tries, the medic gave up running the saline IV. Sommer just thrashed them out.

Broker huddled in the back, wrapped in a blanket next to Milt, who made a cramped pile on the cargo floor beside Sommer. He sipped a sloshing cup of hot coffee gratefully, but he couldn't shake off the bone-deep chill from his last dip in the glacier water. He shivered and figured it was a sign of getting old.

Iker and a deputy sheriff the size of a pro wrestler hunched in the front seat. The way the windshield was catching snow it looked like *Star Trek* when the Enterprise accelerated to warp speed.

"Get ready for a hot belly," the paramedic shouted into her radio. "His pressure is one eighty over a hundred. Pulse is one twenty and he's running a temp of a hundred and four." She listened, rolled her eyes, and poked Iker in the shoulder. "ETA?"

"Fifteen minutes," Iker said.

"Make that one five minutes," the paramedic said. Then she punched off the set and shook her head.

"What?" Broker asked.

"Procedure," she said in a weary voice. "Obviously, the helicopter's out from Duluth, so the administrator wants to throw him in an ambulance and put the ambulance behind a snowplow and ship him down the road to the nearest hospital where there's a surgeon."

"In this weather? What about Falken, the surgeon who paddled out with me?" Broker asked.

"They're arguing about that right now. His license is current and they made some calls."

"So what's the problem?" Broker asked.

"Mike. The administrator. He wants to poll the hospital board before he signs off on surgical privileges. One of them's in Florida."

Iker turned from the front seat and glowered. "Yeah, bullshit! After all we been through, this fucking guy isn't going to croak because of red tape."

"Hey. What the hell," said the huge deputy behind the wheel. His name was Sam and he rolled his eyes. "It's like these Yuppie jerks come up here and tell us how to live. They run up the real estate and open Starbucks and bean sprouts. They tell us where and how we can fish. They want to take our snowmobiles and rifles away. They love the wolves from Minneapolis or Chicago or wherever the fuck they live, never mind the fuckin' wolves eat our dogs on our porches. Then, when *they* get *their* asses in a sling they expect us to hang our balls over the edge and pull them out. And who foots the bill for all the overtime? Them in their gated fuckin' suburbs? No, we pay it out of our dwindling fuckin' tax base."

Sam's rant broke the tension in the Tahoe and they burst into deranged frontline mirth. The truck accelerated, slipped, and sideswiped a mass of overhanging spruce branches. The swerve brought them out of their laughing jag.

"Where'd you get this beast, anyway?" Iker asked, suddenly realizing they weren't in a county vehicle.

Sam grinned. "Tell 'em, Shari."

The paramedic smiled. "The ambulance couldn't handle the drifts. The Suburban was down and we saw this thing parked in front of Vertin's Cafe, had the chains on and everything. So we went in and liberated it off this swampy from the Cities."

They were still wiping tears from their eyes when they saw the fluorescent glow of a deserted Amoco Station, and it looked like somebody left the door open to an empty freezer the way the lights burned white on white. Soon they glimpsed chimney smoke flapping over the rooftops of Ely like tattered sheets and abandoned cars loomed up, mired in knee-high drifts. Nothing moved except the Tahoe and the banshee wind and the reeling shadows of the trees.

Finally they approached Miner Hospital, an obstinate red-brick relic of mining-company medicine that vanished and reappeared in whirlpools of snow. They came closer and saw a bright orange wind sock whipped out rigid as metal sculpture from a corner of the flat roof. And a double garage door opened and the Tahoe lurched inside and the doors closed.

The engine quit and for the first time in three days Broker was in an enclosed, dry, quiet place that smelled securely of radial tires and clean concrete, only more so because it was a hospital with a red cross.

The rear door jerked opened and a woman, a man, and a haggard Allen Falken reached in. The woman wore jeans under her plum-colored smock. Allen and the man wore hospital blue. Broker and Shari helped them lift Sommer's stretcher and transfer it onto a wheeled gurney cart.

In the flurry of movement, Allen looked at Sommer, then called to Milt who did not respond. He turned to Broker.

"Milt said the lump went down an hour ago. Sommer felt better, then he got delirious," Broker said.

Allen shot a look at the other man. "We're up shit's creek for time if he perforated; where the hell's that anesthetist?"

"She's coming."

Then Allen, who seemed taller now, commanded Broker. "You've got to get another gurney and load Milt yourself, the storm caught them at shift change and they're way understaffed. C'mon people, let's hustle," he urged everyone as Brecht, the nurse, and the paramedic rushed Sommer up a ramp, through heavy swinging doors, and into a corridor.

Iker followed them, returned with a gurney, and helped Broker load Milt. Sam the driver stayed behind the wheel, talking into a snarl of static on his police radio.

They wheeled Milt into a small equipment-packed alcove with two treatment tables on the right. Shari came down the hall and supervised while they heaved Milt on the table. Then she waved them away and cut off Milt's wet clothes.

Broker followed Iker down the hall and focused on a wall poster that diagramed potential fishhook accidents and the proper first-aid procedures. Dizzy at the heat in the building, he steadied his arm on a wall, and saw that his cheap wristwatch was still running. The time was 9:45 A.M. They had dumped in the storm a little before eight yesterday morning. They'd left the camp on the point at ten. Getting Sommer out had taken fifteen minutes shy of twenty-four hours. Broker's knees started to wobble. He'd been traveling on rough water, bouncing in rougher air. Now he was having trouble finding his land legs.

Up ahead, they had Sommer in the hall in front of an elevator surrounded by bristling carts stacked with monitors and a tangle of IV lines and electrical cords.

"Where's Amy, goddammit?" Brecht yelled. "It won't be pretty if we have to cut this guy without her."

"We paged her. She's coming."

Sommer screamed as Allen, Brecht, and the nurse freed him from the rigid stretcher in a coordinated surge and discarded it along with the soaked sleeping bag. His eyes rolled, gumdrops of sweat mobbed his face. "HURTS GODDAMN HURTS!" he screamed.

"You're okay, Hank," Allen said. "You're in a hospital. We'll take good care of you." Metal shears flashed in his hand as he cut away Sommer's clothes. The material disappeared in a blue cyclone of activity as electrical leads attached to rounds of tape were thwacked into place on his bare chest. Bumpy trace lines jumped on a cardiac monitor.

"FUCK YOU HURTS!"

"He's delirious. He can't hear you," Brecht said to Allen. Then he called out to Judy, "Get STAT CBC with diff and lytes. I'll get a blood pressure. Start two large-bore IV's antecubital and run them wide open," Brecht slapped on a blood-pressure cuff and pumped it up while the nurse strung liters of saline IV and popped catheters in the hollows of Sommer's elbows.

Broker watched Allen take a stance astride the crisis. Hair askew, still unshaven from the trail, he was a rougher version of his usual self. *He has to be beat*, thought Broker. *I sure am.*

"This guy NPO?" somebody yelled.

Broker turned at the bright female voice and matched it to a young woman with straight-ahead posture who jogged down the hall in jeans sticky with snow stuck to her knees. She shook more snow from her hair, cast off her jacket, and caught a blue smock the nurse tossed to her. She had large gray eyes under tawny, pale blond hair, no makeup, and freckles dotted her cheeks.

Brecht nodded at Allen. "Amy, Dr. Allen Falken."

"When's the last time he ate?" she asked.

"Not since midnight, right?" Allen craned his neck around the huddle of medics and queried Broker.

Broker nodded. "That's what Milt said."

"Is he allergic to any medicine?" She asked.

"Is it . . . ?" An out-of-place guy peered over their shoulders. He wore a white shirt, loose collar, tie unknotted, and his face sagged, blotched with concern.

"It's bad, Mike," Brecht said as he probed Sommer's lower abdomen gently with his palm. Sommer thrashed and screamed.

"Jesus," Mike said.

"It's the real deal. Like a burst appendix."

"You've done an appendix," Mike said.

"I stabilize and ship south. My thing is your kid's ear infection. This is way over my head. We have to open his abdomen and do a small bowel resection."

"Don't lecture me, I know what it means," Mike hissed in a trapped voice, a hospital administrator treading in his worst nightmare. Lawsuits circled his furrowed brow like a halo of hungry sharks.

"He's gotta do it," Brecht said, jerking his head toward Allen.

"Let me think," Mike said.

"No time to think," said Amy, the new arrival.

"What's that supposed to mean?" Mike countered.

"Means you're going to have a *lot* of paperwork to do if this guy tips over because you shipped him," she continued. "There's EMTALA, there's a blizzard. We have a licensed surgeon on board and a guy who's septic with a perforated bowel. Not cool, Mike."

"Amy's right, we try to ship him, he will fucking die." Brecht bit off each consonant for emphasis.

Mike turned to Iker, who shook his head. "I won't put him back out in that weather. No way."

Lastly, he looked at Allen who waited a beat and called it: "We open that belly or he's dead. Make a decision. *Fast.*"

"Okay." Mike hitched up his belt, squared his shoulders, and nodded to Allen. "Take him downstairs to the OR and scrub in. But Amy—I want all your stuff in recovery in case we have to reintubate. I mean, syringes full, everything. No one's going to say we weren't on top of this."

Then Mike saw Broker and Iker standing there leaking puddles of lake water and ice melt. He cleared his throat and motioned to the paramedic. "Shari, get these guys something dry to wear."

As they retreated back toward the garage, Broker watched

Brecht, Amy, and the nurse shove the gurney toward the open elevator. Allen walked last, his hands held high, poised. Amy bent over
Sommer, worked his jaw between her hands, opened his mouth, and
looked into his throat. "Oh shit, this guy's got an airway from hell,"
she said merrily.

"But you can intubate him?" Allen asked.

"I can intubate him anywhere, anytime," she shot back, a little
cocky, a little high on the action.

The elevator doors closed behind them.

Chapter Nine

Milt lay in the ER room cubbyhole draped in a floral-patterned hospital smock with an IV in his arm and an ice pack on his swollen right shoulder.

"That smock had to be recycled from Martha Washington's drapes," Broker said. He was feeling good. Tired as hell but good.

"Oh *please*," Shari groaned. Then she bent over Milt and said, "You probably tore a muscle and went into spasm in the plane."

"I'd rather break a bone than tear a muscle," Milt said as his eyelids fluttered and he struggled to stay awake.

"I hear you," Shari said.

"Hank?" Milt asked, drifting.

"Allen is operating," Broker said.

"For the report, what happened out there?" Iker asked.

Milt twitched, a modified shrug. "Straight-line winds dropped on us. Worst water I've seen on a lake. Hank had a hernia and he paddled his ass off. That's when he blew his gut. He and Broker swamped. Broker pulled him out." His eyes rolled toward Broker. "Guess he got his adventure to write about," Milt said, smiling weakly.

A lean woman in a blue smock and trousers came up silently in tennis shoes. She wound her dark ponytail into a hair net and pulled on latex gloves.

"Some day, eh, Nancy?" Shari said.

The nurse raised her brows, which emphasized the circles of fatigue under her eyes. "I worked all night watching two wards, now I still got them plus recovery when they bring that guy up."

They chatted quickly, then the nurse syringed a dose of pain reliever into Milt's IV, pointed to the puddle of water on the floor, and politely waved them off.

Broker and Iker followed Shari back into the empty garage. Sam and the Tahoe were gone. It was a busy afternoon.

Shari opened a locker, threw them towels, and turned her back. While they stripped and dried off, she rummaged around, clucking, obviously enjoying the fact that the two sweatshirts she heaved back to them were decorated with really hideous logos. Mismatched sweatpants followed.

While Shari made appropriately disparaging remarks, they put on the dry clothes and blue slippers. They went back into the hospital and padded down a corridor walled with floor-to-ceiling plate glass that churned, aquarium-like, with silent snow.

"Worse than the Halloween storm in ninety-one," Iker said. Broker, too tired to comment, plodded on to the staff lounge and flopped on a couch. In less than a minute he was chin on chest in a deep nod. He came up from the nod and heard Iker ask Shari what was going on downstairs in the operating room.

Shari pointed to her stomach and drew her finger down to her crotch. "They cut him open and lift out his intestines. Then they snip out the perforated section and sew it back together. After that they wash out his stomach cavity real good. They have to repair the hernia, but because of the presence of infection, they won't use a patch, so they stitch him up the old-fashion way."

"Ouch," Iker said.

Broker didn't hear the rest of the conversation because he was fast asleep.

"Hey, Broker, wake up, man."

"Wha . . . ?" Broker lurched forward and checked his watch. It was just past noon. He blinked and saw Iker's square, smiling face.

"They're done. They're bringing him up to the recovery room."

They turned through the halls, entered the ER corridor, and

Broker could almost feel the sunbeams peeking around the corner. The only person not smiling was Hank Sommer, who was sprawled out on a gurney, trussed in his own ugly floral gown. The agony that had gripped his face for twenty-four hours had melted away. With his mouth open in a long yawn he looked—if not peaceful—certainly burned-out stoned.

Directly over Sommer, Amy, the gray-eyed nurse-anesthetist, pulled off her bonnet in a triumphal gesture, shook out shoulder-length hair, and pushed the gurney. Nancy, the busy nurse, with her hair coiled in a net, hauled the other end. They steered the bed into a small room and detoured around a tall cart on casters that looked like a Craftsman tool chest with red drawers, and parked him next to the wall.

"What's the crash cart doing here?" Amy asked.

"Mike wanted it prepositioned."

Amy rolled her eyes and nodded at a trayful of tiny drug bottles and syringes positioned on the bed between Sommer's feet. "I hear you, he wants all my stuff ready, too." Then they switched Sommer from a mobile monitor to the bigger monitor bolted to the wall. The wired beep beep beep of his pulse, blood pressure, and oxygenation graphed steadily across the video screen.

Allen shuffled down the hall flanked by Brecht and Judy, the nurse who'd helped unload the Tahoe. They all wore blue tunics, trousers, blue booties over their shoes, and blue bonnets. Like rakish ascots, blue masks hung loose at their throats.

To Broker they seemed to move with the quiet swagger as would a blue-uniformed bomber crew who had just pulled off a dicey mission. And there was no doubt who the pilot was. Allen's throat and a wedge of chest showed through the V-neck of his scrub blouse, and a spatter of Sommer's blood dotted the hem. His strong hands swung at his sides as he took his victory lap along the surgeon track, that fine line between the kill floor and The Resurrection.

Broker added his grin to the wave of admiration.

Allen pulled off his bonnet and ran a hand through his matted hair. The corners of his lips dimpled up and, in a grateful gesture, he held up his right palm to shoulder level and high-fived Broker.

"So he's all right?" Broker asked.

Allen nodded and showed even teeth in a tired grin. "Hey. He lucked out. He had a good surgeon." More seriously, he said, "We caught it in time. He should be fine. Fine," he repeated, and scuffed his feet and tripped off balance, and Broker noticed that as he moved farther away from the OR, he seemed to diminish in stature. To physically shrink.

Broker reached out to steady him and Allen blinked, then squinted as his eyelids trembled. "I'm all in," he said. "Pooped."

"I hear you," Broker said, craning his neck to see into the small recovery room.

"Let the anesthetist make sure Sommer's all the way awake and stabilized. A few minutes," Allen said.

A congratulatory huddle formed in the corridor—Iker, Shari, Broker, Brecht, and Mike, the very comforted-looking administrator. After a moment, Broker stepped away and poked his head into the recovery room and listened to the medical chat.

"He's breathing well, sats good, rhythm stable," Nancy said.

"Okay," Amy said as she scanned the monitors. "Let's rouse him, get him to raise his head, squeeze a finger, swallow." Amy leaned over Sommer. "And wait for the eyelids, the littlest muscles are always the last to come back. Who's got the Narc keys?"

"Got them right here. I've got everything today."

"Get twenty-five milligrams of Demerol and give it IV."

Nancy went to a closet next to the oxygen outlet, opened the locked door, and went in. Amy moved the tray from the foot of Sommer's bed, looked around, and then placed it on a corner of the crash cart. Nancy returned with a slender syringe.

"Wait a sec. Let me get him talking," Amy said, propping her elbow next to Sommer's head. She leaned down and dangled her index finger in the loose fingers of his right hand. "Can you blink? Can you squeeze my finger?" she asked.

Sommer's eyes swam around, fluttered. He pressed her finger and tried to move.

"Take it easy," Amy said, patting his arm. "You've got a few stitches in your abdomen."

Sommer pursed dry lips. " 'peration."

"That's right. You've had an emergency operation that went just fine and now you're in the recovery room."

He blinked, focused, blinked again. "High," he said slowly.

"Hello, yourself."

"No. Stone . . ." He took a breath, wheezed. "Grog . . ."

"Yep. We gave you something. We're about to give you some more of the good stuff."

"Hi," Sommer said.

"Right, you're stoned, huh," she said.

Sommer raised his head and attempted to look around. "No," he said more distinctly. "Hello." He studied her. "You're pretty," he said in a halting voice. Then he squinted at the badge on the front of her blue tunic that read: AMY SKODA, CRNA. "You're pretty, Amy," he said, a little surer.

Amy executed a modified curtsey and said, "Thank you, and you're lucky to be alive."

Sommer blinked, the electric beep speeded up, and his voice sank. "Where?" he struggled to raise his up on elbows. Fell back.

"It's all right," Amy reassured him. "You're in a hospital."

His eyes turned to dark tunnels, remembering. "Storm."

Amy nodded. "Mister, you've had quite an adventure."

"Others?" he whispered, almost inaudible.

That's when Amy saw Broker edging through the door. She backed away from the bed, signaling to Nancy, hooking two fingers, squeezing her thumb in a squirting gesture. Nancy injected the Demerol into Sommer's IV, then discarded the used syringe in the Sharpes Box.

"Sorry, Mr. Broker, if observers are a hindrance, they will be removed," Amy announced as she put her palms on Broker's chest and backed him out into the hall. Then her stern expression relaxed into a smile. "Let him rest a few more minutes." Her hands lingered a beat longer than necessary and then she poked the logo on Broker's garish yellow sweatshirt with a straight finger. "Oh my," she said. A crawly drawing of a plump wood tick with a grinning cartoon-bug face bannered the shirt, with the caption:

Natural Wood Ticklers.
Sexual Aids & Muskie Lures.
Camp's Bait Shop
Hayward, Wisconsin.

"If I didn't have a sense of humor, that might offend me," she said, maintaining direct eye contact.

Broker, never good at small talk—and wondering how she knew his name—asked, "Do I know you?"

Her face went from warmly inviting to snappy attention as her eyes shifted past Broker. "Dr. Falken."

Allen, gray with fatigue, shambled up and gestured with an upturned palm. "How's he doing?"

"He's out of the woods," Amy said with a straight face. "Vitals are normal. He roused, raised his head, squeezed my finger, swallowed, and told me I was pretty."

"Are you treating for pain?"

"Nancy gave him twenty-five milligrams of Demerol. I'm going to get him something cool for his throat."

Amy breezed past and Broker watched her model the possibilities of baggy blue trousers as she walked down the hall. "She's pleased with herself," he said.

"Yes, nice, ah, glutes. Nordic skiing, diagonal stride, would be my guess," Allen yawned. He blinked and continued in a more serious voice, "She was extra careful extubating him and bringing him out of anesthesia. He has a tricky throat to work in. She's as good as or better than anyone I've worked with in Level One, so she's earned some strutting rights." As an afterthought, he said, "She's wasted on this place."

Then he patted Broker on the shoulder and drifted back down the hall and sat heavily on a folding chair. At the other end of the corridor Amy Skoda stopped to chat with Iker. They both looked up at Broker at the same time, and Amy batted her eyelashes, then lowered her gaze, walked away from Iker, and turned out of sight down the hall.

Then Broker nodded out on his feet and came back when he started to lose his balance. Dead-tired, he saw some movement. Iker and Shari started toward the dispatch room across from the ER cubbyhole and the yells started.

"Heads up, gang! We got another one!"

"What now?"

"No problem, relax, a broken arm, lacerations," called Brecht. "A drunk tried to drive a snowmobile through a birch tree. Thing is, that Tahoe they're using as an ambulance got stuck on the street, so we're going to have to manhandle the stretcher in."

Broker went to the garage, slipped back into his wet boots, and went to the street in front of the hospital, where deputy Sam had mired the Tahoe in a drift. Amid much yelling, they hauled another man lashed to a Stokes stretcher into the garage. Lumps of frozen blood the size of jelly beans stuck to the new patient's face and he smelled of alcohol and gasoline. A bloody pressure bandage was wrapped on his head.

Tracking snow, they stomped in through the garage and transferred the guy to a treatment table in the vacant emergency cubbyhole. Milt had been moved deeper into the building.

"This one's mine," Brecht said and he commenced the call for tests and service. Amy appeared at Broker's side, handed him a Dixie cup full of chipped ice, and said, "Hold this a sec." Up close, in addition to the gray eyes, she had long lashes. And she smelled good. Neither medicinal nor cosmetic.

But clean. And just so . . . *there.*

Broker kicked off his snowy boots and put his dry slippers back on as Amy joined the ER doc and bantered for a moment. Then she broke away and returned down the hall. "No big deal, a broken leg," she said, taking back her Dixie cup.

Whoa!

Broker came up sharp on the balls of his feet, his eyes darted. Heard something . . .

"You all right?" Amy asked.

Broker held up his hand. *Stop. Listen.* He stared at the skinny nurse with the black ponytail, who had been watching Sommer and had been out into the snow briefly to help with the new arrival. She was now hurrying up the hall toward the recovery room.

Broker, who could hear his daughter cough across a crowded auditorium, detected it through the medical chatter. Cued by his hard eyes, Amy and the other nurse caught it one beat later. Allen, sitting zombielike in the corridor, lurched up in his chair, raised his head, and turned.

The once rhythmic beep-beep-beep of Sommer's monitor was improvising in a minor key.

Booop . . . booop . . . booop . . .

"Oh fuck!" The color drained from Amy's face and the Dixie cup went flying and ice chips skittered over the waxed linoleum floor as she sprinted down the hall.

Chapter Ten

Booop . . . Booop . . . Booop.

"Shit! Call a code. He's arrested in here!" Amy yelled as she ran through the door into the recovery room. Broker was right behind her and he saw Sommer lying rigid with his eyes shut, his lips and cheeks turning the blue-gray color of the glacier water, and from then on it only got worse.

"Christ, he's in V fib! What the fuck happened?" Allen rushed into the room and his dazed eyes swept the monitor and then fixed on Sommer's face.

"I don't know. He came out clean in the OR. He was fighting the tube. Vitals were fine, train of four. Now . . . he bradied on me," Amy shouted back as she moved behind Sommer, clamped his face in both her hands.

"What the . . . ?" blurted Dr. Brecht, coming through the door.

"He's in bradycardia. Bag him, start CPR," Allen said, crossing his hands over Sommer's sternum. Immediately Brecht reached for the defibrillator that sat on the cluttered crash cart.

With one eye on the monitor screen where a low, bumpy line traced the failing heartbeat, Amy thrust Sommer's jaw up, opened his mouth, and swept a finger in his throat. He hadn't swallowed his tongue. "ABC's, ABC's," she chanted under her breath. "Oxygen." She grabbed the oxygen mask as Brecht checked the defibrillator cords and unwound the paddles. Amy yanked the mask over Sommer's face and pumped the balloon bellows.

Allen pistoned down in a CPR rhythm and burned a question at Amy. "How long?" he demanded.

"I don't know," Amy said between clenched teeth.

"More than four minutes?"

"I don't know, goddammit."

Brecht lowered the paddles and went to the cardiac monitor. "Jesus," he said.

"What?" Allen asked.

Brecht poked a button on the monitor. An alarm began to wail and the Ely doctor erupted. *The fucking alarm was turned off!*

"No. That's not true . . ." Nancy protested.

"Nancy, shut up," Amy said. And Broker, standing back against the wall out of the way, winced at the reflex of damage-control in her voice.

"Christ, Amy," Nancy stammered, "I just went out to help with the accident case, I looked in before I went outside," she protested. "His vitals were normal, he was talking. The monitor was set and he was fine."

"Well, he's not fine," Allen muttered as he pumped down. "He's in arrest. I want to see your charting. I want to know how much sedation he had on board."

"I brought him out clean," Amy declared, the gray of her eyes tightening, going steely.

"What the hell?" Mike, the administrator, lurched in the doorway.

"Get him out of here," Brecht shouted. Shari, the paramedic, stepped in and gently but firmly crowded the horrified administrator back into the corridor. Allen and Amy stared at each other, their faces inches apart as they worked. Brecht returned to the defibrillator and held a paddle electrode in each hand.

Amy shook her head. "He's coming back."

But the line on the monitor was still going a bumpy boop de boop and Brecht hovered, holding the paddles like cymbals. Allen kept up the compressions.

Boop beep boop beep beep beep . . .

"Keep ventilating, he's coming around," Amy said as the white clay of Sommer's chest moved. "I'm telling you, he's breathing," Amy insisted.

"She's right," Allen raised a hand in the first calm gesture since the incident started. "He's back."

Broker caught peeks of Sommer in the blue-clad scurry and could see the faint pink filter into his cheeks, his throat, and into his motionless, thickly muscled forearms.

Allen popped back one of Sommer's eyelids and Nancy handed him a slim penlight. "Mid position, reactive to light. C'mon Hank, wake up, man," Allen whispered.

Sommer lay like a grotesque doll with his smock pulled to the side and his swollen belly bulging in the harsh light. A long splash of Betadine bathed the incision and bled thick orange streaks down his hip and groin. The incision itself looked like a line of flies melted into his skin and, below the cut, his genitals were a heap of spoiled white fruit. Gently, Allen tidied the smock as the steady beep-beep-beep marked time in the silent room.

Allen swayed, regained his balance, and shot a withering stare at Amy. "I want to know all the meds he's had in the last thirty minutes."

"I did everything right." Amy's posture was firm, but her cocky, confident demeanor had deserted her, and her words came out with a dry rasp that grated into irritation. "Doctor, sit down, you're asleep on your feet."

"Answer the question. Any signs of recurarization?" Allen persisted.

"No, dammit," Amy said.

Allen steadied, took a breath, exhaled, spoke in a more normal tone. "I'm sorry, he's a friend of mine . . ." He looked at Sommer, the monitor. He rocked again. Caught himself.

Amy shook her head, disbelieving. The small room was full of sympathy but she found herself at bay, and when she spoke she was speaking to herself, not replying to Allen. "Could he have aspirated when we went after the new patient?" She shook her head, bit her lip. Thinking out loud, she muttered, "God, did I take the airway out too soon?"

Beep-beep-beep.

The doctors and nurses stood in a circle over Sommer as the room took on the acoustics of a brightly lit morgue. When Brecht broke the silence and told Nancy to wheel the snowmobile accident to X-ray, she moved like she was walking underwater. Iker appeared in front of Broker and raised his hands, questioning. Broker shook his head, exhausted. He pushed past Iker and continued down the hall away from the institutional tile, the stainless steel fixtures, the barren whiteness of it.

He shoved through the emergency room door, and paused in the garage to pull on his parka and light a cigar. Then he stepped out into the stinging snow. It was more hospitable than where he'd been.

A moment later Shari joined him. Cupping her hands expertly against the wind, she lit a filtered cigarette with a Zippo. They stood for several minutes, smoking.

"Friend of yours?" Shari asked.

"I just met him three days ago," Broker said. "I don't get it." He couldn't make it fit coming after the storm, the long paddle, the plane ride, the blizzard, the successful operation.

Shari was direct. "The nurse-anesthetist fucked up. Which is a hard call because Amy is really good."

"How? Without the big words."

"Who knows. The guy's got that short, muscular neck, a receding chin, and the buckteeth. He's an anesthetist's nightmare. After surgery, when they take him off the gas, they remove the breathing tube and the carbon dioxide builds up in his bloodstream. That gets him breathing again. What they're saying is his airway collapsed in the recovery room. So maybe he was breathing but still had enough residual sedation in him to come back on him and he went hypoxic."

"Allen said . . . curare something?" Broker asked.

"Recurarization," Shari said, nodding. "It means like reparalysis. If Amy miscalculated the amount of sedation he had on board it could have taken effect again, and he takes a spill off the steep slope of the oxygen-hemoglobin-dissociation curve. That'd do it."

"Jesus."

"Yeah. And nobody was there. He couldn't get air. He started sliding into arrest and no one caught it. Somebody—probably Nancy, who's working a second shift and is covering three jobs today—neglected to calibrate the monitor alarm." She shrugged. "Cut the O's to the brain for four minutes and the guy's a carrot. It happens."

Broker turned away and wandered back into the hospital where people continued to teeter on stilts of shock. Amy stood vigil in the recovery room at the head of Sommer's bed. Brecht, Judy, and Nancy huddled a polite distance from her. It was like a wake in there, so Broker went back in the hall and saw Allen pacing, bent forward, as if he were walking uphill. Allen blinked, focused, and recognized Broker, then walked over and patted him on the shoulder. The fatigue he'd kept at bay to perform the operation now poisoned his face into a haggard nicotine-yellow, and Broker read it all in the surgeon's hollow stare. Save the guy and then . . .

Allen attempted to smile. "I have to tell Milt. You know, he's been asleep through all this."

"What happens now?" Broker asked.

Allen slowly shook his head. "It depends on how long he didn't get oxygen. He's comatose. He could wake up in a few hours or in a few days, or it could be weeks. Or . . ." Allen pursed his lips. "Once he opens his eyes he can be evaluated by a neurologist. Until then, we're only speculating but . . ." Allen faltered, his voice caught. "Jesus, look at him. He's suffered some damage."

"Some damage?" Broker repeated.

"Brain damage."

"You mean?"

"I mean, she shouldn't have pulled that tube so soon in the OR."

"He was talking. They were talking. They were teasing back and forth," protested Broker.

Allen made a weak, erasing gesture with his right hand. "I don't know. It's like . . ." he swatted the air, ". . . stop signs. Nobody obeys them anymore, they can't be bothered to take the time." A sound between a cough and a laugh rattled in his throat. "She was in a hurry, I guess."

Then Allen continued down the hall to the nurses' station and Broker watched him pick up the phone slowly as if the receiver were an anvil. Slowly, Allen pressed in the numbers and waited and then, as he began to talk, his facial expression collapsed inward like a piece of crumpled paper.

Standing ten feet away Broker could hear the stunned, vaguely familiar female voice protest over the phone, "No, what a minute, how could that happen? He was in the hospital, goddammit."

Chapter Eleven

It was still snowing. But softer now, almost out of respect.

"Stop signs, huh," mulled Dave Iker. "He's got a point. World War Three will probably start some hot afternoon down in Minneapolis at a four-way stop."

They were both pretty beat up.

Iker's service belt reeked of wet leather, piled on his desk in the sheriff's office in the Ely courthouse. They were still wearing the mismatched sweat suits from the hospital, and Iker's purple and red sweatshirt bore the crude drawing of a bearded man holding a big grasshopper. The type underneath spelled:

ST. ERHO FESTIVAL, MENAHAGA, MINNESOTA

St. Erho was the patron saint who rid Finland of grasshoppers. Uncle Billie maintained that St. Erho's Day, like St. Patrick's Day, was an excuse to get drunk, because there never were grasshoppers in Finland.

Broker stared out the window at the moderating storm and it all went into a distracted glide, and he mused how lots of Finns had settled around Ely. Maybe because the lakes and forest and six months of winter reminded them of home. Or maybe their national ethic of fatalism attracted them to farm fields full of granite rocks.

Broker caught himself drifting, shook his head, and asked, "That nurse-anesthetist, Amy, she local?"

Iker nodded. "Ummm. Amy Skoda is one of the few who figured how to come back and earn a living." He slowly raised his eyebrows. "She was asking about you, before it all went bad."

"Skoda? She a Finlander?" Broker asked.

"Half Finnish, half Slovene; the cream of the local gene pool." He threw an arm toward the wall where a procession of retired peace officers stared down from framed portraits. "Second picture up there. Stan Skoda's kid." Skoda filled the picture frame like an amiable fireplug and Broker vaguely remembered the man from hunting parties when Broker was in high school.

"Take a hike. I gotta make a call," Iker said. The format glowing on his computer screen gave his face a lime tint as he hunched back to his chair and stared at the number jotted in his spiral notebook.

Broker nodded, got up, and went looking for the gents, as Iker reached for the phone. He had to make the duty call to Hank Sommer's wife and explain the circumstances of the tragedy.

When Broker returned, Iker was predictably more gloomy.

"How'd it go?" Broker asked.

"She said '—but he was in the hospital' three times." Iker shook his head. "Could have been worse. That doctor, Falken, had already called and prepared her. She's got this nice voice," Iker said. "You know, like way down at the bottom of an air conditioner."

Broker nodded. He knew how it worked; the phone rings and a strange cop from faraway invites a wife to take a sudden plunge to where she keeps her personal ideas about mortality.

Iker, who lived thirty miles of impassable highway to the west in Tower, then called his wife, made sure that she and the kids were all right, and explained the day's events and how he was stranded with Phil Broker.

"So now you and your ex-copper buddy have two choices, huh?" another wife's voice rattled in the telephone.

"Yeah, I guess." Iker winced and held up the receiver at arm's length. Broker heard the wife say: "You can shovel snow or get drunk."

Iker hung up, shrugged. "What are you going to do?"

"Get a room at the Holiday Inn."

"I got to finish filing this report. Maybe I'll see you at The Saloon later." Iker tossed Broker his truck keys.

Broker left the courthouse, climbed in Iker's truck, and drove toward the Holiday Inn that overlooked Lake Shagawa at the edge of town. No way he was going to try the unplowed road to Uncle Billie's Lodge in these conditions. Iker's Ford Ranger barely grabbed traction in Ely.

Moving at a crawl in four-wheel low, he went over some of the medical terminology he'd heard thrown around this afternoon: Sommer had suffered a significant "anoxic insult" and was currently comatose—in a coma due to oxygen starvation to his brain precipitated by respiratory complications following surgery. The informal opinion at Miner Hospital was that Amy Skoda had underestimated the amount of sedation in his system and took him off anesthesia too early in the operating room. Perhaps, someone speculated, she'd anticipated that the surgery would take longer, not allowing for Allen's speed and skill. Sommer's being hypothermic may have been a factor. Whatever the precipitating events, he developed trouble breathing in the recovery room.

Nobody was there when he crashed, and the alarm on the monitor had not been set.

As he left, Broker overheard someone console Amy. *It could happen to anyone.* But it didn't happen to anyone. It happened to Hank Sommer, the guy Broker had promised to get out of the woods. The guy he helped deliver to a warm, safe hospital where they preserved his heart and lungs and lost his brain.

Wham.

Broker hooked a frustrated fist at the steering wheel in a tantrum of flash anger, swerved, and almost lost control of the truck. Reflexively, he steered into the skid and came out of the spin. *Take deep breaths through your nose. Check yourself.*

Usually he had a much longer fuse.

The Holiday Inn was a deserted post-and-beam jungle gym with a cathedral ceiling and a bored, snow-hypnotized receptionist who smiled discreetly at Broker's attire. He carried in the duffel he'd retrieved from the dispatch desk, took a room, and went down a stairwell, opened a door, and stepped into a limbo of clean walls, curtains, and hotel furniture that could be anywhere-USA.

And he just wanted to disappear.

But he stripped down out of habit, went to the shower, and applied soap, shampoo, shaving lather, and a razor to peel off the cold outer layer of the last twenty-four hours. He rubbed a porthole in the steamed bathroom mirror and gauged his fatigue by the redness of his eyes. He took out dry jeans, a fleece pullover, and his spare boots.

After he'd dressed, his hand moved toward the phone, thinking to call the hospital and check with Allen, who'd stayed behind to watch over Sommer and Milt. He withdrew his hand.

You don't really know Hank Sommer.

And it was like—all his life he'd worked the sharp end and he'd always been annoyed at the compulsion of people who couldn't resist adding their personal embroidery to the messy edge of tragedy. Now he discovered he was not immune to this character defect.

He was dwelling on it. *If you hadn't hassled Sommer so much during the storm he might not have pushed so hard, might not have ruptured himself.*

Try again, Broker.

You fell apart out there and an injured man had to take up the slack.

Either way, if Sommer hadn't paddled to the max they would have dumped in the middle of the lake, not ten yards from the point. Their bodies would be stiff white logs rolling among the rocks on the leeward shore of Fraser Lake. He'd gone on a canoe trip in only fair physical condition and his strength had faltered when the chips were down.

These were ponderous thoughts to keep afloat in an ocean of fatigue, especially after the narcotic hot shower, and the bed beckoned, but so did the image of Sommer lying less than a mile away with his eyes closed, his heart beating, and his lungs sucking oxygen.

And his head full of static.

Broker lurched to his feet and grabbed his parka. Iker's wife was right. He needed a drink.

The snow had grayed the early afternoon enough to switch on the streetlights and it was a bad day for a drive, but Broker took one, anyway. He pushed the Ranger through the small business district and followed the flashing blue light of a county snowplow out

Sheridan Street to the outskirts of town, where the plow stopped, defeated by drifts on Highway 169. Broker turned around in front of the International Wolf Center and retraced his route.

Ely was end of the road, a departure point for tourists paddling into the wilds. Things were different when Broker was a kid and spent part of his summers here. Then, the iron ore they dug up from the veins that literally ran under the town was so pure it could be welded directly on to steel.

The iron fields were so potent they interfered with radio signals, and the rattle of boxcars full of ore had competed with the buzz of seaplanes flying fishermen into the paradise of northern lakes.

The mines came to grief on the global marketplace. Miners who had landed on Iwo and Saipan were thrown out of work when the steel could be shipped in cheaper from Japan. In the late '70's the government annexed the lake country along the Canadian border as a wilderness preserve and banished the gasoline motor to keep the woods and water pristine. The bitter land-use controversy still flared.

Broker switched on the radio, scanned the dial until he hit WELY. "Sally, your brother wants you to stay put. He's safe, he's made it to town and won't get back until this blow is over."

WELY was one of two American radio stations licensed to transmit personal messages. The other was in the Alaskan bush. He turned off the radio and stared into the storm.

Now the school district was shrinking. Income from vacationers didn't translate into the kind of jobs that supported families. Like his home ground on the Superior shore, another piece of his geography was being changed by '90's Über wealth.

Take it in stride, he told himself, keep moving, don't look back.

Mike and Irene Broker had raised their boy to be a stoic. They had been inoculated against sentimentality by bumping up hard against the Depression and Hitler, and they'd passed the antibodies to their son. Broker understood the cultural message of his time. He'd been raised to fight Communists, and he had. He'd come home from his war refitted with a forty-gallon adrenaline tank.

So he'd joked that he'd worn a badge to feed his action jones. But the fact was, if somebody had to remain vigilant in the night so others could sleep in peaceful beds, it probably should be somebody like him.

A shape jerked at the corner of his eye and he almost wrenched the wheel—*seeing things*—an artifact of shock and fatigue, and he was back to taking deep breaths through his nose to steady down his jumpy thoughts. And he almost had to laugh—Christ, he'd come up here to get away and . . .

He just had to maintain control and forward motion and balance. He used to be good at keeping things separate and filed into their own compartments. But it wasn't that easy to take this one in stride. He'd sprung a leak. Stuff was getting in. Stuff was getting out.

His mom—well, Mom had always worried that he had too much imagination for police work. Peel back the bark, she'd said, and he was layered and impressionable. *Like a ball of wax*, Sommer said, *things stick*.

And the things that stuck were memories from more than twenty years of cleaning up after human beings at their worst. And suddenly he swerved again, but this time it was in his head, and he was back in the middle of the argument with his wife.

And she'd said, *Oh, I see, so it's all right for you to do it but not for me, is that it?*

The memory invoked all the hoarded resentments; she still thought she was indestructible at thirty-three. She took too many chances out there and left him home to rehearse attending her funeral with their daughter Kit . . .

Right now Kit's absence ached in his arms and he could smell her milky sweet-sour breath and her copper curls and see her chubby face that was part Rubens and part Winston Churchill, and he could hear her pure laugh that was so uncomplicated by fear. He experienced a piercing memory of her a month ago as she struggled with the physical limitations of her limited grasp and discovered that she couldn't carry all her stuffed animals at once.

She was going on three and by the time she was four she'd experience the death of something—a cat or a dog or a hamster. She'd find and poke her first roadkill. Fearless, like her mother, she'd probably lift the maggots on a stick.

She was almost ready for *The Lion King*, which he'd screened. She'd see Mufasa trampled to death by stampeding wildebeests and watch little Simba vainly attempt to rouse his father from a permanent sleep.

Eventually, she would pose the question: *Daddy, will you die? Will Mommy die?*

Will I die?

Broker parked Iker's truck in a snowdrift in front of The Saloon on a desolate street in Ely and was in a fine mood when he pushed his way through the door, stamped off snow, and took over a table in the corner. The place was dim as a cave and sparsely populated by a few hardy snowmobilers and a storm-weary bartender and waitress.

Broker was no drinker. For a thirst-quencher he preferred lemonade on a hot day, and his only use for bar culture had been as a fertile recruiting ground for bottom-feeding snitches. He always made a point to leave drinking scenes before the lip sync went haywire and people's expressions became dissociated from their words.

Uncharacteristically, he ordered a double Jack Daniel's and drank half of it. He gagged, flushed with sweat, and drank the rest, then sat back and waited for the numbness.

He kept getting stuck on the inverted sequence of Sommer's mind being suffocated inside his living body, and the image obligated him to reflect on his own fast parade of sudden death.

"Traffic," Broker mumbled to his whiskey glass.

August. Last year, on a sticky, humming, deep-green afternoon he and his father were out for a walk by the state capitol in St. Paul. They'd paused on a freeway overpass with the domes of the capitol and the St. Paul Cathedral bracketing them north and south, and rush hour on Interstate 94 clamoring below their feet. Mike Broker at seventy-nine took long mental vacations and tripped down rabbit holes of nostalgia because in the rabbit holes he was young and doing things that mattered. That hot August afternoon, Dad had looked down at the racing cars and said, "This is what it sounds like when a lot of young people die fast and unhappy in a tight spot. Hundreds of lives go screaming by each minute."

Dad was talking about the first hour on Omaha Beach.

The rush was not that loud in Broker's memory but it was audible enough to prompt ordering another double. After it arrived and he drank it, his thinking wobbled: Okay. The body dies first. Buddhists, Muslims, Jews, Hindus, and Christians could all agree on that much. The problem was—the major religions were designed for a medical reality that didn't anticipate CPR, ventilators, and dialysis.

"Hey," Broker signaled across the dim, nearly deserted room to the waitress at the bar. "Give me another."

Pocketing his change after the drink arrived he noticed that he was losing corners of seconds off his reflexes and that the fine muscle control at the tips of his fingers had turned blunt. But his thinking had profoundly elongated.

So. Here's the deal. Sommer's body didn't die but his mind did, and now his stubborn flesh was holding HIM—his spirit, whatever—hostage inside. Broker shook his head, stymied at the physical geography of where Sommer *was*. And his layman's impressions about biomechanics did not encourage a solution. He understood vaguely that the "human" parts of Sommer's mind had been obliterated because the deeper cortex—the lizard brain—had sacrificed the higher functions to preserve the vital pumps: the heart, the lungs.

Broker envisioned the embers of Sommer's life warming a lidless reptilian eye and he suddenly wanted someone to blame besides himself—so he looked around and, well, no shit, he'd been sitting here for ten, fifteen minutes and hadn't seen Iker hunched over a bar stool at the end of the bar. Iker had traded in his St. Erho sweats for a pullover, jeans, and a heavy leather coat.

Like two aging Earp brothers, their eyes met, paused briefly to check each other's backs, and dropped back to their glasses.

Then, scanning the room more carefully, he spied Amy Skoda sitting at a corner table with her back against the wall. Half her face was blacked out in shadow. The other half was caught in the neon haze from a Budweiser sign. She still wore her blue trousers, now tucked into car boots, and her open anorak revealed the ID badge clipped to her blue tunic.

She moved her head forward into the light, their eyes met, and Broker saw reflected in her face the blame he felt burning in his own.

Chapter Twelve

Amy was not alone. Two snowmobile jocks, mistaking her troubled, fixed stare for an intoxicated cripple, had moved into chairs on either side and were treating her to drinks. And judging by the full shot glass in her hand and the empty one in front of her, she was not protesting.

Broker was smart enough to know there's no fool like an old fool. He was just too burnt and boozed to listen to himself. So he thought—what the hell, why not give forty-seven going on twenty-five one last try? He heaved to his feet playing funky theme music in his head. Like Muddy Waters and Bonnie Raitt. *I'm Ready*. Dumb barroom stuff.

He pushed his chair aside and fixed on the beefy one wearing the Arctic Cat knit cap who'd looped his arm around her shoulder. The guy was a chinless wonder, a regular evangelist for the lite worldview of a beer commercial.

"Aw, c'mon, you can tell me about it," Arctic Cat said with great sincerity as his fingers grazed near the shape of her left breast.

"Aw, God," Amy said, shoving the arm away.

"Hey honey. It's all right." Arctic Cat, tone deaf to the lethal disgust in her voice, took encouragement as Broker came across the room surprisingly light on his feet and appeared on Arctic Cat's blind side.

Amy had the right idea, and she clearly knew her anatomy. This time she grabbed Arctic Cat's hand and cranked down on his wrist. The husky snowmobiler grinned at her attempted armlock.

She'd hit the same old problem—upper body strength. Arctic Cat was just too big.

Broker experienced no such difficulty as he swiftly took over the arm grab from Amy, wrenched the wrist, and threw in an old-fashioned Iron Ranger hockey check.

Arctic Cat's fleshy nose and lips briefly adhered to the wall like thrown Silly Putty before he oozed to the floor, leaving a wet smear down the pine paneling. His buddy stood up and discreetly took a step back.

The man Broker had knocked down rolled over and sat up, holding his wrist; confused, blinking, he wondered aloud, "What's that she got me with? Musta been some kung fu?" His nose and lips commenced to bleed.

"Nah," Broker said, amazed at the callous spring of his anger, "you're just fat, ugly, and slow."

Then Amy was between them with two deep furrows creasing her brow. She jammed both hands on Broker's chest, extended her arms, backed him off, and said hotly, "Hey, don't *hurt* him; take it easy, he didn't mean . . ."

And Iker was there, moving fast and edgy for a big man; he shouldered Broker aside, flipped open his wallet, and badged the two guys. "Go away," he said tersely. "Now."

While Iker soothed the bartender who had picked up the phone, the snowmobilers parleyed, recognized that they had strayed into the dangerous part of the zoo, and made the proper decision.

"C'mon, let's go down the street."

"But nothin's open down the street."

"Let's go there, anyway."

Amy handed the guy with the nosebleed a bar napkin with some ice inside and told him to apply pressure. After they left, Iker peered first at Broker, then at Amy and asked, "You two all right?"

"Yeah, sure," Amy said quickly.

"Hey, no problem," Broker said.

"Sit down, Dave, have a drink," Amy said.

Iker gave them a tight smile. "No thanks, I don't have the energy to get between you two. Not after today."

"What's that supposed to mean?" Broker said.

"Means I know both of you. I'll just finish my drink and go sleep on a desk, thank you." He tipped a finger to his forehead at Amy, grabbed Broker by the elbow, and steered him across the room and out the front door. He did not stop to finish his drink.

No wind now. Just the big quiet and the big snowflakes drifting down like tiny parachutes.

Iker took a stance and eased back his coat so Broker could see the cuffs and the clip-on-hide-out holster on his belt from which protruded the patterned grip of a stubby Colt Python. Dave Iker stood six one, weighed 205, and was no slouch in the physical department, and right now he looked slightly dangerous, like he was working.

"Okay. It's like this. She's a little vulnerable right now." Iker's voice was reasonable, but his cop body language said, *watch the fuck out here*. "I know her family. She's been a perfectionist since she was a kid, so she's going to take this thing pretty hard."

Jesus. "What . . . ?"

"Hey look, age-wise, she's still a kid compared to you. *And* she knows your marriage is on the rocks. And just maybe she's got a little thing for you. And you're not helping matters playing twenty-five-year-old cowboy coming to the fucking rescue . . . so go easy and don't take advantage . . ."

"I wouldn't . . ." Broker protested.

"I know you wouldn't. Just don't. And another thing. I don't know what the story is between you and your old lady but don't take it out on drunks. Not in my town. The body slam on that lush was unnecessary. That was excessive force. Jesus, Phil, you know better. The lone wolf UC days are over. You're a goddamn civilian . . ."

Iker *was* working. Broker was being *warned*. He stepped back, chastised. "Hey, Jesus, Dave . . ."

"Just . . ." Iker gave him a tight cop smile that really was no smile at all and made a pressing down "cool it" gesture with his open hands. He shook his head. "Look. It's been a bad day. Let's not have a bad night." He punched Broker on the arm. Hard. "So, you okay?"

"Yeah, sure." Broker was replaying the shock and fear on the snowmobiler's face when he plowed into him, and seeing Amy, stepping in, with the pained look in her eyes.

"Drop my truck at the office in the morning," Iker said as he turned and walked to a county cruiser. Broker waved vaguely, and he was thinking how none of this was supposed to happen. He came here to hide and wait out his . . . problem. Now there was all this *stuff*.

Shivering, he stood alone on the street and watched Iker's taillights disappear around a corner. Then he went back into the bar, returned to Amy's table, and the words came out before he got them lined up right. "Look, I'm sorry, going off on that guy. I just have a lot on my mind."

"Oh *you* do, do you," she said making her eyes a little wider.

"Well, I guess you do, too. Can I sit down?"

"Sure, as long as you understand I don't need any more of *that* kind of help." The gray eyes, though dipped in alcohol, still cut.

Broker nodded and pulled up a chair while Amy flagged the bartender and held up two fingers. The waitress, eyes lowered, brought the two glasses on a small round tray, put them down, made change, and retreated.

"They know," Amy whispered, looking after the waitress. "This is a small town. Everybody knows about Sommer."

Broker rotated the double shot in his fingers and raised his eyebrows. "Do you always drink like this?"

"I never drink. It's a filthy depressant. Cheers."

He drank and the two burning ounces seared through the roof of his mouth and up his sinuses.

"Now take off. I really don't need any help," she said, squaring her shoulders, sitting up straighter. A gesture that wasn't supposed to be taken seriously.

"Yes, you do," Broker said and he figured she'd been the bright, sharp tack all her life and maybe sometimes she got ahead of herself.

"I do?"

"Yeah, we're linked," Broker said. "You left your post to come out in the hall and chat me up, remember."

Amy shook her head and her hand floated up and touched her hair. "Nancy was with him."

"She left *her* post to get the new patient. Who was in charge?"

She met his eyes on the level from behind her fort of shot glasses, and he could find no excuses in her defiant gaze. She did not impress him as someone prone to making fatal mistakes, and her choice of occupations was an alert exercise in avoiding exactly such an outcome. "No, that's too simple. Something else happened," she said firmly.

"Something?" he asked.

"Look, you should probably leave me alone."

"Sorry."

"What? Are you one of these guys who finds tragedy a turn on?" Amy asked.

"Takes one to know one, huh?"

"I guess." Amy looked away and her profile, big-eyed and cleanly featured in a tumble of bright hair, contrasted with the dull residue of the snowmobiler's blood on the wall behind her chair.

"You're one of his friends," she said.

"No. I rented them the gear and went along to help around camp. I paddled out to get help."

She turned full-face to him, lowered the gray eyes, and raised them slowly, which felt good to an old, married, recently deserted guy who was getting drunk. "You don't look like a canoe guide," she said.

So it begins. He thought to play his part, so he inclined his head to go along. *Huh? What? Me?* But he remembered Iker's warning.

A little clumsy now, Amy said, "You have more . . . range." Her hand drifted out and her cool right index finger floated over the pale stripe on his ring finger. "You, ah, forgot your wedding ring."

"Separated," he said, not sure if it was the right word. There wasn't a word for people in his situation. Fucked, maybe.

She started to say something, stopped, and let the calm finger touch a hollow of bone and tendon above the joint of thumb. "Nice veins," she said.

They paused to look off in different directions while the waitress came to their table, stooped with a small bucket of hot water and disinfectant, and scrubbed the dots of Arctic Cat's blood from the wall and the floor.

When the waitress left they resumed looking at each other and it was clear there was no trivial human clutter between them, and Broker stood on a high board feeling his breath, and he could see it all play out in easy, sexy stages. But it was a game and he didn't play games with women.

"C'mon, cut the crap. Iker told me you were asking about me," Broker said.

She slumped. "Figures, you used to be a cop. You guys stick together." She looked around, furtively.

"What?"

"This isn't smart, you and me having this conversation. I shouldn't talk about . . . things. That lawyer on the trip with you . . ."

"Milt."

"Yeah, I heard Milt is already asking questions half zoned on Percodan." She took a deep breath, let it out. "There's this peer-review process and there'll be a root-cause analysis session."

"An in-house investigation?"

Amy shook her head. "It's not . . . legal—of course Milt would love to hear what's said—but it's confidential, protected from discovery. It's more like this forum for medics to talk through an event and find out what went wrong without fear of punishment."

"So you think there'll be a lawsuit?"

She snorted. "C'mon, of course there'll be a lawsuit, and I'll wind up taking the heat. It's the logical finding. The anesthetist screwed up *somewhere*. But it's not like I intubated an esophagus. I'm not going to lose my license."

She stared mute as the alcohol shut down a whole layer of her facial muscles. With a numb smile she continued, "If you got rid of doctors and nurses every time they made a mistake and croaked somebody in postop, you'd have to close half the hospitals . . ."

Through the veil of booze, Broker tried to listen patiently and get a feel for the person behind the bitter words. Amy was indignant and pissed more than guilty or sad. But he lost his concentration, except to fixate on physical details like the way a sturdy purple vein on her throat throbbed and her habit of making little water circles on the table with the bottom of a glass and then erasing them with her finger.

"It really cracks me up," she was saying. "Remember those guys who got killed in Somalia, that mob dragged them around on TV? You remember that?"

Broker nodded.

"How many was that they killed?"

"I think it was eighteen dead," said Broker, the reader of history.

"And it freaked everybody out. Now we just drop bombs and don't use ground troops . . ."

She lost her place and Broker did, too. Then she leaned forward and wrinkled her forehead.

"How many people do you think die as a result of accidents and negligence in hospitals every year—take a guess?"

"I don't know, Amy."

"Depending whose numbers you pick—how about between sixty and ninety thousand. That's *every* year. Funny isn't it, how we set priorities. Eighteen soldiers die doing their job. It gets on TV and it changes the foreign policy of a country. And we tolerate those kinds of numbers in the health-care system. Hell, we killed more people this year than the fucking army did."

"Amy, I think you're being a little hard on yourself."

She obliterated water rings with the heel of her fist. "You want to see real nightmares, check out an emergency room in the Cities on a Saturday night."

"Saturday nights and summer full moons," he agreed.

Amy sat back, peered into an empty shot glass. "Amen. Emergency room nurse, Hennepin County Medical Center, three years before I went to anesthesia school."

"The kind of nurse who dated cops?"

"Oh, yeah." Her eyes conjured up 5 A.M. in Minneapolis at the end of the graveyard shift. Empty streets. Everything closed. "And I'd come home alone, sad, on the holidays and my mom would suggest I take up some activities, you know, get back into piano. Or dancing . . ."

Amy stretched and slowly leaned her head to the side, which was neat because of the way her hair cascaded slowly, strand by strand.

". . . Mom was always big on lessons. Ballet almost destroyed my ankles. Every year before high school I had to face *The Nutcracker*. Now there's an aptly named show. I was a mouse and worked up to an angel." Her brief smile nicely illuminated a happy childhood. "Mom wanted me to be the Sugar Plum Fairy." She shrugged. "And my dad—he'd look down the table kind of owly over the turkey and say, 'Can't you find a nice boy?' "

Amy composed herself and recited. "The reason I know Dave Iker is because my dad used to bring him home for coffee when Dave was an itty, bitty deputy and my dad was a sergeant. Stan Skoda went from the CCC Camps to North Africa, to Sicily, to Italy. He came home and worked in the mines. When the mines closed he became a cop." She sighed and raised her eyes. "Jesus Christ, Daddy—the nice boys all want to fix my computer."

She plucked a long strand of hair, let it fall, and blew it away. "Any rate, Daddy would say, Get past the excitement and find something that works." She drew her wrist across her cheek and trapped the single tear she'd shed. "Is that what you had, Broker? Something that worked?"

"You're drunk," Broker said.

"Sorry, I never killed anybody before. I'll do better next time."

"You're saying you did it? Premature extubation, whatever?"

Her eyes came to points through the booze. "No way. I was strictly by the book. Something like this is usually a system failure."

"What? A machine malfunctioned?"

"No, a human system. A procedure broke down."

"So it just *happened*?" Broker asked.

"Shit happens on bumper stickers—but nothing just happens in a recovery room. Somebody fucked up and it wasn't me."

With that said, Amy lurched to her feet and promptly lost her balance. Broker was up, none too steady himself, and caught her, and her hair and lips buzzed his cheek as her full, warm weight sagged in his arms.

"Your lucky night," she whispered as her eyes rolled up expressively. "Ever get puked on by a pretty woman?"

Broker dragged her toward the ladies' room.

He was mindful of Iker's stern advice but where would she go in her condition? Where was her car? Where did she live? He just couldn't leave her and, to his current inebriated way of thinking, they *were* linked. Tied in a black crepe bow by Hank Sommer.

So he drove home drunk for the first time in more than twenty years with an unconscious woman passed out in the passenger seat. Tonight, home was the overbuilt Holiday Inn out on the lake.

He made it to the parking lot without incident and put the truck in neutral to sit awhile and balk at the complex intersection of his pragmatism, his innate puritanism, and his sudden need not to be alone tonight. How was he going to get her past the receptionist? She was dead weight. He'd have to sneak her in.

So he drove to the end of the lot, parked, went around to the passenger side, and eased her out and slung her over his shoulders in a rescue hold. His knees faltered, then steadied. Judging by her solid muscle tone, she'd drunk all her milk growing up and did her exercises, too. With her thigh warm under his biceps he lurched off, around the back of the motel.

His room was on the bottom level, with French doors opening on a patio overlooking the lake. But he'd forgotten the number and, pawing one-handed in his pocket and balancing Amy on his shoulder, he discovered he'd lost the card key envelope with the number on it and he wasn't sure the card opened the patio door anyway.

So he lowered Amy carefully into a plastic lawn chair and dragged up another chair to position her feet so she wouldn't fall over. Wisps of snow began to stick to her face and hair.

Only be a minute, he promised.

Huffing, he jogged around the building and into the lobby where the receptionist gave him his room number. Floating through the lobby, he felt like a helium-filled balloon in a parade, but he made it down the stairs and found his room and struggled with the key card and, finally, he was in.

Amy.

He threw back the curtains, opened the patio door, and stepped outside. She was still slumped in the chairs twenty yards away, with a faint beard of snowflakes on her cheeks. Quickly, he carried her into the room, plopped her on the first double bed, and dusted the snow from her hair and her face. He removed her parka and boots to make her comfortable. That's when he saw the blood, a rusty stipple on the front of her tunic and down the hip of her pants.

Sommer's blood was following him.

He didn't like the idea of her sleeping like that, in Sommer's blood. Awkwardly, he positioned her arms above her head and worked with her tunic, easing it up and seeing, feeling, the warm heft of her upper body and smelling the faint shadow of the fragrance of her underarm. The back of his hands grazed the taut straps and the full ivory cups and he saw the single fold across her smooth stomach.

Next he peeled off the socks, then the baggy blue pants, and she had long, well-muscled legs and maybe Allen was right, a cross-country skier, and she had tomboy scars on her chiseled knees and red polish on her toenails. Just his luck to find another Title Nine Lioness.

Broker took the outfit to the bathroom, ran cold water, and tried to scrub out the blood with a washcloth and face soap, but it wasn't going to happen. So he rinsed the clothes, wrung them out, and hung them on the shower rail.

He went back to the bed, blinked at the baby-blue panties stretched between her defined hip bones, and raised his eyes to the bra, and that presented a dilemma.

His wife—he was careful not to think her name because the phonics might cast or break a spell—his wife—well, she had smaller breasts, for one thing. And the stretch marks ironed on her stomach. Yes. But what he was getting at was, she never slept in her bra. He was almost certain of that.

He studied the garment, which was nothing flashy. A sensible Maidenform. He eased up her shoulder. Just the two eyelets in the back. Now. He'd placed her on the first bed coming in from the patio which put the other bed between her and the bathroom. And he'd be in that bed if he didn't move her. So. First he had to transfer her to the bed closer to the john. That way she wouldn't have to deal with going past him in the dark, which might make her uncomfortable waking up in the middle of the night in a strange room.

It was different picking her up with most of her clothes off; the sheer abundance and scent of her hair and her flesh and the carnal breath of alcohol combined to make him dizzy. Especially the smooth, warm way she slid in his arms. Carefully, he hoisted her to the second bed, turned down the covers, and eased her between the sheets. Then he raised the shoulder and unsnapped the bra to reduce the constraint. He did not remove it. Leaving her privacy intact, sort of. He tucked the covers up to her throat.

He gently reached down and pulled a strand of hair across her lips and cheek and went back and touched her cheek again with the back of his knuckles. Pretty girl. Broker shook his head and felt it all drop on him. What had happened to Hank Sommer was worse than death. The problem with having a highly developed code of duty was the flip side—the shame when you screwed up.

Had Amy screwed up? Had he?

He had to shake these doldrums. Write it off to lingering shock and the unaccustomed booze. He took two steps back and lowered himself into a chair because the bed was too far away right now. No, that wasn't it. The bed had become fearful.

He could shut his eyes. But would he ever open them again?

He watched Amy's chest rise and fall peacefully, which caused him to yawn. To fight off the lethargy he sat bolt upright and reached for the small writing table next to the chair and clamped his hands on to the edge.

He held on so tight his fingertips blanched white, because he had to stay awake, because the sleep he now imagined was bottomless, laced with black bubbles, like his look down into the glacier water. Because he'd never take sleep for granted again.

But his eyelids pressed down and the bubble of his willpower burst, and sleep opened its arms and waited with the patience of gravity. He finally slumped forward through the ether of an alcoholic dream and pitched toward the floor in a slow-motion fall, but the floor had turned to transparent glass beneath his feet and he crashed through, down into the private catacombs where he walled off his dead. And he saw Hank Sommer's long, quiet body in its own private room and Hank's sightless eyes startled open and looked up.

And a whole heap of bodies stood up in a forgotten place called Quang Tri City. They were schoolboys from Hanoi and farm boys from the provinces and they formed a circle and he saw that their hair and fingernails had grown long since 1972.

Nimble as spiders, they swept in to get him.

Chapter Thirteen

Nina Pryce.

If ever a name destroyed sleep. He lurched up, ducked, and discovered he was in bed wearing nothing but his shorts. How'd he . . .

Amy Skoda appeared next to his bed smiling, with her eyes mostly clear and her hair in place. She held a coffee cup out to him and he saw the room-service tray with a coffee carafe on the bureau next to the TV.

"Actually I know more about you than I let on last night. I know you married Nina Pryce," she said.

Broker studied the T-shirt she wore, which he'd last seen folded in his duffel. The black one with NEW ORLEANS spelled out in white alligator bones. Below the hem, lamplight glossed the blond fuzz on her thighs.

She cleared her throat and handed him the coffee. "After Desert Storm, Nina had a small following. Not quite Mia Hamm, but loyal. I almost went into the army because of her."

Broker grimaced slightly at the subject of his wife. Amazon-Dot-Kill: she had achieved a certain female-soldier notoriety in the Gulf. He took the cup and sipped. The coffee helped his hangover, which was less overt pain than a massive energy drain. "So why didn't you?" he asked.

"Hey, I'm out there but I'm not *that* cutting-edge. Nina wants to fight next to the men."

The words were rote and spun from his mouth. "She didn't just fight next to the men in the desert. She led a company of them against three times their number of Republican Guards and she won. It sort of alienated the patriarchy." He cleared his throat. "That, and the fact that she wouldn't suck titty with the Witch Hook Feminists. She caught it from both ends and they ran her out of the army."

"But she got back in. She's in Bosnia."

Macedonia, actually. Probably Kosovo. He didn't know exactly. The unit she was in now, Delta, didn't officially exist. "Clinton stuck his nose in," Broker said, employing the name like an all-purpose subject, verb, and object. He waved the subject away. "I, ah, don't remember getting in bed."

Amy shrugged. "I got up to pee and found you passed out on the floor. So I tucked you in."

"You picked me up?"

"You're big but you're not that big."

Broker found her style distressingly familiar.

"I took your pants off, too. Don't worry," she said, "I'm not pregnant and your virginity is intact."

He let that one slide, too, and just stared at her. "You don't look hungover."

"Oh, I'm hungover; I just don't whine about it."

He couldn't win, so he knuckled his frizzed hair, gathered the sheet toga-fashion around his waist, grabbed his jeans, and went into the bathroom. When he emerged, shaved, showered, and dressed, she had changed back into her rumpled hospital duds.

"Thanks for collecting me last night," she said frankly. "I would have tried to walk to my car and wound up in a snowbank."

He nodded and opted for brevity. "Bad night."

"Do you want to know the kicker?" She flung open the curtains and Broker winced at the roar of sunlight and the cloudless blue sky. Lake Shagawa twinkled placid as a millpond. Then she said quietly, "I called in. They're flying him down to the Cities in half an hour. Thought you might want to say good-bye."

The plows had left the parking lot iglooed with piles of snow. As they threaded toward Iker's truck, Broker, feeling achy and fogged over, reached for a cigar.

Amy laughed.

"What?"

"The eyebrows. And the cigar. You look like a cross between Sean Connery and Groucho Marx."

Broker grumbled, threw the cigar away, got in, started the truck, and drove into town through a convention of yellow county snowplows. All around, Ely's residents wore Minnesota weather-cowboy grins and were chipping away at the drifts with shovels and snowblowers.

A block from the hospital Amy touched his arm. "Better let me out here. It probably won't look right, us walking in together." As she got out of the truck they heard the whack of a helicopter on approach at the hospital helipad.

The chopper had triple tail fins, which made it a BK 117 American Eurocopter; it was dark blue with white diagonal stripes and the letters SMDC on the fuselage. It carried a pilot, a registered nurse, and a paramedic.

It was the kind of expensive ride only real sick people take.

Broker drove through the shadow of the Eurocopter and into the lot where the plows had created white cubbyholes with twelve-foot walls. He parked in one of them as the chopper landed on the other side of the white maze, and he got out of the truck and walked toward a knot of people standing on the hospital steps. Milt, wearing a borrowed sweat suit under his parka, his arm in a sling, with a barely civil smile on his face, stood like a man on a mission. He was listening to an officious-looking woman in a pants suit. She was talking but she was clearly on defense, arms crossed over the briefcase clasped to her chest.

Nearer the door, in the shadows, Allen slumped against the brick wall in his blue parka and baggy loaner jeans and a sweatshirt. His hair drooped to complement his sunken eyes and the twenty-four-hour beard that darkened his face.

The stunned woman standing next to Allen looked like all the mothers Broker'd ever seen who had lost their children at the state fair.

Jolene Sommer, the trophy wife, was not the Barbie Doll Broker had expected. She was neither blond nor tanned. Her dark hair, olive skin, and restless green eyes flew Mediterranean flags against her white-trash name. In her bittersweet glance, he glimpsed something rare that had been shattered when she was a kid and cheaply put back together.

She was in her early thirties, stood about five eight, and weighed maybe 120 pounds. The dark hair twisted in natural curls around her shoulders, and her cheekbones were wide under the broken emerald eyes, and her lips were full and her nose straight. She wore no obvious makeup to complement the quiet shades of gray and charcoal of her turtleneck sweater, slacks, tailored wool coat, and the soft leather of her boots. She had removed her gloves. A simple gold band marked her left hand.

Broker instantly disliked the young guy wearing shades who stood next to her; he disliked the way they looked so good together; he disliked their palpable aura of familiarity.

Further, he disliked beauty in a man; the torch-singer glow of a Jim Morrison or a young Warren Beatty who hid cocaine secrets behind aviator sunglasses. He disliked the casually tousled thick blond hair, every strand of which seemed individually groomed and placed. He disliked the insouciant hip-slouched promise of youth, the easy sex in either pocket. And he disliked the man's flat-bellied athleticism, so innocent of aches and pains.

Mostly, he disliked his own disapproval.

This had to be the old boyfriend. Broker was painfully reminded of all the lean young army ranger officers who rubbed elbows and flirted with his wife half a world away.

Ex-wife?

Whatever.

If Jolene was Bonnie, this had to be Clyde. Okay. He was a six-footer and python-smooth and strong. Looking more carefully, Broker found his flaw; this was a guy who couldn't maintain his cool. It was the way he'd dressed for this occasion that gave him away. His black suit, black shirt, black tie, and the glasses looked like an early Halloween costume or the garb of a limo driver who'd booked a really good ride. And in contrast to the other people gathered here, he put out such a fulsome cloud of barely suppressed well-being, he almost sparked.

Allen crooked his arm and summoned Broker with a nervous wag of his finger, shouting to be heard over the helicopter.

"Broker, come over here, Hank's wife wants to meet you. Jolene, this is Phil Broker, the guide. He paddled us out to get help." Allen's voice was controlled and grave and his eyes stayed focused at knee level.

"Heads up, Jolene; this is the canoe guy," echoed the young man in black as he took her elbow and steered her. Allen immediately acquired her other elbow and both of them attempted to squire her forward. It looked like a tug-of-war over the spoils, and Hank's brain wasn't even cold yet.

Broker felt the heat go to his hands. He had no right to be indignant. But he was.

He became more irate as they continued to hang on her arms as Jolene Sommer reached for his hand. She moved like a person really eager to meet new people, and her sweaty clasp was more a grab for something solid than a handshake. "I truly appreciate what you did," she said, searching Broker's face.

Broker wanted to convey something but, rather than grope for words, he remained silent and Jolene continued to hold on to his hand. Looking too deeply, almost impolitely, into her eyes, Broker blinked and stepped back. She still had Allen holding one elbow, the smooth young guy clamped on the other.

His impulse was to pull her away, take her aside.

But he was the stranger here so he nodded, released the handshake, and stepped farther back. The guy in black then effortlessly moved in, squeezed Broker's elbow, and took a long billfold from his inside jacket pocket. With one-handed flash he manipulated three $100 bills and tucked them into Broker's hand. "For your trouble, fella; thanks again."

He's dealt blackjack, thought Broker, who wanted to see his eyes.

So, slam-bam-dismissed. Okay. But old radar started to track. While he studied what was wrong with this picture he remained low-key. He slipped the bills into his pocket, like they expected a humble canoe guide to do, and folded his hands below his waist like an usher, and waited.

Milt concluded his nontalk with the lady in the pants suit, who retreated inside the hospital. He spotted Broker and walked over with the forward momentum of a slightly damaged armored vehicle. They shook left hands. Milt extracted a business card and said, "I'll be in touch. I can reach you at the lodge, right?"

Broker nodded, took the card. "Who's the lady you were talking to?" he asked.

"Oh, her? She's small-fry. The risk management flak for this place. Fortunately, they're part of the Duluth system and Duluth has deep pockets."

"Lawsuit," Broker said.

Milt narrowed his eyes. "Word is two nurses heard the anesthetist admit she took the breathing tube out too soon."

Broker nodded politely—like it was all over his head— and then pointed toward Sommer's wife and her sleek companion. "How'd they show up so quick?"

"Charter out of St. Paul."

"Who's the guy?"

Milt narrowed his eyes a fraction tighter, as if this were more information than a loyal canoe guide needed to know. After a beat he said, with a ripple of distaste, "Earl Garf, he's the remnant from her checkered past we discussed."

"Uh-huh. What's he do now?"

Milt shrugged. "What all the smart young ones do, computers." He adjusted his sling, turned: "Well, ah, Christ, here comes Hank."

An ambulance pulled out of the garage toward the waiting helicopter.

"Got to go, thanks for everything," Milt said; quick handshake, fleeting eye contact. He was leaving Ely and the tragic vacation, locking back into the gravitational pull of his high-speed, high-stakes world. They all were. He stepped back to join Jolene and Allen as the gurney bearing the blanketed mummy bumped toward the helicopter door.

Eyes shut, Sommer's face jutted under a clear plastic oxygen mask like carved Ivory Soap.

Broker's lower lip went a little stiff as he recalled the tramp of ritual. Bagpipes at cop funerals. Taps sounding over rows of empty paratroop boots. He had wanted to thank Hank Sommer for saving his life.

But he was just the hired help so he kept his place amid the tragic procession. Sommer's Ford Expedition was still at the lodge. The keys were hanging on a peg by the fireplace. All three clients had clothes and gear strewn from Ely to Fraser Lake. Clearly the departing friends and family were too preoccupied to collect belongings. He had Milt's card.

The cortege escorted Sommer to the helicopter medics who

loaded the gurney into the chopper. Mrs. Sommer, Allen, and Milt embraced awkwardly. Garf smiled directly into the sun.

Then Garf escorted all three of them to a waiting cab and they drove away. Broker squinted into the bright sky, and the wind sock on the hospital roof hung limp, and the only danger nature posed today was the flash of mild snow blindness.

The helicopter lifted off and in its place, on the far side of the helipad, Amy Skoda stood at attention, her hands balled loosely at her sides. She watched the helicopter, and Broker watched her until the engine faded and the plane itself receded into a dot in the southeastern sky. Then Amy turned away and came across the parking lot.

Broker coughed three times. Then he sneezed. The sneeze blew the sharply stacked sun-and-shade design of the brilliant day into runny watercolors. Dizzy, he put his hand out and felt Amy's firm grip steady him.

"Must be hungover," he mumbled.

She rested a cool hand on his forehead. "I don't think so. You went swimming in ice water in a blizzard. You fried your resistance paddling out. You've caught a cold."

Chapter Fourteen

It's all shadows now.

Sinking. Velvet suffocation.

Darkness fills in like ink. Shadows twist. Are they sparks or are they bubbles? Do they rise or do they burst? Don't know. Ego sorts through the debris and finds the drawers of memory. Ego rearranges and sifts. Robust memory responds. There was icy water, then pain. Now bright lights. Halos of concerned faces hover. Ego assumes personality. Personality discovers some of its baggage.

Hurt. Dying. Dead.

But stuff still moves inside his head. Drowned in the dark, he grows gills and discovers he can breathe the black. Somewhere above, on the surface, murky storms of human weather barge around; garbled people in white coats who move, poke, talk, shine lights.

Better to avoid It. Them. Up there's where the pain lives. Better to roll over and dive and meander along the bands of shadow where the lacy patterns of light sway like kelp.

Enchantment is not out of the question.

Everything else sinks but life is a stubborn bubble that persists in rising to the glow that is brighter and brighter and like—hey—

See . . .

. . .

A kind of seeing. Dream-seeing. A shadow man and shadow woman in fuzzy outline, filled with black. They stand, facing each other, and the man slouches forward heavily. He holds one palm up and with the finger of his other hand, he strikes the palm, sadly counting items off a list.

The woman bows her head and pulls a hand through her hair. Her other hand presses into her chest over her heart.

Still not clear, like peering through screens, veils, mist. Just shapes. Tense, worried shapes. And some precocious part of his mind is piping up that this is how Homer described shades in hell.

A bell rings and they walk away. Now there's nothing to look at but a shadow couch, a fireplace to the left, banks of windows, and beyond the windows a spidery lacework of barren branches under a slab of veined marble sky. Hello?

The woman returns and stands before the windows. She raises scissors and she could be a figure from Sophocles the way she methodically saws at her long dark hair. Clumps fall to the floor and on her shoulders until all she has left is a plucky cap the color of wine. With a broom, she sweeps the shorn hair into a dustpan. Then she is gone.

His eyes can move but they steer out of control; they roll, tipsy, and hit the curb of his vision and rotate back. His shoulders heave, the muscles of his neck jerk. He hits restraints. Straps maybe. Nothing else moves.

Nothing moves.

Paralyzed?

. . .

Maybe just broken. Say broken.

Okay. Fix broken later.

. . .

No color. Everything grainy, gray on gray—ashes after fire. The air itself is a mist of blowing soot. Hell again, a dream without sound. At the bottom of the dream two bare feet stick out from a sheet. They sprawl on the edge of a mattress covered with a crinkly cover. The kind of rubbery thing that goes on a baby bed to protect it from getting wet. The feet aren't attached. They are just more shadow furniture, like the couch.

Feet. Not feet.

Here. Not here.

The situation calls for discipline. A point of origin.

Ego. I.

Me.

Hank.

. . .

From the angle of *his* vision *he* cannot find the rest of *himself*.

He tries real hard. He can feel his chest rise and fall as his lungs fill and empty, and he can hear the drumbeat of his heart. He can see arms, inert; just lying there. He sees the coral snake tattoo on his wrist from that night in Columbus, Georgia, after he got his jump wings.

So. You are stuck.

Just asleep. Just asleep. Stay calm.

Wake up. Wake Up. WAKE UP!

. . .

The bubbles lied. No up, no light. Still stuck in between. Not awake, not asleep. Just entombed here inside this living suit of a body.

And he senses a wry flutter behind his eyes. A . . .

Smile. Because isn't everyone trapped inside themselves?

Okay, be serious.

Stuff is connecting up. His mind scurries for a fix. You cannot move today. One day at a time.

But his imagination and intelligence are running more in step now—more like him—and they are running scared because they've already made the leap. What has no body and can see? Five-letter word starts with G.

No longer merely a camera/recorder, the voice inside is his voice now and can still laugh at a joke.

Hey man, it's like you're dead.

And then. *What if you are dead?*

How would you know? *You've never been dead before.*

C'mon cut the Buddhist shit, this is serious.

What's that? Tunnels of sound. Drains unclogging. Whoosh.

"Jesus."

Jesus. Someone said "Jesus." An echo like . . .

Wait a minute here.

Oh, shit, oh, shit, what if Aunt Louise is right and Jesus is wait-

ing at the end of the long, dark tunnel to pull me over and stick the God flashlight in my face and check the expiration on my spiritual ID—not the historical Jesus who was some right-on, squat, big-nosed, splay-toed, swarthy rabbi who was bucking the system. No, it's the Anglo-Saxon, blue-eyed Baptist Methodist Catholic Lutheran Episcopalian Presbyterian Jesus, the only man in '50's America allowed to have long hair, and Eisenhower is God and heaven is really a white-church picnic in Mississippi.

"So when they nailed Jesus to the cross . . ."

Oh, shit, oh, God. Somebody *was* talking out there, not in here. No bullshit. Shadows talking out in shadow land. Two shadows talking close.

"No. No. Take my word, it just wouldn't work that way."

"But that's how they show it in this painting. And this book costs . . . look at this, a hundred and forty-five bucks."

"That painting's from some religious Flemish fanatic's imagination three hundred years ago. Absolutely incorrect. It would never happen. Spikes through the palm would not support the weight of the human body. They'd tear right out."

"Hmmmmm," shadow number two said. "You're saying they just made it up."

"I don't know about that. Crucifixion was practiced by the Romans as a form of state execution. And the Romans were, above all else, engineers. They were always very practical in their planning."

"So how would they have nailed him up, you know, live?"

"Live?"

"Like, in real life."

Real life. Real life. Bodies that move. *Hey. I'm here. I'm—listening.*

"Probably they just used rope and strung them up. It would have been more efficient and cheaper. What killed them was exposure, starvation, and the hanging, the cramping of the shoulder and chest muscles disabled the lungs until the condemned person slowly asphyxiates."

"Like they couldn't breathe anymore."

I can breathe. I can breathe.

"That's right."

"But if they did nail them up what would be the ideal way to do it? Give me your best-case scenario."

"There's an anatomy book on the reference shelf over there. Go get it."

Get it, get it. I'm here. Can't really see them yet. Like behind Venetian blinds. Come out, come out.

"Okay, here are the bones of the forearm and hand. The logical place to pin the arm is through a foramen."

"Forearm, right."

"For-a-men."

"Say what?"

"A natural opening in the body. And on Hank, that would be here, see?"

Oh, God. Touching. Touching me.

"At the terminus of the radius and ulna bones. Above the wrist. See this opening in the tendon? Called the interossesous membrane."

"You mean, ah, here?"

I can feel that! I can feel that. They're touching my left wrist. Poking it. I can feel it and I can breathe and I can hear.

"Right here, there's a natural opening between the bones."

"Just give it the old kabosh right there and nobody's going anywhere, right?"

"Not unless they tear through a lot of nerves and soft tissue, and especially not if the nail has a head on it."

. . .

Gone. They're gone. Come back.

I'm here.

Me, Hank.

Come back.

Chapter Fifteen

"**I don't suppose anybody** brought in the other canoe, did they? I'd hate for it to sit out there all winter. Freeze-up will probably stove it in." Uncle Billie was calling long distance from Arizona golf heaven and when Broker didn't respond, Billie continued on, "Well, I guess not. Don't worry about it. I'll write it off. And the tents. And all the gear . . ."

Several seconds ticked by during which Broker did not volunteer to go back into the canoe area and round up Billie's lost items. Billie cleared his throat and resumed talking. "Just goes to show you. Hell, kiddo, we all figured it'd do you good to get out in the woods. Get some fresh air, work out your heebie-jeebies."

"Yeah, yeah, go cut a rug," Broker shot back in Billie's Kilroy lingo. "Let me talk to Mom."

Irene Broker came on the line. "How are you doing with all this?"

"I got a cold," he said, avoiding the question.

"Heat up some cider, lemon, and vinegar."

"I know, I know; listen, Mom—have you, ah, heard anything? I know she's got the number out there."

"No calls." He waited while his mother searched for the right words. "Maybe she's waiting for you to call her. You have numbers for her over there."

"Right. How's Dad?"

"He's taking a nap, should I get him up?"

"No, just say hello; look, someone's here, I gotta go."

"Take care."

He placed the phone back in its cradle. No one was here at the moment, but Amy was on her way, bringing supplies to the shut-in. He just didn't want to talk. Being sick mocked and trivialized him, and his darkest thoughts all ended in a comic sneeze.

He stared up at the stuffed moose head over Uncle Billie's fireplace. Damn thing was too big for the main room and it swooped out with horns like the wingspread of a Stone Age bat. The glass eyes followed him.

And he kept seeing Jolene Sommer being led off by Allen Falken and that Earl character. He wondered how *she* was doing with all this.

It was four days later. The weather had turned dismal and Broker's cold exaggerated all his doubts. Between Kleenexes, he scourged himself with shoulds: *Should have been more responsible on the trip. Never should have been caught in open water by the weather like that.*

Never should have unloaded on that slob in The Saloon.

More specifically, he never should have thumped the guy in front of Amy Skoda, who now worried that he was extra-deeply troubled, which added a mighty tweak to her caretaking instincts and brought them up to full erect. So she dropped in every day to check on him, to bring groceries, provide company, and offer her strong but also very soft and warm shoulder to buoy him up. Taking some vacation time from work in the aftermath of the "event," she reminded him that she was just a call away . . .

He made camp in the lodge's main room with the moose. He'd folded out the sleeper couch in front of the fieldstone hearth and surrounded himself with tissues, tea, and lemon, cough drops and VapoRub. Days unwashed, his hair was a greasy thicket. He lived in baggy long johns and Uncle Billie's ancient blue wool robe.

He turned away from the telephone, picked up the TV remote, and clicked to CNN on satellite feed. He watched the news until they showed the gritty color images of corpses in a weedy ditch for the tenth time today. Kosovo: UN monitors expelled, refugees running to the mountains, winter coming on. He averted his eyes from the image of a dead child.

He tapped off the remote, went back to the phone, and punched in his voice mail at home. No new messages.

He swore out loud, which caused him to have a wracking coughing fit. When she'd heard his cough, Amy worried about secondary infections and had mentioned pneumonia. She wanted him to go in and have it checked.

Pneumonia was for infirm old people.

He drew the line at pneumonia and antibiotics.

Onward.

He went to the kitchen where two large kettles simmered on the ancient Wolf stove, and turned the heat up under the smaller one. When the loose sage and eucalyptus in it bubbled, he draped a towel over his head tent-fashion and inhaled the steam. He was trying to think positive when he heard a car.

He crossed to the windows and saw Amy's green Subaru Forester pull up the drive and park. Her choice of vehicle revealed a lot. Knowing her a little better now, he gathered she was a serious student of *Consumer Reports*. Impulse-buying was not in her nature. She did her research, budgeted her priorities, and then moved decisively to get what she wanted.

And if *Consumer Reports* posted an index for independent, thirty-something women she would rate first in her class in reliability and crash-worthiness.

And persistence.

Hatless, wearing a tidy blue parka with gray sleeves, she swirled in from the cold with her freckles and her hair bright as Celtic metalwork. She carried a shopping bag in her arms and a saddlebag purse slung over her shoulder.

"How are you feeling today?" she asked, heading for the kitchen.

Broker coughed hello.

"I think you should go in and have that checked," she said over her shoulder.

"In all due respect, I won't be going near a hospital for quite a while, thank you."

"Fine." She dumped the bag on the kitchen counter.

"You get it all?" he asked, hobbling after her.

"I bought all the hippie cures they had in the co-op."

"Think you know everything, don't you?"

"I know some of this stuff has merit as prevention but you're full-blown. I know a serious lung inflammation when I hear one."

Grumbling, Broker unloaded the bag: Vita-C, cider, vinegar, oranges, limes, lemons, echinacea, goldenseal, and Siberian ginseng. Cough drops and two boxes of Popsicles. He put the Popsicles in the freezer.

She went to the stove, avoided the cloud of sage, and sniffed the other pot, picked up a hot pad and lifted the cover. "What's cooking?"

"I found some venison in the freezer so I'm making stew."

She covered the pot and took off her jacket and hung it on a kitchen chair. Her sweater and jeans were practical and lived-in. He wondered if she ever wore a dress. Probably not. She crossed her arms, looked around at the cozy stocked shelves, the pots and pans dangling on a steel butcher's rail, and said, "Kitchens."

"What?" Her tone of voice put him on guard.

"My dad always said you have the best talks in the kitchen."

"What?" he repeated.

"Your Uncle Billie and my dad are hunting buddies, you know."

"Uh-huh," Broker said.

"Well, they talk." She paused. "About you."

"Jesus," Broker grinned awkwardly.

"Well, it doesn't hurt to talk."

Broker scrubbed his knuckles in his frazzled hair. "Like about my life, up to and including the present train wreck with Sommer?"

Amy shrugged her shoulders agreeably.

"And talking about it is going to make it better?" Broker nodded his head. "Usually when women say that, it means *they'll* feel better if they get you to talk. Okay, let's talk."

"Fine. Tell me about your marriage," Amy said.

"That's easy. My wife has this Joan of Arc complex. She intends to be a general. Does anybody ask what it's like to be the general's *husband*, home taking care of the kid? Or at teas with the officer's wives?"

"Women did it for years, why can't you? Where are you at with being separated from your daughter?"

"I've been with my daughter every day for two years. She's probably due for some full estrogen immersion."

"Aren't we light and breezy today, and so adept at small talk," Amy said.

"That's me?" Broker gestured offhand. "Food, eat; gun, shoot; woman, copulate."

Amy planted her hands on her hips. "You know, down in the Cities you might be a bad motherfucker. But up here, guys like you are a dime a dozen."

"What's that supposed to mean?" Broker drew back, a tad defensive.

Amy shook her head. "Sort of sad when a guy like you is reduced to bullying overweight drunks, like that guy at The Saloon. That was all out of proportion. Dave and I talked about it."

"Great. So now it's amateur-shrink hour."

"Dave thinks it's all coming down on you; your wife takes off, you're getting older, being on your own, not having any—well, structure in your life."

Broker grinned. "Lucky for me I got Amy Skoda standing here with the structural integrity of a small skyscraper."

Amy raised an eyebrow and swatted a denim-clad hip. "Check it out. This is not exactly a cornerstone."

Broker lowered himself to a chair at the kitchen table and mumbled, "I'm old enough to be . . ."

"I know—my brother," Amy dismissed him with a wave of her hand and plopped into the chair across from him.

"So how was *your* day?" he asked.

"Oh, wonderful. We had a preliminary root-cause analysis session."

"Sounds grim."

Amy winkled her nose. "Allen Falken sent a tape-recorded statement. He said he wouldn't come in person because his friendship with Hank Sommer could be perceived as coloring his judgment. He did a beautiful job of making me look like a hick."

"That bad?"

"Pretty bad. But friendly, more like. How do you staff for a five-hundred-year storm if you routinely staff for light fishing accidents in the summer. So it's like my fault, but he can sympathize because I'm not really up to speed."

"Really?" wondered Broker. "Right after the surgery, before it happened, he made a point of telling me how sharp you were."

"I guess he had a change of heart. So the consensus is that Hank Sommer wound up a vegetable because the nurse-anesthetist miscalculated somewhere and the attending nurse failed to monitor in postop."

Amy's finger traced invisible water rings on the tabletop. "They're not sure *exactly* where things went wrong. He was hypothermic and cold is always a weird variable and can effect the way the body metabolizes drugs. Like it could sequester and hoard them in a sluggish circulation system and release them at odd times."

She tossed her hair. "Whatever. And Nancy Ward, the recovery-room nurse, was having a bad day; she'd had a fight with her husband and she'd worked all the previous night. Technically, she'll catch the brunt of a malpractice suit. It looks like she neglected to program Sommer into the monitor. So she takes the blame for leaving him untended. But I was in charge. So it comes back to me."

"You agree with them?"

She crossed her arms across her chest.

"You don't agree with them?"

She uncrossed her arms, then recrossed them, stood up, and changed the subject. "There's this rumor how you smuggled two tons of buried gold through Laos into Thailand and banked it in Hong Kong? Dave says if you didn't have connections in the FBI, the IRS would be all over you."

The rumors. Broker waved his hand. "Hell, I should pull it out of the stock market, put it all back into bullion, and bury the stuff again."

"Bury it? Like a *pirate?*"

"Exactly." He heaved up and went to the counter, selected a knife from the rack on the wall, and sliced an orange, then a lemon, followed by a lime. The tart citrus circles tumbled off the blade and laundered the air; orange, yellow, and green in a pile like tropical doubloons. He dumped the slices into another large pot, added a quart of cider, a generous splash of vinegar, two tablespoons of honey and a cinnamon stick, and set the flame.

Amy got up, joined him at the counter, and looked over his shoulder. "You're going to have the most expensive urine in Minnesota."

"Mom's home remedy."

"Whatever." She held out her left hand. "Look, see that?" She pointed at a faint white line on the edge of her palm.

It was an old scar. He said, "So?"

"Thirty years ago, the summer you helped Billie put in the boat dock." She pointed out the window toward the old, hump-backed dock jutting into the lake. "You cut a fishhook out of my hand. You were eighteen. I was seven." She appraised him. "You don't remember."

He didn't recall the fishhook. He remembered building the damn dock, though.

"You're no fun today," she said as she put on her coat. "I have something else for you." She removed a bag from her purse and handed it to him. It contained a cardboard and cellophane toy box and a copy of the outstate edition of the *Minneapolis Star Tribune*.

"What's this?" There was a kid's action-figure called *War Wolf* in the box—plastic wolf head on a pumped-up body, dressed in camo fatigues.

"Way uncool, Broker; everybody's heard of *War Wolf*, the poor man's *Star Wars*," Amy said, patting his cheek. "You know what else Dave said? He said you were lost in the modern world. I'll bet you've never seen *Seinfeld*? *Ally McBeal*?"

"Hey, knock it off, I read *Doonesbury* every once in a while. And I watch *The Crocodile Hunter*." He held up the toy and hunched his shoulders, questioning.

"Read the paper, there's an article about Hank Sommer in the feature section folded on top."

Amy touched his cheek lightly once more, told him to keep washing his hands, and outside, clomped down the steps, got in her practical, reliable car, and disappeared into the early evening. She probably drove the speed limit when nobody was around.

As he turned his mom's cider remedy down to a simmer he wondered if she kissed with her eyes open.

It was not much of an article, with just a tiny picture of Hank squeezed into the type. A bigger picture showcased the plastic toy.

Creator of War Wolf in Coma.

Timberry writer Hank Sommer was diagnosed as being in a coma due to complications following emergency surgery in Ely, Minnesota, last week. After a daring boundary-water seaplane rescue in a violent storm, Sommer was operated on to repair a rupture and perforated bowel suffered during a canoeing accident.

Milton Dane, prominent St. Paul attorney, is representing Sommer and his wife against the Duluth Medical Group that manages Ely Miner Hospital.

According to Dane, "Ely Miner violated the standard of care with respect to Sommer's post-operative treatment. It is ironic that Hank survived the storm, the hypothermia, the rescue, and the surgery, only to be deprived of oxygen in a hospital recovery room."

Irony has stalked Sommer throughout his writing career. His first two novels garnered critical attention but little in the way of sales. Then he wrote *War Wolf*, a satire in which a returning veteran afflicted with dioxin poisoning becomes a vengeful Communist werewolf.

Director Bruce Cook found a copy of *War Wolf* three years ago in the remainder bin. The movie—which earned over ninety-three million dollars—established Sommer's career as a novelist. It also produced a financial bonanza for the author, who shrewdly negotiated lucrative deals on other *War Wolf* spin-offs, including the action figure and video games.

Broker shook his head, pushed up off the couch, put on his parka, and selected a cigar. Brandy seemed like a good idea, so he raided Billie's liquor cabinet and poured two inches into a cup, hit the play button on Billie's CD player, went out on the front porch, and sat down on the steps. Through the open door he heard Jay and the Americans kick in as he popped a match.

Cigar smoke clawed his throat, so he took a soothing drink by way of a solitary toast: Whiskey, Women, Work, and War—to Hank Sommer, who wears a coral snake on his wrist, who saved my life, who takes second billing to a kid's plastic toy . . .

C'mon, Broker, tell the truth, you voted for Ventura, didn't you?
Yeah, Hank, damned if I didn't. Just to spite the suits.

He looked out over the dark lake and shivered. Damn, it was cold for October this year. Tiny glints clamped down along the shore; there'd be a skin of thin ice in the morning.

Uncle Billie's porch faced north up Lake One and as the night filled in, the edges of the pine crowns feathered out and melted into a black sky. As the tree line disappeared so did perspective. Broker was alone with a star dome virtually unblemished by artificial light and, except for the occasional airliner and the seldom satellite, it was the cosmos of the ancients.

The Big and Little Dippers hung high to the north around the polestar, and Orion hugged the eastern horizon. The summer triangle of Deneb, Vega, and Altair slipped away to the west a little more each night.

Mom, hoping he could be the artist she had never been, tried to nurture in him a sense of discovery, and never missed an opportunity to slip a few coppers of wonder into his piggy bank of instincts.

See the shapes of animals in the clouds. The constellations.

Dad taught him to find the real animal in the forest; the deer by his tracks, where he bedded, where he fed; by his rubs and scrapes. Honoring both his parents, he'd let his practicality cross-fertilize his imagination.

The Cities, stacked with high-rise humans, had never been his home. This was home and, as always, the wilderness beckoned with silent beauty, absent mercy. Broker sipped his brandy and mused how the death traps in nature were always feminine: oceans, mountains, deep woods. Which was as it should be because their victims were usually young, romantic, dumb men.

Jay and the Americans called it accurately:

Come a little bit closer
you're my kind of man
so big and so strong . . .

Moved by the rhythm of the old music, he didn't have to travel far to find the memory of Jolene Sommer's green eyes.

Broker stood up, poured out the rest of his drink, grimaced at the cigar, and threw it away. Getting cold, he went inside, shut the door, and placed another log on the coals.

He dippered out a cup of his mom's cider, settled back on the fold-out bed, took a sip, and let the citrus mix of honey and vinegar trickle down his sore throat.

The damn newspaper stared at him again, and he was about to toss it across the room when he caught the headline below the fold on page one.

ACCOUNTANT FOUND DEAD, CRUCIFIED IN WOODS

"Crucified?" he said out loud. They gotta be kidding.
But they weren't.

A bow hunter found a frozen body in the woods northwest of
Marine on St. Croix yesterday afternoon. The deceased, identified
as Timberry financial planner Cliff Stovall, had his left hand nailed
through the wrist into the stump of an oak tree with a six-inch
pole barn-spike. Sources close to the sheriff's office said that a
hammer and evidence of heavy drinking had been located at the
scene. Stillwater resident Jon Ludwig discovered the body while
deer hunting.
    Stovall's partner, Dave Henson, told the Washington County
sheriff's department that Stovall had gone to look at some property. Henson also explained that Stovall was distraught over a
recent separation from his wife.
    An anonymous source in the sheriff's department said Stovall
had been treated in the past for alcoholism and self-mutilation.

Broker slowly sat upright. The flu lost its grip as he calmly
worked back through the delirious landing on Snowbank Lake. Distinctly, he remembered Sommer raving:
    Tell Cliff to move the money.

Chapter Sixteen

Directory assistance listed the number of Stovall and Hensen Associates in Timberry, a suburb east of the Twin Cities. Broker didn't have to get past the receptionist.

"I know this is bad timing, but an acquaintance, Hank Sommer, recommended Cliff Stovall for investment counseling. And now, well, I thought maybe his partner . . ."

"Of course, Mr. Sommer is—was—is one of our clients, I guess . . ." her voice caught. "I'm sorry, it's a little crazy around here."

"I, ah, understand, maybe I should call later."

"No. I'm sure Mr. Henson will talk to you. It's just that these tragedies have hit our office kind of hard. Cliff and his wife were friends of Mr. Sommer and Dorothy . . ."

"Were?"

"Well, before Mr. Sommer remarried. And, ah, before Cliff and his wife broke up."

Dorothy? "Dorothy Sommer, right," he said.

"No, she was—well, she'd never changed her name. So it was always Dorothy Gayler."

"Right, is she still . . . ?"

"At the St. Paul Pioneer Press."

"Of course. You know, I think I will wait awhile and call later. Thank you."

Broker hung up and drummed his fingers on a yellow legal pad. Freshly showered and shaved after ten hours of healing sleep, he doodled circles bisected by crosshairs on his notepad. Then he printed "Sommer." Under Sommer's name he printed "Stovall." He drew a circle around Sommer and Stovall. Then he printed "Trophy Wife— Bonnie (Parker?)and Clyde." He drew a crude open arrow around Bonnie and Clyde and aimed it at Sommer. In a third column he wrote: Dorothy?

He went back to directory assistance, got the newspaper's number, and punched it in. The switchboard passed him to the features department where he listened to Dorothy Gayler's voice mail. The businesslike voice on the recorded message revealed nothing: "I'm not here; leave a message." He hung up, poured another cup of coffee, and had better luck on his second call.

"Dorothy Gayler."

"Dorothy, you don't know me, my name is Phil Broker. I was on the canoe trip with Hank Sommer."

"Yes." Crisp, the perfunctory voice was precise as the strike of a typewriter key.

"I'm calling from Ely. I'm not a friend, I was the guide."

This seemed to warm communication. "You went for help, with Allen Falken; I remember now," she said.

"You know Allen?"

"I've met Allen. I wouldn't say I *know* any of my ex-husband's new friends." Distancing.

Broker speeded up his voice, reaching to catch her flagging interest. "Well, I was just doing a job and I got caught in the middle of that lake and pooped out. The fact is, if it weren't for Hank I wouldn't have made it. I'd be dead."

"How refreshing." She was making up her mind whether to talk to him. "Mr. Broker. Everyone else has talked about the ironic tragedy of Hank's . . . situation. You call me up and express a kind of gratitude." Her voice strayed close to sarcasm and closer to Broker. Okay.

He continued quickly. "Except the way it turned out, I can't say it to him." He paused, then said, "I'll be in the Cities the next few days. I wondered if you'd be willing to have a cup of coffee tomorrow?"

"Why?"

"I want to know who he was. I saw this article in the Minneapolis paper but it didn't feel like the guy I met."

"The father of the toy, you mean. Ours wasn't much better. Well, that's what he turned into but that wasn't who he was when I knew him." She paused, then said, "What time tomorrow?"

"Lunch?"

"Make it one P.M.; I work out at lunch. I'll meet you on the street, in front of the building. How will I know you, Mr. Broker?"

Broker looked at the coatrack by the door. "I'll be wearing a fleece jacket, sort of blaze orange."

"Of course; it's getting toward that time of year," Dorothy said.

Broker thanked her and hung up.

Picking up momentum, he thumbed through Uncle Billie's permit applications and found Sommer's number. Deep breath. Slight shuffle of nerves. Jolene Sommer picked up on the third ring. He let the breath out.

"Hello?"

"Mrs. Sommer?"

"Yes."

"My name is Phil Broker, the guide on the canoe trip with Hank." Broker heard a click as someone picked up an extension phone in the Sommer house.

"Earl," Jolene said, "put down the phone. I've got it." They waited. The other person on the line did not put down.

"Is this, ah, a bad time to call?" Broker asked. Earl evidently didn't waste any time moving in.

After a pause, Jolene said frankly, "When's a good time?"

"How is he?"

"He's comfortable," she said in a controlled, tired voice as if she decided on these words after many conversations. "Milt Dane suggested I surround him with familiar things so I set up his bed in his office where the windows overlook the river. And he can see his desk and books. He's got a feeding tube now. So . . ."

A little shocked, Broker blurted, "He's at home?"

"It's become a little complicated, financially," she said, in a quick, defensive burst. Then more slowly, "Actually, I think he's better off. Since I brought him home I get the feeling he's looking at me. Of course, everyone says that's impossible."

After an awkward silence, Broker said, "Ah, I've still got his truck up here."

"Oh God, I'm sorry, a lot of things have been falling through the cracks. I'll send . . ."

"Actually, I'm coming down to the Cities. I could drop it off."

"Oh."

"Say tonight, around four or five P.M.?"

"I guess . . . that would be fine." She gave Broker directions which he wrote down on the pad. After he said good-bye he doodled more circles and crosshairs. On the trip Hank had been arguing with her about money. Now he was at home and not in a hospital because of money. In the seaplane, Hank's last words were about money. Broker printed in big blocky letters—FOLLOW THE MONEY.

He sipped coffee, debated briefly, then picked up the phone again and called a number in Lake Elmo, a rural township on the eastern fringe of the Twin Cities metro area, near Timberry. On the second ring he got a woman's voice.

"Hi, Denise, is J.T. there?"

"It's him," he heard her call out, and he knew she had rolled her eyes in that expressive way. "You know, *him*."

The guarded but also curious deep voice of J.T. Merryweather came on the line. "Uh-huh?" In the background Broker heard Denise whisper: "Find out why Nina split."

"Hey J.T., I need a little help."

"Hmmm," J.T. said. "You know, so do I. Maybe we should give a call over to Manpower, get us a temp. And by the way, hello, how are you, how's the family."

Broker smiled. He and J.T. came out of the service around the same time. Bored with ordinary life, they took the civil service test and were rookies together in St. Paul. They'd partnered together in narcotics and homicide before Broker went to BCA and specialized in guns. J.T. made it up to captain in St. Paul where he flunked office politics and took early retirement to go into business for himself.

"Very funny. Look, could you do me a favor? Call John E. over at Washington County and get the word on that crucifixion in the woods last week." John Eisenhower was the Washington County sheriff. Also a graduate of the St. Paul Police Academy in the same class with J.T. and Broker.

J.T. said, "Wasn't no crucifixion. Newspaper got carried away. Guy nailed his hand to a stump. You can't call, huh?"

"I don't really want anybody knowing I'm around."

"Uh-huh. Just can't shake the old peek-a-boo UC habits?"

"There it is."

"You use people you know."

"Yeah. Like how I used you to get a sore back hauling all those hay bales last August. Like I used you, leaving my truck to for *you* to use."

"Humph. You only come around when you need something."

Broker grinned. "Actually I could use a place to hang out because I'll be nosing around in Timberry."

"Timberry, that's some serious Yup; I was over there at the mall and saw my first Humee. Cute little blond kid driving it looked about fourteen. Yeah, sure, c'mon by. Denise would love to talk to you."

"Won't work, J.T. I'm not in the mood."

"I hear you, Broker. I don't give a shit about your sorry personal life. But Denise wants to know, and she wields power over this place. Woman swings that vaginal wrench of hers around like a goddamn scepter."

In the background, Broker could hear Merryweather's wife scold him roundly—something about bad influences and people who refused to grow up.

"Call John E. and schmooze him up," Broker said. "I'll see you later this afternoon." On the verge of laughter, they rang off.

Then he glanced at the canoe trip applications strewn on the table with his notes. Sommer and Allen Falken both lived in Timberry, which was as far away from Ely as you could get. It was an instant bedroom community that nineties' wealth had erected in Washington County. The last time he drove through he'd been amazed to see a whole forest of evergreens transplanted from a nursery to screen the new homes going in.

Broker was up, pacing. Sommer's keys hung from a peg on the clothes rack next to the door. He glanced out the window at the parking lot, where Sommer's Ford Expedition waited, hunched and gleaming against the wilting snow like a black enamel bison.

After about ten seconds of debate he reached for the phone again and called Amy. As soon as she answered, he asked without preamble: "Is it weird that Sommer would be at home so soon after the accident?"

"Are you kidding?"

"I just talked to his wife. He's at home."

"Something's off. He needs a full-care nursing facility at minimum."

"She said he *watches* her."

"C'mon."

"No bullshit. You interested?"

"Maybe."

"So, what are you doing?"

"Coming over to your place."

"I'll make another pot of coffee," Broker said.

Chapter Seventeen

Jolene Sommer hung up the phone and paused for a moment with her palm on the plastic receiver where his voice had been.

Broker, the guide.

She sat at the kitchen table, exhausted, taking refuge in a cup of coffee, staring out the window. At the edge of the backyard patio, a red cardinal was inspecting an empty feeder that dangled from a barren tree limb. She knew what Sharon Stone wore to the Academy Awards last year, but she didn't know what kind of tree it was. She never caught the knack of feeding the birds. She barely remembered to feed the cat.

Hank had . . .

She looked away and restarted her thoughts. Broker. She had a notion of him from up north, paddling with Allen through the night in an effort to save Hank.

He was not smooth and all tucked in like Allen. He had a deep-set tongue-and-groove muscularity and he was at home in his body, which was important. He had a quiet voice; simple perhaps, but direct. She tried to remember his weathered face, the light, courteous touch of his hand that day at the hospital.

Jolene was good at first impressions. She was also good at puzzles, the ones with pieces. She wasn't so good at crossword puzzles—yet—because her vocabulary needed work. She believed you liked a person in the first seconds when you met them or you didn't.

She had liked Phil Broker. He possessed a solid, old-fashioned quality, like he'd been made to last.

Her eyes moved across the spacious kitchen and back out the window past the bird feeder to a jumble of oak rounds strewn on the dead grass by the woodshed behind the garage. A heavy splitting maul was imbedded deep in one of the upright rounds. Rust had formed an orange scab on the wedged blade.

A muffled crash echoed up from the basement and that was Earl dropping his barbells on the carpet. Earl had installed himself downstairs, where, like a bilge pump, he'd siphoned away just enough of the bills to keep the house—and her—afloat.

Earl was a creature of habit. And so, to her regret, was she. When things fell apart, when she realized she was facing this crisis literally broke, with nothing for resources but a couple of credit cards—she'd reached out to Earl.

Which had been a large mistake.

Jolene rubbed her forehead with her fingertips. After all these years about the only thing she could say about Earl was that he'd peaked early and still looked good with his shirt off.

They just couldn't seem to break the pattern—she'd go off on her own and wind up drinking too much. Earl would step in and pull her back from the brink. Her part of the deal was to manage Earl's temper so he didn't go berserk on people.

This dynamic spun in circles for more than thirteen years, since high school; except for the year and a half when Earl went off on his own tangent in the army. That was after the mess out in Washington. He'd signed on to Desert Storm, trekked deep into the Iraqi desert with the 24th Mech, eager to redeem himself. Spent six months battling nothing more serious than sand and fleas, and he came home without any real medals, just one sandy case of the clap. All his life Earl just couldn't catch a break.

Until now.

Jolene finished her coffee and put the cup in the dishwasher, added detergent, and tapped the start button. Then she paced the kitchen, touching up the table, the island, and the counter with a damp washcloth. Her life had turned into one of those ads from a woman's magazine at the check-out counter. *Be thinner, richer; live in a beautiful house . . .*

Right.

The first few days she had been stunned and needed Earl to guide her. But now she was over the initial shock and not real sure she wanted Earl back in her life, living in her basement, playing his mind games, waiting for her to lose it and start drinking again so it would be old times again. Him calling the shots.

Well, she wasn't going to drink today. She had fourteen months of sobriety in the bank. And not a penny more. Hank had tied up every cent he owned in the trust.

Trust had sure turned into a funny word around this house.

Jolene took a deep breath. Earl always started out intending to do it by the rules. Just trying to help, he'd taken Cliff Stovall off for a heart-to-heart, to convince him to open the trust. She didn't know the details, but she could guess. Earl got mad. So far, no cops had come snooping around.

And the bills . . .

Jesus Christ, when she faced the idea of the bills she thought of the scene in *Jaws* when Roy Scheider first sees the shark and he jerks back—like whoa. Now, like Roy, she needed a bigger boat.

She shook her head and let her eyes drift back out the window to the woodpile. She could not imagine Earl yanking out the maul, splitting the wood, stacking it in tidy rows. He enjoyed watching it burn, all right, in the fireplace but it never occurred to him to go out and split more when it ran out. For all his pampered muscles, Earl refused to sweat outside a gym. He was the future, he'd said. In the future, the third-worlders would do the physical work. Mexicans, probably.

She looked out the window for a few more moments at the hungry cardinal and the brown leaves and the gray sky. The morning was like a moody song from an oldies station: sentimental. Perfect for feeling sorry for herself. Perfect for stinking-thinking.

It was one of her favorite alcoholic fantasies: being rescued. And a lot of men had come to grief on it, walking into a dark barroom and seeing her marooned on a bar stool.

That's what had been so perfect about meeting Hank. She met him sober. *I know I was bad, but just give me this one chance and I promise I'll be so good . . .*

Hank had rescued her, all right, but Jolene saw right away that his ex-wife had handled the finances. Hank was lost around money.

The hammer fell about ninety minutes after she got to the intensive care unit at Regions in St. Paul. A neurologist had been called in to evaluate Hank; his workup and consulting was costing hundreds of dollars a minute.

Then this square-shaped lady in a maroon and black business suit had trampled though the blue-garbed medics like a rhino trashing a patch of petunias. She had pointed out that Hank Sommer's Blue Cross policy had lapsed because of nonpayment of premiums.

Private pay.

Boy, those two words could empty a hospital ward of smiles real fast.

Well, no way could she keep him in the hospital at two, three grand a day. Milt Dane protested, said she couldn't just take him AMA—against medical advice. Jolene, mad, said, "Watch me." Hank had already had a feeding tube inserted, so Earl borrowed a wheelchair and they brought Hank home in Earl's van.

A bad move that almost alienated Milt, which she could not afford to do. Now she was smoothing that over; in the meantime, until Milt put Hank in a fancy nursing home, she was working round the clock, playing nurse. And while she was sure that Milt worried about her not sleeping, the real reason he wanted Hank in that home was so he could check on him without running into Earl, whom he despised.

Riiiinggg.

An alarm went off. Every two hours alarms went off. Feeding alarms, turning alarms, range of motion alarms, bathing alarms. She heard Earl coming up the basement stairs.

"Great. Another nice guy who just wants to help out. Oh, I can drop off the Ford, no problem," Earl said, mimicking Broker's voice. "I hope him and Allen don't trip all over each other."

Earl wore an electric-yellow T-shirt with a *War Wolf* logo in Day-Glo blue. He'd scissored out the sleeves to show off his biceps. The shirt was a size too small and clung to his torso and wadded around his hips, clearly revealing the deep-cut ripple of his abdominal muscles and the curve of his belly above the tops of his jeans which he wore without underwear and very low on his hips, with a shadow of pubic hair peeking up and over.

Earl was unshaven and his hair was moussed and he was into looking like Brad Pitt in *Fight Club* this week. The stud in his ear and the cannabis shine to his blue eyes had the same tight sparkle. Jolene didn't really care for Earl swinging his abs back and forth in her kitchen. "You're losing your pants," she said.

Earl smiled. "You didn't used to mind that."

"Why don't you grow up," she said.

"Aren't we sounding grandiose today," he quipped back. He knew all the AA jive and where all her buttons were. He'd started patrolling the house, peeking in cabinets and drawers, looking for hidden bottles of vodka.

A static sound between a dry-heaving pant and a raving growl shushed their little spat. The sound came from a white plastic baby monitor on the counter. The monitors were Jolene's idea; she had placed them throughout the house to help her keep track of Hank.

Earl said, "C'mon, it's feeding time."

To him it was a fairy tale. He was Jack and he'd climbed the beanstalk and had stumbled on the mythic goose and now all he had to do was keep the goose alive until it squeezed out the golden egg. Hank's care and feeding were a serious, round-the-clock commitment.

They went down a flight of circular stairs, through the bedroom, and out on the full-season porch that ran most of the length of the back of the house.

Hank was pink-cheeked and clean shaven, with spittle drooling down his chin. He wore a pair of diapers and a hospital gown and was propped up in a railed Hil-Rom hospital bed, fidgeting slightly back and forth. His neck twitched, his eyes rolled back and forth in their sockets. He could move his lips and tongue. The feed bag hung on an IV tree above him and a strap buckled his chest as a precaution against pitching off the bed. Allen said the movements were just spasms, involuntary. Sometimes Hank's eyes would burn on her so intensely that she was sure he was in there, watching.

Jolene squared her shoulders and went into the room.

Actually, it was good that he lurched around; it gave him a fighting chance against the bedsores. For the last five days she had followed a strict schedule that included turning and repositioning Hank side to side every two hours—feeding and hydrating him, manipulating his arms and legs in passive range-of-motion exercises twice a day, bathing him, constantly swabbing his mouth and gums with a suction wand, and changing his diapers, which Allen referred to as adult pads.

First she wiped his chin and checked his throat. She picked up the electric suction wand and cleaned away excess saliva and mucus from his teeth and gums.

Earl took a can of Ensure from a case of the product, opened it with a church key, and dumped it in the continuously running gravity drip which spiked off the bag that connected to his stomach tube.

He tossed the can at the wastepaper basket by the door. Missed. The empty clattered on the hardwood floor. Earl licked a finger. "Yum, yum. Prune dip, my favorite."

"Knock it off, Earl," Jolene said. "And pick up the goddamn can."

Earl grumbled and retrieved the can and tossed it in the basket, backhanded. "He scores."

She cut him with a stare.

He sneered back. He didn't like it when she'd sheared off her hair. Or when she'd brought in the single bed to sleep next to Hank at night. He thought the hair and the single-bed routine were overwrought theatrical gestures.

"Hey, c'mon; we need a little gallows humor to break the mood around here," he said. Laughing, he backed off and then, goddamn him—just to be coarse, he tipped a few books from the bookcase as he was going out the door, like a mean little kid.

Jolene smoothed a hand through her shorn hair, took a deep breath to steady herself, and, as she swung her eyes around the room, she met her reflection in the mirror framed in the bookshelves. She was sunken-cheeked, haggard. Red around the eyes like a speed freak on a long burn. Still . . .

Mirror, mirror on the wall.

She'd known she had it when she was about seven. By the time she got to high school it could ripple over her face like a dark wind.

Even now, strung-out exhausted, she had it. For half a beat she engaged the rare expression before it sparked away. It was something a good photographer had to sneak up on because she couldn't duplicate it on cue. This was America—so the way you really knew you had it was if you could sell it.

She had logged some shoots and she had a portfolio. She'd been told that, if she put in the work, she could give New York a try. But she kept waking up in cheap rooms with a hangover and Earl in the bed next to her.

And then she met Hank.

Jolene turned from the mirror and studied the wreckage of her husband.

Once she'd thought the worst thing in the world could only happen directly, physically, to her. Now it had happened to someone else, and she was definitely feeling it. She'd cut her hair to honor the emotion.

"That's a change. You taught me that," she said under her breath.

As she reached over and eased the sweaty mop of hair away from Hank's wild eyes she wrinkled her nose. She was getting used to the diaper smell. Dutifully, she changed him, and, as she wiped him clean, she noticed how the muscle tone was already turning to taffy. Her hard old Hank was spreading into a puddle of flesh.

She deposited the diaper in the diaper caddy and kneaded the residue of white talcum powder between her fingers. One of life's safe things. For a moment, she almost remembered the fragrance from infancy, from before walking and talking. She pursed her lips. "Hank, you tough old fart, now that you're not here anymore I think I'm starting to appreciate you."

Chapter Eighteen

He'd grown up fascinated with the war-soaked fiction of Heming-way, James Jones, and Norman Mailer; so, like many wanna-be writers out of that tradition, he'd conducted a love affair with near death. He'd hung it out there more than most and returned from the edge with a fair scrapbook.

Now he knew he'd just been a tourist.

There was only so much of him left. Left here at least. Portions of him were missing and sometimes he suspected they had moved on to somewhere else.

All he could manage now was the sensation that the inside and the outside were merging; that the things he thought were him were blending slowly with the things that weren't. He had the distinct feeling that he'd been wearing his skin like a blindfold all his life.

Storms of human weather still took the form of shadows that brought food and nourishment. He vaguely knew the slosh was being inserted into his feeding tube. Inside, he felt his stomach rip-ple in anticipation and the drool beaded on his tongue but he couldn't control his tongue, it just crawled around in his mouth, wagging at nothing.

. . .

Sometimes there was more than nothing.

Glimpses.

Damaged snapshots from a burned family album. All alone in

*the dark theater of his head, he became a child again, waiting for the
show to start.*

I remember . . .

And suddenly he was there with his first memory . . .

Mom.

*She was strongly made, a dark-haired farm girl with large
hands, on a rubber pad on red linoleum, scrubbing, down on her
knees with a can of Babbo and a pail at her side. She'd put out the
front page of the* Detroit News *to keep Hank off the wet floor, and
the grainy picture on the newsprint was gritty black and white and
showed soldiers raising a flag above a scrub of brush.*

*She was first-generation American, with cousins fighting for
Hitler and a husband in the Pacific killing Japs. He remembered the
cool, sticky scent of lipstick, powdery cosmetics on soft leather, and
the smell of Chesterfields in her purse. The war was everywhere.
Like fat, black victory germs, the endless factory smoke sprinkled
down on the snowbanks.*

*At play in the summer backyard, among tomato plants that
grew up in humid green waves down in the hot tickling dirt, under
the leaves, in the emerald-filtered light, he dug holes for his toy soldiers. Tiny khaki vinyl men. Dappled shadows.*

*Like the island jungles on the other side of the world where his
dad . . .*

First song. An old scratchy 78.

"Feudin', Fussin', and a Fighting" by Dorothy Shay.

*The song played on the night his dad came home from the
Pacific. Dad was hugs and tumbling on the floor, a smell of tobacco,
alcohol, and sweat. Whiskers.*

*Two years later they were both gone, instantly, in a head-on
crash. Mom's sister raised him after that. Holy Roller Church four
times a week to keep him out of trouble.*

*Sister Wolf at the young people's meeting on Friday night would
work her pimply congregation with guilt and shame, and then close
the sale with cold-war terror. The bombers, she would say, have left
Russia and are coming to drop their atom bombs. You better give
your soul to Jesus tonight. And during the altar call he learned to go
forward in the second wave, so the preachers were busy laying
hands on the first rush and he'd slink on his knees right through the*

thrashing of the Holy Ghost and creep out the back door of the basement auditorium and sneak a cigarette in the alley.

First bike. Schwinn. Red. With fat, treaded tires pebbles got stuck in and clicked on the sidewalk.

First woman. Halloween night, 1960, his freshman year at Wayne State in Detroit. She was older, a high-breasted Canadian graduate student down from Toronto for a party, impressed enough with his persistence to take on his sexual education. Set the bar real high for all the slow American girls to follow.

. . .

The first man he killed . . .

. . .

But then he heard the words . . .

"So here's the thing," Jolene thought out loud as she ran the suction wand over Hank's gums and around his tongue. "Whatever I did before, I haven't done any of it since I've been sober.

"Remember what you said about drunks being lucky because they can reinvent themselves? How they can lump all the bad stuff they did together and flush it down the past. What I'm shooting for here is to see you through this thing to make my amends. The problem is goddamn Earl doesn't seem to get it."

She fluffed the pillows behind his neck. "Earl doesn't think people can change. For sure not me. He's sort of the original antipersonal growth hormone in that regard." She fingered his chin and touched his cheek. "And you. I think you're due for a shave."

She left and returned with a plastic razor, shaving cream, a bowl of hot water, and a towel. As her hand glided the razor over the familiar contours of Hank's face, her eyes wandered the room, remembering how they'd worked together, Sheetrocking and taping the walls, building the bookcases, both of them in T-shirts and jeans spotted with paint, eating ham and cheese on rye, drinking Cokes.

They both tried to quit smoking the first time in this room, after they'd fooled around on the floor amid piles of books.

All those books. Had he really read them?

Could she someday? Before she met Hank the most she'd read at one sitting was *People* magazine.

"We had a pretty good time for a while," she said, carefully wiping the lather from his face and neck. She clicked her teeth and hunched her shoulders. The house surrounded her like an expensive train wreck.

Her train wreck, goddammit.

She patted Hank on the cheek and walked over to the books Earl had tipped to the floor. She stooped, collected them, and methodically put them back on the shelves. That was Earl for you. He threw tantrums. He could be a violent child.

Then, after the temper subsided, he would be sweet. But he never apologized for the tantrums. The good and the bad alternated. There was no—Hank's word—synthesis. No learning from experience.

Like she was trying to do.

Jolene felt the amputated craving for a cigarette. She shoved her hands in her pockets.

She and Earl had been born on the same day, the same hour, in the same hospital in Minneapolis. They had the same astrological pedigree. Mars conjunct Pluto. Biker stars, Earl called it. Deep, powerful urges for both good and evil. They were biker's stars because Earl said the Hell's Angel's credo meant you had to know the difference between good and evil.

And choose the evil.

She knew all this because they'd had their charts done by Lana Pieri who lived down the block when they were high school sophomores in Robbinsdale. "This is some heavy shit," Lana said. "You guys could go either way."

"Or both ways at once," Earl said, grinning.

There was this part of AA where you admit to God and one other person the exact nature of your wrongs, and she had told Hank how she'd had a part in killing a man once during her wild phase.

She knew about the jokes that Allen and Milt told about her and Earl being Bonnie and Clyde. Well, Allen and Milt were pretty perceptive guys. Because that freezing night outside of Bismarck, North Dakota, at that isolated convenience store with the one sorry gas pump out in front, that's exactly who they were. Driving straight through from Minneapolis on no sleep and no food, a nickel bag of grass, two six-packs of Blatz, Earl's guitar, an amp, and one suitcase.

They were hungry and broke, working mean drunk-dares back and forth inside a stolen '89 Camaro. And it was so cold it made you crazy. Colder than Minnesota, if that was possible.

This time she was going in with the gun because she just wanted to get warm. So Earl handed her the gun he'd stolen from his uncle, a Colt .45 automatic, a big military keepsake that weighed as much as her mom's klunky old handheld electric mixer.

So she went in and the guy behind the counter licked his lips and hitched his cowboy belt buckle up under his round cowboy beer belly and grinned at her like she was Sheena of the Prairie or something, for sure the best thing he ever saw come swinging into his graveyard shift. And she didn't really enjoy the frog-eyed, dry-swallow gulp of sheer animal fear the big pistol produced on his startled face. And she understood exactly the problem with guns when instead of handing over the money from the till he reached right through his first fear and under the counter for a gun of his own.

The thing about guns was, if you took one of them out and pointed it at a person you better be ready to use it.

Which bang she did before he did, point-blank. Knocked him over into the racks of Skoal and Red Man chewing tobacco and beef jerky. Jolene didn't see any blood but she remembered distinctly the gritty scuffed silver soles and the metal taps on the heels of his cowboy boots as the big slug knocked him for a flip.

"I killed him," she explained to Earl who came running in as she was cleaning out the cash register.

"No, you didn't, he's still moving," said Earl who took the pistol and sent her out to the car. And she could still remember how big and cold that night was, with the gas station lit up like a big candy machine under all those stars and how lonely those two last shots sounded, muffled behind the glass. She vowed she'd never go back to North Dakota, ever.

"I didn't kill him," she said.

"You didn't kill him," Earl said.

Jolene had hugged herself and shivered. "God, it's cold."

"Absolute zero," Earl said. "At least it is for that guy back there." Jolene had stared at him. And Earl had grinned. "The tem-

perature at which everything stops—minus 273.15 degrees Centi-
grade. I got straight A's in physics, remember."

And they talked about it as they turned off the Interstate and
drove a jigsaw down back roads north of Bismarck to Theodore
Roosevelt State Park where they ate bologna sandwiches on the
shore of Lake Sakakawea and counted out $135.74, which was
what that clerk's number amounted to when it came up.

They'd talked about God and if he were there and always
watching, and would he hold it against them, and about karma
coming around on them, which was different than God, but still
definitely payback.

They'd finished their sandwiches and both agreed. They'd take
their chances with God and karma over witnesses any day.

Chapter Nineteen

Allen, almost jaunty, swung a black satchel bag in his left hand. It was an old-fashioned doctor's bag, and he was on the kind of professional errand that surgeons never perform. Certainly not these days.

He was making a house call.

The bunched clouds threatened rain and the air was the color of damp cardboard. But the day was easy on his eyes. Every needle in every soggy spruce tree punched up bright as miniature green neon.

Allen crossed the Timberry Trails Hospital staff parking lot and walked toward his car, thumbed his remote, and heard the door open with a snug chirp. It was a light-paperwork morning and he had offered to sit with Hank Sommer while Jolene went into St. Paul for her first office meeting with Milton Dane so they could restart their bumpy relationship and get Hank into a full-care nursing home.

Seat belt. Ignition. He tapped the CD console as he steered his three-year-old Saab out of the lot into the tangle of midmorning traffic. He hummed and moved his shoulders experimentally along with the earthy cross-rhythms of Ladysmith Black Mombazo.

He could learn to loosen up.

Yes, he could.

Toward the end of his surgical residency at the Mayo Clinic, Allen had a recurrent fantasy that he would go into the hospital one day, walk across the red line, and never return. The red line was a literal line painted across the corridor that marked the boundary between the germ-infested world of the patients and the blue, sterile, controlled world of surgery.

In this fantasy his life would be one long procedure, and when it was over he would have operated on everyone who'd ever lived.

Allen saves the world. The End.

Now he was amending his fantasy.

Allen saves Allen.

He identified his problem and appreciated the irony. In surgery he space-walked on a tether of pure clinical knowledge. He manipulated precision instruments to fix the broken parts of the people who lay motionless under his hands. But when he took off the blue clothing and stepped back across the red line he returned to earth and was warped by G's. By the time he reached the sidewalk he was a fallen medical astronaut. He and the patients had traded places. On the street, he was the one anesthetized. Numb to the world.

Since Hank's accident he was obsessed with learning how to leave his work brain in the OR and just go out and live. And he was on his way to take his daily dose of the risky treatment he had prescribed for himself.

In a few minutes he'd cleared the traffic lights and was streaking down a secondary road between fields of standing corn. Beyond the corn, the tree lines hovered in a damp Impressionist mist. The chlorophyl dipstick was way down, the carotene was up, and the leaf change was in full glory.

Then he rounded a turn and his pastoral vision disappeared as the Timberry development blob munched its way through the woods, vomiting out rib cages of blond timber and farting out concrete cul-de-sacs.

He had joined the Timberry Medical Group to escape this very congestion. He only had to park his car once a day. He could walk from the clinic to the hospital, and to the health club. Some docs he knew had to commute all over the whole Minneapolis/St. Paul metro to three of four different hospitals a day.

Allen veered and accelerated past a queue of cars lined up for a left turn. Too many people were moving in. On his right, bulldozers scuttled like maggots on the remains of the forest and the fields. Lowball Mexican carpenter crews banged away, roughing in more new homes.

He disdained traffic. They should have a two-tiered road system, he mused—one for busy professionals and another for the patients to play bumper cars.

Hank Sommer's house sat back from the road on a bluff over the St. Croix River behind a screen of two-hundred-year-old white pines. From the road it looked like a small lake cabin, but as Allen wound down the serpentine driveway between the thick tree trunks the house revealed itself stage by stage in levels that cascaded down the bluff.

Hidden, subtle; quirks that Hank appreciated and Allen did not.

The weather-streaked cedar-plank walls and the rough shake roof were silver-dark, as were the thickets of frost-tortured ferns and hosta that clogged the walks of liver-colored cobbles. Canadian hemlock and Japanese yew grew in the shade like prickly green shadows. That was Hank for you, drawn to shadow as the better part of light.

Allen would cut it all down. Let in some light. Put in a tennis court.

Earl Garf's boxy green Chevy van sat like a guard dog in the turnaround in front of the garage. Allen parked behind the van, got out, and noted a bubbling of rust along the driver's side of the van's rocker panels. He was expected, so Earl would stay in the basement, out of sight until summoned to drive Jolene into town. But he'd make enough noise to intrude, to let Allen know he wasn't far away. That had been the daily drill every time he'd checked in on Hank since they'd foolishly brought him home.

Allen mounted the simple brick porch and pressed the bell.

Jolene opened the door and Allen sniffed. The secondhand smoke of Hank's Camel straights still lingered inside the house.

Seeing her, he wanted to take her all at once, like medicine. Like tonic. But he controlled himself and disguised his disappointment at the way she had renounced makeup and shorn her long hair. He was used to the suffering look that bleached the faces of families of terminal patients. But he didn't like seeing it on her.

This morning, fresh from the shower, she wore gray sweatpants and a blue, armless T-shirt. It was very warm in the house so she was barefooted.

"Hello, Allen," she said, very friendly.

"How're you doing, Jo." His eyes flew to the firm white magnets of her bare upper arms. Veered away.

She merely nodded, letting the weary smile play across her lips as she took his coat. He kicked off his shoes as she hung his coat in the hall closet, and as she turned back to him he was minutely aware of the entire volume of her body, the air it displaced and the smooth way it moved. She was all surface, image.

It occurred to him that he could only visualize the interior of anesthetized draped bodies on an operating table. He could not see past the surface of moving bodies. This insight bothered him slightly.

"I really appreciate this," she said.

"No trouble at all," Allen said.

As usual there was no mention of Earl down in the basement.

She led him through the living room. He approved of the way the house was a little cleaner every time he visited. More of Hank's clutter had been pruned and removed to the basement and the garage.

Seeing the light filter into the house through the slats of heavy wooden Venetian blinds, and the black Bakelite plastic rotary phone on the living room desk, Allen understood that Sommer had been born twenty years too late. On more than one occasion, he had heard Hank quip that he would have liked to jump into Normandy with the Airborne and kill Germans, but he was only two years old at the time. Spiritually, Hank belonged in the tar pits with the generation of blue-collar smokers who'd fought in World War II.

They went through the kitchen and down the circular stairway. "The canoe guide called," Jolene said. "He's bringing down Hank's truck this afternoon."

"Broker," Allen nodded. "He's a good guy. Doesn't say much."

"I'd completely forgotten about leaving it up there."

"It's all right."

"No, it's not, it's a detail. Details are important."

"Yes, they are. For want of a nail," Allen recited.

She stopped and cocked her head. Allen explained, loving the bare slate of her face, "It's an old saying, from a poem. 'For want of a nail the shoe was lost. For want of a shoe the horse was lost. For want of a horse the rider was lost. For want of a rider the battle was lost. For want of the battle the kingdom was lost.' "

She nodded, filed it away, and they resumed moving through the master bedroom, past the open door of the bathroom where the mirror was still beaded with the moisture of her shower. The king-size sleigh bed looked like it hadn't been slept in for a week.

Then they turned into the spacious studio where Hank Sommer's loose body was arranged on a cranked-up hospital bed. Allen startled at a flurry of gray movement on Hank's lap.

"Just the cat. She likes to curl on his stomach," Jolene said.

Allen watched the gray, short-haired animal dart from the room. He disliked cats and he hated surprises, so he especially hated this cat's name: Ambush.

Hank wore a baggy blue shift and as they entered the room his eyes lurched back and forth. His hands clenched up, strangled invisible tormentors, and fell down.

Allen smiled tightly at the narrow single bed at the foot of the hospital bed where Jolene kept vigil. She had never been this devoted to Hank when he was whole. Now she kept to the care schedule like a martyr, and he had a real worry she'd hurt her back, moving him through the turning and ROM exercises.

It was more denial. Like the radio and TV and the vase of fresh flowers that sat next to the bed and that she changed every other day. Some days she tuned the boom box to his favorite oldies station. On other days it was C-SPAN or the History Channel.

It annoyed Allen the way she clung to hope.

A diagram of instructions for turning and feeding was taped to the wall. She'd set up a regular baby-changing station on a cart next to the bed. Diapers, baby wipes, oil, talc, Desitin for rash. The most ironic of her makeshift innovations was the baby monitor with speakers positioned throughout the house.

Her hand drifted up and touched his forearm, and Allen felt a jolt of excitement. It curdled to pique when she said, "He always does that when I come in, like he's looking at me."

"Random eye movement; he blinks, he drools, he grunts. It doesn't mean anything," Allen said stiffly.

"Well," Jolene said, "sometimes I come into the room and his eyes pick me up." She approached Hank's bed, stopped at a distance of one foot, and stared into him like he was a department store window.

Allen's face flushed slightly. He folded his arms tightly across his chest and kept his voice low and under taut control. He gave it to her straight and clinical, and then some.

"We had the best man from HCMC neurology evaluate him. He found 'no visual pursuit.' That means his eyes cannot fix and follow an object. Diagnosis: persistent vegetative state. We can run CAT scans, MRI's, EEG's; they will probably show brain shrinkage."

Jolene pointed. "Look, he did it again."

Allen went on, a little heated. "The eye movement is a primitive auditory response, just electricity firing down in his brain stem. It's not human, it's reptile. Remember what the neurologist told you—the diving-seal syndrome." Allen paused, visualizing the image of Hank plunging into blacker and blacker arctic depths. "The deeper the seal goes, the more nonessential physical systems it shuts down."

Jolene wrinkled her nose.

"Look, I, ah . . ." Allen stammered. Immediately he recovered, overcompensating with a technical barrage: "When Hank's body reached a crisis it had to choose between supplying oxygen to his brain or to his core organs—the heart and lungs. Peripheral functions lose to core functions. Unfortunately, in that scenario, the cerebral cortex is a peripheral function. And brain cells die within four to six minutes without oxygen. So along with consciousness, the voluntary motor fibers that control the face, the arms, and legs were wiped out. The involuntary muscles continue to function, intercostal muscles and the diaphragm survive to support the lungs which powers the heart."

"All I know is that he looks at me," she said as she went to the bed and fluffed the pillow behind Hank's head. As she stepped back she fingered his thick hair. "Okay. I fed him and changed him. He doesn't need turning for two hours."

"I'll be just fine," Allen said.

"Well, I have to get dressed."

Out of habit, Allen threw back Hank's gown and checked the incision. There was no sign of infection, it was healing normally. As was the feeding-tube insertion. Then he opened his bag, removed a blood-pressure cuff and a stethoscope, took Hank's blood pressure, and listened to his lungs. The vital signs were regular. One hell of a resilient lizard fought for life within Hank's human husk.

Then he took a pencil light from his shirt pocket and moved it back and forth in front of Hank's eyes, which blinked rapidly as the pupils tightened normally to the light. Allen dismissed this lizard reaction, more attuned to the rustle of material on skin and the lily scent of body lotion coming through the open doorway to the bedroom that adjoined the studio.

Hank's blue flotsam eyes sloshed from one side of his head to the other. His hands spasmed, clenched, and dropped. Just the lizard again, some nerve pathway twitching.

Allen heard heels strike hardwood. She stood in the doorway wearing a simple gray dress, panty hose, and half-inch heels. The white-faced widow.

"I'm not sure exactly when I'll be back. Milt mentioned having lunch after we meet."

"Go," Allen said. "You need to get out of the house."

She turned and disappeared and Allen overheard some muted conversation as Earl ascended, troll-like, from the basement. The door closed and Earl's van started, and a moment later Allen heard the tires spit gravel against the tree trunks as he swerved down the long, twisting driveway.

In the more immediate vicinity he focused on the music playing in the background: Bob Dylan singing "Blowin' in the Wind." Allen walked to the radio and punched the off button.

They were alone.

Not they. It was a curious gray area. The definitions were inexact. Hank was more an *it*. Legally, *he* was dead. Clinically, *it* was alive.

He walked up to the bed and—Jesus—a needle of pain pierced his right ankle and snagged in his sock. Allen lurched back and kicked at the husky gray fur ball. The goddamn cat had snuck back in the room and had been hiding under the bed and had lashed out a paw.

The cat evaded the kick, which infuriated Allen who aimed another powerful kick. Missed. The animal skittered in a scramble of claws on the polished oak flooring and disappeared into the hall.

Allen pulled down his sock, inspected his ankle, and found a thread of blood and a scratch. He rubbed the spot and hoped the cat had its shots. Then he turned his attention back to Hank.

"She's gone into town to talk to Milt. He'll flirt with her over lunch, I expect. We all do." He patted Hank's knee. "But you knew that. I think you even enjoyed it. Remember the first time you showed her off? You'd discovered her at the AA group and brought her to the poker game. You were still married to Dorothy. The fact was, we all thought she was a hooker."

He'd started talking to Hank the last time he was here alone, doing an examination. Now the sound of his voice didn't seem so odd. It was almost natural. And it was a little like being in a confessional.

There'd been no provision for confession in his Lutheran education. Just him and God. No intermediate buffer of priests to barter sins into doing rosary laps. The older he got the more the notion of indulgences made sense. Right now he could use a spiritual litigant to plea-bargain his dilemma.

How many commandments had he broken?

The one about coveting your neighbor's wife for sure.

"You shouldn't have flaunted her, Hank," Allen said. "You shouldn't have made a game out of it."

Allen eased Hank's leg aside and sat down on the bed.

"You were always so sure of yourself, you figured you were the only one who could take risks. We were all just—what did you used to call us—college boys.

"Well, Hank, I really want to thank you for upgrading Jo from X-rated to PG 13. You won that little wager."

Allen got off the bed and paced to the bank of windows over-looking the river. He leaned forward, hands on the sill, and peered at the dusky color on the far Wisconsin shore. Then he turned.

"Hank, you know, at first I was certain it had been an accident. I was fatigued and hypothermic. Paddling out with Broker damn near killed me."

Allen clicked his teeth. "Oh, he's coming to visit. Phil Broker, the canoe guide. He's bringing your Ford down from Ely. I'm surprised Earl overlooked it. I think the green van's days are numbered."

Hank's head slumped forward and his brow furrowed. The lizard perplexed.

"For fifteen years I've trained myself to be immune to fatigue," Allen went on conversationally. "Except for small details, I've never had a major slip in the OR." Allen paused and stared at Hank who rocked sightly and whose throat made a slight hiss.

God, it was so sad. Like talking to a corpse with living eyes.

"I mean, I'd just pulled off a very clean procedure under less than ideal conditions. I was working with a strange scratch team in a podunk surgical suite. I pulled you through.

"And then . . .

"You were in recovery and I talked to the anesthetist and she said you were awake and strong and I thought, okay, let him rest a minute, and I dropped my guard and the fatigue was really coming on then. But they got this new patient, the snowmobile accident, and I saw everybody run out the door and I thought, oh shit—this hick nurse has gone off and left you alone.

"So I went into the room and I saw this loaded syringe sitting there on the cart next to your bed. And that's when the fatigue locked up my brain because I couldn't remember—had the nurse given you the Demerol?

"So I picked up the syringe and shot it into the IV and then, looking at the syringe again, I saw the anesthetist's red stick-on label and—my God—I had just given you a shot of succinylcholine from the anesthetist's intubation tray. It's impossible to mistake that syringe for Demerol. But that's exactly what I'd done.

"Believe me, I was shaking more than you were and you were shaking plenty when that muscle relaxant hit your bloodstream."

Allen replayed it. His first instinct should have been to reintubate, to administer oxygen. To save the patient.

But Hank was the patient. Jolene's husband.

He'd been battered by shock and self-preservation. It had been his first major mistake as a surgeon and now he realized it had been a turning point in his life.

"The fact is, Hank, *I don't make mistakes*. And now I wonder if my fatigue had freed my inhibitions." Allen's voice shook with sudden passion. "Maybe I was doing what I really wanted to do. Maybe I never wanted to save your life. Maybe, standing there, watching your muscles shake and then go flaccid, I realized how much I wanted you gone.

"And I saw how it could happen. How the sucs would be out of your system in minutes without a trace. It would look exactly like a respiratory collapse in recovery, which would make sense with your difficult airway. And being left unattended.

"No one was watching. I had blundered into the perfect crime. So perfect that it couldn't have been accidental. It had to be destiny.

"And I remembered how we'd had this conversation; I'd asked you how I could find a woman like Jo and you just laughed and said, 'You have to be willing to take a chance,' and how I was a control freak and I'd never take a chance.

"Well, check it out, Hank. I drew off some saline from the IV to refill the syringe and put it back on the tray. I turned off the alarm on the monitor and then I went back down the hall and slumped back in my chair. I knew the anesthetist and the attending nurse would be held accountable."

Allen shuddered. There, he'd purged it and now it took a moment for him to bring his breathing back to normal. "There," he said aloud. "So now you know." Then he patted Hank's inert knee almost fondly. "The only thing I didn't foresee, old buddy, was that you would live through the episode."

Chapter Twenty

When Amy wheeled into the parking lot, Broker, antsy, was pacing at the end of the boat dock puffing on a cigar. She walked out to him and noted the vital color in his freshly shaved cheeks and his alert eyes. He wore his coat casually half zipped. No hat.

"You're feeling better," she said.

"What if . . ." Broker began.

Amy held up a gloved hand. "Hold on. What are we doing here?"

"What if there's a reason they don't have Hank Sommer in a hospital?"

"You mean he isn't as wasted as they say he is?"

"You tell me," Broker said.

"That's wishful thinking." Amy shook her head. "First, I've been briefed by our risk-management people. Milton Dane is a top-of-the-line malpractice attorney. No way he'd jeopardize his reputation in anything duplicitous. And second, Hank has been examined by the insurance company doctors, too. There's no dispute about the diagnosis."

Broker studied the look in her eyes, which was the same methodical, intelligent look that good investigators always had in their eyes when they demolished his hunches.

Procedure, they would say. Go slow, they'd say.

Right on cue, Amy said, "These things follow a certain protocol."

"Yeah, but what if the wife is right about him looking at her?" Broker pressed.

"Unlikely. It's normal for a bereaved spouse to grab at straws."

"What if I could get you in to see him?"

Amy expelled an explosive, mirthless breath. "The defendant in a lawsuit approaching the plaintiff? They'd pull my license. I'd never work again."

"So why'd you drop everything and come over here?"

Amy bit her lower lip, looked down the lake. "Did you make that coffee?"

Ha, thought Broker.

They went inside and took off their coats. Broker poured two cups of black coffee from Uncle Billie's Braun. Amy took a chair to the kitchen table and made room for her cup in the litter of Broker's notes, permit applications, and the newspaper she'd left last night.

Broker thumped a knuckle on the Stovall article in the *Star Tribune*. Amy sipped her coffee and read. Her tongue meditatively probed one cheek, then the other. She looked up. *So?*

"The dead guy is Sommer's accountant."

"Weird."

"It's past weird. Sommer's luck giving out in the hospital after he lives through a cliff-hanger rescue is weird. Then his accountant coincidently dies the same week? Check this out—when the seaplane plopped down in Snowbank, the last words Sommer said to me were 'Tell Cliff Stovall to move the money.' Five days later you hand me a newspaper and I read that Cliff Stovall dies in the woods under bizarre circumstances."

Amy considered the doodles on the notepad. The names, the address. The directions. The block letters: FOLLOW THE MONEY. "So those doodles—what does 'follow the money' mean?"

"It's a cliché. But a very durable one. People being who they are, it never wears out."

"Be more specific; exactly what does it mean, in this circumstance, associated with Hank Sommer's name?" she asked.

Broker cleared his throat. "When somebody draws five fouls in the first quarter, what's the first thing you think."

"Too many things going wrong for normal play," Amy said. "But that's hypothetical law-school bullshit. Give me facts."

"Okay, that morning at the hospital, when Sommer was choppered out. His wife was there."

"Yeah?"

"Did you notice the young stud who came up with her?"

"Broker, I sort of kept my distance that morning."

"Mrs. Sommer isn't just a young, sexy trophy wife; she comes with heavy baggage, like her old boyfriend, who has apparently now moved into Sommer's house."

Amy raised her cup and studied the faint coffee ring it left on the table. "So? She observes briefer decent intervals than the rest of us." She raised her eyes. "It's only the oldest story in the world."

Broker continued, unfazed. "On the trip, Sommer and his wife were fighting about money. They were feuding on his cell phone. At one point he got so pissed he threw the phone in the lake. Dane and Falken said he moved all his finances into a trust because she was giving money to the boyfriend. It involves money," Broker insisted.

"What does?"

"The accountant's death."

Amy reread the article. "It says here he had a history of drinking and self-mutilation."

"I don't buy it. He was sitting on Hank's estate which the wife wanted. She had to take Hank out of the hospital because of financial difficulties."

"They were married. There's probate. Where the hell are you going with this?"

Broker pursed his lips. He kept seeing the smug young guy standing next to Jolene in the hospital parking lot, his handsome, gloating face. Like he'd just won the lottery. "The boyfriend," he said.

"C'mon, Broker. The wife is now a de facto widow. So she decides to seek the comfort and support of her young stud/ ex-boyfriend. It might be sleazy, but it's not breaking any laws. Is it?"

Broker brooded under his thick eyebrows. "I'll bet if I toss the boyfriend he comes up dirty."

"If that's all you've got, you don't have much," Amy said.

"Actually I have less than that." Broker stood up and walked from the kitchen area through the main room to the coat hooks near the door. With a swipe of his index finger he speared Sommer's key ring off a hook. "All I've really got is Sommer's Ford Expedition, which I'm returning today. To his house. That means I'll get to go in and pay my respects, check out the wife, check out the boyfriend, and check out Sommer. What if I get in there later this afternoon and he looks me dead in the eye? What then?"

Amy squinted at him suspiciously as he came back toward the table. "I see what you're trying to pull."

Broker, aghast, held up his hands in protest. "What?"

"You're trying to suck me into this project of yours."

Broker smiled. "How am I doing?"

Amy raised her chin. "Maybe I'll tag along just to prove I'm right and you're full of shit?"

"But what if I'm right?" Broker countered.

Amy's features conducted a mobile tug of war between practicality and curiosity. "And you can get me in to see him?"

Broker nodded. "Shouldn't be too hard. The wife never met you. You could be anybody. Hell, you could be my girlfriend."

Amy smiled politely. "But what if the wife isn't dumb. What if she sees I'm way too smart to get mixed up with some lame-duck, middle-aged, half-married guy?"

"Ha," said Broker, grinning.

"Ha, yourself. If we take the Ford down, how do we get back?" she asked.

"I have a buddy who runs a farm near Sommer's place. He's got my truck. I've been meaning to bring it back up north."

"How long will we be gone?"

Broker shrugged, "A couple days?"

Amy thought about it and said, "I get one day at the Mall of America; it'll save me a trip and I can get some shopping out of the way."

"Deal."

"Okay, I'll go to keep you honest," Amy said.

"Great. Let me throw some things in a bag, then we'll go to your place and drop off your wheels," Broker said.

Amy's barely winterized rented cabin overlooked Lake Shagawa on the outskirts of Ely. As Broker came through the door he saw a computer, lots of books, cross-country skis, snow shoes, a pile of busted-out running shoes. He also smelled something. Propane gas.

It never failed to amaze him how natives could ignore every rule of winter survival, from going out in sub-zero temperatures in tennis shoes to living with leaky gas connections on their stoves.

Immediately Broker went to the sink, mixed some dish-washing detergent with water in a glass, crossed to the stove, and dabbed the suds on the connector stem, and saw bubbles blister up in the suds. "Do you have any wrenches?" he asked

"What?"

"You're streaming gas. You're going to blow up."

And Amy, who had mastered the life-and-death complexities of an anesthesia machine, said, "Oh, the stove always smells a little." She pointed. "Wrenches are in the drawer to the right of the sink. There should be some Recto Seal there, too."

While Amy threw clothes into a duffel, Broker turned off the gas, unthreaded the valve, regooped the fitting, retightened it, tested it, and went to the bathroom to wash up. She'd hung a grotesque poster on the back of her bathroom door that showed the gross folds of a ridiculously obese human face. Mouth open, tongue out, its sex was impossible to determine. A hand-lettered caption over the picture announced: INTUBATE THIS!

As he dried his hand she moved in next to him, opened the cabinet, and removed several slim jars of various face oils and emollients. Then she picked up a palm-sized plastic wafer—her diaphragm—passed it under his nose, weighed it briefly in her hand, and dropped it in a cosmetic bag.

Broker frowned mildly at her clowning.

"I could always get hit by lightning," she said airily, spinning on her heel.

He bet she was a demon for detail in the OR, but she was lax in her bathroom. He snagged her elbow, pulled her back, selected the tube of Gynol vaginal lubricant from a shelf, and tossed it to her. "Just in case it's not greased lightning."

Amy pursed her lips. "And I had you figured for a prude."

Broker shrugged. "Hey, I was young once. You know how it goes: you drink too much, you wake up in a strange apartment with a lizard nesting in your mouth and her big scaly sister snoring in bed

next to you, so you stagger for the bathroom, grab for a tooth-
brush . . ." He made a face. "I've brushed my teeth with that stuff at
least once in my life."

For the first time since they'd met, they laughed.

Broker relaxed behind the steering wheel of Sommer's big Ford and
debated whether to empty the ashtray. He decided to leave it. The
crushed cigarette butts were like Hank's cold fingerprints. They
were just a few miles down the road when Amy asked.

"So, did you go on hunches like this when you were a cop?"

"I was a lousy cop," Broker said.

"Really?" Amy raised her arms, reached behind her head, and
pulled her hair back in a practical ponytail.

"I mean I was good at what I did but I was a lousy cop," Broker
said. "Take Dave Iker, now he's a good cop: responsible, a demon on
details, street smart—but." Broker poked a finger in the air. "Ninety-
nine percent of the time he'll get there after *it* happens. Then he'll
follow procedure. If he's lucky, he'll squeeze a snitch or a suspect to
squeal on somebody. It's worked that way since Cain killed Abel."

"Dave says you were an adrenaline addict, that you never could
go the speed limit."

"There you go, procedure. Most cops are rigid about authority,
they like to enforce rules."

"And you?" Amy asked.

"I preferred to get there *before* it happens. That's what deep
undercover is all about. If you're really going to catch monsters you
go hang where the monsters live."

"And maybe become a bit of a monster yourself?" Amy asked.

Broker held her gaze for a beat, then held up his hand with his
thumb and forefinger a measured inch apart. "Maybe just a little."

"Right, like a little pregnant," Amy said.

After that, they exchanged normal information about attending
the University of Minnesota in different eras. Amy mentioned the
doctor she almost married in Minneapolis. Broker skirted the subject of his first wife.

He drove Highway 169 out of Ely and crossed the Laurentian
Divide just north of Virginia, Minnesota. He got on 53 and took
that into Cloquet where he stopped and filled up the Expedition at

the landmark Frank Lloyd Wright gas station with its hovering witch's-hat roof.

They bypassed Duluth and stopped at the Black Bear Casino for lunch. Then back on the road, Interstate 35 fast-forwarded them toward the Cities at seventy-five-plus mph. The traffic thickened and the evergreens gave way to mixed hardwood and fields around Hinckley. The Expedition purred powerfully on eight cylinders, and soon they were running a gauntlet of billboards and tract houses.

Then they skimmed the northern edge of the Minneapolis/St. Paul metro and angled off east and took 95 south along the St. Croix River through Stillwater.

Then they entered the Timberry mall-sprawl and cul-de-sacs with names like Hunter's Lane and Oak Ponds. Broker turned again, into the countryside west of the river.

"Where are we?" Amy asked.

"Lake Elmo," Broker said. "I'm going to drop you with J.T. and then I'll take the vehicle over to Sommer's. I assume somebody will give me a ride back."

"So who's this friend?"

"J.T. Merryweather. Ex–St. Paul cop. Used to be my partner a million years ago. Now he's into raising poultry."

Twenty minutes later they arrived. Amy laughed out loud. "Since when are *ostriches* poultry?"

"J.T. says they're the beef of the future."

The objects of her surprise drifted big-eyed, short-beaked, long-necked, and very long-legged behind six-foot fencing. Flocks of gray-brown females and a few taller black-plumed males. They stood between seven and nine feet tall, and some of the males could weigh four hundred pounds. There were almost a hundred of them in the fenced paddocks, anomalous against the flaming maples and red oaks of the Minnesota countryside.

They turned into a drive past a country mailbox positioned on a setback so a snowplow wouldn't knock it down. They passed a sign that spelled out ROYAL KRAAL OSTRICH, J.T. MERRYWEATHER, PROPRIETOR.

The snug two-story farmhouse was separated from a red barn by weeping willows. The door opened and a tall denim-clad man wearing cowboy boots and a Stetson walked out to greet them.

"He's a black guy?" Amy said.

"Makes sense, huh? Both J.T. and his birds originated in Africa."

Amy looked at the paradoxically ungainly but graceful birds floating across the cold afternoon shadows. "Those birds are a long way from Africa."

Broker threw open the door, got out, and walked to meet J.T. They clasped hands, locked thumbs, and dapped it down, old style.

For five years J.T. had been putting his farm together; like most of the cops close to fifty in St. Paul, he took the early retirement. He'd dropped the twenty pounds he'd gained when he quit the cigarettes and his face had lost that puffy desk-bloat. Some men age into roundness. J.T. and Broker shared a genetic predisposition toward edges. And farm work and fresh air were putting the taut angles back into J.T.'s Ethiopian cheekbones.

"Hmmmmm," J.T. said, big hands on his hips, as Amy came around the Ford and waited to be introduced.

"J.T., this is Amy Skoda," Broker said.

"Uh-huh," J.T. said, appraising Amy.

"It's not like that," Broker said.

J.T. nodded. "Far be it from me to judge people," though in fact J.T. believed in enforcing the rules with the ardor of an Old Testament Jeremiah. He grinned and tipped back the brim of his hat with more than a little theater. "Hell, I'd fuck around myself except my wife would beat me to death with a number-twelve Weber cast-iron skillet when I was sleeping." He extended his hand. "J.T. Merryweather. Pleased to meet you."

Amy took the handshake, looked around. "So what's it like going from law enforcement to ostrich farmer?"

J.T. grinned slowly. "Comes naturally. I keep them in cages." Straight-faced, he added, "Actually, my family was heavy into agriculture for quite a while in Georgia, in the eighteenth and nineteenth centuries."

"Gotcha," Amy said.

Denise Merryweather walked out on the porch in just a blouse and jeans, hugging herself. She was a well-put-together woman over thirty and under fifty, who was successfully playing hide and seek with age. She had a width of Cherokee blood to her dark face, strong brown eyes, close-cropped hair, and a cross on a chain at her throat.

As a general proposition, she had never approved of Broker.

"Phil Broker," she said in a noncommittal tone. "Will you and your friend be staying for a while?"

"Hi, Denise, this is Amy Skoda. Amy, this is Denise," Broker said.

The two women met on the stairs and shook hands.

"It's not like that," Amy said. "We are, like, friends."

"I'm glad," Denise said. "Because we only have the one spare bedroom. Broker, you get the couch."

An awkward silence followed Denise's remark. Amy cocked her head at a distinctive rattling rebound sound from the barn and changed the subject.

"Hoops?" she asked.

"Uh-huh," said J.T. "I tore out the milking stanchions in the back basement of the barn, poured a new concrete floor, and put up a backboard for my daughter."

"You did, huh?" Broker said.

"Okay. You helped."

"Come on inside, honey," Denise said. "Let these two men whine about getting old." Denise motioned Amy into the house.

"We are getting old," Broker said.

"I'll never unhook a 38D triple-eyelet bra one-handed in under three seconds again, cruising in a '57 Chevy, that's for sure," J.T. said.

"Why, Jarret True Merryweather, I didn't know you could count past twenty." Denise flared her eyes as she disappeared through the door with Amy. When the door was shut J.T. scrutinized Broker.

"So who's the woman?" he asked.

"That thing up north, the guy who got brain dead in the Ely hospital . . . Hank Sommer," Broker said.

"This guy," said J.T. pointing at the Ford Expedition.

"Yeah," Broker said. "She was the anesthetist."

"You fucking her?"

"No, of course not." Broker was careful not to sound too indignant.

"So what are you doing?" J.T. asked.

Broker chewed his lip, furrowed his brow. "The guy nailed up in the woods by Marine . . ."

"Uh-huh. I made some calls. Stovall, the accountant."

"Stovall was Sommer's accountant," Broker said.

J.T. moved his hands back and forth trying to make invisible pieces fit. "Yeah, so?"

Broker debated whether to go further.

J.T. said, "Uh-huh. You're not quite sure what you're doing but . . ."

"I got this feeling about something," Broker said.

"I recall a conversation that started this way in eighty-nine. Two hours later I got whacked with a machete."

"It was the flat of a machete," Broker protested.

"It was a machete. It broke the skin," J.T. insisted, starting to hitch up his coat sleeve.

"Look," Broker said. "I have to take this car back."

"You need me to follow you, give you a ride?"

"Nah, I'll hang out with Sommer's wife for a while. She'll give me a lift back here."

J.T. thought for a moment, then squinted. "You're holding out on me," he said.

"A little," Broker said. He turned and walked toward the big Ford.

Chapter Twenty-one

The Buddhists say—*the mind is a monkey chasing its tail, suffering and desire going round and round. Hank had that monkey scampering inside his skull, treating his brain like a television remote. Pushing buttons. Throwing it down. Picking it up, chewing on it, drooling on it. Peeing on it. A goddamn electrical shitstorm of neurons and electrons blazed behind his eyes.*

Then, something clicked. The static cleared and the picture came on.

Came on big-time. Snap, crackle, and zap. Digital high res, fiber-optic, surround-sound. ON.

Lights, camera, action. And what a picture. Almost like his perception and intelligence have become more acute in feverish overload. Burning up the wires. You and me, Jerry Lee.

Great balls of fire.

And he sees and hears.

His buddy, Allen Falken. Dead-Eye Doc himself.

A whole corridor of emptiness now filled up with detailed memory. The last face he saw before the icy black ink pumped out of his heart and down-flooded him inside until only his mind survived, hooked to the aqua lung of his heart and lungs and cast him into inner darkness to float in the nonspecific blackness inside his skin.

Last face. First face.

Allen. Smooth, Teutonic Allen, every hair in place and looking like a young, fit Billy Graham.

Handsome but not too handsome. Vain but in moderation.

There was some split screen going on, some interior backfill of images, the moraine of his life, the clutter of his personal album. But memory insisted on being very vivid, painfully boosting the resolution.

And it was like one of those Yogi Berra Zen pronouncements that illuminate a universe of everyday pain and comedy and hopes and dreams. The "This Is It" of your life.

Allen, sitting there, talking in his best bedside manner.

There was a sensation like when the roller coaster slows at the end of the ride, and Hank felt the loopy circuit of his eyes start to steady down, then stop. Hank rotated his eyes consciously, blinked consciously. Allen, absorbed in his casual soliloquy, missed it.

Missed it because Allen, good ole cautious, quiet Casper Milquetoast Allen, was saying that he finally took a chance.

No one's looking. The syringe. Succinylcholine. A paralytic. Then turn off the monitor.

I see. At first it's a mistake. Then it's more like an accident on purpose. Uh-huh. Then it's deliberate.

The nurse and the anesthetist take the blame.

The linx.

Blond woman. Young. Sharp and a little sassy. Liked her.

Allen. Fucker. Sitting on the bed. Patting my knee.

First you saved my life, then as an afterthought you killed me. I see. The first covers the tracks of the second.

Thought it would kill me. That's the antiseptic thinking of the surgeon. But it's hard to kill a man, Allen. Only sure way is to cut off his head.

Allen babbling on. Allen trying to come to terms with homicide. Didn't mean to. Did. Didn't mean to. Did.

She loves me. She loves me not.

Am I getting this right? And now the way is clear for Allen to court Jolene?

Allen and Jolene?

Think back to what he said. Okay. Jolene's having lunch with Milt.

Now Milt must have a really big case.

Really big.

And Hank sees what Allen left out.

Whoever winds up with Jolene is going to get a lot of money.

It was information; and like Yogi said, it's déjà vu all over again. The old wager he had with Allen and Milt. Is the information of your life a cage that imprisons you or raw material for change. Nature or nurture.

Can I take this cockney wretch and turn her into a lady.

My Fair Lady.

In a tight spot, Hank. Well, no shit. You have to make the right move.

It's a gift.

Maybe, just maybe, you get one last fight.

As sneakily as he could manage it, Hank eyeballed the casual, smug Allen, let his demented eyes rest on him for one burning second.

I'm gonna come back from the teeter-totter and add you to my body count. I'm gonna find a way.

Okay. Can't quit.

Gotta.

Go.

All the way.

But for now, he has to keep his eyes moving in the blinky, loopy pattern. Even though all the voltage in his mind screams to focus and use his eyes to let the outside world know he is in here. It's the hardest thing he's ever done.

But if he focuses and winks and blinks consciously, then Allen will know he's alert. And Allen has just confessed to him. Allen will turn him the rest of the way off.

Hank makes his only move.

He rolls his eyes.

Keep the eyes moving. Blinking randomly. Drool. Run laps. Let Herr Doctor Falken think you're the vegetable. His creation.

Gonna.

Come.

Back.

Motherfucker.

Chapter Twenty-two

Broker had always taken back roads and harvest fields for granted, but now he saw that Washington County was running out of them fast. Not more than two miles from J.T.'s place the lumber skeletons of new houses haunted the farmland.

That was global warming for you. The Minnesota winters used to keep the population down and the riffraff out.

Getting closer to the river, he referred to Jolene's directions, found the turnoff, and took it to a left turn. "It's a dead end," Jolene had explained without irony on the phone. The last leg of road was semiprivate and the lots were three hundred feet deep, butting on the river. Broker drove past two fenced tennis courts and a putting green, and came to the house number on the mailbox.

Sommer lived in his own small woods of mature white pines. As Broker came down the shadowed, twisting drive he estimated some of the trees were two feet in diameter. Hundreds of years old.

He approved of the way the sprawling cedar home blended into the trees and the river bluff, camouflaged in thick beds of hosta, ferns, and low evergreens. Seams of moss patterned the cobble paths through the shade garden.

A green van and a silver-gray sedan were parked in front of the three-car garage. Broker parked, got out, went to the door, and rang the bell.

Almost immediately, Earl Garf opened the door—like he'd been waiting and had watched him arrive. Garf was off his hygiene today, disheveled in a studied, expensive way, his hair thick with mousse and his beard stylishly grown out. He wore baggy jeans, a loose T-shirt, and bulky cross-trainers.

"Mr. Broker," Garf said in a crisp parody of politeness. "Jolene's expecting you, she's in the kitchen. This way." Courteously, Garf showed him through the hall into a long living room. This was a different Garf from the man who'd stood beaming in the snow outside Ely Miner Hospital. This was Garf playing butler with an actor's conceit.

Sommer's house still smelled of paint and sawdust—not quite lived-in. His taste ran to dark wood and shade inside, just like outside. Then they were in the brighter kitchen. Garf, the mannered joker, announced, "Mr. Broker is here." Then he silently withdrew.

Broker was surprised to see Allen Falken sitting at the table with Jolene, hunched forward, talking over blue coffee mugs.

"Broker, hey," said Allen, rising from the table. Allen looked more relaxed than Broker remembered, dressed in an open-collar beige oxford shirt and jeans. Jolene's face was pale and blurred with strain. The thick Mediterranean hair was gone—with extreme prejudice. Christ, she looked like the French Resistance had cut it. She wore a gray dress, nylons, and she had kicked off a pair of low heels.

Allen stepped forward, and he and Broker shook hands warmly. "So how you been keeping yourself?" Allen asked, finding just the right tone of restrained familiarity. A more robust Allen, more centered.

"I've been all right," Broker said. He placed the car keys on the table.

Jolene also got up and raised her hands, and when Broker extended his, she took it in both of hers. Her hands were unexpectedly soft, surface-cool melting to very warm in his palm and covering the back of his hand.

"Thank you so much," she said.

"No problem," Broker said. She smelled damp with nerves and very serious, like lilies, stained glass, organ music, and caskets in a church. She had pronounced lavender circles of fatigue and worry under her eyes. On her they looked good. A faint flush crept up his neck and into cheeks. Must be hot in here, he thought.

"Did you have any trouble finding the place?" she asked.

"Perfect, ah, the directions were . . . fine."

"We were having some coffee," Jolene said.

Broker made a stiff, waving-off gesture. "Stuff keeps me up if I drink it in the afternoon." He shifted from foot to foot and placed his hands behind his back, winding up in an almost formal parade-rest position.

Allen and Jolene nodded sympathetically.

"Ah, Jolene just got back from her first serious meeting with Milt Dane," Allen said, keeping the conversation going.

"The lawyers for the hospital will play a waiting game," Jolene said.

"That's pretty typical at the beginning," Allen said.

Jolene twisted her lips slightly. "They'll wait to see if Hank dies. Milt says if he dies, it's cheaper for them." She shook off the D word, worked at a smile.

Broker cleared his throat. "I was wondering what he's doing here at home. So soon, I mean."

Jolene crooked her finger. "Come this way," she said. "I'll show you something." He followed her through a doorway into the living room which was tiger-striped with Venetian-blind-filtered light. An alcove set off through an archway contained a long desk table which literally overflowed with paperwork. "Here's where Hank pays the bills," she explained.

Then she trailed a hand through the surface papers. Broker glimpsed a legal format.

| STATE OF MINNESOTA | DISTRICT COURT |
| COUNTY OF ST. LOUIS | FOURTH JUDICIAL DISTRICT |

Case Type: Medical

Harry Sommer, by and through his wife and guardian, Jolene Sommer,
Plaintiffs

Malpractice
File Number:
Judge

vs.

Duluth Health Services.
Defendant.

INTERROGATORIES TO DEFENDANT, SET 1

Jolene said, "Somewhere in this pile are two or three premiums from Blue Cross he forgot to pay."

"Ouch."

"We found out an hour after we got him to Regions," Allen said.

"Absentminded," Broker said.

"Big-time," Jolene said as she plucked a bill that was held to an envelope with a paper clip. "This one's for the helicopter ride. St. Mary's Life Flight out of Duluth. Fifty-five hundred bucks."

Allen stepped in helpfully. "You recall the cell phone conversations?"

"Oh, yeah," Broker said.

"We were fighting about these," she said, pointing to the bills. "He didn't like the way I was pushing to get them paid off, so he and his accountant moved all his money into a trust, to teach me a lesson, I suppose. He was the trustee and his accountant was the alternate trustee. Now Hank's incapacitated. The accountant died. Two point three million dollars and I can't touch a cent. Milt says it will take a month to bust open the trust in probate. And it was costing three thousand bucks a day to keep him in the hospital. So I brought him home."

"Milt's putting Hank in a nursing home next week," Allen added quickly. "It just got off to a bad start."

"I . . ." Broker searched for a word.

Jolene waved her hand in a dismissive gesture. "Yeah, I know. Un-fucking-believable." She stepped forward and took Broker's elbow. "Let's go see Hank," she said.

"I'd like that."

"What do people call you?" she asked. "Phil?"

"No, ah, Broker, usually."

"This way, Broker."

A hall off the kitchen dropped into a tight circular staircase to the next level. Going down it, Broker thought of castle scenes. Someone should be carrying a torch. They came out into a master bedroom, king-size sleigh bed, dressers, armoire, all in cherry. Sweatpants and a T-shirt had been tossed on the bedspread. The faint lily scent was preserved in the damp towels in the adjoining bath.

"He's just next door," Jolene said. They went through another doorway into a large four-season porch that was bunkered with books. A cold fireplace was black with soot and smelled of ashes and neglect.

Solemnly, Broker stepped into the room and was immediately startled by Hank Sommer's brilliant blue eyes and the gravitas with which they blazed point-blank into his own.

Broker.
Hank let his eyes focus for a second. Then he saw Jolene and Allen come through the door behind Broker and he forced his eyes to continue into their elliptical orbit.

The eyes rolled away, caught in the corner of the sockets, and slowly wandered back. Hank's brow was furrowed, his hair furiously mussed, the eyes, two wobbling ice fires, his beard had been removed, and his chin was shiny with drool. Broker thought of paintings of famous angry men. Moses descending the mount, dashing the tablets. John Brown.

Hank lay on his side in a hospital bed cranked up like a recliner. A pillow was positioned between his knees and a baggy gray gown covered him. A heavy canvas strap buckled his chest and his hands were clenched beneath a large gray cat. Broker divined weariness in the twisted sheets on the narrow cot at the foot of the bed.

"Jesus," his chest heaved. He'd anticipated seeing Hank sick, his body snarled in tubes and electrical monitors. There was just an IV tree that held a suspended sack of liquid and a tube that snaked into Hank's gown. There was a bed table with a vase of fresh wisteria and a large TV and a radio tape player on a rolling stand. But basically it was just him, there on the bed. Looking almost normal.

With a cat in his lap.

The cat had avocado eyes and black diamond pupils and a wild, regal guardian demeanor. Vaguely, Broker recalled that the Egyptians worshiped cats.

He cleared his throat. "Kind of throws you, seeing him so normal."

"He doesn't need a tracheal tube, it's the only reason he can be here," Allen said.

Jolene crossed the room to the bed, picked up a Kleenex, and wiped Hank's chin. Quickly she ran the suction wand around his mouth. "I keep expecting him to just get up and want a cup of coffee."

Hank, watching from the moon, from Mars, was amused. Not coffee, Jo. What I'm dying for is a cigarette. He'd thought about this and he'd decided that if someone held a Camel to his mouth and closed his lips around it, he could manage a drag.

And Hi, there, Broker. How you doing? You already know Allen, the assassin. And Earl Garf is lurking somewhere. Abe Lincoln had Earl in mind when he said a certain congressman would steal a hot stove. Right now I'm assuming Jo is a victim of circumstances, but the vote's out on that, so I'll just continue to snoop and poop here in the weeds.

The cat stretched on its side and extended its paws and flourished claws at Broker's approach.

"Watch out, the cat has this habit of leaping out and scratching you," Allen cautioned.

"Hey, kitty," Broker easily reached down and tickled the cat under her chin.

"She only attacks certain people, isn't that right, Ambush," Jolene said, carefully lifting the cat off the bed. With the cat in her arms she started for the door. "Take as long as you want. We'll be in the kitchen."

Now there were two sets of lungs breathing air and two hearts pumping blood in the room. Broker understood he was alone. But he didn't feel alone. Was that intelligence or just ambient electricity he had seen firing in Hank's eyes when he first entered the room? Hank gave no clue, he just lay unmoving, blinking, as his loopy stare wandered out the windows.

Broker felt weight press his lungs. Hard to breathe. The air turned heavy. So he turned from the bed and inspected the room. A stiff-backed Shaker chair sat in a corner. Broker got it, brought it over, positioned it next to Hank's bed, and sat down. Should at least say his name. But his voice balked and he began to sweat.

"This is hard for me," he began.

"I need to thank you for saving my life. Which is funny because I figured I was there to take care of you." He exhaled some of the heavy air and his voice sounded hollow and shaky, alone and not alone in the room. He laughed nervously. "Sort of what I did all my life, look out for people. So you surprised me. And the fact is, I wasn't—am not—in the best shape. The fact is I'm going through this thing with my wife . . ."

Broker felt his lips start to tremble, and his carefully constructed, all-purpose mask of a face, the one he'd worn to hell and back a few times, began to crumble. The wave of failure and remorse welled up in his chest again and this time it threatened to rise through his throat and lap past his eyes. *Jesus. Talking to a dead man.*

"You see, I thought I had it all figured out. And then it turned out, I didn't."

He had to do something physical. Now. Or he would liquefy into a puddle.

His eyes tracked the room. Books, files, a computer, of course. And a few framed photos on the walls. Broker got up and walked the shelves. Scanned the pictures. Teenage Hank in a ducktail hairdo, lean and tan, standing in front of the obligatory '57 Chevy. There was a black-and-white framed cover from *Life* magazine from the forties. And Hank again, a few years older, in faded jungle fatigues squatting with a group of soldiers who wore Screaming Eagle patches.

Then he walked to the black maw of the fireplace, where a damp log had drowned in a slush of ashes. Nobody had cleaned it. There was no room for oxygen to circulate under the grate, the wood couldn't burn.

The wood box was empty. The least he could do was clean out the fireplace and bring in a load of wood. He took the ash bucket and a small shovel and brush from the fireplace that sat next to the hearth. Methodically, he shoveled out ashes, filled the bucket, and used the stiff wire broom to sweep out the hearth stones.

He took the bucket to the sliding patio door, opened the door, and stepped out onto the deck. Side stairs led to the lawn along the bluff and the back of the garage. As he carried the ashes toward the bed of frost-killed ferns and hosta next to the garage he walked past the kitchen windows and glimpsed Allen and Jolene, two shadows illuminated by the light over the table.

When he dumped the ashes he saw the heaped rounds of unsplit oak and the empty woodshed built along the side of the garage. Instinctively, his hand reached out and easily unfroze the heavy splitting maul with one hard slap and a yank. Then he kicked aside the damper sections of oak at the top of the pile and found several drier pieces. He put one on top of the chopping block, planted his feet, hefted the maul, and swung. The cold oak shivered and divided like balsa.

For several minutes Broker lost himself in the rhythm of the work, keeping warm, swinging the maul. Then more carefully he split several of the pieces into smaller strips. When he had a pile of kindling, he loaded an armful, turned to the deck, and saw Jolene standing on the steps watching him. Allen stood inside looking out the kitchen window.

"You don't have to do that," she said. She had pulled a bulky blue sweater around her shoulders and wore a pair of scuffed leather slippers that were many sizes too large.

"Kind of hard to have a fire without wood," Broker said.

She hugged herself. "Hank brought in this stuff before he went on the hunting trip and it's just been sitting."

"You have at least two cords of good oak there," Broker said as he carried his load up the deck back to the studio. Jolene ran ahead to hold the door. Inside, Broker filled the wood box and found a hand hatchet next to the wood box which he used to splinter off some tinder.

Jolene stood over him with her arms folded across her chest. A pile of old newspapers lay next to the hearth and Broker crumpled several sheets in the grate, added the tinder, and stacked smaller pieces of wood, pyre-fashion, spacing them so the fire could breathe. He took out his lighter, lit the paper, and set the flue. The hot flame from the newsprint was sucked up the chimney. In a minute he had a good fire crackling.

The flicker from the flames put a hint of color in Jolene's face. "Nice to have a fire," she said.

Broker stood up and dusted off his hands. When he turned he had another of those uncomfortable impressions that Hank Sommer was watching him. Almost like . . . But when he looked more closely he saw that Hank's eyes were wandering and rotating. The eye business engaged his curiosity. He needed more time, here, in this room. He needed a reason to come back.

"I have to get going. I'm going to need a ride. It's not far; I'm staying at a friend's farm about eight, nine miles away," Broker said.

Jolene nodded. "Of course. Allen will give you a lift."

For a moment Broker stood looking at Hank. He exhaled. "Words don't come close, do they," he said.

She smiled a utilitarian smile, then walked across the room and straightened the framed *Life* magazine cover. Broker followed her and inspected the June issue from 1942 that featured Vinegar Joe Stillwell's face in black and white, looking like a weathered American Mars.

Jolene smiled and pointed to the date. "I found it in an antiques store; it came out on the exact day Hank was born. I probably shouldn't have straightened it. What if it was the last thing he touched in this room?" She shifted her feet and started to lose her balance.

Broker raised his hand to steady her. She caught herself and said, "Thank you; I'm just a little tired."

As they left the room Ambush the cat darted through their feet, crossed the floor, and smoothly leaped up on the bed. She curled against Hank's motionless hands, and then slowly began to lick the fingers of his right hand with her pink sandpapery tongue.

Hi, Ambush, looky here; Broker is Prometheus, he brought us fire.

Broker found his reason to return as he followed her up the circular stairs. "You should get that wood split and out of the weather," he said.

She turned, studied him, and simply said, "Yes."

"Why don't I drop by tomorrow afternoon and take care of that," he said.

This time she just watched him and said nothing.

"About two," he said.

"I'll make a pot of coffee," she said, and then they continued into the kitchen. Broker washed his hands in a bathroom off the kitchen while Jolene explained his transportation problem to Allen.

Allen had put on his coat and shoes and was holding Broker's coat. "Let's get going, I have to get back to the hospital and check on some folks."

Jolene and Broker said good-bye. They did not mention chopping wood in the morning.

Allen drove over the speed limit but was very competent behind the wheel. For the first few minutes they chatted, catching up. Broker asked about Milt. Allen described again the insurance fiasco and the weird money-bind Jolene was in because of the trust. Then he delivered a flat, factual overview of Hank's condition. "His involuntary muscles seem to function perfectly. But Jolene misinterprets his random blinking and eye movement for focused sight." Allen turned to Broker and grimaced slightly. "It gives her false hope that he'll recover."

"She looks pretty done in," Broker said.

"She's watching him around the clock. So far, her jury-rigged home care plan is working. In a few days Milt will have him into a full-care nursing home. Otherwise, he's as good as his heart and lungs, and they are working just fine."

"So he could go on for quite a while?" Broker said.

Allen pursed his lips and they remained quiet for a few miles. Broker asked finally, "The guy who answered the door? He was at the hospital up north."

"Exactly," Allen said. "Well, life's a come-as-you-are party, and that guy—Earl Garf—is a visitor from Jolene's previous life. I have to say that when she discovered she was broke, Earl was Johnny-on-the-spot to help her out. On the other hand, he, ah, also moved into the basement."

"Maybe he smells a big malpractice settlement," Broker said.

The remark caused Allen to study Broker's profile for a few beats. "Yes, the thought has occurred to Milt and me."

"Doesn't look like the kind of person Hank would keep around," Broker said. Some of the animus he felt against the younger man weighted his words.

"Believe me, if Hank was on his feet, Garf would be gone," Allen said. "They had a fight once. Hank threw him out of the house."

"Doesn't sound like a good scene," Broker said.

"I don't think they're intimate, if that's what you mean," Allen said tightly.

"Still," Broker said.

"Right," Allen said.

Then they arrived at J.T.'s and, seeing the birds gathered in a pool of barn light against the wire fencing, Allen said in a distracted voice, "Ostriches? They're a healthy alternative to beef."

They shook hands. Broker was hoping that Amy wouldn't come walking out the door. Allen Falken was thinking that he was saying good-bye to Phil Broker forever. He turned his car and drove off with a final wave.

J.T. let Broker in and they went into the kitchen where Amy was helping a six-foot-tall thirteen-year-old set the table.

"Unca Honky, wazup?"

Broker narrowed his eyes at Shamika Merryweather. "You're not suppose to be talking like that. It's definitely not PC."

"Certainly not in mixed company," Shami said straight-faced. "And certainly not at school where it would be abusive and insensitive. But here at home I'm still under my daddy's strict control, and my daddy says that's your name."

"How tall are you now?" Broker countered.

"Six foot. How tall are you?"

"Six foot."

"Yeah, but I still have another five years to grow," Shami said.

Amy walked up looking very sane and healthy to Broker after his visit to Sommer's house. "How'd it go with Hank?" she asked.

"It's hard to tell. He could be looking at people. But Allen Falken doesn't think so."

"Oh."

"Right, that was him in the car. He just dropped me off. Which makes it harder for you to go Sommer's house, because Allen can ID you."

"So what's next?"

"I'm going back tomorrow for another look."

"Okay, can I take your truck to do my Mall of America junket?"

"Sure." Broker rubbed his chin. "Basically, it's pretty grim over at Sommer's."

"You don't look grim," Amy observed.

Chapter Twenty-three

Broker was not one to dream.

So the sudden flash of Sommer's startling acetylene eyes jolted him awake and left him sitting up in the dark on the fold-out couch in J.T.'s unfamiliar living room.

Shadows strummed the wall above him as the wind pushed the willows back and forth. New night sounds murmured: the creak of the eaves, the furnace fan whirring on.

Sitting in the dark in one strange house he thought of another strange house. Sommer's. Multileveled and full of people. Especially Garf, the wild card in the basement. Broker tried to imagine Jolene and Garf together in the cherry sleigh bed while Sommer treaded water in the next room.

He rejected the image, reformulated it, and put Garf back in the basement and saw Jolene, alone in the king-size bed. Did she sleep soundly or did she toss? Or did she really sleep in the narrow bed at Sommer's feet?

Was she a diamond in the rough, or just an opportunist?

Jolene, Garf, Sommer, and the dead accountant were human puzzle pieces that he couldn't make fit. And he wondered if Sommer would now be counted among the things he'd never know. Like where his daughter was sleeping tonight. He didn't even know what country she was in.

What he did know was that he wouldn't get back to sleep, so he felt around for his jeans, pulled them on, and carefully made his way between the shadowy furniture toward the kitchen.

Red digital numbers on the microwave stamped 5:29 A.M. in the dark. A moment later an appliance clicked on with a watery gurgle—J.T.'s preset coffeemaker. Upstairs, on the same schedule as the coffeepot, people stirred. Doors opened and closed. Water ran in pipes.

Broker went back to the living room, got his travel bag, and took it to the half bath off the kitchen. When he emerged shaved and dressed, he smelled brewing coffee and heard soft footsteps coming down the stairs.

J.T. padded through the doorway wearing jeans, a blue flannel shirt, and wool socks. He flicked on the light. "Amy's still asleep. Denise and Shami are coming down for breakfast, so let's take some coffee into the barn. Feed some birds."

J.T. poured coffee into a thermos, sat down, pulled on a pair of work shoes, then got up and reached for a lined denim jacket. Broker took his coat and boots from the mud porch and soon they were walking toward the barn, testing the icy pre-dawn air in their lungs.

J.T. handed Broker the thermos and two cups, then withdrew a pipe and a pouch of tobacco from his chest pocket. "Even in Minnesota, I can still smoke in my own barn," he said as he filled his pipe and squinted into the distance over Broker's shoulder. Broker reached for a cigar and they lit up like two truant kids.

J.T.'s eyes had acquired a new habit of focusing beyond the person he was with and resting on a point in the sky. Even a blank night sky. He used to be a close watcher of people, and they had pretty much lived up to his expectations. Now he preferred to stay far away from most of them, to get beyond them. Growing his own corn, oats, and alfalfa he'd become addicted to the constant examination of wind, clouds, humidity, and the color of air.

They walked out to the paddocks, fed the birds there, returned to the barn, and continued to scoop feed into five-gallon plastic buckets and dump them in feeding troughs in one of the two pens that sectioned off the lower level of the building. Broker moved in easily among the leggy hens who drifted away and cautiously returned after he'd dumped their feed.

The barn was new territory for Broker, with its musty scent of oats and corn fermenting in cold wooden bins and the loft above, heavy with alfalfa bales. He had grown up north of Grand Marais on Lake Superior. He knew something about fishing, hunting, logging, and iron mining. But there were few real farms in the granite bedrock of Cook County, Minnesota.

"Watch out. They peck at glasses, watches, rings, pens. Shiny stuff attracts them," J.T. said. Broker shouldered through the birds. He wasn't wearing a watch. He sure wasn't wearing a ring.

Then J.T. held out an arm to bar Broker from entering the second pen. In that pen, a solitary four-hundred-pound male stood nine feet tall, with his thick black plummage flexed, tipped with white feathers. The stubby wings and tail feathers came up and he coiled his long neck at them.

"Popeye's my big, ornery male," J.T. said "When he gets his wings out and his tail up, never get in front of him. He's getting ready to attack. Always stay to the side."

"How come you have him all alone in here?" Broker asked.

"I, ah, haven't figured out how to move him back into a paddock. Last time I tried, he cornered me and almost kicked me to death. So I'm going to wait till he's way, way out of season to try again."

The reinforced plywood door to the pen shuddered when Popeye threw a kick as if to echo J.T.'s remarks.

"Jesus," Broker said.

"Yeah. Ostriches throw a mean knuckle. They're the only birds that have two toes on their feet. Check it out."

Broker snuck a look into Popeye's pen. Two toes, but one was little and one was real big with a thick ugly claw on it. "Ow," he said.

"It's no joke. They can kill a lion with one kick. He could disembowel a man, easy."

After all the birds were fed and watered, J.T. led Broker through his incubator and hatchery rooms, now closed down because the birds quit laying their two-pound eggs in September. J.T. and Broker climbed some stairs and entered a long, comfortable studio paneled with barn wood.

A counter ran around the room and one side held an ammo-loading press and shelves of gunsmith paraphernalia. Farther down the counter a screen saver on a Gateway PC trailed bubbles, sting rays, and an occasional shark. Two space heaters were in place as backup, but J.T. crumpled some newspaper and tossed some kindling in a Fisher woodstove next to his computer desk, and soon had a fire crackling.

The other side of the room was outfitted with more counters fanning out from an industrial Singer sewing machine and racks of leather-working tools. Sheaves of tanned ostrich leather in black, maroon, and gray—some with a scale pattern, some with quills— hung from the walls. A picture window behind the sewing machine was an ebony mirror, filled with night.

Broker took the rocking chair by the stove and J.T. sat on the stool at his work counter. J.T. tossed a leather checkbook case to Broker. "You want to trade up?" he asked.

J.T.'s first prototypes had been stiff, the stitching not sufficient to hold the leather. He'd brought in a commercial sewing machine, learned a few tricks, and started backing the ostrich with calfskin, and now the items were supple. This new one was a little slicker than the one in Broker's hip pocket.

"Shiny leather," Broker said.

J.T. nodded. "An experiment. Out of a South African shipment."

Broker handed it back. J.T. tossed it aside and picked a sheaf of printer paper from the counter. He poured more coffee and relit his pipe.

The calm expression of the ostrich farmer was overprinted by the suspicious frown of J.T. Merryweather, former homicide detective.

"I downloaded this stuff from Washington County: Cliff Stovall was a fifty-six-year-old white guy, a CPA. He died of exposure complicated by self-mutilation . . ."

"So they're set on this self-mutilation theory?" Broker said.

"There it is. The coroner made notes more about what was on the outside of Stovall's body, than what he found inside."

"What'd he find inside?" Broker sipped coffee.

"Traces of Antabuse and a lot of alcohol. Blood level out of sight."

"Okay, give me the outside," Broker said.

"Thirteen significant self-inflicted wounds caused by cutting and piercing going back over twenty years." J.T. raised his eyebrows. "In a world of seriously fucked-up individuals, this guy was a standout."

"Nothing about foul play?" Broker said.

"Nope. Self-mutilation," J.T. reiterated. "I'm getting pictures sent of the pre-autopsy so I can show Shami the downside of body piercing. She wants to get a nose ring."

"So this isn't the coroner making a diagnosis?"

"No, they pulled this guy's medical records. He wasn't some teenage kid taking a roll-around in the tackle box. The coroner called him an aristocrat of the cutting culture. He was a regular inpatient at the St. Cloud VA on the neuropsychiatric ward."

Broker frowned. "I don't buy it."

"You want to see all the reports?"

"Screw the reports; I don't buy it." Broker said.

J.T. leaned forward and poked the air with the stem of his pipe for emphasis as he read from his notes. "You're just being contrary. Stovall was an alky on Antabuse. And he took Trazadone to go to sleep and Prozac to smooth him out in the morning. The record mentions severe childhood trauma complemented by post-traumatic stress disorder. And his wife left him and filed for divorce six months ago."

"So what are they calling it?" Broker asked.

"Misadventure."

"Jesus, not even suicide?"

"Uh-uh. See, the way they interpret this stuff, Stovall was a mass meeting of self-destructive disorders, so borderline and numbed out, the only way he could feel things was to cut and stick himself. They figure he fell off the wagon, drank his way though an Antabuse reaction—which is hard-core because Antabuse and alcohol are a recipe for projectile-vomiting like in *The Exorcist*—then he kept drinking and was playing dangerous games with a hammer and a spike."

J.T. tapped a sheet of faxed paper on the desk. Broker recognized it as a police report. J.T. said, "July ninety-six, Washington County responded to a nine-one-one from Stovall's wife. He'd gone off the wagon and nailed his wrist to the bathroom door in the basement of their home. Paramedics used a Wonder bar to get him free. Same wrist. Like this."

J.T. picked up a pen and then positioned his left forearm on the counter, palm up, and then curled his wrist back, aligning his thumb and fingers so the pen pointed back into the hollow of his wrist. "They figured he was playing this kind of game again."

J.T. pounded the pen down into his wrist with an imaginary hammer in his right hand. "He went a little too far and he got, pardon the pun, stuck in the woods with the weather turning bad, and he froze to death. Not suicide."

Broker shook his head. "Well, thanks for the trouble."

"No problem." J.T. tossed the pages aside and said, tongue in cheek, "I know how you benefit from a steady hand when you go off on a tangent."

Broker ignored the jab and rocked silently back and forth and stared out the picture window where the blackness had dissolved into pale streaks of purple and vermilion.

"So you really went for this thing; why is that?" J.T. asked.

"We were bringing Sommer out in the seaplane. And he started raving about telling Stovall to move the money. That's what got me going after I saw the article about finding Stovall in the woods."

"Raving, like in delirious?"

"Yeah, he was delirious. He was pissed at his wife. So he moved all his money into a trust where she can't touch it. The alternate trustee was Stovall, who checks out the day after they discover that Hank Sommer's health insurance has lapsed."

J.T. stroked his chin. "Her lawyer is Milton Dane. She's not without resources."

Broker nodded. "True. Milt's arranging for a nursing home, and he's busting open the trust."

"So she panicked and now she's covered," J.T. said. "You went with your gut and arrived at a conclusion and worked backward, trying to make events fit. Uh-huh. Typical Broker. You always were a prosecutor's nightmare. But they put up with your bullshit because it helps to have someone around who'll walk into the lion's den with a pocketful of raw steak. That last bust, you bagged those National Guard guys selling machine guns all over the Midwest, that got a lot of people promoted. Not just at BCA, but at the Bureau and ATF. The word on the street was, they left you out there about five years too long."

"You getting into giving speeches in your old age?" Broker said.

J.T. squinted. "Yeah, I'm into speeches and simple shit like knowing where my wife is. She's in the kitchen eating Total Raisin Bran with my daughter, getting one hundred percent of her vitamins

before she goes to work. And this is your problem we're getting to."
J.T. leaned forward. "Can you tell me where your wife is? Where
your kid is?"

Broker grimaced. "C'mon J.T.; not first thing in the morning."

"You can't, can you?" J.T. said. " 'Cause you don't even know.
And you know why? Because *you married yourself*, you dumb shit.
Only difference between you and Nina Pryce is she's younger, so
she's got bigger balls."

"Having fun, aren't we?" Broker said.

"I'm just warming up. See, the way I have it figured out is those
other women you knew bored you, and then here comes Nina who
doesn't bore you. And you actually thought that because she had
your kid and married you, she'd toss off her Wonder Woman
bracelets and stay home and knit." J.T. rubbed his hands together
and smiled. "Looks like *she's* the one that got bored with *you* this
time." J.T. grinned.

"What is this? Tough love or shooting-wounded?" Broker asked.

"You tell me," J.T. said. "Nina left your shit weak and some
writer guy had to save your ass. And you've got yourself so turned
around that you show up here looking like the poster boy for the
Peter Pan Principle, with your snappy young nurse."

Broker had to protest. "Peter Pan Principle? When did you
stoop to psychobabble?"

"Actually it's Denise's term," J.T. sniffed. "You know, for guys
who never grow up."

And then Amy, who had been standing in the doorway unob-
served, nursing a cup of coffee, enunciated precisely: "That's snappy
young nurse-*anesthetist*."

"Hmmm," J.T. said, slightly deflated, coming off his roll.

Amy entered the room and said, "Okay, while you guys are
solving the problems of the world I need to borrow a vehicle and do
some early Christmas shopping."

"Hmmmm," J.T. said again.

"Right," Broker said, glad to change the subject. "So where's
my truck?"

J.T. cleared his throat; wrinkles appeared on his neck as he drew
his head back between his broad shoulders and tried to stand up
and scratch his forehead. "I been meaning to talk to you."

"My truck?" Broker insisted.

"It's in the Quonset," J.T. said, pulling on his coat and moving toward the door.

Broker and Amy followed J.T. back out into the cold and they tramped after him across the yard to the large equipment shed. J.T. pushed open the doors and flipped on a light. A tractor and a John Deere bailer were parked in the foreground. A bobcat sat beyond them, and parked in the rear was the shape of Broker's sleek Ford Ranger, shrouded in a huge blue tarp.

Broker walked forward, grabbed a handful of tarp, yanked, and then groaned. The windows on both doors were gone, nothing but pulverized shatter-glass hanging in the corners. The door panels were caved in and so were the fenders and wheel wells. The sides of the truck bed were cratered. The tailgate was dimpled.

His truck looked like a Roman legion had hauled it in a field and used it for catapult practice.

"I can explain," J.T. said as Broker began to space out his cussing.

"Goddamn mother fucker . . . I let you use this to bring in *hay*?"

"Well, it involved hay—straw actually. See, I was taking bedding straw into the paddock where I used to keep Popeye and . . ."

"Son of a bitch, shit!"

". . . and the sucker decided to take on the truck. Amazing he could kick that high."

"Kick?" Broker voice was strangled. "A *bird* did this?"

"If it helps any, I damn near didn't get out of that pen intact," J.T. offered. "It's not like you paid full boat for the thing. I remember how you had the fix in at the police auction. You had your eye on that truck since the time you confiscated it on that meth bust up in Pine County."

Broker growled and stomped out of the Quonset and paced back and forth. He noticed Denise and Shamika standing on the porch. After making fleeting eye contact they both diplomatically scooted to Denise's Accord and drove away.

Hearing J.T.'s boots crunch up on the cold trap-rock behind him, Broker walked to where J.T.'s glossy Chevy Silverado was parked next to the house. "Well," Broker announced, "I'm going to need to *drive* something."

"Uh, wait. No way, man. You can't use the Chevy. I sort of promised that to Amy to go shopping. But, ah, you can use the Cherokee."

"The Cherokee?" Broker swung his gaze to the ten-year-old boxy red Jeep that sat next to the Chevy. It looked like an experiment to determine how much rust could be balanced on top of two axles.

"The Leper Colony?" Broker protested.

"Not much to look at, I agree; but everything under the hood is rebuilt, got new rubber, heater's good. Oil changed every three thousand miles," J.T. added.

Amy smiled and patted the fender of the Silverado. "So which of you guys is making breakfast?"

Chapter Twenty-four

After breakfast Amy took off on her shopping errand and Broker had some time to kill before his coffee date with Sommer's ex-wife. So he helped J.T. rearrange bales in his hayloft for a few hours. Then he washed up, changed his shirt, started up the old Jeep, and headed for St. Paul.

Broker picked up Interstate 94 coming in over the St. Croix River from Wisconsin just west of the Hudson Bridge. Then he drove twenty miles to where the city of St. Paul was rising from the hundred-year blahs. The talk was all about the Minnesota Wild's new hockey arena that would dominate the redeveloped riverfront. St. Paul was swinging her tail after decades of being eclipsed in the shadow of Minneapolis.

Broker was aware of this primarily because he had trouble finding a place to park. On his third try, he squeezed into a ramp and then walked to the newspaper building on Cedar Ave.

Dorothy Gayler was tall and lanky in a long dark coat, with shiny black hair cut in a precise page boy that brought to mind Prince Valiant from the Sunday comics. The hard October light emphasized the faint lines that branched off her eyes and down her cheeks. She made no effort to disguise any of it with makeup.

She picked him out easily from the busy early afternoon street crowd. He did not have a cell phone jammed to his ear. He wore jeans and the blaze-orange fleece jacket.

"Mr. Broker," she said, extending a lean, knuckle-prominent hand. They shook. "There's a coffee shop in the skyway, shall we?" He nodded and she led the way. They went in the newspaper lobby, mounted a stairway, and entered the skyway, which was a covered, elevated walkway system that connected all the downtown buildings and allowed St. Paul residents to travel between buildings out of the winter weather.

"Are you located in Ely?" she asked.

"No, my uncle has an outfitters there. I was just helping him out."

"And what is it you do when you're not guiding canoe trips?"

"I have a small resort on Lake Superior, north of Grand Marais."

"So you don't get down to our city much, do you?" she asked.

Broker smiled at her cordial, city-mouse condescension and followed her through the busy skyway past banks and boutiques and into a coffee shop decorated with JUST DO IT Nike posters and swooshes and lots of chrome.

Several highly caffeinated young people jerked their eyes up from their laptop computers, perused Broker's rustic attire, then returned to their screens.

Dorothy ordered coffee, insisted on paying, and they found a table. After she sat down, she shook off her coat and scarf. The muscles of her neck and throat were firm and clean. He caught a whiff of chlorine. A swimmer, he thought.

She came directly to the point. "You said on the phone you wanted to know more about Hank, because he saved your life."

"Yes."

"Well, if he did save your life then you have the essence of who he was; you see, he was all about taking care of people. Oh, he tried to be a reporter for a while but it wasn't his nature."

"Oh, really?" Broker, who rated reporters about equal with hyenas, was curious.

"Hank always said a newspaper is a place where reporters wait for something bad to happen to someone else, for someone to tattle on someone. Then they swoop in and do a trim job on reality to fit their byline and a deadline."

Broker's expression showed amused surprise.

"Oh," Dorothy waved his reaction away, "I'm no cherry. Twenty-six years in the trenches. I admit, when I was starting out I thought I would have a *career*. But, as Hank never tired of pointing out, here I am, chained to the copy desk in a word factory, stamping word widgets toward a pension like all the rest of the hamsters." She smiled. "That's what he called people trapped inside corporations."

"Running in those wheely things," Broker offered.

"They're called exercisers," Dorothy rectified, then continued. "That's why he got involved with the Newspaper Guild and became the business agent. Reporters amused him, calling themselves professionals," she allowed herself a small smile. "The National Labor Relations Board classifies them as skilled tradesmen." Dorothy tossed a profligate hand. "So he was our junkyard dog who protected us from management." She fixed Broker with a stare. "But it wasn't enough."

"You mean the money?" Broker asked.

Dorothy's eyes evaluated him. "Were you in the war, Mr. Broker?"

"I was a little old for the Gulf."

"That was not a war, that was a TV show. The last real war."

"I see. Yes. I was."

Dorothy sipped her coffee and pursed her full lips. "Hank used to say there are two kinds of soldiers: the kind who fight and the other kind."

"Keep going, I'm with you so far," Broker said.

"Have you heard of a place called the Ashau Valley?"

"Yes, I have." He recalled the Annamite Mountains which bordered Laos emerging out of morning mist.

"There was a hill in the Ashau that was briefly infamous in 1969," Dorothy said.

"Hamburger Hill."

"Yes. Hank was a buck sergeant in the 101st. He took his squad of twelve men up that hill. When they all became casualties he was issued ten replacements. Nine of them became casualties. That's a casualty rate of 190 percent. He went up the hill five times."

Broker nodded. "The red teardrops tattooed on his forearm."

Dorothy smiled. "Hank lived a contradiction. He wanted to take care of people but only if they were engaged in extremely destructive behavior."

"You mean?"

"I mean, obviously, his marriage to Jolene *Smith*." She paused on the common name with a twitch of scorn. "Have you met her?"

"Yes, she's, ah," and here Broker paused a beat too long.

Dorothy's steady brown eyes glinted. Then the shine evaporated and she batted them. Coy. "Younger? And very attractive. With a touch of true grit that Hank apparently found irresistible." Dorothy smirked at Broker's polite frown.

Broker lowered his eyes and took a sip of his coffee.

"Oh, come now, Mr. Broker, let's not be shy. How old are you? Forty-five?"

"Forty-seven."

"So I have three years on you. Big five-oh." Dorothy smoothed her fingertips down her cheek. "Ten years ago I was still attractive. Twenty years ago I was downright sexy. Now I'm—what would you say? Striking? Well-preserved?"

Broker drew back instinctively from her flash of claws and soft venom.

Dorothy smiled, hitting her stride. "Have you noticed how aging leading men are paired with hard-body bimbos in the movies—Sean Connery, Harrison Ford?"

"I don't see that many movies," Broker said.

Deftly, Dorothy pointed at the naked stripe on his ring finger. "What happened there?"

"My wife and I are separated."

"First marriage?"

"Second marriage."

Dorothy's eyes locked on like missile radar. "How old is she?"

Broker cleared his throat. Dorothy raised her eyebrows in merry expectation. Broker said, "She's thirty-three."

"And why did you break up?"

"So she could pursue her career."

Dorothy flashed a steely smile. "Well, good for her."

For a moment all Broker heard was the natter of keyboards at the surrounding tables. He struck back. "Bitter," he observed.

Dorothy cocked her head, insinuating her face a little to the side. "I stuck by him. I edited his hopelessly purple, overwritten copy. I held his hand when he was insecure. And then, as soon as he made some money, he left me for a hot little bitch." Reflex smile.

"I'm not bitter, Mr. Broker; but sometimes I cannot help but feel the comfort of a certain justice."

Broker thought, but did not voice, another cliché that would never die: *Hell hath no fury . . .*

As quickly as it came, the ice storm passed on Dorothy's face.

"Of course," she said, "Jolene was very much in need of rescue. Very much in need of someone to take care of her," she delivered these words with the deliberate cadence of a woman who could clearly take care of herself.

"Are you saying he put himself in jeopardy marrying her?"

"Oh, *premeditated* jeopardy. Have you been to the house since they brought him home, AMA—*against medical advice?*"

"Yes."

Dorothy pursed her lips. "I visited once. I thought the baby monitors were a nice touch. Did you notice a big, buff lout lurking in the basement named Earl Garf?"

Broker cleared his throat. "Perhaps she observes a shorter decent interval than the rest of us," he said, stealing Amy's line, which went over big because Dorothy's voice swelled rich with malice.

"Oh, that was very good for . . ."

"A resort owner?" Broker smiled. Dorothy smiled. And their eyes rattled together briefly like crossed foils.

Enjoying herself, she lowered her eyes, and when she looked up she had leaned forward across the table and tilted her head slightly so her eyes revolved. One hand drifted up and touched her hair.

"Have you ever heard of the old badger game?" she asked.

"Young woman hustles old guy. Young boyfriend in the wings. It crossed my mind."

"Because it's the truth. Hank knew it from the start. It's what attracted him, don't you see?" Dorothy smiled. "Mr. Broker, do you believe people can change?"

For an ex-cop it was a no-brainer. "No way."

"Me either. But Hank believed people could change. He thought Jolene could change. So that was his lion-in-winter delusion—that he could help her change before she took him to the cleaners."

Broker rotated his coffee cup in his fingers. "So the accident up north just accelerated things."

Dorothy raised her eyebrows. "And tremendously upped the

odds. Now she will reap a huge malpractice settlement. She won the lottery."

"You seem to have accepted all this?" Broker wondered.

"He was guilty. He gave me a very generous divorce settlement. And, despite everything, I knew how unhappy he was. He wanted to be a writer, you see."

"I thought he was?"

"*War Wolf*? My God, he did that as a joke. A satire," she rolled her eyes. "The fact was, he just couldn't tell a story that wasn't totally encrusted in bullshit. Then this bizarre windfall of Hollywood money fell on him. He left me. Bought the river house, found a new group of friends, started drinking again, and went back to AA where he discovered Jolene. Don't you see . . . "

She leaned forward. "He couldn't *write* a decent story so he bought one to *live* in. And now Jolene Smith—who never graduated high school, by the way—is writing the ending."

Broker looked Dorothy straight in the eye. "In the plane, coming out after the storm, he was raving. But he distinctly said to me, these exact words, 'Tell Cliff Stovall to move the money.'"

Dorothy shrugged. "I know Cliff's wife. She told me Cliff was restructuring Hank's finances off-limits to Jolene. She was already writing checks to Garf, the boyfriend."

Broker leaned forward. "But Stovall is dead in some weird scenario in the woods. The same week as Hank?"

Dorothy apparently accepted Stovall's death with equanimity. "Have you spent much time around drunks, Mr. Broker?"

"No." Only as much time as he had to. He'd gone through the treatment-therapy motions with some cops when they tanked. But no.

"Do you subscribe to the disease theory of alcoholism?"

Again he balked. And she finished for him.

"No, of course, you're old school. You might pay lip service to the fashionable babble but underneath you think it's a moral weakness, don't you?"

"I think that if you've got a drinking problem and you don't have good health insurance to pay for inpatient treatment you're shit out of luck in the enlightened state of Minnesota."

"But is it a moral weakness?"

"Yeah," Broker said. "If you're sick all you can do is get well. If you're bad you can redeem yourself and be good."

Dorothy laughed. "You and Hank would have gotten along just fine. But whether you believe it's a disease or a stigma, in the end, it kills people in very ugly ways. Hank, Cliff, and Jolene Smith met in an AA group. They were drunks. You know what they tell alcoholics in treatment? They tell them that one out of three will make it clean and sober. One will struggle back and forth between relapse and recovery. And one will die a pretty horrible death. And that's exactly what Cliff Stovall did."

Broker nodded. It was a familiar description. "The guy on either side is going to get it."

Dorothy raised her cup in a salute and said, "Well, Mr. Broker; it certainly looks like Jolene Smith was the guy in the middle." After a moment, she sniffed, "Probably not the first time she was in between two men with her ass and her mouth on the same axis."

Chapter Twenty-five

Broker drove east on I-94 and tried to see Jolene as a lush who was one drink away from insanity and death. Dorothy was right; he didn't have a lot of insight into conditions like chronic drinking. He'd been one of life's shock troops. He'd met problems fast, in your face, on the street. He knew how to cuff them and collar them; how to stop the bleeding, clear the airway, and treat for shock. Other people toiled over the long haul, behind closed doors, to mend the collateral human damage.

Dorothy's barbed comment about men who marry younger women still quivered—right next to J.T.'s Peter Pan Principle remark—and he found himself wondering what happened to old shock troops.

He turned off the freeway, drove aimlessly for a few minutes, and wound up on a desolate country road. The steering wheel jerked and the Jeep bounced around like a steel tray full of rocks, and the rusty suspension found every bump and pothole in the stiff gravel road, and each jolt was a shot of gravity reminding him that—although he'd lived an interesting life—right now he was on his way to turning into a statistic. He was joining the forty-five percent of American couples whose marriages would end in divorce.

Broker ran head-on into Doubt on a lonely country road between two chilly, whispering cornfields.

He couldn't make the pieces fit for Sommer. Was he on a tangent, trying to relive an exciting part of his life?

So maybe it was time to play the cards in his hand, which did not include a wife and a child or any particular detective brilliance. He'd chop some wood and stack it neatly. He'd look at Sommer one last time and make his gesture and bid farewell. He'd go home and wait for the phone to ring.

There was Amy. Well, she had to live with it. There would be no closure on Sommer; there'd always be a place that hurt when you touched it. Like a dead child.

Onward.

Broker drove east toward the only landmark he could see, the tall NSP smokestack south of Stillwater, and found his way back to the main roads.

After getting his directions straight, he pulled up into Sommer's drive and parked the Jeep next to the Green Chevy van. Then Earl Garf stepped out on the porch wearing a big smirk and baggy skater pants, and all Broker's good intentions went to hell, because if ever there was a wrong guy in the picture it was Garf. Look at him, so pretty and immortal.

Broker got out of the Jeep and stalked up the steps.

"Hey," Garf grinned. "It's the Tin Woodsman. How you doing?"

"What's that supposed to mean?" Broker asked in a level voice, in no mood to be trifled with by assholes. Even assholes who went about 220 and lifted weights.

"The Wizard of Oz, you know. It's a little joke. You came to chop some wood, right." Without waiting for a reply Garf sauntered down the steps and inspected the Cherokee. "Wow, what'd you do? Drive this through a rust storm?" Genial contempt caked Garf's voice as thick as the gunk he wore in his hair, and Broker felt his shoulders loosen and drop slightly and his hands started to get hot and his fingers flexed open and closed.

Reacting to Broker' body language, Garf raised his hands in a mollifying gesture. "H ', take it easy. Jolene and I really appreciate what you're doing." Smoothly Garf inserted two fingers in his jeans pocket and withdrew another of his hundred-dollar bills. "For your trouble, man."

Broker didn't think. He reacted and snatched the bill and deftly stuffed it down the neck of Garf's funky Calvin Klein sweatshirt. "Go ride your bike. Mug an old lady."

Garf's smile crumbled and was replaced with a reluctant resolve as he shook his head and said, "I'm opposed to beating up old guys on principle, but . . ." He moved into a stance. "Just so you know. I've got a black belt."

Broker nodded. "Uh-huh. I heard of that. It's for people who never learn to fight growing up." A flourish of righteous anticipation swelled his chest and chased away the blues. Here, at least, was something he *could* understand: putting the hurt on this young asshole.

"Earl." Jolene's voice shaped the name so it sounded like "bad dog." She appeared in the doorway wearing jeans, a denim jacket, a light gray turtleneck tucked in, and scuffed leather shoes. No wrinkles or bulges showed anywhere unless they occurred naturally in material.

"This guy . . ." Garf started to say.

"*Earl*. Go inside and wipe Hank's chin."

Garf grinned tightly. "Some other time, maybe." He made an accommodating gesture, skipped up the steps, and went past Jolene into the house. She closed the door and joined Broker in the drive.

"He has a good side," she said. "But you kind of have to lead him to it."

Broker said nothing and they observed his silence carefully. And he knew that she knew that a lot of guys would have left by this point.

It was just nippy enough to encourage them to keep moving, so, after about thirty seconds of looking each other over, they walked around to the back of the garage. She took the lead. Broker approved of the way her jeans were not too tight, more like a comfortable second skin with a pair of leather work gloves tucked in the wallet pocket.

Around in back, a tray sat in the empty wood lean-to built under the eaves of the garage. It held a fat thermos, two cups, a creamer, sugar, and two spoons. She poured a cup. Broker shook his head when she pointed to the cream and sugar.

It was the kind of very good coffee that made you want to stay in her kitchen forever. So he sipped and surveyed the pile of wood. The rounds were uniformly cut from straight trunks. "This is really clean oak," he said. "You found a good supplier."

"Hank cut it on his friend's land." She paused. "Late friend. I guess he committed suicide, but the cops didn't call it that. The accountant. I told you, remember?"

"I'm sorry," Broker said, who definitely remembered. He was tempted to ask about Stovall but that would be out of character. Instinctively, he was back playing a role. He'd wait.

"It's pretty gruesome all around. See, Hank had two sets of friends: his old screwed-up AA buddies and his new poker-party friends who he goes on his extreme vacations with, mainly Allen and Milt. Cliff, the dead guy, was from the AA group." Then she added, deliberately, eyes steady, "I met Hank in that group. He used to say AA was a spiritual journey."

Broker cocked his head at her language.

She smiled briefly. "He'd say the difference between religious people and spiritual people is religious people are afraid of going to hell. Spiritual people have already been there and meet on the road back."

Broker nodded. "So you're in the program?"

"I don't go to meetings anymore."

"Sounds like it wasn't a real lucky group you were in," Broker said.

"I hear you. But, the fact is, I've been sober for fourteen months."

"It must be working, you look healthy; tired but healthy," Broker said.

She smiled bleakly and said, "Considering." She put her coffee cup back on the tray and pulled on her work gloves. "I'll stack."

It was turning into a nice afternoon. A residue of frost glistened on Broker's boots and there was just a faint ghost of condensed moisture trailing off his breath. He pulled on his gloves, picked up a round, set it upright on the block, and hefted the maul.

Jolene watched Broker work and saw how he was a natural, easing into a steady rhythm; each swing of the maul originating from his planted feet, bent knees, whipping up through his hips, and smoothly arcing into his arms. Whack. The oak split and flew apart. He set the halves up and gave them another lick, making each round into four pieces of kindling. When he positioned a new log, she picked up the split pieces and took them to the shed.

After five minutes he striped off his jacket and she got a better picture of how he moved. He was like Hank—his body didn't telegraph his age. He could be anywhere in his forties.

And she thought how a lot of men self-consciously attacked work, among other things, with a jerky, almost angry, intensity; what Hank had jokingly called the need for man to demonstrate his mastery over nature. Broker had progressed beyond the amateur need to audition for her benefit. Or his own.

He was just a little too good to be true, with his killer Wolfman Jack eyebrows.

Given her experience, he should therefore be rejected out of hand as suspect. But this morning she had dressed carefully, choosing a practical look, just the simple jeans and shirt. She had caught herself starting to reach for a tube of lipstick and stayed her hand. Cosmetics were not appropriate right now, and she decided they were not necessary for Broker. In fact, she figured the opposite.

And she had allowed her heart one skip against her rib cage when she saw him hose down Earl with wolf pee. But she'd tucked her heart back in its Valentine envelope and coolly appraised Broker. And she was thinking how maybe Earl had run into someone out of his league, someone who was quietly and competently dangerous. Clearly Broker didn't get that way of moving on people in a gym.

So why did he come back?

Maybe, like Allen, he was lonely and had found a woman in a vulnerable situation. No. This was not simple boy-girl. So maybe, like Earl, he smelled the pot of gold at the end of Hank's tragedy. If so, he was very good at concealing his intentions. Or maybe he was just performing a samaritan courtesy, putting up a winter's wood.

What intrigued her was that she couldn't tell.

And she sensed a hint of melancholy. The first thing she'd noticed yesterday was his newly naked ring finger; the dent of the missing wedding band still pressed into his skin. So that was the loose string she'd pull on when the time was right.

So far he was looking good at chopping wood. She wondered how he'd be at trimming Earl down to size.

Intuition told her Broker could accomplish that task. But the roots of her intuition were still soggy with booze. She had to be careful. And even if he could chase Earl off, at what price? So she'd see if Broker could be useful. So no double messages. No games. She'd just see if there was a next step.

So she stooped, picked up, carried, and stacked the kindling. She ignored the pain in her arms and lower back. She assumed he was like Hank and put a premium on the ability to perform manual labor with a minimum of complaint. A quality that was fast departing from the realm of TV babies and PC nerds.

When half the shed was filled, Jolene straightened up, removed her gloves, and patted at a flush of sweat on her forehead. Broker put down the maul and said, "You'll feel it tomorrow, using muscles in a new way."

She smiled and arched her back. "Coffee break. It's in my union contract," she joked. He nodded, removed his gloves, and reached for a cigar as she poured coffee into two cups.

"You mind?" he asked, holding up the cigar.

She responded spontaneously from the brief happy life she'd known before her dad left when she was seven. "Actually, I kind of like cigar smoke. It reminds me of my dad and the old Met Stadium. When I was a little kid we'd go see the Twins. It smelled like beer, peanuts, and cigar smoke."

Broker smiled, approving of the remark.

They sat side by side in the unfilled half of the woodshed. She had taken pains to make sure the other half was stacked with industrial precision. Jolene took two sips of her coffee and made her move.

She touched his left hand, the ring finger. "Kind of shouts," she said.

He held the hand up, fingers out, inspected it, then let it fall into a fist. "Yeah," he said. "I thought of putting a Band-Aid over it."

Jolene raised her eyebrows eloquently, mocking, *Does it hurt that much?*

He waved off her concern, "I married a younger woman," he said.

"A lot of that's going around."

"There's risks."

"Yeah. Younger men," she said.

He nodded. "In my case, about twelve of them."

That stopped her and it was his turn to grin. "She's in the army, the only woman in a squad of guys."

"Oh." Jolene didn't see that coming.

And their eyes tangled up in that specific way when two people know they are both thinking the exact same thing about losing a person. About being lonely.

He held up his hand. "You know all about me. I don't know anything about you," he said.

And she said, "All I know about you is that you used to wear a ring on that finger and it's not there anymore."

He poured out the dregs of his coffee, stood up, pulled on his gloves, and nodded toward the woodpile. "Let's finish this," he said.

"And then?" she asked.

He looked into her eyes and they shared another quiet moment that began to throb in her temples like the Mormon Tabernacle Choir. And she thought, this guy is trouble and you have enough trouble, but she didn't turn the music off.

And after a Hallelujah Chorus worth of eye-fucking, he said, "And then we'll see if you need any more help around here."

Chapter Twenty-six

Hank toured hells he had known—Detroit got him ready for the hill, in the hammer shop at Huron Forge and Machine. Twelve drop hammers blowing out your eardrums in an acre of fiery steel forgings. The men and machines all hot, loud, dangerous, dirty, and sharp.

Mainly he thought Sartre was right in No Exit; *hell was just other people, especially if they were Jolene, Allen, and Earl Garf.*

Right now hell was Wisconsin, which was all he could see out his studio windows, and the Wisconsin river bluffs looked like a mass grave of dead technicolor porcupines.

And then, along came Garfinkle. The made-up man who hated his name and his past and was trying to reinvent himself as Brad Pitt from The Fight Club *or Keneau Reeves from* The Matrix.

He walked up to the bed and greeted Hank with the nickname he thought was so funny: "So how's the Big Lebowski today?"

All Earl's wit came from the movies, and Hank figured that's what Earl and his whole slacker generation had instead of experiences. But he had not seen The Big Lebowski, *so he was at a loss. It was the least of his problems.*

"Know what?" Earl said. "Your old lady has another suitor. First Doctor Allen and now the canoe guy from up north . . ."

The canoe guy.
Broker's back.

". . . he's out there in back of the garage knocking the wood in little pieces. I think he's practicing up to knock a piece off of Jolene. Just like Allen is. But, for my money, I think the sleeper candidate has the inside track. When I took her to Milt's office yesterday, Milt kissed her hand. It was very suave."

What's Broker doing back here? This could be a case where Earl was right.

"At any rate, we'll know who rings the bell." Earl walked over to the bedroom doorway and Hank could barely see him fumble around at shoulder level on a bookshelf next to the doorjam. He moved some books aside and pointed. "State of-the-art miniaturization, batteries, and transmitter. This baby is what the CIA uses. I cut a little hole in the wall and trained this camera on her bed. The camera transmits to long-playing tapes on a VCR in the basement. Forget voyeur TV; this is the real thing. I was thinking lighting would be a problem if it happens at night. But you know what? Jolene always sleeps with a night-light. So I upped the wattage in the night-light bulb. When she does the dirty, we'll have broadcast-quality audio and pretty good video. Unless, of course, she does it in the cot at the end of the bed. I didn't think of that."

Earl scratched his head briefly, then grinned, proud of himself as he tented the books back over the concealed camera. "You know what would have been good? I should have got your buddy Stovall on tape. He was a riot, a regular worm. Except he loved the hook.

"It was his fault, you know. I gave him every out. All he had to do was come up with some bread to pay the hospital bills. You know what he said? He said, not as long as I was hanging around. Can you believe that shit? *I* rented that hospital bed you're laying on. Me."

Earl pointed an accusing finger. "I mean, she didn't have shit. She couldn't pay the fucking mortgage, man. Jolene told me about his hangups so I left his dumb ass pinned to a tree so he could think about it. I figured if he did it, he could undo it and Jolene could get access."

Earl paused. "It was kind of a mellow day when I lured him out there. You know the place. Where you cut wood. In fact I used a trunk from a tree you cut down. And I left him with the hammer and two quarts of Johnny Walker Red."

Earl grinned. "I thought that was a nice touch." He shrugged. "Any rate, I never figured it'd snow and get below freezing. I thought of going back out there but I didn't have the right shoes, and I figured the van would get stuck. Besides, snow is good. It covers evidence. They already closed the investigation. They aren't even calling it suicide, man. He just fell in over his head getting his weird kicks. You sure know some real degenerates."

Suddenly Earl frowned and stared at Hank and Hank realized that he'd stopped roaming his eyes and was glaring at Earl. He let his eyes droop and roll. Then, like a tiny yellow cloud, the smell of urine seeped up from his diapered crotch. Just a few drops.

"Lookit you, you pig; you're pissing yourself, aren't you," Earl accused, wrinkling his nose. "This is where I draw the line, like I told Jolene, I'll turn your ass, feed you, and wipe your drool, but I definitely don't do diapers."

What a horrible experience it was to watch an idea slowly form on Garf's face.

"On the other hand, maybe I do," said Earl as he crossed to the windows and looked off to the left. Reassured, he came back to the bed and pulled Hank's gown aside and opened the Velcro stays on his diaper.

"That was hardly a sprinkle, so tell you what I'm going to do." Earl swung his eyes in a mischievous look over his shoulder and unzipped his fly. "This is for the time you fucked with me, Lebowski."

Hank watched Earl take his Average White Boy dick out of his pants and aim a stream of pee onto Hank's crotch.

I can feel that, fucker.

The urine splashed hot-chrome yellow and smelled like greasy rotten eggs. It pooled briefly between Hank's thighs and then soaked into the thick, absorbent material. Earl went up on tiptoes and stretched forward to shake off the last few drops. Then he put himself away and refastened Hank's diaper and straightened the gown. Very satisfied with himself, Earl picked up the TV clicker off the cabinet, zapped on the TV, and thumbed up the volume. Carefully, he inserted the remote under the clay fingers of Hank's right hand.

Another of his little mockeries.

Then Earl left the room.

Fucker pissed on me.
Helplessly soaking in Earl's urine, Hank tried to remember in detail the night more than a year ago when this cyber punk had walked into his house for the first time. Like some pimp, he'd ordered Jolene out into his car. Called her bitch, cunt, whore.
Called Hank geezer.
Yeah, well—a few minutes later Earl wound up on his ass in the driveway with a bloody nose—Hank's attention suddenly wrenched away from the pleasant thought of thumping on Garf. Christ, his hand was on fire.
This stinging in his right hand. Jesus, his right index finger, like something hot was under the skin squirming to get out.
Hank tried to turn his eyes into a magnifying glass and his mind into the sun. He tried to concentrate his thoughts into a beam of flame on the finger. If. If . . . he could move his finger an inch he could . . . hit the red button on the top of the remote—the one with the two letters: TV—and turn the sucker off. The red button was right between his first and second fingers. If he could do

that, he could message. He could communicate. Maybe find a way to fight back.

Then he shut his eyes and drove his thoughts into his dead flesh. He visualized wrecking crews beating through debris, pushing against collapsed tunnels and fried nerves, searching for something that could hook up.

Just give me one thing. One thing.

Nothing.

Just Earl's taunts and his wet piss.

And the cryptic snatches of Jolene's and Earl's conversations that confirmed Cliff was dead. Lost in the woods in his special pain, with the cold shadows lengthening, the snow creeping over his shoes, and the booze for comfort.

Allen, Garf. They were coming in with cold, blunt noses, sniffing like jackals, tearing off hunks of him, thinking he was a corpse.

The question mark was Jolene; would she land heads or tails? She'd shown signs of empathy since his accident in the way she attended to him, talked to him, played music for him, left the TV on. She kept looking into his eyes and believed that he was looking back.

Could he trust her?

Or Broker?

Okay. Okay. Get squared away. Nothing good is going to happen. It's a question of how much bad you have to eat before it ends. Those are your options.

If he didn't dangle just so on his single thread of sanity it got like Auschwitz in his head. C'mon, Hank, don't overwrite, he chided himself.

Cliff was dead but he'd done his job. But Jolene wasn't strong enough to stand up to Garf. He'd take everything if it wasn't locked away. Milt would score his legal settlement. Allen had seen to that.

Then Ambush the cat appeared in midleap, lightly dropped on the bed at his side, sniffed the wet diaper, and moved a distance. Then she curled up at his hip and purred like a big, warm fur cricket.

Hey, kitty. At least we're still pals.

Ambush stretched against him and nuzzled the hand that cov-
ered the remote. Then she concentrated on the first two fingers, lick-
ing them methodically with her tongue.

Needles.

Jesus. I felt that. More than before. An excruciating but won-
derful thawing sensation in his index finger brought on by the pink
sandpaper of Ambush's tongue.

C'mon.

Hank sent all his thoughts back into the dead spaces of his
right arm and commanded them to fight their way down through
the wrist and the palm to link up with the painful tingle in the
finger.

Right now it all seemed to depend on a cat's tongue. Keep it up,
Ambush. Good kitty. And then he was gone—deep inside again,
with random movies flickering in his head.

After the hill.

Her name was Mai, a slender former medical student at the Uni-
versity of Hue, who spoke French and English and left it all behind
to get rich running the laundry concession at Camp Eagle. Mai, who
sometimes threw a fuck his way. She didn't really need the carton of
cigarettes he brought for her.

But it wasn't going to happen, maybe never again. The hill had
definitely busted his dick string, so she lounged back and smoked a
Salem while he tried to explain that Americans were going to the
moon.

"Bullshit, Hank."

"No, I swear, in July they're going to the moon."

"How can you go to the moon? You can't even go to the Ashau
Valley? You can't even get a hard-on."

And then in July he came out alive and was back in Michigan, in
a darkened motel room, not sure who the naked woman asleep next
to him was, not remembering her long white body or her long
brown hair. The TV was on just like it was the day he left to go to
the war thirteen months before. Back during that time he'd come to
and squinted through the dirty windows of another hangover, and
they kept showing the pictures over and over and the volume was
off and it took him forever to get up and focus, and then he realized
he was looking at the churning footage of Bobby Kennedy lying in a

pool of blood in the kitchen of a Los Angeles hotel and that was the going-away party.

And this was his coming home. A discarded champagne bottle on the floor blew its cork and he came up all jangled and alert just in time to hear Neil Armstrong say that's one step for mankind.

Chapter Twenty-seven

Most of the wood was split and stacked when Earl stepped onto the deck outside Hank's room and waved at Jolene.

"He smells like a Porta Potty at the state fair. I'll feed him and wipe his nose but I'm not changing diapers, uh-uh," Earl said.

Jolene removed her gloves. "I'll be back in a minute." Broker nodded and resumed work. She followed Earl inside and the first thing she reacted to was the blaring volume on the television. Immediately she searched for the remote. "Very funny," she said when she found it where Earl had comically inserted it in Hank's limp hand. She picked it up, clicked off the set, and said, "You know how much he hates the Fox News Channel." She eyeballed Earl to see which face she was dealing with.

"C'mon, he isn't there. Allen says if you keep up that kind of talk you're going to have a problem with acceptance," Earl said.

Okay. It was his mean face. "I already have a problem with you," Jolene said flatly.

Earl moved on an oblique angle to her defiance and threw a menacing arm in the cat's direction. "You should do something about that goddamn cat." Ambush was now up, back arched at Earl's loud voice. "If it was up to me, I'd nail that damn cat to a tree."

. . .

The idea of Earl harming Ambush filled Hank with a normal anxiety that he found comforting compared to the bizarre terror he inhabited. Run, kitty, he thought. Get away from him.

Which Ambush did. She jumped lightly to the floor and sped from the room.

"I'd watch running my mouth about nailing things to trees," Jolene said under her breath.

"You know what they say?" Earl grinned. "To a man with a hammer everything looks like a nail."

"I'd watch my mouth if I were you," Jolene repeated, louder.

"Or what?"

"You said you were going to *talk* to Stovall," Jolene strained the words through set teeth.

"I did *talk* to him. He wouldn't talk back."

"So you got mad."

"Jolene, whatever I did I did for you. We're in it together. You told me all about his cutting hangups because he talked about them in AA. How the cops had to come unnail him from the bathroom door in the basement. Same wrist. I used the scar for a guide."

"You didn't have to waste the guy, goddammit."

"Me? He fucking *froze* to death. It wasn't suppose to get that cold."

"It was dumb and wrong and unnecessary," Jolene said. "Milt will be into the trust in a month . . ."

"Maybe, maybe not," Earl countered. "Hank's got an ex-wife in Michigan and one in St. Paul. They could tie it up."

"We're just lucky no cops have been going around interviewing all Stovall's clients," Jolene said.

"Hey"—Earl stabbed with his finger— "if I ever have to do any explaining, I'll explain the part about you feeding me his cutting habits first. Maybe we don't make it anymore, honey, but we're still linked at the hips—just like NoDak."

North Dakota. As always, Jolene recoiled from the memory of the ice age cold and that cowboy clerk's scuffed boot soles doing their backward flip. So she changed the subject. She took out a fresh diaper, a baby wipe, and talcum powder. She said, "How could you grow up and never change a diaper?"

Earl made a face. "That isn't a baby's butt; that's a rude old guy's."

Efficiently, Jolene peeled away Hank's gown, removed the diaper and, as she carried it to the diaper caddy, she wrinkled her nose. "Something's different," she said, weighing the sodden weight in her hand.

"Yeah, him out there, he's different," Earl said, jerking a thumb toward the muffled sound of splitting oak.

"He's handy," Jolene said. She dropped the diaper into the can and let the top fall. Then she swabbed Hank with a wipe and dusted him with talc. Then she scooted an arm under the small of his back and levered him up to slide the new diaper under him.

"The Yellow Pages are full of guys who are handy," Earl said.

"I kind of like this one," Jolene said, pulling Hank's gown into place.

Hank watched Jolene smile sweetly, undeterred by Earl's glower. Something was going on. Maybe some of the things he'd been trying to teach her the last year had taken root.

"Hey, look," Earl said, "you're almost a rich widow. You have this big house and you're surrounded by these guys who want to get into your pants. Allen for sure, maybe Milt, now this Broker guy . . ."

"Yeah, so, tell me something I don't already know," Jolene said.

"How about you need some protection. And guidance."

"Earl, what I'm trying to tell you is I don't need your kind of protection."

"Hey, wait a minute here, *you* called *me* up. You were all freaked out till I showed up," Earl protested.

Jolene smoothed wrinkles out of Hank's sheets. "True. I was. But now I'm better. And I don't need your protection," she repeated firmly. "That's why I have a lawyer."

Her last remark clearly alarmed Earl. "Hey, Jolene, word of advice. You try going from Wal-Mart to Nordstrom too fast, you're going to get the bends."

"Oh yeah? How'm I doing?" Jolene asked, sticking out her chin.

Now Earl threw his change-up and became genial. "Jolene, honey," he said, coming forward, arms wide as if to embrace her, "who's always been there for you?"

She moved in swiftly and poked a stiff finger into his sternum. "Right. And I appreciate it." Another poke. "And I'll make sure you're taken care of," she said.

"Taken care of?" Earl slapped her hand away, his expression curdled. "That sounds on the minimal side."

"Not at all. I kept track and wrote it all down in a notebook, the amounts you spent putting me through treatment and what you gave me the last few weeks. We'll come up with a figure we agree on. See?" And she let him have another sharp poke.

"Ow." The annoyance on Earl's face quick-fused to anger. He reached out and grabbed her hand below the wrist before she could poke him again. His knuckles blanched white and purple as he powerfully wrenched her toward him.

"You're hurting me," Jolene said between clenched teeth.

They glared at each other, Jolene up on her tiptoes, yanking her hand to free her trapped wrist.

Earl pointed out the window with his other hand, in the direction of the woodpile. "Cut the shit, Jolene. Now you get rid of him or I will. And if I do, it won't be pretty." He released her hand.

Jolene stepped back and triumphantly massaged the bruising already evident on her wrist. "You know what? I think you better watch yourself around this guy."

An awkward amount of time passed. Too long for a simple bed check. Broker had finished the wood and now waited, sitting on the chopping block with the maul across his knees. When Jolene left she'd been breezy and confident. When she finally stepped back out onto the deck and approached him she had washed her face and put on lipstick. And her posture and gait were guarded. She held her right arm tucked close, protectively.

"I think you better go," she said. Her eyes did not quite rise to his. "It's got a little tense around here."

"Uh-huh." Broker got to his feet.

"I don't know exactly how to put this." She glanced back at the house. "I'm afraid you could get hurt."

Broker ignored her last remark and tugged at the cuff of her right sleeve and saw the bracelet of blood bruising on her wrist.

"That's going to show," he said.

"I'll wear long sleeves."

"I owe your husband a big favor, more than chopping wood can repay," Broker said slowly.

Jolene shook her head. "Earl's my problem. And I have to learn how to handle him."

He could still walk away. But maybe this was his entry into the curious dynamics of this house. So he said it and went over the line. "How about I just teach him some manners."

After another of their loud silences, he reached in his pocket, pulled out his wallet, and removed a card on which was printed:

Broker Fixes Things
Carpentry, Electric, Plumbing
Landscaping

The card was history—an artifact of his undercover persona. He was following his reflexes but he was working in midair, without a badge, without authorization.

But it felt good.

He took a pen from his jacket pocket, crossed out the old Stillwater address, and wrote down J.T.'s phone number and handed her the card. "I'll be at that number for the next two days. You think about it."

Jolene looked at the card, then at him. "You sure?"

Broker nodded. "Like I say, you think it over. Now, I'm going to put this away and leave." He hefted the splitting maul, which weighed twenty pounds of forged steel. He carried it into the house and searched for the basement stairwell and followed a rising column of loud music and a steam of sweat, dirty laundry, and a faint under-scent of cannabis down the stairs off the kitchen.

Earl had converted the finished part of the basement into a computer crash pad. He had a futon, bench press, and weights in one corner. The rest of the space was a spaghetti junction of cables and lines connecting up two computers, two video monitors, a scanner, a TV and VCR, and a CD player set up on three tables. Piles of disks and software manuals littered the carpet.

Earl sat at his central computer nodding to the beat of 'NSYNC. Broker did not know the name of the group and vaguely understood that it was teeny-bopper music, and he wondered why a grown man was into those sounds.

Earl was selecting blocs of numbers off his screen and saving them to a file. Broker took a discreet step closer and studied the spreadsheet. Names. Addresses. Social security numbers. Sixteen-digit numbers grouped in fours. Then the heading: mother's maiden name. And names, hundred of them.

Hmmm.

Because of the music, Earl did not hear him approach, so Broker watched for a few moments as Earl scrolled up more columns of names and numbers. And it looked to Broker's cyber-challenged, but suspicious, eyes that Earl was in possession of a whole lot of other people's credit cards.

Broker reached down and took an envelope with Earl's name and a St. Paul address from a pile of bills on the desk and tucked it in his pocket. Then he leaned over and tapped off the CD.

Earl spun around, momentarily startled. Broker smiled and said, "Working hard, huh?"

Earl quickly moused an X in a box and closed the screen. "Code," he said.

"Code, huh?"

"Yeah, I'm consulting on an encryption project for this firm in Bloomington."

"Sounds complicated."

"Some people find programming elegant. Actually I think it's pretty fucking tiring," Earl said slowly, carefully watching Broker casually swing the maul in his right hand back and forth like a Stone Age intruder in Earl's little high-tech pod.

"I wouldn't know," Broker said.

"Tiring and stressful," Earl said. "Gets old pretty fast when you go through two million lines of code to find one comma out of place. I used to work for Holiday, you know, the chain of gas stations. Trouble-shooting their network."

"Sure, Holiday," Broker said.

"They own you twenty-four hours a day. Beep you in the middle of the night. You're not your own person." He positioned his feet to get up, and leaned forward and found the wedge blade of the maul jammed against his chest. "What the fuck?"

"Hey, that's one of those new, thin-screen jobs," Broker said, nodding at the trim-line monitor. "That must have cost a few bucks."

Earl started to get up again and this time Broker thumped him on the chest with the maul, causing him to drop back in his chair.

"I'm done with the wood, thought you'd like to know." Broker jabbed the maul harder.

Earl was not intimidated. He grinned and shook his head. "Take a minute to think, old man. When you came down those stairs you were looking at a bloody nose. Now you're headed for intensive care."

"Nah," Broker said, "I think you're just another of those point-and-click pussies." Broker heaved the maul, and the cool, liquid glaze of the screen exploded in a puff of glass and sparks in Earl's face. The maul handle clattered, overturning his keyboard.

"You, you," sputtered Earl as he knelt and yanked the monitor cords from an outlet box.

"Sorry, must be my Luddite tendencies coming out," Broker said.

Earl was puffed with fury but his shirt and eyebrows and hair and lap were dusted with sticky pieces of broken glass. His hands, which had balled into fists, now opened to wipe the debris away from his face and eyes.

"Don't touch her again," Broker said, then he whipped out his wallet, fingered out the hundreds that Earl had given him up north, and flung them in Earl's face.

Then he turned, walked up the stairs, out of the house, and got into the Jeep. He waited for a minute, watching the door to see if Earl would come out. It occurred to him that he probably needed a weapon if he was going to play these kinds of games again. But Earl didn't show. So he scribbled Earl's license plate on a scrap of paper, shifted into reverse, backed up, put it in first, and drove away.

Broker was smiling, enjoying the memory of the shocked look on Earl's face when his computer monitor turned to glitter dust. For the second day in a row he had come to Hank Sommer's house for the last time. He had a feeling he'd be back.

On his way to J.T.'s, Broker detoured through Timberry's main commercial drag and spent half an hour purchasing some items in a CompUSA.

Chapter Twenty-eight

Earl looked funny with shards of computer glass dusted in his hair and his eyebrows, so Jolene left him sputtering in the kitchen and went downstairs. She saw the chopping maul lying in the havoc of the computer screen like a collision between Earl's and Broker's worlds, and she laughed harder. Coming back up the stairs she continued to laugh. So he yelled at her to clean up the mess and she told him to go fuck himself and he started to come at her.

So she stabbed the straight finger in his chest again and said, "See, dummy, I told you not to mess with this guy."

Then that mean glower came over Earl's face that made him look like a blond Klingon on *Star Trek*. And he stomped off, and to make some kind of point he took the keys to Hank's Ford Expedition and drove off and left her alone.

Which suited her just fine and she had to smile. Broker, swinging his axe.

Feeling a little light-headed, she wandered into the living room and allowed herself one twirl. Whee. Sort of. When Hank had been . . . normal, the house was more like school and he was the teacher she got it on with between classes. Not really hers.

Now she liked being alone in the house; well, alone with the wreckage of Hank. She liked to walk through the rooms, trying them on.

The idea slowly forming.

Her house.

She turned the volume up on the baby monitor in the kitchen so she could hear Hank. Then she paced the living room and touched the old-fashioned couch with its fat arms outlined with fat brass tacks. For months they'd trolled the St. Croix Valley and western Wisconsin, hitting all the antiques shops, finding Mission Oak furniture and Tiffany lamps. Funny man. He'd worked hard to make the whole place look like an old Humphrey Bogart detective movie. She understood what Hank was trying to do, how he had made up this house like a movie set and arranged her among the furniture. He had reached a certain age and made some money, and he had tried to live his life like entertainment. Which was similar to trying to stay high all the time. Trying to make your life into a story that was smoother or more exciting than it really was.

What, in treatment, they called delusion.

The thing about stories, she thought, was that they have beginnings, middles, and tidy conclusions where they wrap up all the loose ends. But what if you're thinking you're in the long, happy middle and real life suddenly comes along.

She'd cut hair with a perky born-again named Sally during her hair-stylist phase, and Sally had two neat kids and a dutiful husband, and one day she opened her kitchen cabinet to reach for the cornflakes and found Death sneering her in the face.

Breast Cancer. Snap. Just like that it zipped through the lymph glands and into the lungs, the liver, the pancreas. And Jesus turned out to be on a different page of her story. Maybe he could raise the dead and turn water into wine in the Bible. But through a frigid Minnesota February he sat back and watched Sally wither and die in slow, irradiated nausea.

At the end of Sally's story they had to pour gas on the frozen dirt to warm it enough for the backhoe to dig her a hole to be buried in.

"Poor Hank," she said. She wasn't sure what Hank believed in, but she didn't think it was anywhere near Jesus.

To get sober you were supposed to admit you were powerless over alcohol and turn it all over to a Higher Power who could restore you to sanity. So far she'd faked her way through the Higher Power part, saying it was just other people. Mainly it had been Hank. Now he was gone and she wasn't sure about God, big G.

God sounded like another man she'd have to deal with at some point down the line.

So, with Hank gone, it was just natural that her Higher Power was going to be the Almighty Dollar. Until something better came along.

But right now her Higher Power was playing hard to get.

She walked through the living room into the alcove den and confronted the stack of bills on the desk. She'd sorted the envelopes into two piles. The first contained all the maintenance expenses that kept the house running, that Earl had paid for the month of October: mortgage, NSP, phone bill, cable TV, garbage and water, and three VISA cards.

The biggies went in the second pile; the hospital bills from Ely and Regions; the helicopter, the neurologist workup; and the consult, the MRI, nerve testing, the stomach feeding tube. They all had three zeros after the commas.

It all came down to the money. Hank knew that. Realistically, would she have married him if he were going to AA twice a week, working on a loading dock, and holding on by his fingernails?

Her dad had been like that—a good guy who drank a little too much and worked with his hands. Mom changed the locks and got a lawyer and then, when Dad was gone, she went to work as a secretary for the lawyer. Jolene was seven.

When she was ten, Mom married the lawyer and they moved from North Minneapolis to Robbinsdale. Mom had a bigger house with plastic covers on the upstairs living room furniture; she had new friends, she had parties and vacations.

When Jolene was fifteen the lawyer's eyes would follow her up and down the hall as she got dressed in the morning to go to school. But the lawyer never touched her. Neither did her mom. Jolene always had clean clothes and food and shelter and about a foot of Plexiglas between her and Mom. Jolene broke the suburban plastic pattern and ran away with Earl when she was sixteen.

She stirred the bills with her hand, willfully messing them up. She'd seen this show on the Discovery Channel; these experiments with orphaned chimpanzees where they'd put the apes in cages with mother surrogates which were these constructions and one of them, the wire mother, had food and water but was made of cold steel mesh. The other, the cloth mother, had no food but was heated wood and fabric. The baby chimps would go to the warm mother and hug her and stay there even when they started starving.

And that was the bottom line on drinking right there, it was hugs in a bottle.

Yeah, well, the last Jolene heard, her wire mother was living in Sarasota, Florida, and the lawyer had oxygen tubes in his nose, and fuck her for giving up on Dad.

Jolene fluffed her short-cropped hair, straightened up the bills, found a note she'd written to herself, and said "details." Then she picked up the phone and called the information desk at the Timberry Public Library.

An hour later, she was in the studio sickroom, turning Hank when the phone rang.

"Jo, it's Allen."

"How are you doing, Allen?"

"Well, Earl called me and he said he was a little worried about you. Apparently Broker came back today and they had a run-in."

"Yesss," Jolene said slowly.

"Earl did some checking. Have you heard of NCIC?"

"The national crime computer." She chided herself for knowing the answer a little too quickly.

"Well, before he was a friendly canoe guide he was something else. He's in the computer. Or someone with the exact same name is who did time in Stillwater Prison in 1989 for assault. There's some other charges about drug possession and stolen property."

"And?" Jolene was cautiously curious. A reformed con was a nice concept but was pretty much a liberal myth.

"I just want to make sure you're all right. Do you want me to drop by?"

Jolene evaluated the courting urgency just below the surface of Allen's voice and clicked her teeth. Dutiful Allen. Useful Allen. Everybody assumed Hank would die.

What if he didn't, what if he stayed there for years and years. What were her options, medically?

Allen could tell her when the time came, maybe help her

through IT. Briefly she imagined Allen, naked, in bed and she wondered if sex was more natural for him because he was used to putting his hands inside people's bodies.

"So you think it's serious?" she asked frankly.

"A police record is nothing to joke about."

"I could make a pot of coffee if you can get free."

"I'm in the clinic today, so I could come over for a while in
about an hour," Allen said quickly.

After Allen hung up Jolene turned to Hank and said in a practical voice, "I have to think about the future now. And I don't want
you to suffer any longer than necessary."

Jolene brewed up another pot of coffee in Hank's Chemex, following
the procedure Hank had taught her. She ground the beans—
Cameron's Scandinavian Blend, distributed in Hayward, Wisconsin—
for exactly seventeen seconds. Then she put one of the round white
paper filters in the glass beaker pot that looked like something from
her high school chemistry lab, added the coffee, and poured in the
boiling water.

She stepped back for a minute to let the grounds bloom.

It was the second pot of coffee for the second male visitor of
the day.

Moving right along. Her timing was perfect; the last of the coffee was dripping into the pot as Allen's Saab roared down the drive.

Okay.

She met him at the door wearing her brave smile but, when they
came into the kitchen, he saw the twinkle of glass on the floor. Must
have dropped from Earl's clothes and she'd missed sweeping it up.
She told Allen what had happened and, at the end of her story, she
leaned forward and rested her forehead briefly on his chest.

Like the hot water and the coffee grounds, Allen bloomed.

Then they sat down at the kitchen table and had their coffee,
and she confided in him. She told him how she'd got off to a bad
start letting Earl back in her life, and now, Broker was just trying to
help out and send Earl packing.

She hoped it didn't get rough.

She said she was really getting tired of having these kinds of guys in her life. Then she and Allen took their coffee to the study and Allen quickly did an examination of Hank, whose lungs were still clear and whose blood pressure was still normal, and clearly he was going to live forever that way.

And so Jolene just blurted it out, not caring how horrible it sounded, how she was afraid when all this was over, the court case and everything, how Hank could go on and on and she'd be—a few real tears creeping out now—a nun married to breathing cadaver for the rest of her life.

And she let Allen take her briefly in his arms. "Don't worry," he murmured, "I can help, if it comes to that."

"Shhh," she placed her cool finger to his lips and felt them flutter in a faint kiss. "Not now," she said. "Someday, but not now."

She could see Allen conjure intimacy in the tone of her voice and in her moist eyes.

Jolene withdrew her finger from his lips and took a step back. "Details," she said, brightening, blinking away tears. "And all for the want of a horseshoe nail."

"What?" Allen asked.

"The poem you mentioned, remember? It's anonymous. A doggerel, not really a poem, it's part of the *Real Mother Goose Rhymes*. I looked it up."

Allen was impressed.

As he drove away, he placed his right hand across his heart, like a civilian saluting the flag; except he was touching the place where Jolene had rested her head against his chest.

She had definitely reached out to him on a very delicate matter. And it wasn't as simple as a Do-Not-Resuscitate or a Do-Not-Intubate order. Hank's heart and lungs showed no signs of failing.

And he wasn't hooked to a ventilator, so it wasn't a case where the care provider could elect to end medical support and flip a switch.

Jolene could try to get a court order to withhold nutrition but that looked mercenary, and there would be a gruesome time element.

But if she did get a DNR-DNI order as a precaution against a

future incident, and if he discreetly induced a respiratory arrest—
that would work.

Yes, it would.

Earl came in around supper time smiling sweetly and carrying a
deluxe Domino's pizza and an armful of flowers, which he proceeded to place in makeshift vases around the kitchen. She gauged
the depth of his insecurity by his needy cow eyes; he was actually
watching her for signs that she might be willing to fool around
with him.

"What do you have now, friends in the cops? How'd you get on
the national computer?" she asked, ignoring his eyes tracking her
movements around the kitchen.

"Allen must have called," Earl said in a distracted voice, arranging flowers, sniffing them like Ferdinand the fucking bull.

"How'd you come up with a police record on Broker?" Jolene
asked as she turned on the oven.

"Easy. Those ads on TV for the online background checks: 'See
if anyone you know has a criminal record,' " Earl mimicked a hyped
broadcast voice. "Well, they're jacked into NCIC, so, since Broker
came on a little stronger than your run-of-the-mill canoe guy, I
typed in his name." Earl folded his arms and looked very concerned.
"I think you have to be real cautious around this dude."

"He *likes* me." She held up her bruised wrist. "It's assholes who
molest women that he's down on." She put the pizza in the oven.

"Ah, I'm thinking, if he gets rough again, I may need to bring in
a war elephant."

"Who?"

"I was thinking Rodney."

Aw, God, a name that brought back the dumb old days. While
she drove, Earl and Rodney would act out their comic-book fantasies with the guns, and they picked off three desolate 7-Eleven's in
the outer-ring burbs before she and Earl went off on their own and
had the bad experience in North Dakota that ended their stickup-
artist phase. Jolene shook her head. "Earl, Rodney's in jail. Remember his bright idea about stealing machine guns from the National
Guard?"

"He copped a plea and gave up a bunch of redneck militia types in Alabama, so he's on probation."

She shook her head, then narrowed her eyes, calculating. "Rodney's got bad genes, he's a second-generation crook, and, for my money, I see him as way too slow to handle Broker."

"What? Are we taking bets?"

"I'm just saying, Earl, that Rodney is a muscle-bound klutz, and I see Broker as quicker and smarter. And another thing, I don't want him anywhere near this house. I don't want Rodney to know where I live."

"C'mon Jolene. He's a friend."

"He'll eat everything in the refrigerator, then he'll sleep on the couch. When he wakes up he'll steal all the major appliances. No way."

"I'm still going to talk to him."

"I don't like it," Jolene said. But it held appeal as a test. Broker would have to prove himself in the street. She'd alert him, of course, then she'd settle back and watch. She innately understood playing people off against each other, but Hank had explained it was a popular business practice in corporate life, where they cut throats with paper memos.

They called it creative tension, and there was plenty of it to go around in this house.

"How's that pizza doing?" Earl asked.

"In a minute," Jolene said, her brow furrowed, thinking it through. Broker gets rid of Earl. Allen does the right thing by Hank. Then, hopefully, after a long, decent interval, Broker and Allen would both get lost in the long shadow of someone with real future potential, like maybe Milton Dane.

One floor down, Hank marshaled all his willpower to thaw his fingers. He felt sensations, little tickles, imbedded deep. Jolene was just a shadow wiping his chin, suctioning his mouth, bringing him his slosh. She flitted in and out of the room.

Hank focused all his energy. C'mon fingers.

C'mon.

Chapter Twenty-nine

Amy's shopping bags were stacked on the mud porch and she met him at the door. Before he could open his mouth she reached out and plucked a sliver of computer screen from the folds of his jacket and held it up. Then she cautiously dusted a fine sparkle of the glass from his chest.

"Broker, stay put. You're covered in broken glass," she said.

J.T. came through the door, observed that Broker, in fact, was sprinkled with tiny bits of glass, and said, "Hmmm."

Amy tilted her head. "What happened?"

Broker studied her and thought how she and Jolene were close in age but the comparisons ended there. Amy was someone you'd trust to watch your daughter and Jolene was the one you'd run off to South America with after you'd embezzled a million dollars and abandoned your family.

"There's this predatory dude camped out in Sommer's basement and he and I had this minor altercation," Broker said.

"Uh-huh, and why's he there?" J.T. asked.

"Well, he's the wife's ex-boyfriend."

"Uh-huh, and he sort of slid back in the picture after Sommer became a vegetable," J.T. speculated.

"The wife," Amy said with a sidelong glance to J.T. "I remember her at the hospital. She was what you'd call hot."

"She cut off her hair, she don't look so hot now," Broker said.

"So why did you and this guy get into it?" J.T. asked.

"Well, he sort of manhandled her . . ."

"And you didn't find her boring," Amy said with a wry down-turning of her lips, "and you came to the rescue. How gallant." Practical, she picked up a short broom J.T. kept in the corner of the porch and thrust it into Broker's chest. "Go outside and dust yourself off."

As Broker tidied up on the front porch, Amy came out in her parka, walked past him, descended the stairs, crossed the yard, and proceeded to walk back and forth along the fence next to the barn. A half-dozen female ostriches floated behind her like moody gray animations.

"You really have this way with women," J.T. said, coming up behind Broker. "She's getting ready to bail on you."

"Yeah, yeah." Broker handed J.T. the notepad with Earl's license number and the envelope with his name and his St. Paul address.

"What's this?"

"Could you run this guy for me, see what turns up?"

"You run him. Call John E. at Washington county. He'll do it for you."

"You still have a computer link to downtown. If I call John he'll want to know why. And if he finds out I'm snooping around he'll get curious about that, too. Next thing, unmarked cars will be following me around."

"Which is, like, their job—you know—sworn officers, they do shit like that if they pick up on suspicious behavior," J.T. said. "But, fact is, I could use your help around here over the weekend, so I'll do your scut work."

"Help?"

"I'm taking some birds to the slaughterhouse in the morning. The nearest USDA ostrich-approved butcher is in Iowa. And Denise's sister's place is on the way, so I'll spring Shami from school one day and take the family for a long weekend. Leave in the morning, be back Sunday night. If, that is, you'll feed and look after the stock."

"Three days," Broker said, liking the excuse to stick around.

"Friday, Saturday, Sunday."

"I can do that. I don't know about her." He pointed to Amy, who continued to meditate back and forth along the fence.

"Tell her you'll have the place to yourself, the two of you. You know, during the day you can go over to Sommer's and rescue the hot wife, then you can come back here and play house with her. Get in a lot of practice that way." J.T. smiled.

Gingerly, Broker approached Amy and chose his words carefully. "J.T.'s asked me to keep an eye on the place until Sunday night," he said.

Amy took her time, with a sweet smile. Then she reached out and tapped him once on the chest. "I agreed to ride along for your hunch. But I'm going to skip your midlife crisis."

She pulled a Mesaba Air Lines schedule from her pocket. Mesaba was the commuter air link from the Cities to points north. "I stopped by the airport on the way back from the mall. I'm going to see about a flight tomorrow. You will give me a ride to the plane?"

"Of course."

"If you were smart you'd go back with me," she said. "It doesn't sound like a good situation over there, Sommer being at home instead of in a full-care facility. It sounds, well, dysfunctional."

She was right, of course. When he didn't respond, she continued. "Scenes like that tend to have these messy internal dynamics. They tend to drag well-meaning outsiders down to their level."

Broker looked up at several female ostriches who bobbed their heads in big-eyed agreement behind Amy. After her sensible advice had faded, he asked, "So tell me something?"

"Sure."

"Why does he look at me when I first walk into the room. I mean, right in the eyes. Just like somebody you know. Then his eyes start to roam."

"That could be primitive reflexes, a reacting to shapes and sounds. Residual brain-stem stuff."

"What do you look for if you think someone's coming out of a coma?"

"False hope in the eye of the beholder," Amy said.

"C'mon."

"Okay, you look for signs of conscious thought and motor control. Blinking in patterns comes to mind. One for yes, two for no. If you have that you can progress to an alphabet board and communicate."

J.T. appeared on the porch holding a cordless phone. "So what's the plan?" he called.

"She's catching a flight north tomorrow. I'm staying to watch the birds," Broker yelled back.

J.T. waved and went into the house talking on the phone.

Broker said, "I need to stay and help him out."

Amy nodded. "You guys are pretty good friends."

Broker thought about it. "We were partners, we respect each other, but I don't think we were ever good friends," he said.

Amy inclined her head. "Why not?"

Broker shrugged. "We've talked this out over the years. Maybe it's semantics. But we figured it's a stretch for an intelligent white guy and an intelligent black guy to call themselves friends in this country. Especially if they're cops."

"But you get along great," Amy said.

"Yeah, but would our *friends* get along, see? The problem is always other people," Broker said. "As long as we've known each other, after work, we'd go unwind in different bars, we went home to different neighborhoods. It's like two religions that coexist but can't really mingle and still be themselves. So we belong to different-skin religions. It's the term we made up to simplify things."

"I don't know if I like the implications of that way of thinking," Amy said.

"I can dig it. You can afford to be liberal. You're from Ely, where the biggest minority is timber wolves, with tourists a close second."

They walked back toward the house. Halfway, she stopped him with a hand on his elbow. "I was right, wasn't I, Sommer's wife doesn't bore you?"

"Amy, I won't play games with you."

She shook her head and released her fingers from his arm and said, "You won't answer me, either."

J.T. walked Broker through the feeding and watering routines. He'd already mixed his feed and run hoses. All Broker had to do was scoop and dump and turn spigots. Before supper, Amy and Broker helped Shami and J.T. load nine birds in a horse trailer. Loading involved selecting and moving birds from the outdoor holding pen into one of two smaller stalls inside the barn. The door on the stall was chest-high, inch-thick, reinforced plywood hinged to swing out away from the stall into the lower level of the barn where J.T. had backed up his trailer. When the door was open, it formed one half of a funnel; the trailer door supplied the other half.

If a bird was passive they moved in on either side and grabbed a wing and steered her into the trailer. And seven of the nine ostriches went easily. Two of then were touchy and aggressive. So J.T. gave Broker a long-handled barn shovel to fend off an attack by placing the blade across the bird's breast if she charged.

He repeated his warnings about staying beyond the kick radius. And moving to the side of a bird, never frontally. As Broker held the bird at bay with the shovel, J.T. danced in and grabbed the head and quickly slipped on a black sleeve. Once hooded, the bird became docile.

As they maneuvered the second feisty female into a corner, hooded her, and put her in the trailer, the walls of the adjoining pen shook with sledgehammer impacts.

Popeye, the truck killer, was announcing his presence.

They closed the door of the left stall and J.T. pointed to the identical door of the right stall. Popeye hovered and hissed, his angry eyes nine feet above the floor, his wings up and out in a rampant threat display.

"I don't want you going into his pen when I'm gone. Just drop the feed over the door into the side of the feeder and turn on the faucet. I'm serious. Don't open this door, and you *never* want to be in front of him when his wings are up," J.T. lectured.

In the house, as they were washing up for supper, the phone rang and Denise called out. "A call for Mr. Phil Broker from a Mrs. Jolene Sommer."

Amy, helping set the table, did not look up. She shook her head slightly and continued placing silverware. Broker took the phone from Denise.

"Broker?"

"Yes."

Jolene said, "Earl did some checking around and found a Phil Broker in a police computer who did time in Stillwater in 1989 for aggravated assault. Anybody we know?"

Broker exhaled audibly and did not answer.

"Yeah, well, Earl's feeling a little lonely and threatened and is off looking for a friend of his whose brains are all down in his neck, if you know what I mean. I just thought you should know it could get rough if you're thinking of coming back over here."

There was this interesting new edge to Jolene's voice. Daring him.

Broker could feel Jolene gauging his silence on the other end of the connection. After an interval, she asked, "Are you?" she paused, then added, "Thinking of coming back here?"

Her voice skipped pretense and caution and cut straight to the danger. And it was Jay and the Americans in Broker's head, and she was defying him to come a little bit closer. And she knew he knew it. It was just that simple.

And he was just that dumb. And she knew that, too.

Do it. Go.

"How about in an hour?"

"I'm here." She hung up.

Broker hung up, turned, and Amy was standing two feet behind him.

"For what's it's worth, I think you're headed for trouble," Amy said simply as he stepped around her.

Good. About time something happened.

Broker had lost his appetite, so he walked out to the Quonset hut and levered open the door to his mangled truck. He reached behind the seat, under a tarp, and removed a winter-survival pack containing some highway flares and clothing. Then he took out a 12-gauge shotgun, shells for it, and a sack of cleaning tools.

He sat on the bent running board and disassembled the old Mossberg, a practical, no-frills farm gun with a cut-down, barely legal, barrel, which he swabbed, and sprayed some WD 40 on the slide and the safety. He reassembled the piece and worked the slide, thumbed the safety on, then off, and cleared it. Satisfied it was in working order, he stuffed four double-aught rounds into the magazine, wracked one in the chamber, set the safe, and wrapped it in a blanket. Then he took the gun and the survival bag to the Cherokee loaner. He folded down the rear seat, making a handy compartment so he could quickly reach back, flip up the prone rear seat backrest, and access the weapon. Then he tucked the box of double-aught shells and his survival kit in with the gun.

As he shut the Jeep door and turned around he saw J.T. standing in front of him with a manila folder in his hand.

"This guy isn't that heavy," J.T. said.

"Really?"

J.T. opened the folder and handed Broker a sheet of fax paper. He squinted at the smudged writing on the ruled form. It was a fax of a photo negative, an old police report from Redmond, Washington.

> Officer responded to report of a fight at the Microsoft offices. Subject was a programmer who had an argument with a superior and assaulted the CEO who tried to intervene. Subject was arrested and escorted from premises and held overnight. No assault charges filed.

"So nothing, so that's it?" Broker said, smiling slightly, but not entirely relieved. His instincts told him Earl Garf was still trouble.

"But look where it happened. Microsoft. So, for the hell of it, I called out there. They're two hours behind and I got a sergeant in records who remembered the incident."

"Good memory."

"Not exactly, what he said was, 'Oh, yeah, the guy who took a swing at God. He'll never work in the computer industry again.' "

"God, huh?" Broker said.

"Yeah, your boy Earl tried to punch out Bill Gates. Know what else the Redmond cop said? He said that if he would have controlled his temper and kept his nose to the grindstone he'd be a cyber millionaire now. He was in on the ground floor. They fired him and rescinded all his stock options before they were vested."

"That's interesting. But this guy is still an asshole," Broker said.

"But not exactly a heavyweight," J.T. said. Then he paused with droll apprehension, "unless . . ."

"Unless what?" Broker grinned.

"Unless he's the vampire," J.T. said, raising his eyebrows in mock-foreboding. The vampire was their lingo for the hypothetical perp who didn't cast a reflection in mirrors, who left no trace, no fingerprints or tracks. Who was way too smart to get caught.

They both laughed. And Broker said, "I don't think so. He's just another asshole who deserved to be jammed up, and that's what I'm going to do. I'm going to chase him off and give Sommer's wife some breathing room."

"So, you want some company so you don't fuck this guy up too much?" J.T. asked with a flavor of the old days in his tone.

"It's not like that," Broker said.

"Right. Story of your life. Nothing is what it looks like, huh?" J.T. shook his head.

Broker climbed into the Jeep and turned the key. "I'll be back tonight."

"Sure you will," J.T. said.

Chapter Thirty

The constellation Orion tilted on the horizon like a sideswiped road sign, and Broker was driving way too fast and thinking how his whole life had been a struggle to stay within the rules. His distaste for procedure had turned his stint in law enforcement into a personal method-acting spree. No one had ever stayed undercover for ten years. But he had. In local cop gossip, the Broker Syndrome superseded the Stockholm Syndrome.

And apparently Earl had pulled up some relic of Broker's old undercover persona that was still floating around in the computers. Obviously, the "revelations" had favorably impressed Jolene Sommer. Broker, driving seventy mph down a winding country road, wasn't about to discourage her.

Even his idea of settling down had been extreme, marrying a woman who wanted to be Joan of Arc. But he had tried to live in a conventional world of rules. *I do. For better or worse. Daddy.*

Didn't work.

The cold fields and tree lines sparkled with willful diamonds of excitement in his high beams. He was playing with other people's lives. Yeah, well, he didn't belong pulling a plow, did he?

So take a break. Take a chance. Blow the carbon out of your pistons.

You're bargaining. That's what Nina would say if she were here.

She wasn't jealous. She knew the score. The world was complicated. Stuff happened. *But we do believe in consequences, don't we?*

Jolene was a passing opportunity, and latching on to her could be a revenge game. Was he getting back at Nina? Maybe.

Probably.

And as he turned into the driveway and snaked between the old pine trees he thought how this wasn't for Sommer anymore, was it?

This was for him.

He looked around. No sign of Earl's van. It could be in the garage. Broker didn't care. Bring him on.

Before he got out, he saw her silhouette framed in a rectangle of light in the open doorway with a hip against the jam in the oldest posture in the world.

And as he came up the steps, still not able to see her face, just her shape, he wondered who she was and would he ever find out. And it wasn't like adultery because he was separated and she was basically a widow, and like Amy said, she just observed a shorter decent interval than most people. And apparently, tonight, so did he.

"So," she said. No perfume. No candles, no wine, no fire in the fireplace. She looked careworn in a pair of old jeans and a faded green blouse, and her short hair was frazzled and her green eyes were beyond weary. Just—*so, here we are.*

Fast through the darkened house, wordless down the stairs into the bedroom. Broker looked once at the closed door to Sommer's studio, then he winced at the baby monitor on the bedside table. The deep, distant sound of Hank Sommer's breathing rose and fell like surf.

"He's asleep," she said as she reached over and turned the volume down on the monitor.

"Earl?"

"Off brooding. Probably plotting against you. I don't expect him back until late tonight, if at all," and she turned off the light. And it was just her shape again, defined by a night-light. Like in the doorway.

When he reached for her she pulled back long enough to look seriously in his eyes and say, "Just never lie to me, okay?"

It was the only pause before they got at each other.

· · ·

"I'm starting to think sex is like a shakedown cruise. It's how you really get to know somebody," Jolene said to the darkened ceiling when her breathing returned to normal.

"I never thought of it like that," Broker said. He was surprised at how tentative their physical introduction had been. He'd come at this thinking it would be impulsive, like feeding time at the tiger house. Everybody definitely getting their whiskers wet. Yet, while the lovemaking was carnal, the intimacy was chaste. She had been fragile, almost like she was holding her breath the whole time. Now she looked vulnerable and double-naked in the faint light. Dutifully, she'd turned the volume back up on the monitor, and now Hank's sleeping breath haunted the dark room.

And Broker was thinking how when you're young and in bed with a new woman it was an occasion for ego and vanity and it was all surface sensation. Because when you're young, basically, all you own is your body.

But when you grew older and had been knocked around in a couple marriages, it went deeper than your skin. Now he felt like a trespasser in someone else's life. And he'd taken a flyer on impulse and overlooked precautions. He was very aware it wasn't his bed. Broker looked around to make sure he knew where the exits were.

Jolene sat up and hugged the sheets around her. "I used to think sex was about people possessing each other. I'd get jealous. I needed a lot of reassurance." She smiled a wry smile and touched the hair on his chest. "Of course, I was drinking then."

"It's okay," Broker said, and immediately he regretted the words because they were the same tone and weight of feeling he used with his little daughter when she suffered a minor hurt. "I mean . . ." he started to say.

"Shhh," she stilled him with a cool finger to his lips. "It's not okay. When you're dependent, you do things. Things . . ." She shook her head and her eyes swam up, conjuring. Quickly, she masked the brightness in her gaze with a raw expression. "I worked as a dancer in this scummy joint once. I took it all off and stuck it in their faces. And they'd tuck dollar bills in my . . ." She grimaced, looked away. "Dollar bills. You'd think I would have held out for fifties or at least twenties."

"Jolene." Broker sat up, simultaneously feeling an urge to hold her and to run. Like a lot of things lately, this was not turning out the way he'd pictured it.

She grinned at him and it was the kind of grin that would be cruel if it wasn't on a wild animal that didn't know better. "Sobriety changes you, all right," With a faint curl to her lip, she said, "I used to have a pussy. Now I have a vagina." She raised an eyebrow. "That's progress."

"Take it easy," Broker said.

"*You* take it easy," she shot back, coming up off the sheets, suddenly sharp and brittle. "You're only the second guy in my life I've ever been in bed with sober. You got that?"

In the awkward silence that followed they both pulled away a little and covered themselves with the sheets. Broker had the distinct impression they were both wishing they could smoke a cigarette. She was the first to break the silence, speaking to the ceiling.

"Earl's waiting for me to give it up, start drinking and crawl back to him. Christ, Allen; he's like a little kid waiting for a cookie. You—you're not so easy to figure," she said.

"What's hard to figure?"

Jolene turned on her side, propped herself on an elbow, and her hand unconsciously explored the missing waves and volume of her shorn hair. She said, "How many guys show up to return a car and wind up in bed with the lady of the house in two days?"

The lady of the house. So that's who she was.

Broker sat up in full-blown character and scratched his chest. "You mean guys who go to work and do what their asshole bosses tell them to do, who drive the speed limit, who watch their wives get fat, and who sneak dirty movies and beat their meat?" He cocked his head at her, reached out, and gently tapped her lips with his index finger. "You opened the door, not me."

She brushed the remark aside. "The thing about you is no flaws, no character defects. You've never really been weak or sick, have you?" She sat up and the sheet fell away from her breasts and, like Allen had predicted, they were perfect 36 Cs that stayed tucked and pointed on their own. "Can we cut the bullshit?" she said.

"I'm all for that."

"You spent time inside, right?"

"C'mon, I spent twenty-three days in Stillwater; I was barely through with orientation when my lawyer got my conviction thrown out."

"Technicality?"

"Hell, no. The cops got a snitch to lie."

"And?"

"Some people I know got him to tell a different lie. What's the big deal? It was a long time ago. And that's not who I am anymore," he said emphatically.

"But you did things."

"Did things?" Broker frowned. "What is this? You'll show me yours if I'll show you mine?"

"We already did that. You did things," she repeated.

"I did things," he affirmed.

"What things?"

"Look, Jolene. Some people, when they're young, they don't go in for nine-to-five, you understand?"

She squinted at him. "Answer the question."

Inwardly excited, he smiled. He was auditioning, like he was on the job again. But he wasn't working. That part of his life was over. So what was he doing?

Pretending?

Broker winced. "Okay. Probably not the kind of things that you think. I arranged things."

"That's a little vague," she said.

"I used to believe people should have the right to smoke grass and own guns, okay?"

"Your conviction is for assault."

"When you arrange things, you guarantee the bona fides of the seller and the buyer, and you secure the transaction. If someone gets out of line, you have to straighten them out."

Jolene again evaluated his words and matched them to his expression, to the relaxed potential of his body. "But you don't do that kind of stuff anymore?" she inquired.

"These carloads of very heavily armed black guys started showing up from Chicago and L.A. Crack changed the whole street scene and I got out ten years ago. I made some money and socked it in a little resort up on the North Shore before real estate went through the roof. It was a good investment and I'm comfortable. I suppose getting older had something to do with it."

"But you still keep your hand in?" she asked.

"Say what you mean."

She sat up straighter and swung her head, tossing hair that was no longer there. "You said you owed Hank."

"I owe Hank."

"I need you to arrange something."

"Go on," Broker said cautiously.

"I need you to get rid of Earl."

"Wait a minute." Broker held up his hands. "I don't do . . ."

"No, no, silly; I mean I want you to put Earl back where he was before Hank's accident. Which is at a polite distance and respecting boundaries. I don't want him hurt. At least not hurt too bad. And I want him to understand I'm going to pay him what I owe him."

Broker was relieved at the genuine sound of her request which fit the dimension of the debt he owed her husband. And he was consoled that his guilty little fling had now moved on to a practical next step.

"So?" Jolene prompted him.

"I can do that," he said.

"There's one thing I want you to understand," she said. "I want you to remove Earl from my life. I do not want you to replace him."

"Jesus," Broker grinned and shook his head. "You don't exactly go through a lot of Kleenex, do you?" He reached for his pants.

"I have feelings," Jolene said circumspectly, "but I keep them to myself."

They stood on the back deck, collars turned up as the evening chill syphoned off the baked-bread warmth of the bedroom. Broker smoked a cigar and watched the running lights of a solitary boat on the slowly freezing St. Croix River. When he turned, he could see into Hank's studio sickroom through the patio doors. Hank was illuminated in his bed by a lamp—still life with coma.

Like when he was working and trampled on people, he rationalized the twinge of guilt, telling himself he was out to get a bad guy.

"Earl and I did things, too," Jolene said. "But we never got caught. I guess we were social criminals," she reflected. "Sort of like social drinkers, you know; they quit when it starts interfering with their lives."

"What things?" Broker grinned as he mimicked her voice and tone.

"Remember that movie *The Color of Money*? Mary Elizabeth Mastrantonio and Tom Cruise, you remember them?"

Broker nodded. "I remember, they were two punks and Paul Newman taught them to be hustlers."

"Two *talented* punks, thank you. Well, that was us completely. Especially Earl. He was this brash, talented jerk. And I guess he still is. And I even look a little like Mastrantonio, don't you think? There's some Italian on my mother's side."

Broker studied her. "She has more hair, you're taller. What things?"

She squirmed away, evading in a wheedling voice. "You *know*, stealing things, selling dope. Dumb kid's stuff. Then we moved to Seattle and Earl got real heavy into computer code on the ground floor at Microsoft. For a while it seemed like we'd straightened out, but his temper got him in trouble. We split up for a while when he joined the army. He was in Desert Storm, all dressed up with nowhere to go. He felt cheated. Then he came home and we disappeared into Seattle during our Kurt Cobain–Courtney Love period. Earl meddled in coke and cyber crime and I got very heavy into drinking."

Broker shook his head. "Kurt who?"

She smiled and patted his cheek. "That's what I like about you. Anyway, we woke up one morning and I decided I had to get clean, so we came back to Minnesota."

"And that's when you met Hank?"

"My hero." Jolene smiled fondly. "The thing about heroes is first they save you, then they try and change you. He tried to explain to me that you don't have to settle for the life they give you. He said that's what this country is all about. It's why people left Europe and came here in the first place. They were criminals and were persecuted, but they came here because it was this new thing in the world, in history . . ."

Jolene stretched her hands and attempted to grasp something in the air.

"I didn't really hear what he was saying until after his accident. Now I'm beginning to understand. Being sober is my New World. People can change. Look at you, you changed, didn't you?"

Broker, blindsided by her earnest language, didn't trust his voice and remained silent. She continued talking.

"Except I made one big mistake. I panicked when Hank left me in this money bind. Now Earl thinks . . ."

Broker shrugged. "Can you blame him? Any man you take up with right now is going to have one eye on a huge malpractice settlement."

"Including you?"

"I just said it." Broker nodded his head toward the house. "But this isn't me."

She regarded him from the corners of her eyes. "So you don't want the money and you don't really want me . . ."

"Hey, I don't want to put my suitcase in your closet. But I wouldn't mind seeing you again," he said.

Jolene laughed and unburdened the thought that was on her mind. "The problem with you is you're too good to be true."

Broker shivered at her words, the way they sailed into the dark on her silken breath. He shied away when she poked a finger into his ribs. "Just another hero, huh? Like Hank. He never expected us to go the distance. He said it's one of the big stories in life. People grow at different speeds. He figured I'd outgrow him the way I outgrew Earl." She squared her shoulders and the cold night air was all the makeup she needed. "I'm just getting started," she said.

Broker asked, "So you figure out where you're headed?"

She inhaled, exhaled. "Just so we understand each other, I like you and I want to see you again, but I don't see us, like, together long-term. The next guy I get involved with seriously will be somebody with fewer rough edges. Somebody *safe*."

"Somebody you can control?"

"I didn't say that." She came up on tiptoes and kissed him, a frank, direct kiss midway between friendship and everlasting damnation.

When the kiss ended she was practical. "About Earl—sometimes when he's upset he can get, well, violent. And he knows some pretty thuggy guys."

"What I have in mind doesn't involve rough stuff," Broker said. "But I need to get at his computer for a couple of hours. Are you sure he won't be back tonight?"

"Pretty sure."

"I had a peek at his computer screen and it looked like he was collecting credit card numbers."

"Credit unions. He hacks into credit unions and cleans out all the credit cards and sells them on the web." Jolene smiled. "He swears he only drains off money from very wealthy people, like Robin Hood. What are you going to do?"

"I have a set of disks for his Zip Drive in the car. If you'll play lookout, I'll copy his hard drive. Then, if he agrees to move off from you an appropriate distance, say after a few years, he can have the copies back. He doesn't agree, we go to plan two and the disks wind up with the computer-crimes investigator at Washington County, and your basement will be full of cops and Earl goes away."

"Not bad," Jolene said.

Chapter Thirty-one

Jesus, it was a dump. A dump on Arcade on the east side of St. Paul where the mooks went to watch women get naked and rub up against them. And the air was poisonous with cigarette smoke, and he could see some very questionable substance fouled in the nap of the cheap orange carpet next to his shoe which wasn't even dry yet. There was a bar and tables, and these alcoves with overstuffed chairs where the dancers did their thing.

And that's where Earl found Rodney, sunk in one of the chairs under a lap dancer who was chewing gum and working her hips to the beat of the Righteous Brothers, "You've Lost That Loving Feeling." Earl looked away. He was off human intimacy for the time being. He preferred to jack into high-shock plastic and a thick glass screen where the action was kept crisp, internal, and sanitary. People were just too messy. Even perfect-looking people like Jolene could be messy. Even Jolene leaked once a month.

Fluids. Sweat. Tears. He thought briefly of Cliff Stovall in the woods.

Blood.

Pissed and shit himself, too. Disgusting.

His fault. Not mine.

Earl went back to watching Rodney and thought, *I should throw him a fish. This should be a cow humping a big seal. Rodney should be going arf, arf.*

"C'mon, Rodney, we got to talk, man."

Rodney was stretched out on the divan chair, arms alternately bracing on the fat cushions or twitching at his sides. There was a sign on the wall: PATRONS AREN'T ALLOWED TO TOUCH THE GIRLS WITH THEIR HANDS. But he could squirm his hips as much as he wanted. So his legs were spread and an ample G-string-and-pasty-clad transplant from West Virginia named Mavis was lashing him with her long, braided blond tresses as she straddled his hips and pumped him in sync with the music.

Earl knew who Mavis was because this wasn't the first time he'd met Rodney here and had to sit though one of her dry humps. She had bruises on her thighs and they looked about to pucker. All right for now, but headed for the cottage cheese shelf.

Rodney's head was thrown back and a silver chain glistened on his fleshy neck, and every time Mavis socked it to him, the Thor's Hammer medallion on the chain jiggled in a fold of sweat.

Like the governor's, Rodney's shaved head tapered smoothly up out of his overdeveloped neck. When the feds had him sweating down in seg at Oak Park Heights, he'd panicked. He'd imagined he heard moans in the dark and he felt the walls go clammy with nightmare sweat. In one of his worse moments, he had tattooed a swastika on the end of his prick with a tiny safety pin and a Bic refill. He did this as a token of goodwill toward the Aryan Nation. Any minute now Rodney hoped that his Nazi logo would squirt ecstatic black spiders.

"Rodney?"

"Almost," Rodney panted. "I'm close."

"C'mon, Rodney, this is taking all night," Mavis said. "You're into deep overtime, my man."

"Just a little more," Rodney said.

"Rodney, baby, like—I'm getting all chafed raw. You can't leave that zipper open like that. You know the rules." She gingerly climbed off him and kissed him on his shiny skull. "Better luck next time." Rodney held up a handful of bills. She plucked them and jiggled off into the gloom.

Rodney watched her go, pouting, "Thirty-two, man, and it's all over. Just can't get it up anymore."

Earl shook his head. "Give up the steroids, Rodney. They're shrinking your testicles into snow peas."

"Yeah, yeah." Morosely, Rodney zipped his fly and struggled to his feet. Six foot three, 260, twenty-four-inch arms. He could bench six hundred. Earl's war elephant. "C'mon," he said, "let's get some grease."

They cruised and debated restaurants and settled on a Famous Dave's.

"You're buying, right?" Rodney asked as they settled into a booth.

"Sure. Go for it."

When the waitress arrived, Rodney recited, "I'll have the giant slab of ribs, double cornbread, two cobs of corn, and bread pudding for dessert."

They made small talk about the weight room until the food arrived. Rodney was always more agreeable eating. Halfway through the rack of ribs, Rodney looked up and wiped his chin. "So what exactly you want to do?"

"Scare a guy," Earl said.

"How scared you want him?"

"Like a broken-knee scared. Louisville Slugger scared."

"What'd he do?"

"He's bothering Jolene. I want him to go away."

"Jolene." Rodney's eyes revolved and were dreamy for a moment. "She still quit getting high?"

Earl nodded. "Started going to meetings."

"Yeah, and married some old guy?"

"Uh-huh, except the old guy's dying and this other dude is bothering her."

"And this is something you can't handle on your own?"

Earl leaned forward. "I just want you for backup. I don't want to work up too much of a sweat."

"Right," Rodney smirked. "You're the brain, this messy physical stuff is beneath you."

"I'm the one using the bat, Rodney."

"Sure, right. So who is this guy?"

"He's from up north, he guides canoe trips in Ely." Earl was about to explain the connection, but he decided not to. Rodney had been spooked in Oak Park Heights and had been doing a lot of coke. He didn't follow stuff the way he used to.

Like right now. Rodney was staring at the carnage of rib bones on his plate, his eyes kind of misfiring and trying to focus. He said, "You know, I gotta be careful."

Earl nodded his head. "Look. This guy is going to take one look at you and shit his pants."

Rodney squinted at him. "Yeah? There's two kinds of guys who shit their pants. There's the kind who shits and freezes and there's the kind who shits his pants more like—what it is—a figure of speech that floods him with testosterone and adrenaline, you dig?" Rodney spread his lips in a lazy shark grin with strings of pork and gristle stuck between his teeth. "Then this second kind of guy comes over and kicks the living dog shit *out of you.*"

"Not this guy," Earl said. "This guy is over the hill, almost fifty. He'll be scared. I guarantee. Then I'll touch him up a little with the bat and he'll head back for the sticks."

"You ever seen the inside of Oak Park Heights?" Rodney asked suddenly.

"Christ, Jesus, no," Earl said indignantly. They sent people who did his kind of crime to Sandstone, the federal lockup north of Hinckley which was a country club compared to OPH. In fact, Sandstone was like a postgraduate seminar in computer hacking; they had some sharp operators in there. A guy could learn a lot.

"It's like this big rectangular basement, four levels of meatlocker buried in the ground, and down in the middle they have this yard. There's a baseball diamond and all, but it's hardly ever used, and you look out through this narrow window with these two fat bars called mullions and there's three tiny flower beds and this one tree they just planted. This one skinny little sapling that probably will never make it through the winter. And that's what you see for the next twenty years."

Rodney shook his head. "One fucking little tree. Man, growing up in Minnesota, I always took trees for granted."

"Rodney," Earl said firmly, trying to bring the guy back on task. "Tomorrow night. I'll pick you up."

"And go where?"

"He's staying out on this farm in Lake Elmo."

Rodney's eyes balked and his broad forehead furrowed. "Canoes? Farms? This really is not my preferred line of work."

"Look. We get him alone, he sees you and is paralyzed with fear. I whack him around a little and give him his walking papers and that's it. You earn three hundred bucks for just standing around. How's that?"

"That's fine, if it goes down like that." Rodney held up a greasy rib bone and gestured. "But if it looks in any way funny, I'm out. If I look sideways they're going to bust me. I ain't gonna get raked over on account of something pissant like this." ·

"Don't worry. Look, I need one favor. Trade cars with me tonight. I have to snoop around to make sure where he's staying and he knows what I drive."

Rodney shoved his car keys across the table, caught Earl's toss.

"Take it easy on the wheels, it's Jolene's husband's Expedition. And here," Earl slipped him a folded hundred. "Go back and get your lap wet. See you tomorrow."

"Yeah, and yeah," Rodney said, snapping a rib bone between his molars and sucking on the end.

Earl took 94 east to the river, then turned south on 95 and cruised the house in Rodney's Trans Am. He turned off his headlights and slowly rolled down the driveway. Uh-huh. Like he figured. Broker's busted-down Jeep was still there. Settling in.

Okay. His mind raced ahead. First get rid of Broker. That would give Jolene some space to climb down off her high horse. She'd come around. She was bound to come around not sleeping for a week. He just hoped she didn't start hitting the bottle again.

So Earl backed up the drive and went up the dead-end access road and waited in a small park where the road intersected the highway. Where he'd have a good view of passing cars. He put on his Walkman and ran some Eminem.

Three times through the tape, more than an hour later, Earl was shuffling his shoes in the compost of Burger King wrappers clogged around Rodney's accelerator when a pair of high beams cut the gloom: the beat-up red Jeep. Okay.

"Got in the cookie jar, didn't you, you fuckin' hick," Earl said grudgingly as he eased onto the road and followed the Jeep, still keeping his lights off, seeing by the faint light of a sickle moon. "So you're feeling pretty good."

He and Jolene weren't that way anymore and hadn't been for years. More like weird siblings. Whatever. Think of something more pleasant. Like what a boost it was going to be swinging the bat into Broker's knee. He visualized the patella and tibia powdering. He would see Broker crawl. See him cry.

The fantasy brought an agreeable flush.

This was what he wanted. Screw Microsoft and all the time he spent in that fucking desert over there, never once firing his weapon. Sometimes he figured the only real thing he'd done in his life was finishing off that gut-shot store clerk in North Dakota after Jolene messed it up. He didn't count Stovall as a kill. That was an accident. Either way, it was Jolene who got him into both of those scenes.

Just like she was getting him into Broker, who, he hoped, would take a cue and go away with just a broken leg.

Well, he'd know pretty soon.

By now the ride was getting tricky, and Earl had to let his fantasies go and pay more attention to following the Jeep through a back-road grid until it finally turned into a darkened farm. Earl drove on by and parked behind the first tree line past the house. Just a hundred yards away, he watched the lights come on in the house, probably the kitchen, then the bathroom, then they switched off.

He waited another ten minutes, then he walked back toward the house, past the tall shadow of the barn where some kind of animals were moving around behind a fence. Earl shivered, nervous now, worried about dogs. But there were no dogs and he used a pencil flashlight to copy the number off the mailbox. Then he stepped onto the lawn and wrote down the fire number. He'd driven UPS delivery in the sticks and knew that fire numbers were the most reliable way to quick reference a residence. Just call up the local sheriff's office and tell them you're a lost UPS driver and give them the fire number; the rural cops' dispatcher would talk you right in. And that's what he'd do tomorrow.

Sleep tight, sucker.

Half an hour later he quietly let himself into Hank's house and tiptoed down to the basement. Immediately, he hit the rewind on the long-playing videotape in the VCR that recorded from the hidden camera in Jolene's bedroom.

He tapped on the monitor and punched play, got an empty bed illuminated by just enough night-light to make it interesting, even arty. He ran rewind, hit play, more bed; so he went back and forth until on his tenth or eleventh try . . .

"Oh, wow."

Chapter Thirty-two

Something shook him and he opened his eyes.

Oh-oh.

Right in front of him, a man and a woman grappled in the dark. His eyes rolled past the flickering carnal image, then lurched back. Really worried now—not sure if he was dreaming or awake, or even alive.

Worry ran into panic.

It was a sign. Get ready, it's time.

Stay calm. Stay calm. The only part of his life he had any control over was the moment he left it. He understood he must stay alert and focused.

But it was hard to concentrate because his eyes were fixed on clutching knees and a sweaty, plunging back. He could almost smell the hormones popping in their armpits.

The watching made him dizzy and dizzy was sensual. Almost like moving. His thoughts strained for sensation, to rise up and swarm, like fruit bats he'd seen once, leaving a jungle cave at sunset. He yearned to touch the sweaty skin.

With the whole goddamn black void to aim at, he was drawn to one hot spot of jerky flesh.

Distractions.

He'd tried to prepare for this moment. He had meditated on the mechanics. And now it was unfolding just like the Buddhists said it *would. Leaving the physical body, he was distracted from his journey to a higher plane by scenes of intense intercourse.*

These were the diversions.

Hadda be. So this was IT.

The big night jump.

Don't mess up your death with distractions, Hank. Stay focused one hundred percent in the moment.

> . . .

The last blinders of shock crumbled and Hank recognized Jolene out there tugging on Phil Broker's business, with one elegantly muscled leg crooked in the air, like a snob's little finger as she held a dinner fork. Except that wasn't no fork she was holding.

Broker. Comforting Jolene the widow not widow to Hank's dead not dead. And, like back in the canoe during the storm, Broker paddling hard, trying his best to keep up. Hank could sympathize.

Then—

"I could kill you now and these pictures would be the last thing your brain would ever see. God, I wish you could see them."

Pictures.

Earl's voice established perspective and Hank realized the screwing was confined. Screwing in a box.

Earl had <u>recorded</u> it, like he said he would, and now Hank was watching the video on television.

"Okay, Lebowski," Earl said. "Sit back and enjoy the show. Just for you, I'm going to run the part again where she blows him."

So Hank treaded in his ebbing life and watched Jolene's deathless youth flicker on the screen. He could almost hear her voice again.

Shit! He did *hear her voice.*

"What's going on in here?"

Jolene stood in the doorway; her bare shoulders licked by the silent, shimmering video in which she wore nothing at all.

Earl grinned, getting off on seeing her, split-screen; doing Broker on the video and, in the flesh, in the doorway a few feet away. She couldn't see the front of the set and had no idea. Then Earl stopped the tape. Blip. Hit the reject on the VCR. Took it out.

"Ah, nothing; just checking him. I thought I heard something but he's all right." Earl polite, smiling. "I, ah, see you're sleeping in your own room tonight."

Jolene waved vaguely and went back to bed.

Earl, as usual, switched on the Fox Channel, muted the sound, and left Hank with the TV remote stuffed in his dead fingers.

Ha-ha.

Hank, alone now, worked a venomous edge, lashed on by the silent fulminations of Sean Hannity. Then he steadied his eyes, looked beyond the TV, and fixed on the blackness out the windows.

He wondered how many more times he would see the sun rise over the Wisconsin river bluffs. He felt no rancor for Broker. He pitied the man his innocent lust because he could not attribute innocence or spontaneity to Jolene.

What's she up to?

Hank focused the fury he felt on his body mass. The body was mostly water, wasn't it? And water conducted electricity. His thoughts became electric swimmers, thrashing toward the first and second fingers of his right hand.

Just before the indifferent sun heaved up, the dead flesh of his index finger moved a fraction of an inch.

Thank you, Earl.

Thank you, Allen.

Thinking about killing you is the only thing keeping me alive.

Chapter Thirty-three

Jolene slept through the alarm and missed turning Hank three times. Now, as a thin spoke of sunlight eased between the drapes, she stretched out on the king-size bed, lazing in and out of the first good night's sleep she'd had since . . .

She sat up and hugged herself, and she could feel the memory of Phil Broker's body still imprinted in her arms. Another comic-book hero, like Hank. Briefly she fantasized that he would put Earl Garf back in his place, back in her past. And then . . .

"THE DOW JONES CLOSED DOWN FOUR HUNDRED POINTS IN REACTION TO A SHARP RISE IN OIL PRICES . . ."

The burst of frenzied audio catapulted her upright in bed. Jangled, she stared at the door to Hank's studio, muttering "Earl" under her breath. Had to be. Playing his TV games with Hank. Not even taking time to pull on her robe, she scrambled off the bed and stalked into the next room.

". . . AGREE THAT ONLY EXTERNAL FORCES CAN THROW OFF MARKET FORECASTS . . ."

"Goddammit, Earl," Jolene yelled.

Huh?

The raucous blare and the driving musical background vanished the moment she entered the room. And there was no Earl in sight.

Just Hank, propped on his side in bed, staring right at her with
Ambush curled in the curve of his lap and the TV remote where Earl
had left it, jammed in his fingers as a joke.

Jolene. Naked.
Even with the short hair, she was a serious meditation on origi-
nal sin.
Hi, honey.
And in his head he was playing "Thus Spake Zarathustra" from
2001, like when the ape figured out he could use the tapir bone as a
weapon, because Hank was using his index finger to traverse the
buttons of the TV remote a big half-inch and touch the mute con-
trol. The set sizzled on at max volume. A hyper verbal group of Fox
talking heads were in full cry, puzzling over lurching stock prices,
unrest in the Middle East, and terrorist attacks on a U.S. barracks in
the Gulf.
Smug Yuppie pukes having their adventures in capitalism; they
really thought life was a fucking Mercedes ad. Too bad. Globaliza-
tion wasn't running like a smooth computer program guaranteed to
enhance their portfolios. Hank coldly wished them several million
tough, bitter, third-world peasants armed with AK-47's.
Back to Jolene. He switched off the set.

Jolene said, "Wait a minute." She peered at the motionless figure on the bed. She took a few cautious steps forward.
Hank's eyes did not depart on their usual loopy circuit; instead,
they remained fixed, burning, on her. They were riveted in a way
that made her aware of her nakedness, so intense was the stare that
she began to feel the sweat drip cold in her armpits and dribble down
her rib cage. It smelled like the fear of men she'd learned in puberty.
Pissed, hungry eyes, looking right at her.

Tap.

The TV came alive again in a shout of static.
Jolene screamed and ran from the room.

.   .   .

Allen had expected more than this for fifty bucks.

It was his first private tango lesson and he assumed there would be a little flavor of the slums of Buenos Aires—dark hair, cleavage, at least black tights and posters on the wall. Something sexy, like the dance itself. He found himself standing in a spotless Scandinavian kitchen. The windowsills were lined with cactuses, and beyond the prickly pear, Allen had a view of an exhausted gray sky, shredding birch trees, and a smudge of White Bear Lake lying flat as a dirty mirror.

The instructor, Trudi, was a well-preserved, petite matron in her sixties whose perfectly coiffed white head barely cleared his shoulder. She wore a white sweater and gray slacks and looked more like a senior Lutheran angel than an aficionado of a steamy dance that originated in Argentine whorehouses. Her only concession to the dance was pointed black dance shoes. Allen was in his stocking feet. He got her number from a Timberry adult-education brochure. In this, his first stab at self-improvement, he didn't want other people watching, as in a studio class. He'd wanted anonymity.

He watched Trudi move her kitchen table against the wall to make her dinette into a dance floor.

Her husband sat in the den just down the hall with the door ajar. He was watching the History Channel and so, instead of pulsating Latin music, Allen heard the rumble of massed Soviet artillery spelling doom for von Paulus's encircled Sixth Army in Stalingrad.

Okay. Allen resigned himself to it. He had to start somewhere.

"The Argentine tango begins in the center with a stable upper-body frame," Trudi said. She touched his sternum. "This is your center."

So far so good. Still no music.

"We'll start with side-to-side steps." They faced each other, holding hands. "Move your center over your left foot, move only about six inches."

Allen shifted to the left.

Trudi frowned. "You're too tight. You're pumping your shoulders, your upper body must remain relaxed and upright. It's all in the legs." They tried again. He moved left and then right, and this time

Trudi floated with him. "Better. In tango, the man must lead and the woman must follow, and the man must lead from the center."

That was more like it. But what he had in mind were the lunges and dips he'd seen Al Pacino execute in *Scent of a Woman*. And where's the music?

Allen chose the tango because it was a male-controlled, choreographed seduction and therefore conformed to an elaborate fantasy that featured Jolene Sommer.

"Again," Trudi said.

Allen stepped to the side and lost his balance.

"Patience," Trudi said.

Allen winced gamely. He was a long way from Al Pacino. Still. He couldn't resist asking, "How long before we get to, you know?" He leaned forward and circled his arms around an imaginary woman.

Trudi smiled. "That might take a while. Let's try some silver boxes."

The silver box was a six-step pattern. They'd wait on the eight-step box because, Trudi explained, *la crasada*—the crossover step—would only confuse him at this point.

Still no music.

Three moves into his tenth silver box, Allen felt his pager vibrate against his hip. He excused himself, checked the number, and his heart skipped. It was synchronicity. It was Jolene. He walked over to the window with the cactus fringe, flipped open his cell phone, tapped in the number, and suddenly the dull day came up keen as the cactus needles.

"Allen, it's Hank, please hurry," Jolene shouted into the phone. Full-blown panic. Dammit, he must have stopped breathing and she caught it late.

"Call nine one one."

"It's not like that, just hurry, okay?"

"I'm on my way," Allen said.

Allen ignored stop signs and ran two red lights. Coming down the snaking driveway to Hank's house he jammed the brakes and fishtailed and dented his rear left bumper on a tree trunk.

Couldn't be helped. He grabbed his medical bag and sprinted for the door.

Jolene met him in her robe. And although her eyes were bright with alarm, they were also very clear and vital. In fact, she looked much better than he'd seen her in a long time—rested, color in her cheeks, even her short hair had a plush spring to it.

She led him through the house toward the studio. Garf was there, of course, unshaven, looking barely awake but amused, in a T-shirt and a pair of sweatpants. He spooned a bowl of cornflakes close to his chest and rolled his eyes. There was a damp spot on his shirt where'd he'd slopped milk.

"And then," Jolene said, "just as I was waking up, the TV came on in Hank's room. And I went in and he was looking right at me."

"Gee, you mean like he knew you did something," Garf said, defying Jolene's furious glare with a mild grin.

"Just relax," Allen said. "Take a deep breath and tell me what happened."

"Earl thinks it's funny to leave the TV clicker in Hank's hand. *He* turned the TV on and off."

"Earl did," Allen said, getting a little perplexed.

"Hank did," Jolene said.

Hank resolved that this—his last story—was one time he couldn't afford to screw up. This time he intended to do justice to his characters. And here they came. He couldn't reach out and touch them but he'd heard their confessions. All the ingredients were present for them to start fighting among themselves.

He just had to figure out how to get the party rolling.

He could move one finger a half inch and he could control his eyes. So he could communicate. He took a chance contacting Jolene, but her reaction had been to call the other two. He had to control himself; what he did was spite after seeing the tape.

He'd have to think out the next move. Make it count.

For now he was going to lay low and be the best vegetable in the garden. So his eyes rolled. His fingers, with their mighty new muscles, were as motionless as white banana peels on the TV remote. They drew near the bed. Allen and Jolene stood on the right, Earl was on the left, munching cereal.

. . .

"He was just like that with the clicker," Jolene said.

Allen leaned over the bed and carefully inspected Hank's eyes and his hands.

"This is exactly the way he was?" Allen asked again.

Jolene bit her lip. "No, actually, now that I think of it, Ambush was on his lap."

Garf giggled and backed away, gamboling like a jester and humming the jangled *Twilight Zone* theme.

"The cat?" Allen said. Confounded, he moved his hands in a jerky pantomime, acting out a miniature drama. "Cat on lap," Allen said slowly, sounding like Dr. Seuss.

"No, no; it wasn't like that. It was *him*." She pointed at Hank.

Allen steepled his long fingers and raised them slowly to his lips. With the attitude of a thoughtful prelate, he stepped closer to Jolene.

"Jo, I think the strain is getting to you."

She shook her head. Allen started to place his hand on her shoulder, saw the swell of her bare throat and collarbone, and, hearing a rush of the tango music Trudi never played, held it back.

"Why don't you get dressed, let's go sit down in the kitchen and have a cup of coffee," he suggested gently.

"Good idea," Garf said, chewing with his mouth open. "I'll watch Hank and make sure he doesn't jump in the river."

"You're not helping things," Allen said, a little testy. He turned back to Jolene and raised his eyebrows expectantly.

Jolene dropped her shoulders. "Okay."

"Good," Allen said. "I'm going to go wash my hands." He walked through the bedroom into the bathroom and shut the door.

Garf moved in and nudged her shoulder. "Better take a shower, girl."

"What's that?" Jolene narrowed her eyes.

Garf smiled. "You don't want to be staring into Allen's eyes talking about the meaning of life and have Broker trickle down your leg, now do you?"

Jolene swung her right hand to slap Garf in the face but he caught her hand easily. She narrowed her eyes, questioning.

Garf winked. "Hank told me."

"Oh, yeah?" she shot back. "What he told me was that Broker copied your whole hard drive, especially your ambitious banking records."

"Bullshit."

Jolene smiled sweetly.

"When?" Garf squinted when he saw she wasn't kidding.

"Last night." She hunched her shoulders like a starlet and let them drop. "Afterward," she said coyly, "he made a duplicate copy off your Zip Drive."

They glared at each other. Then, as Earl backed off, he said ominously, "Broker's ass is grass."

"Don't be selling *me* wolf tickets, and if I were you I'd be real nice to Broker to make sure those disks don't wind up in the wrong hands," Jolene mocked.

Allen and Jolene traded places in the bathroom and, while Jolene showered, Allen paced back and forth in front of Hank's bed. He was aware of Garf, leaning against a bookcase next to the doorway, eating the last of his cereal, watching him.

Garf crossed the room, finished the bowl, placed it on the writing desk, ran his hand along a shelf of video movie cassettes, and asked, "You really kind of dig her, don't you?"

"Maybe," Allen said. It wasn't the right word, but then he resented the direct question coming from someone like Garf.

"I'm going to give you a little advice," Garf said.

"Really," Allen said.

"Really." He pulled a rectangular movie container from the shelf, came across the room, and handed it to Allen.

The film was entitled *The Blue Angel*. On the cover, Marlene Dietrich wore a top hat at a rakish angle and a skimpy cabaret girl's costume. She sat in a provocative pose, hands clasped over one carved knee.

"I've heard of it," Allen said.

"If I were you, I'd watch it very carefully," Garf said. He then turned and left the room.

Slob. Forgot to take his cereal bowl, Allen observed.

Alone now, he resumed his pacing. He was satisfied that the incident that had upset Jolene was just a fluke caused by the damn cat. Still, it left a spooky aftertaste.

It was clearly time to relocate Hank. Jolene needed some therapy or some medication to deal with the strain. And having a smart-ass like Garf around certainly didn't help.

He glanced at the movie Garf had given him; B&W, 1930, German dialogue with English subtitles. He dropped it in his bag. He'd been glib, he had no idea what the film was about; only that it was referred to as a classic.

Chapter Thirty-four

J.T. and his family left for Iowa before dawn, towing the trailer full of ostriches. So, when Broker and Amy woke up in their respective bed and couch, on separate floors, they had the house to themselves. About nine A.M., Broker heard her thump around in the upstairs guest room, then the bathroom pipes banged in the wall as he made coffee.

She came downstairs barefoot in a burgundy terry-cloth robe too bulky to have fit in her travel bag, and Broker figured it was Denise's. She sat at the kitchen table and he saw she had painted her fingernails and her toenails a moody purple. He stood at the counter. There was no "good morning," no "hey, how you doing?" He held up a coffee cup. "Black? Or there's Coffeemate."

"Black."

He poured two black coffees, brought the cups over to the table, sat down, and they faced each other. Her freckles were lifeless gray and her gray eyes were shot with red; her face was puffy, unshowered, just splashed with wake-up water; her usually tawny hair was a snarl of platinum wire sticking up.

By contrast, his eye were clear and calm. His face was smooth and ruddy. His hair was happily tousled. "So," he said, "did you get your flight?"

"Yeah . . ." she stared at the navy blue cup in her hands that was stamped with the legend RAMSEY COUNTY SWAT. Then she snapped her tired eyes on him. ". . . And did you get what you were after?"

The remark smoked past his ear with the incendiary velocity of a .50-cal tracer round, blew out through the wall, scorched a dry cornfield, and streaked out over the curve of the earth. Broker veered away from the comment, which pained him because, after sidling in a little too close to Jolene last night, he was happy to have escaped with all his fingers and toes.

Jolene had been disfigured with alcoholic stress fractures. Amy, even frizzed with pique, remained clean and attractive—a rounded female who looked like she could bounce as opposed to sticking like a dagger.

But probably it was a little late to discover how much he appreciated her. "I have one last thing to do and then I'll be going back to Ely," he said quickly.

"Uh-huh," she said in a neutral tone.

"Just got to talk to a guy, that's all."

"The boyfriend?"

"Yeah. I'm going to explain a few things; kind of truth and consequences, and then I'm done."

"You mean threaten him."

"Okay, I'm going to threaten him. But no rough stuff."

A quick peek directly into Amy's eyes gave Broker the impression she could literally smell Jolene on him. So he took his coffee upstairs and soaked in a long, hot shower. When he came down she was still sitting at the table.

"You had a call," she said. "There's a number by the phone. From that lawyer, Milton Dane. The *wife* gave him this number."

Glad for the distraction, Broker went to the phone and called the number on the pad.

"Law offices."

"Milton Dane," Broker said.

"Whom shall I say is calling?"

"Phil Broker, returning his call."

Broker poured another cup of coffee, sipped; Milt came on the line.

"Hey, Broker, I heard you were in town."

"I brought Hank's truck back."

"That's what Jolene said."

"How's the arm?"

"Ibuprofen. And reps with tuna cans. Story of my life. How long are you in the Cities?"

"Over the weekend."

"Look, could you drop by my office today? Take a quick deposition? It would save me the trouble of driving up north."

"Sure," he glanced at Amy. "I could be there, say—at ten."

"Good. I'll assemble the usual suspects."

After getting Milt's location, he said good-bye, hung up, and turned to Amy. "When's your flight?"

"Six-thirty, check in at five-thirty."

"You want to get out of the house, go into St. Paul?"

"And take a chance on running into Milton Dane, who is going to sue my ass off? No thank you. I'll pack. Just get back in time to give me a ride."

Driving west on 94, he decided it was time to let it go and head back up north. After seeing Milt, he'd call Jolene and nail down a time to have a sit-down with Earl Garf. Maybe someday he'd figure out a way to tie Garf to Stovall. But not today.

Then he'd take Amy to the airport.

When he got back to Ely he'd call her up. Dinner maybe.

And the idea of staying at Uncle Billie's held a certain appeal as opposed to returning to his empty house, with children's books and toys gathering dust in the corners. So, he'd stay in Ely for at least November. Go deer hunting with Iker. Try to kick back for a while. Let things develop.

He entered St. Paul, parked, and found his way to the twenty-second floor of the American National Bank building where Milt had an office.

The pert blond gatekeeper told him to go right in, that Milt was expecting him. Broker went through a door next to the reception desk. Milt appeared at 'he end of the corridor and waved him into his corner office.

Gingerly, they shook hands. Milt was clearly still favoring his arm. The corner walls were primarily glass and, twenty stories down, the east side of St. Paul spread to the horizon like an Amish autumn quilt. In the foreground, the window ledges were lined with travel souvenirs: African carvings, Southeast Asian brass dragons, and South American masks. Framed pictures on the walls portrayed Milt strapped in a life jacket, glowering through whitewater, swinging a kayak paddle.

And there was this tall guy in a gray suit, with beetle brows and a widow's peak, sitting in one of the chairs in front of Milt's desk. A guy who did not get up to greet him, who did not smile.

His name was Tim Downs and he'd been a homicide investigator with St. Paul and had gone to law school at night. He'd quit and hung out his shingle. Downs had been a cop with a nose for politics, the kind who kept track of everyone and everything.

Not missing a beat, still smiling, Milt said, "You two know each other."

"Yeah," Downs said, getting up.

"Yeah," Broker said, nodding at Downs.

Downs nodded back and walked from the office, leaving Broker in flat-footed appreciation of Milt's understated style.

"So, have a seat," Milt said. "You want some coffee?" Milt asked. Broker shook his head.

Milt now extended Broker the courtesy of addressing him as a player and a peer. "So Allen calls me up the other night and says Jolene's houseguest, Earl Garf—alias Clyde—had a run-in with you . . ."

Broker, caught off guard by Downs's appearance, went on the attack. "Hank belongs in a nursing home, he needs full-time, skilled care. She's working herself ragged."

Milt reacted frankly, hands open, fingers spread. "I couldn't stop her, she went ballistic when the Blue Cross tanked. Look, Allen's been monitoring him every day. He's in remarkably good shape for a . . ."

"Vegetable," Broker said.

"I didn't want to rush her. I also had to get a feel for working with her . . ."

Broker said, "What's the matter? Afraid she might jump to another lawyer?"

Milt said, "Monday I'm moving him into a full-care facility."

"Who's paying?"

"I'm paying. I'm also on the calender in probate in Washington County. It might take a month, but Jolene will be appointed Hank's guardian and executor of his trust. We all just got off to a bad start on this thing."

"Too bad. Garf wouldn't be there if she hadn't come up broke because of Hank's trust-fund antics," Broker said.

Milt said, "I *know* that. If he would have listened to Jolene and paid his bills on time we wouldn't be in this mess. But he didn't listen to her, he went to his AA buddy. You know about that?"

"I know about Stovall," Broker said.

The preliminary fencing ended and they both backed off. Milt glanced at his hands and inquired diplomatically, "Don't like surprises, do you? Like Downs being here?"

Broker changed the subject and pointed to a medical monitor the size of a breadbox that sat on the desk. "What's that?"

"That," Milt said, "is our case. It's a GE Marquette, it monitors vital signs; what they had Hank hooked up to. I rented one." Milt reached across the desk and fiddled with knobs and dials. "And this is what I think happened: they had one nurse watching Hank and, to be fair, half the other patients in the place, plus covering the ER. Once you attach the leads to the patient, the monitor starts graphing vital signs. But if you don't program the machine for a new patient, the alarm doesn't activate.

"So I'm thinking the anesthetist miscalculated the amount of sedation she gave Hank throughout the operation and took him off the gas too soon. They get him up to recovery—but the nurse is busy, she hooks up the leads and forgets the programing procedure; she sees the wave forms going across the screen and thinks everything's all right. She gets distracted, leaves the room, Hank stops breathing, and nobody knows."

Milt picked up a manila folder full of forms and dropped it on his desk. "The case is very strong."

Broker said, "Jolene insists he looks at her."

Milt nodded. "She told me. We've had experts. Allen checks him regularly for visual pursuit. There is no indication of voluntary reflexes." He paused and then focused his full attention on Broker.

"So, let's talk about you. You thumped Garf and he checked around and came up with some interesting background on our trusty north-woods guide; like you did time in Stillwater, and so on. That's when I got ahold of Downs, who investigates this kind of stuff for us, and I asked him to check you out.

"And he just laughs and says, 'Good luck,' because you were only the most freewheeling undercover operative in Minnesota cop land and the longest-running one. Apparently fragments from your undercover days are still scattered through the system, and that's what Garf found in NCIC. You were with the state Bureau of Criminal Apprehension, right?"

Broker remained silent, utterly unreadable and unflappable; it had been his most useful talent as a cop and his least endearing quality to civilians.

Milt, in no way intimidated, leaned forward across his desk. "Right?"

Clearly Milt was no cherry, and he had mouse-trapped him with Downs. So Broker said, "Yeah."

"Among other things"—Milt raised an eyebrow—"like rumors, you're stringing for ongoing deep-shit federal stuff nobody is willing to talk about. Which is why you're still carried in the system."

Broker cleared his throat, crossed his legs, and scratched his cheek. "What else did Tim have to say?"

Milt leaned forward a little more, grinning, "That you're a misfit, a maverick, and maybe a shade more outlaw than cop—not a team player, at any rate." He seemed intrigued by these revelations. Even amused. And something more. Broker sensed the lawyer was a quick study who spotted a passing advantage. He asked, "Can I still get some coffee?"

"Sure." Milt tapped the intercom. "Kelly, could you bring us two cups of coffee."

Broker inclined his head forward. "Did you tell Allen any of this?"

Milt smiled. "Allen, the invincible surgeon? Of course not. I love to keep that guy in the dark."

"So Garf still thinks . . ."

"You have a checkered past. Like he does. Which is how you're playing it with them, I suspect." Milt straightened up when his assistant brought in a tray with cups, carafe, cream, and sugar. When she withdrew, he doled out coffee, then he turned back to Broker. "Naturally—once I learned about your background, I'd been thinking about the difference between omission and commission."

"Say what you mean, Milt."

"What are you doing hanging out at Hank's?"

"You mean, like Allen? And maybe you?"

Milt opened his hands and pursed his lips. "Jolene's in a tight spot. We all feel bad."

"She's the fucking Lorelei." Broker pointed to the white-water pictures on the wall. "I'd plug my ears and mind the rocks, if I were you."

"You haven't answered my question."

Broker sipped his coffee and watched a Cessna traverse Milt's windows on approach to the St. Paul Municipal Airport. "Are you going to win?" he asked.

"Nothing's for sure. But, yeah, I'm going to win."

"Big?"

"Pretty big.

"How will the money be disbursed?"

Milt picked up a handspring from his desktop and squeezed it methodically. "Most of it will go into a trust for Hank's extended care. Some will go to Jolene directly; she has a claim to loss of consortium."

"What's that?"

Milt shrugged. "It compensates for the loss of aid, comfort, and society of the injured party. But as the spouse she has a lot to say about administering the trust."

"Along with her lawyer," Broker said.

"Of course."

Now Broker leaned forward. "Let's say you do win big and the money gets paid, and then, when it's all settled, Hank conveniently dies the rest of the way. What happens to the money?"

"She gets it all. What's your point?"

"I don't see Jolene shackled to bedsores for the long haul. Too many men are interested in her." Broker paused for emphasis. "And love always finds a way."

"That's melodramatic," Milt said, lowering his eyes in distaste.

Broker paused a moment. "You're not married, are you?"

"Not at the moment," Milt said, getting up, turning his broad pinstriped back to Broker. He stared out his windows. "I take it you've been in among these rocks you're talking about?"

Broker couldn't see his face. "Close enough to know when to get the hell out, after I take care of one little detail."

Milt's shoulders tensed slightly. "Which is?"

"Persuading Garf his self-interest lies elsewhere. The way I see it, I owe Hank a favor for saving my butt out on that lake."

"Can you do that?" Milt turned just a fraction too fast.

Broker almost felt sorry for Garf: more and more he was being cast as the main speed bump on the way to Jolene's bounty. Like everybody, Milt wanted him gone. But he didn't want to get his hands dirty and he didn't want to see the messy part. He just wanted it to be made nice and clean; the pretty woman all alone in the big house with all the money.

Broker shook his head. He'd had enough of the Cities. "When I worked the streets, back in the Dark Ages, we'd rough up the riffraff for bothering their betters and call it asshole control. Now, of course, everybody is empowered, especially assholes, and you have to be more civil."

"And?"

Broker chose his words carefully. "You and me have sort of detoured off the record here?"

Milt nodded. "I'd say we're pretty much operating on your old turf."

"Okay. Consider a hypothetical—"

"We're just talking, right?" Milt said.

"Yeah," Broker said. "What if Garf has this excessive, electronic financial profile involving more credit card numbers than he charges items to? What if someone made a copy of his hard drive, but it was too complicated for him to figure out. Of course, Washington County and St. Paul have cyber cops who might have a different opinion, if the disks were to fall into their hands."

Milt nodded. "All speculation, of course; but a simple quid pro quo."

Broker nodded. "Garf moves out of the house and out of Jolene's life. After a certain interval, he gets to watch me destroy the disks. No police involvement. I think Hank would approve. I get the impression he wanted Jolene to have a chance to outgrow the likes of Garf. I'm going to try and give him his wish. But, if Garf goes, there has to be provision for the money Jolene legitimately owes him. I want to be able to tell him that."

"Understood. After Garf's gone, I'll take it up with Jolene," Milt said.

Broker watched Milt tug at his lapels, straighten his tie. "So, do you think people can change?"

"Do you?" Milt bounced it back.

They explored each other's faces for a few beats, then Broker stood up. "What about this deposition?"

Milt came around his desk to walk Broker to the door. "You know, I don't think you're the kind of guy I want to put on the stand."

"You mean, where the other side can cross-examine me," Broker said, mock-serious.

They shook hands.

Driving east out of St. Paul, Broker took less and less relish in the prospect of hassling Garf. It had degraded to the level of an onerous duty, like carrying out the garbage. And it reminded him that one of the reasons he'd lost interest in routine police work was the time spent shooing human rubbish away from the tidy lives of the Milton Danes and the Allen Falkens.

He shook his head, concentrated on driving, turned off the freeway, and threaded through the congested traffic and sprawling strip malls until his wheels struck country gravel. Driving the solitary back roads was an exercise in nostalgia—trying to make time stand still and hold on to the world he'd grown up in. Sometimes he thought that if he stayed out here on the margins long enough, he might come back into style. But truthfully, he knew now that even Garf was part of something new that was passing him by.

Chapter Thirty-five

Amy left a note tacked on the door: WENT FOR A RUN. Her bags were stacked on the porch, ready to go. So Broker phoned Jolene, got the machine, and left a message inquiring when Garf would be home.

Then he went back outside and walked down the gravel road that curved past the barn toward the fields and the paddocks. The wind had picked up. Overhead, fast-moving clouds jammed a busy sky. Sunlight and shadow alternated, slap-dash, on the paddocks' bright tin roofs and the red barn lumber and the mowed green alfalfa fields. Standing on the high ground behind the paddocks, he spotted a flicker of blue and made her out, running the gravel road in a wind suit, on the far side of a long, undulating parcel of standing corn.

He tried to imagine Jolene running. Couldn't see it.

Just wasn't her style.

He lit a cigar, enjoying the bite of the smoke and the chilled scent of alfalfa stubble. A broken V formation of Canada geese passed high overhead, their wild calls plunging down the cold air.

He timed his walk back toward the house so he'd meet Amy as she jogged down the driveway, past the swaying willows. She slowed to a walk and watched him approach as she pulled an ear-warmer strip from her head and shook out her hair.

Broker held up his hands and inclined his head. Teeth together in a wayward smile, he said, "I was thinking . . ."

She measured him with a stare.

He continued, "Maybe next week, when I get back to Ely, we could have dinner."

Amy placed her hands on her hips, not necessarily because of what he'd said; more like that's the way she walked it out, cooling down from a run. But she moved in a wary semicircle around him and her voice was apprehensive. "You were, huh?"

"Sure. You know, go out to a restaurant."

Her chin rose in measured intervals. "You mean, take me out to dinner?"

"That's what I said," he said.

"No. You said, we can have dinner." Her diction was deliberate, hammered.

Broker composed himself. "Amy, could I take you out to dinner?"

"You asking me to go on a date?"

Broker exhaled. "Yes."

"I'll think about it," she said, tossing the reply airily over her shoulder as she walked toward the house. Then, louder, she asked, "Have you had lunch?"

He followed her into the house and they wound up back in the kitchen. She removed her wind jacket and he could smell the sweat simmer in the navy blue fleece that molded her torso. Looking for something to do, he approached the red light on the Mr. Coffee and poured the inky dregs into the cup he'd used this morning.

"That's been warming all day," she said.

Broker shrugged and continued to pour.

She fluffed her hair and faced the cupboards. "It's always a challenge, finding your way around a stranger's kitchen."

Broker took his evil coffee to the table and sat down. She moved to the refrigerator, opened it, and inspected the shelves. She took out a plastic container.

"Ostrich chili?"

"Sounds good."

The social temperature in the kitchen gradually warmed as she found a pot, put it on the stove, played with the gas settings, then pried the cover off the Tupperware container. After she gave him a second medium-stern look, he finally got it and rose from his chair and searched the cupboards for bowls and silverware and glasses, which he arranged in two place settings on the table.

"So, how did it go with Milton Dane?"

"We talked," Broker said.

"Did you give a formal deposition? I mean, did he ask you questions about me?"

"Like what?"

"You saw Nancy leave her post. You were in the recovery room after it happened."

"No," Broker said. "We never got around to that. Not today."

"The wife," Amy said, spooning globs of cold chili into a black pot.

"You got it. The wife, the boyfriend, the money. Hank adrift in limbo."

She turned. "You left yourself out of the cast."

"I don't belong in it. I'm just passing through."

"What about the accountant?"

"I think he was the victim of foul play, I think it involved Hank's money, and I think her ex-boyfriend was in up to his neck. But I can't prove it. So I have to let it go for now."

Amy set the flame under the pot and looked through the clipboards until she found a package of Saltine crackers. She twisted her lips in a wondering expression and went to the refrigerator. "I saw this article in *The New York Times Magazine* about black people's kitchens and white people's kitchens."

"Yeah?"

"Whites have Coke in the refrigerator. Blacks have Pepsi." She opened the door. There was a two-liter, plastic bottle of Diet Pepsi in the lower door shelf.

They both shrugged. The small mystery contributed to the gradual warming in the kitchen: tiny taste bursts of tomato sauce and chili powder popped over the simmering pot; a film of steam blotted the corners of the window over the sink.

"You're different today. So what's changed?" she asked.

"I figured out the difference between attraction and propulsion."

"Oh, boy, physics." Amy evaluated him warily.

"Sometimes if you find yourself hurtling toward someone it might not be attraction so much as what you're running away from."

Amy smiled cynically. "The wife."

"No, someone," Broker protested.

"So this is hypothetical?" she asked.

"Not exactly."

"The wife," Amy repeated.

"Okay, for the purposes of argument. Say I go over to Jolene's place to return Hank's vehicle and I have suspicions about the accountant's death which I can't make pan out. But I'm feeling bad about what happened to Hank and I see her dealing with these problems so I sort of step in . . ."

"Step in?" Amy was amused.

"Yeah, you know . . ." Broker gestured with his hands.

"I got an idea what you stepped in," Amy said.

Broker objected. "That's not the point. What I'm trying to say is I have all this . . ." His hands attempted to manipulate an invisible object in the air. ". . . stuff in my life that's hanging fire—Nina leaving with my kid, my marriage—and I wasn't dealing with it. So I'm rebounding off that. It explains, but does not excuse, getting involved too quick in—"

"Oh, so now you're involved?"

"No, I mean, if my life were in order I probably wouldn't have stuck my nose in."

"Oh, now it's your nose?" On the stove, the chili was starting to simmer.

"You're not listening to me," Broker said, getting a little hot himself.

"Sure I am," she said too casually. "You went to bed with her; what's the big deal?"

"Amy?"

"That's not an answer. You went to bed with her and now you feel bad about it and you expect me to give you . . . sympathy? Now suddenly you want to take me to dinner."

Amy flipped the box of Saltines across the room. It hit Broker's chest and spiraled to the floor. "Make your own goddamn lunch."

She paced the length of the room, wheeled around, and quipped, "So what did you do with Hank? Stuff him in the closet?"

"I thought we were having a serious conversation," Broker said, standing up suddenly, rattling the bowls and silverware on the table.

"How can we have a serious conversation when you won't tell me the truth," Amy said.

They stared at each other as a cloud of scorched chili reared in the air.

"The truth," Broker said with a perplexed look on his face.

"A basis for trust," Amy said, speaking in her best practical voice.

"Look," he gave in, "it only happened—"

"How typical," Amy smiled sweetly as she spun, walked from the kitchen, through the living room, and up the stairs.

The pot on the stove puffed out black fumes, the smoke alarm on the ceiling began to shriek. He heard her footfalls continue to stomp in the hall upstairs. A door slammed. Broker got up on a chair and hit the reset button on the alarm. Then he jumped off the chair, grabbed the pot of burnt chili, and—Ow—immediately drew back his hand. He looked around for a towel, found one hanging over the sink, grabbed the pot handle a second time with the towel, and carried it out to the porch. When he came back in, the alarm was screeching again, so he opened the window over the sink, searched for the switch to the ceiling fan, found it, turned on the fan, then climbed back on the chair and turned the alarm off.

Wreathes of smoke hung in the air like the aftermath of battle. Okay. Get out of the house. Feed the birds.

The nimble clouds of an hour ago now massed into cold gobs. The wind had acquired knuckles.

Hunched over, Broker walked through little squalls of swirling leaves toward the outer paddocks. As he neared them, a crowd of curious hens drifted along the fence line, their stubby wings slightly lowered to warm their long legs. Their big eyes fixed on him like cartoon question marks.

He glanced up at winter clouds in October and very much wanted this detour in his life to be over. He ducked into the first paddock and was soon busy, elbowing his way through clumsy hens who crowded around him as he dumped five-gallon plastic buckets of feed into bins. The bigger males hung back while their harems fed. If one put in an appearance, mindful of J.T.'s warnings, Broker exited the pens and just heaved the feed sidelong at the bins over the gates. In each paddock he checked to make sure the water reservoirs were full.

Half an hour later he came back up the gravel path toward the barn. A grind of downshifting gears drew his eyes toward the road and he saw a flash of an auto chassis streak over a dip and disappear behind a tree line. Then a gust of wind stood him up and he looked at the sky which was darkened to the point where he wanted to check out the weather channel. He'd lost track of the speeding car. Probably the wind.

His last chore was to feed Popeye in the barn.

"How you doing today, you and hit-and-run punk," Broker said, as he carried a last bucket of feed toward the pen and saw Popeye's big stupid eyes bob more than nine feet in the air at the end of his skinny neck.

The wind groaned through the barn's wooden walls and somewhere hanging farm equipment clanged like Gothic wind chimes, and at first Broker didn't hear it. Then he did—the sound of something hard pounding the fender of the tractor parked behind him. A mean cadence, off the rhythm of the wind.

He turned. The source of the noise was a shiny new baseball bat in Earl Garf's hand.

Another guy stood behind Earl, a big guy who also wielded a bat. Broker looked past Earl, at the big guy who was wearing a baggy leather bomber jacket, extra large to allow room for his massive arms. There was a fake bomber-group insignia on the left breast of the coat. A diving vulture. Broker had seen the jacket before.

Rodney had been wearing it more three years ago when Broker busted him for selling machine guns.

"Hiya, shithead," Earl sang out. "I believe you have something that belongs to me." Earl had dressed for the occasion in black leather—a long belted trench coat. As Broker's gaze shifted from Rodney to Earl and back again, Earl loosened the belt on the coat and flexed his shoulders.

"Binds the arms," he said. Then he raised his bat like a hitter warming up and took an experimental swing at the air. His tongue played along his lower lip in anticipation. Earl didn't see Rodney, behind him, getting a good look at Broker and crinkling his wide forehead in surprise.

"Eyebrows?" Rodney said. "Oh, fuck me."

Chapter Thirty-six

Eyebrows.

Broker's nickname in the world of snitches, gun dealers, and dope entrepreneurs, where his last official act had been to arrest Rodney. And he now recalled Rodney's parting words, screamed as they stuffed him into a cruiser—"I'll kill you, motherfucker, if it's the last thing I ever do."

Now here was Rodney shifting a bat in his ham-sized hands. Teamed up with Earl. Getting his wish.

Not good.

But then—Rodney developed instant eloquent possibilities as a mime; recognizing Broker, he shook his head, pleaded with his eyes, and took a step back all in the same second:

You don't know me, I don't know you; this is a mistake; I'm outa here.

Broker nodded ever so slightly and Rodney started backing away, flipping a very abbreviated wave good-bye, close to his hip and behind Earl's back.

"What'd you bring him for, Earl—to block the sun?" Broker asked, encouraged by the changing odds. His eyes took in everything in the barn garage in half a second and came up with a plan. He had one chance not to wind up in an emergency ward, or worse. Even with Rodney opting out, barehanded, even in his prime, he couldn't go up against a bat wielded by a street monster like Earl and hope to come out unscathed.

"I don't like it," Rodney yelled, backing away. "I highly suggest we get the fuck outa here."

"No way; it's gonna cost him at least a knee." Earl stepped forward in a modified batter's stance, gauging his target.

Broker was not about to show Earl anything like fear. He was pissed about his spat with Amy. And he could still smell burnt chili. So he stuck out his chin and taunted, "Earl, be a good little computer nerd and take his advice, because this is just the wrong time to mess with me."

The facts of his situation were far less nonchalant. So, as he moved back to keep the same amount of distance between himself and Earl, he raised the bucket of feed to port arms, to protect himself. He was exactly where he wanted to be—within an easy reach of the dead bolt that fastened the gate to Popeye's pen.

J.T., buddy; I hope you weren't putting me on.

Earl stepped forward, menacing. The bat gleamed in the overhead sodium vapor light. Brand-new, not a scratch on the scripted logo or the clean-grained ash. Earl heaved his shoulders, feinting a swing. Broker moved as Earl moved, tossing the feed bucket at Earl's face.

Whack! Earl swung. Feed pellets exploded from the shattered plastic container.

"Yeah," Earl giggled, an hysterical wheezing giggle on the far edge of control. He had feed pellets in his hair, he had a pale, berserker light in his eyes. Broker instinctively realized why Earl had brought Rodney as extra muscle.

It wasn't to help work Broker over.

It was to pull him off when he lost control and was beating Broker to death.

But Rodney had disappeared out the door into the gray afternoon and Earl, sans backup, had cocked the bat again. Trembling with pleasure and rage, he took another step forward.

Okay. Life had become very simple. If he tried to close the distance and grapple, Broker would for sure take at least one blow going in. So that was out. He needed to get something between his skull and that bat. Broker's hand reached back, seized the bolt, yanked it, and pulled the thick, chest-high gate open.

Earl let go a blinding overhand swing and Broker went to his knees, ducking as the bat smashed down, denting the framing on the top of the gate just above and behind Broker's head. As Earl recovered, Broker scooted around to the other side of the gate and pulled it full-arc on its hinges, so he was squeezed behind it, tight against the plywood outer wall of the pen.

"What a chickenshit," Earl sneered, trying another overhand swing that harmlessly glanced off the gate and thumped the wall. Broker was contorted sideways, one shoulder back, flattened against the wall; his other arm folded against his chest, his hand gripping the simple handle under the bolt, holding the door against him.

Earl could prod into the limited space with the bat, but he could no longer swing. So he tried to pummel Broker, but Broker grabbed at the end and tried to twist it away. With difficulty, Earl yanked it back out of the cranny.

"Give it up, Earl!" Broker yelled. "Walk away now and you won't get hurt."

"Can you believe this guy, Rodney . . ." And then, "Rodney?"

And then.

The high hissing sound Earl and Broker heard was all the more unnerving because its source was not mechanical but animal, because it issued from the quilled throat of an infuriated four-hundred-pound male ostrich. Popeye's massive thigh muscles trembled, tensing, at about the same level as Earl's shoulders. The bird's wings flung up, rampant, and the stiff plumes lashed the doorway of the open stall.

"Now what the fuck is this?" Earl muttered as he looked up into Popeye's bloodshot eyes. Fearlessly ignorant of his situation, he taunted Broker, "Won't work, hiding behind Big Bird. Uh-uh."

Broker came up to look over the gate as Earl shifted his feet to take a swing at the hissing bird. He let go an indolent one-handed swat aimed at Popeye's head.

Like shoo.

The ostrich's right leg cocked and shot straight forward, the scaley big toe with its claw knuckled. Earl was lucky; because of his wide haymaker swing he was rotating and Popeye struck him a glancing blow in the chest, ripping buckles and buttons off the leather trench coat. Even off target, the kick connected like an electric shock and sent Earl flying back against the tractor, and then rolling on the floor.

He scrambled to his feet, holding his ribs with one hand and reaching for the dropped bat with the other. "Son of a bitch," he gasped.

The bird stepped into the garage and Broker lowered himself eye-level with the top of the door. Popeye's ominous grace was an optical illusion. His long legs seemed to be moving in slow-motion when in fact they weren't. They were lining up on Earl again.

Less bellicose now, Earl's face was working overtime on the proposition that a mere bird could kill a man. He gripped the bat and assessed the distance to the open garage door. Instinctively, he tried to go around the high-stepping bird.

"No, no," Broker yelled, safe behind his thick gate. "Stay in front of him. They kick to the side."

Wide-eyed, shaken, Earl changed direction.

Dumb shit.

This time Popeye hit Earl squarely in the left upper arm. Earl screamed as he smashed against the concrete. The kick shredded the trench coat sleeve. Dots of blood stippled the floor. Earl's ragged shoulder flopped like a rag doll's.

Serves you right.

Then someone turned his name into a high-pitched, infuriated indictment: "Bro-*KER!*"

Amy stood in the doorway waving her arms to distract Popeye.

"Do *something*, he's gonna to get killed!" Amy hollered.

Popeye's tiny head rotated on his long neck, big-eyed and comic in contrast to his lethal feet, which shifted on the cement. Amy continued to wave her arms. Earl, his left arm useless, lay collapsed against the tractor tire like the statue of the Dying Gaul.

Broker would have liked to see Popeye get in a few more licks. But now, worried that Amy would get within Popeye's kicking radius, he scrambled from the shelter of his plywood gate and saw the long-handled bar shovel leaning against the wall of the pen.

"Please . . ." Earl moaned.

"Get behind that tractor," Broker shouted at Amy.

"What about . . . ?" she shouted back as she took cover.

Broker sprang for the shovel, grabbed it, and thrust it at the bird. J.T. had told him that male ostriches were territorial. No way Popeye would just walk away.

He shouted to Amy, "I'm going to distract him. You gotta come under the tractor and pull Earl out of range, get him outside, and close the door. Do it."

Amy darted under the big John Deere. "Crawl toward me," she shouted at Earl.

"Huh?" Earl shook his head, confused.

Broker advanced with the shovel extended. Popeye gauged this new intruder's approach, shifted his stance, and stepped back into a tangle of loose wire that lay on the floor.

The bird kicked to free his foot from the coils. Old tin cans threaded in the rusty wire made a racket when Popeye snarled his leg. Tangled in the rattle wire, Popeye's demeanor totally changed. Spooked, he bolted for the open door.

Broker watched the bird accelerate across the yard in bounds so powerful, they looked like special effects. Zero to forty in three seconds, J.T. had told him. Trailing tin cans, Popeye tore around a tree line and vanished.

Back in the barn, Amy was already stooped over Earl. "Get me a knife. Something to cut the coat with."

"First I want to talk to my buddy Earl, here," Broker said.

"Christ's sake, man," Earl grimaced in pain, hunching away.

"Broker," Amy ordered, "I have to see this arm. If it's compound and has bone sticking out we could sever an artery moving him."

"Move him?" Broker feigned laughter. "Fuck him, leave him where he's at." He tugged Amy to her feet, took a firm grip on her arm, walked her outside.

She pulled away, furious. "That guy . . ."

Broker cut her off. "He's not critical. He's got a broken arm. So I'm going to mess with him a little. He's the boyfriend, and he just tried to brain me with a bat and he brought some help."

Amy's eyes flashed, she licked her lips. "I saw the other one run." More eager than cautious, she asked, "Are there more of them?"

She was back in her element; she liked the action and she liked being in it with him. Broker got the powerful impression the ruckus cleared the decks between them.

"Why'd the other one take off?" she asked.

And the answer to that, Broker didn't know. He shrugged and said, "Because he came to break a leg and got a full, frontal view of a charging male ostrich."

"Why break your leg?"

Broker grinned. "To chase me away from Jolene."

Amy grinned with him.

Earl moaned in the barn, "Jesus Christ, will somebody call nine-one-one?"

"Hey, Earl, look out for the rats, there's these big barn rats in there. I think they got rabies," Broker yelled, then he turned back to Amy. "Okay, J.T. keeps a first-aid kit on the mud porch. Do *not* call nine-one-one. We'll run him over to Timberry Emergency after I have a little talk."

"You know what you're doing?"

"Sure, Earl and I are both doing the same thing: trying to scare each other off. He blew his shot. I won't."

"Okay," she squinted at him. "But no more rough stuff. That's a bad arm."

Broker held up his hands, palms out—an innocent. "Amy, I never touched the guy."

She evaluated the look in his eyes. "You would have let that bird kill him," she said evenly.

"Nah," Broker grinned. "Not kill him, maybe kick him a few more times, though."

She turned and jogged to the house. Broker went back in the barn, searched for a moment, and found the bat. To announce himself he swung the bat viscously against the tractor fender. Every time the bat landed, Earl cringed on the floor.

He extended the bat and poked Earl in the ribs. Earl moaned and gritted his teeth.

Broker shook his head. "For some reason, Jolene doesn't want you hurt too bad, so it can end right here. If we can understand each other."

"I need to go to a hospital," Earl said between clenched teeth.

"Listen carefully," Broker said. "I copied your hard drive. Jolene assures me there's enough on there to interest the feds. Credit unions are federal, Earl. You with me so far?"

"Okay, okay."

"Jolene's lawyer guarantees you'll get every cent she owes you—if you back off. You can be friends, but she gets a chance to live her life. That's the deal."

Earl's left cheek and eye were starting to puff black and blue. Shock turned his skin sticky gray. With a face full of blood and dirt, he didn't look so pretty anymore. "What about all this?" he said.

Broker smiled. "This was just testosterone gone awry."

"I mean, what are you going to tell them at the hospital?"

Broker shrugged. "I'm watching my buddy's farm for him, I know you, you wanted to see the birds, you came out and there was an accident."

Earl sighed in resignation. "Friends with Jolene."

"But no manipulation. No games," Broker said.

"Okay," Earl said. His eyes stayed fixed on the door. Amy came jogging back in with J.T.'s first-aid kit, a knife, and a bedsheet. He asked, "Who's the chick?"

"Friend of mine. Lucky for you, she's a nurse."

Amy quickly cut open Earl's jacket sleeve and assessed the lacerated shoulder. "Looks worse than it is, superficial muscle damage." She applied gauze pads to the bleeding and felt around. "The left humerus is snapped, at least once, but it hasn't poked through the skin. He probably has some cracked ribs."

Amy decided to immobilize the arm against his chest with the sheet. Broker helped her sit Earl up and tie the makeshift restraint. Then she gave him some Tylenol. Once the arm was secured they hauled him to his feet and walked him to the Jeep.

As they got in, Amy scanned the empty fields and pastures. "What about the bird?"

"Maybe they come home when they get hungry," Broker said.

Chapter Thirty-seven

After a solitary dinner in an overcrowded restaurant, Allen got away from people and drove toward his town house, deep in one of Timberry's meandering cul-de-sacs.

His efficient two-bedroom row house was somebody's idea of a New England design, clad in white clapboard and black trim. He had a garage, a basement, a deck, and a view. His association kept the outside tidy. He took care of the inside.

Untidy reminded him of his ex-wife, Sharon, who had remarried and moved to California. Like Annette Benning in *American Beauty*, Sharon sold real estate. Unlike Annette Benning, she had never cleaned a house in her life.

They had trudged dutifully together until the end of his residency at the Mayo Clinic.

At the clinic, residents were required to make rounds in starched white coats, suits, and a tie every day. The dress code bolstered Allen's innate fastidiousness, and the more pressed and creased he was at the clinic the more aware he became of Sharon's slovenly habits at home.

Thank God they never had kids.

But then, how could they? Buried alive in the heavy pleats of Sharon's lovemaking, Allen had imagined his spermatozoa suffocated. She had possessed a certain sluggish beauty, if you enjoyed watching heavy whipping cream pour from a spout.

They'd been high school sweethearts. He had been deceived by the household Sharon grew up in, by its snug, scrubbed security. Only when it was too late, after he'd married her, did he realize that the order in that house was the work of Sharon's mother, but none of the mother's precision had rubbed off on the daughter. And this didn't truly manifest until they had moved out of student housing into a town house in Rochester. One of his Mayo colleagues came over after a round of handball and spilled a beer on the scuffed kitchen linoleum. Immediately, he offered to clean it up. "I'll get it," he said to Sharon, "just show me where you keep the mop."

"I don't think we have one," Sharon had said, in effect.

Allen aimed the garage-door clicker, opened the door, drove in, shut off his car, and closed the door behind him.

Thank you, Minnesota, for no-fault divorce.

He unlocked his door and went inside. Jolene had never visited his place. The last two women he'd dated—a lawyer and an investment banker—had given him the impression that his living quarters were too small. He'd already forgotten the personal details of both of them. He did remember that they were compulsively skinny, and the main difference between them was that the lawyer took Zoloft and the banker took Prozac.

Allen could imagine Jolene getting drunk in her past life and fucking her whole high school football team. He could not imagine her taking Prozac.

His town house had originally been chosen for its convenient location, a mile from the hospital and clinic. When he'd moved in two years ago, his deck overlooked wetlands and a woods. Now a golf course provided a deeper shade of sizzling chemical green.

He cared about the environment. He was not a flashy person, he reminded himself, as he walked through the comfortable two-bedroom unit. His furnishings were sparse and functional, well made but not extravagant.

He was not a bad person.

He was not shallow.

He'd made only one mistake in his life.

One.

And he was doing his best to learn from it.

He put a bag of popcorn in the microwave and set the timer. Cub Scout popcorn, sold door-to-door. Sure, here kid.

Not a bad person.

Not.

He left the kitchen, went into the bedroom, and selected a pair of freshly laundered blue scrubs from his dresser. Clothing kept turning up in his exercise bag and he kept forgetting to return it. When he was home alone and didn't expect guests, like now, he wore them as lounging pajamas.

He put on the soft shirt and loose trousers, went back to the kitchen, transferred the popcorn from the microwave to a bowl, and went into the living room. The movie Garf had given him lay on the coffee table. Allen shook out the tape, inserted it in the VCR, and tapped the play button. While the leader played out, he turned *The Blue Angel* jacket over and read the tag line on the back. "A middle-aged professor is degraded and led to his destruction through his infatuation with a heartless café entertainer."

Hmmm. He'd give it a try, to see if there was a point to Garf's insolence. He settled back on the couch and began to eat his popcorn.

The movie was an early talky that creaked across the screen in seventy-year-old black and white. Dr. Immannuel Rath, a portly professor, fuddled his way through the pranks of his students and wound up following some of them to a seedy nightclub where Lola Lola, the Dietrich character, strutted her stuff.

Allen squirmed a little and licked the greasy popcorn residue from his fingers. Very funny. *I'm supposed to be the socially maladroit academic being swallowed alive by the hot nightclub singer. Is that it, Garf?*

But the character that stuck in his imagination was not the professor or the entertainer. As the doomed romance developed backstage in the nightclub, a clown wandered through the scenes with wistful eyebrows and a sad smile painted on his face. The clown's purpose was to underscore Professor Rath's folly. In fact, the professor, ruined by his love for the singer, joined the vagabond traveling troupe and wound up donning the clown costume himself.

The clown was the only character who knew what was going on.

The movie ended with a melodramatic death scene. Disgraced, Rath made his way back to the schoolhouse and collapsed on his old headmaster's desk.

As the film rewound, Allen considered Garf's intent; was it an ironic caution or a threat? Either way, it was a clue that more intelligence was cooking behind Garf's blue eyes than Allen had previously assumed.

Garf had to go, of course. Milt was leery about underwriting Jolene as long as Garf was living under her roof.

And now it appeared that Garf was suggesting that Allen had to go. Allen smiled a tight little smile, got up, and experimented with a six-part silver box tango step. Garf underestimated him, of course. As had Hank.

Allen slid the movie back in its jacket, took the popcorn bowl to the kitchen, washed it, and put it in the cupboard. Then he spent half an hour going over his notes on tomorrow's surgery schedule. Satisfied, he filed the notes back in his briefcase, brushed his teeth, flossed, washed his hands, and went to bed. As always, he fell immediately into a deep, dreamless sleep.

Allen woke punctually at 6:00 A.M., rolled out of bed, donned a wind suit and Nikes, stretched, drank a tall glass of water, and went on a five-mile run.

On his way back, at about mile four as he jogged past a long stand of fiery staghorn sumac, he had his revelation. It started with an awareness about the unself-conscious way his body was moving. For the first time in his life, outside of surgery, he felt fluid, as if his work brain had finally melted and now dripped warm and active down into the rest of his body.

The new perception was simple: the accidently-on-purpose-snuffing of Hank Sommer had not so much liberated Jolene as it had freed him. He, not Jolene, was more alive. Almost as if he sucked Hank's ferocious life force out with a straw and digested it.

He'd finally made a mistake and the disaster had set him free. He didn't need to possess Jolene. He didn't need to *do* anything. He just simply had to *be* himself.

The red line had been erased.

Allen ran home, showered, and then, standing with a towel wrapped around his waist, razor held aloft, his lathered face centered in the steamy bathroom mirror—he thought, No. *Let's let it grow and see how we look in a beard.*

On the damp tile bathroom floor Allen took a few stylized steps and bent over an imaginary tango partner. He dressed, ate cereal in a warm blur, and drove to the hospital.

It was Friday, which was his favorite day because he spent all day in surgery. As he parked and entered the building he mentally put on his work cap to begin to focus on the day's procedures.

But he was not so intense that he forgot to take the time to smile at the nurses, to say good morning to a janitor. And the staff locker room didn't feel like a decompression chamber this morning. Just a changing room.

Capped, wearing blue booties over his shoes, with a mask loose around his neck, he sipped a cup of black coffee in the staff lounge. A small audience had gathered at a table around Lenny Merman.

"So what does it mean if you find a lawyer buried up to his neck in cement?" Merman asked

"Groan," Allen said.

"Shortage of cement," Merman said. More groans.

Merman was a burly ortho guy, so passionate about his work that colleagues joked he'd probably tear his way into a body with his bare hands if the surgical tech was late with his instruments.

"Okay, here's another one. Why are lawyers buried at twenty-six feet instead of at six feet?" Merman would not be deterred.

"Boo, hiss," Allen said.

"Way down deep they're really good people," Merman said.

Allen rubbed the stubble on his cheek and smiled when he caught his reflection in the mirror next to the bulletin board. They wouldn't approve at the Mayo Clinic.

The charge nurse came in and posted the room schedule, and the blue pack of surgeons went off to the surgery suites. Allen walked down the corridor not even paying attention to the red line, went to a sink, and meticulously scrubbed his fingers, hands, and forearms with antibacterial soap.

Allen was a belly man. His domain was the region located between the crotch and the diaphragm, the area in which lay the liver, the spleen, the pancreas, the colon, the small intestines, and the reproductive plumbing. The internal structure, shape, and color of these organs were more clearly visualized in his mind than the faces of the people they belonged to.

He walked into the surgery and held out his hands like a matador to be draped and gloved by the circulating nurse. The team assembled. Allen greeted them—first his resident, Durga Prasad from Bombay, the surgical tech, a circulating nurse, and an anesthetist. Allen, Durga, and the tech worked in direct contact with the patient and observed the sterile barrier. So they were gloved and gowned. The anesthetist, the circulating nurse, and the anesthesiologist—if she wandered in—were not sterile.

The first patient shuffled in, a middle-aged man wearing a hospital gown. Allen matched the face to the procedure on the surgery schedule: bilateral inguinal hernia repair.

They eased the patient onto the operating table. He looked up a little wary at the huge circular AMSCO quantum surgical lights hovering over him on jointed arms, like the wings of a robotic angel. Next, the patient eyed the anesthesia machine which sprouted pumps, dials, tubes, and digital screens.

"You're going to be just fine," Allen said.

Then the anesthetist ran his IV and hooked up his monitor leads and injected Versed in the IV, which he followed with a shot of Sublimaze. The patient was masked, pre-oxygenated, and then was put under with Pentothal.

All smooth, amid casual banter about *The Blair Witch Project,* which Jeannie had just seen on video.

"Really, really overrated," said Jeannie, the circulating nurse.

"Fakey, I thought, the wooden stuff hanging in the trees," said Jerry, the anesthetist.

"Smart, though," offered Allen. "Remember the way they hyped it on the web?"

After Pentothal, the muscle relaxant, succinylcholine, was administered. The patient shuddered. Behind his mask, Allen clicked his teeth. It was the same kind of muscular spasm that he had caused in Hank Sommer.

Allen took a deep breath and waited as the patient lost control of his muscles and went flaccid. Expertly, the anesthetist fitted a plastic shield over the patient's teeth, then inserted an instrument like a stainless-steel, right-angled trowel—a laryngoscopic blade—into the sedated man's throat. The patient's head shifted as the blade was levered forward and upward to elevate the epiglottis and expose the glotal opening. Then the anesthetist inserted a plastic tracheal tube, hooked up the breathing circuit to the machine, and pumped nitrous oxide into the patient's lungs.

Allen directed everything that occurred in the OR with verbal instructions. Nonverbal cues were conveyed through the eyes, the only feature that showed above the surgical masks. Surgical teams were close watchers, especially of their surgeon leader. Now all the eyes in the room keyed on him, to sense his mood, to see what kind of day he'd have.

He heard them whisper that he hadn't shaved this morning and what did it mean?

The patient's stomach was draped with sterile blue sheets. Another sterile blue sheet separated the patient's head from the operating field. The human shape became abstract. Allen's target was an anonymous shaved square of belly which had been designated with a rubber stamp: LEFT.

The tech unwrapped and positioned a sterile tray that contained the instruments for hernia repair, the square of exposed flesh was washed with orange Betadine disinfectant. One last point of etiquette remained: the choice of music on the CD player that sat on a table along one wall.

The eyes over the masks turned to Allen who always selected the music.

"Jeannie, pick us some sounds," Allen said casually to the circulating nurse.

Allen could feel the slight lift in the room as Jeannie spun some Sheryl Crowe. Allen held up a gloved hand, the scrub tech firmly put a scalpel in it, and he made the first incision.

And so the day proceeded under the hot surgical lights. In between procedures, Allen moved between the pre op suites, where he interviewed his next patient, and the consult room, where he spoke briefly with the family of his last procedure.

A hemorrhoidectomy.

A left-breast biopsy.

Time out to consult on a patient in emergency, then back down to surgery to remove another suspect lump from an elderly woman's breast and run it though Radiology.

Lunch was interrupted by a page to consult on a man admitted with a numb, discolored leg and a history of heart problems. Allen jogged up two flights of stairs, saw the patient, and agreed with the internist to give the man a clot-busting drug.

The hours floated by with soft intensity like a long, almost weightless parachute drop.

And soon it would end, after the last scheduled procedure, a laparoscopic cholecystectomy. The lap choly was a routine gallbladder removal using a laparoscopic wand that contained a miniature video camera and lights.

After the patient was intubated and breathing on the machine, his abdominal cavity was inflated with carbon dioxide gas. A tenmillimeter sheath was poked inside through a port incision above the navel. Then the camera was inserted in the sleeve.

Two television monitors were positioned on either side of the operating table, so Allen and his resident could both easily view the liver and gallbladder.

Three other ports were incised higher in the stomach wall on the patient's right-hand side, just beneath the liver. And sleeves were inserted. Two for the resident to handle his forceps and one midbelly, for Allen to use the dissecting forceps, in this case an electric cautery.

Laparoscopy was essentially a spatial-orientation video game played on a living person. Allen held the rotating, pistol-grip forceps controls in his hands and coordinated the working end of the forceps to the image the camera projected on the television towers.

The glistening coral-colored formations of human inner space reminded Allen of spelunking, going into underwater caves with Aqua-Lung and handheld lights—something he hadn't tried yet. Maybe Milt would go for it?

"Lights," Allen said. The powerful overhead lights were turned off.

"Music," Allen said. Again Jeannie chose. Bruce Springsteen belted out "Born to Run" as the resident gripped the gallbladder with a forceps and positioned it against the liver. With exquisitely fine muscle control and timing, Allen clipped the cystic artery and duct with titanium staples, then severed them. He then carved the gallbladder free from the liver bed with the cautery. Before removing it through the umbilical port, as he tidied up some minor bleeders with the cautery, he had an attack of sheer whimsy.

Or perhaps inspiration.

To underscore the new boost in his mood, or perhaps to honor the secret transgression that had launched him out of his rut—Allen acted on impulse in a fleeting moment when no one was watching the video towers. With a deft whirl of the cautery controls he seared two letters into the patient's abdominal wall:

AF

His own initials up on the screens.

No harm done, it would heal in a few days. It was just a tiny flourish. He would have preferred Vivaldi trumpets instead of Clarence Clemons's saxophone, but, hey, what the hell . . .

Allen stripped off his last sterile gown of the day and tossed it in a hamper. Then he dictated his notes and was on his way to the locker room when he met Merman in the hall.

"So how do you code an ostrich kick?" Merman asked.

"What's this, another joke?" Allen was mildly intrigued.

"No way. ER just admitted a guy with a transverse fracture of the left humerus. Bam. One kick."

"Where did it happen? At a zoo?"

"No idea. C'mon, take a look at his arm, the nurse in ER said the kick tore a hole in a heavy leather sleeve and you can see the scale pattern of the bird's toe knuckle in the mangled skin."

"That'd be worth seeing," Allen said, genuinely curious. He kept pace with Merman as they left surgery, went around the pre op admitting desk, and headed down the corridor to Emergency. They turned a corner and, ahead of them, a group of nurses and the ER doc were gathered around a man on a gurney and—

Allen immediately stood absolutely still and let Merman continue on alone.

The patient was Earl Garf.

And Phil Broker was standing at the edge of the medical huddle.

And right next to Broker, holding on to his elbow real friendly-like, was the nurse-anesthetist from Ely, Minnesota: Amy Skoda.

Allen's surprise escaped his lips in a nervous stammer: "Wha-what . . . ?" Ashamed, he backed down the hall and around the corner with his hand clamped over his mouth.

What the hell was going on?

Chapter Thirty-eight

After getting Earl admitted to the emergency room at Timberry Trails, Broker used a pay phone in the waiting room to call Jolene.

He told her that Earl was her friend again, like she wanted, and he'd be moving his stuff out of her basement. And maybe she should send him some flowers because he'd just been admitted to the hospital after having his arm broken by an ostrich.

"That's what I said," he repeated. "An ostrich."

He said he'd be at the farm until Sunday afternoon, and then he was returning to Ely. He said he hoped everything turned out all right.

He said good-bye. Then he realized something and turned to Amy. "You have a plane to catch."

Amy shrugged, grinned. "Let's blow it off. We have an escaped ostrich to find, remember?"

"Right. How do you find an escaped ostrich?"

They laughed, then, remembering Rodney in the barn, Broker made a fast call to John Eisenhower at the Washington County sheriff's department. After quick pleasantries, Rose, John's secretary, said she could squeeze him in for ten minutes if he hurried.

Rushing through the hospital parking lot, Broker explained, "I know that other guy who ran. Rodney. I need to check something with the local sheriff."

On the road, he said, "John and I go way back. I was working on his task force when I arrested Rodney three years ago. He's supposed to be in jail."

Pushing the Leper Colony, he drove eighty mph on back-county roads, leaving Timberry, skirting through Lake Elmo and Oak Park Heights, and turning onto Highway 36 where it made its turn approaching the St. Croix River on the outskirts of Stillwater. A few minutes later he turned into the parking lot for the Washington County Jail and the sheriff's office.

"This will only take a minute," he assured Amy. He jogged into the red-brick jail complex and was buzzed through a security door. Rose waved him in. "Make it quick, he has to talk to the Elk's Club in ten minutes."

John was standing in front of his desk in gray dress slacks and a T-shirt breaking starch on a fresh white dress shirt. Broker hadn't seen him since last May when he'd come up to Broker's Beach for the fishing opener. John was running for reelection next month and he'd been spending time in the gym. He had trimmed his blond mustache and the ten desk pounds that he used to wear around his waist had migrated back to his chest and shoulders as muscle.

They shook hands warmly. Then John's hand went to his pocket and he handed Broker a campaign button: REELECT THE SHERIFF.

"Kind of Nixonian," Broker said.

John struck a pose, and framed an invisible subject in the air with parenthetically cupped hands. "I considered going with 'Reelect Ike,' but decided that was a little over-the-top." He finished buttoning his shirt and tucked it in. "I heard about that business in the canoe area . . ."

Broker nodded. "Reason I'm in town; I brought the guy's car back."

John walked around his desk and took two ties from the back of his chair. He held them up next to the charcoal suit coat hanging from the shelves behind the desk.

"I'd go with the blue one," Broker said.

John nodded and began to knot his tie. "I, ah, also heard from Tom about you and Nina splitting the blanket." Tom Jeffords was Broker's neighbor, the Cook County sheriff.

"Our latest standoff," Broker said, clipping off the words.

"Not real good for your kid," John observed.

"I hear you."

John snugged up his Windsor and reached for his coat. "So what's up? You didn't pop in to help me pick ties," he said.

"About two hours ago I ran into Rodney on the street. You remember Rodney."

"Oh yeah."

"I thought he was doing some serious federal time?"

"Don't quote me on this, but law enforcement is still a pretty snitch-driven business. After you left the picture, everybody—local and federal—was hurting statewide for a contact in the outlaw end-of-the-gun culture."

Broker grimaced, disbelieving. "Rodney flipped?"

John grinned. "Yeah, he's kinda, like, the new you. He's working deep informant to reduce his sentence."

Broker groaned but he now understood Rodney's disappearing act. Rodney wouldn't be telling Earl anything.

A black phone sitting off to the side on John's desk rang.

John eyed the phone, checked his wristwatch. "Shit." He picked up the phone and spoke in the receiver, "I'm tight for time. Whatta you got?"

Broker watched John's eyes roll up in a *Why me, Lord* expression. "So?" he fumed. Then he shook his head. "How the fuck should I know." Then after a moment, he jerked alert. "*No, no, don't shoot it.* The animal-rights nuts will be all over my ass, especially with the goddamn election."

Shaking his head, John lowered himself to his chair, planted his elbow, and knuckled his forehead. "Try and keep track of it and call the DNR. I know it's not wild, but they have tranquilizer rifles. Ask to borrow one. Okay, okay. Page me in an hour and let me know. Right. Later."

John dropped the phone to its cradle. "You talk to J.T. lately?" he asked after a few beats.

"Sure," Broker said in a neutral tone.

"Is he missing any birds that you know of?"

"Can't say," Broker said. Carefully.

"Well, there's only couple ostrich operations in the county and one of them is missing bird because this really big-ass ostrich just did some broken-field running through traffic on I-94 near the Manning Trail and we got a twenty-car fender bender. Luckily just cuts and bruises so far. Hey, Rose," he yelled. "Get me J.T. Merry-weather's phone number."

"I think I better go; you look kind of busy right now," Broker said.

Over a quick beer at the Trapper's Lounge in downtown Stillwater, Broker struggled to keep a straight face as he recited John Eisen-hower's one-liners: "Is he missing any birds? Well, call the DNR."

"What are you going to tell J.T.?" Amy asked.

"I don't know."

"How are they going to round up Popeye?"

"Probably nail him with a tranquilizer dart. So we better get back to the farm. The phone's bound to be ringing. And I'd just as soon you answered in case it's John who calls."

"Okay, I'll help you till we get the bird back. You did tell me to shut the barn door and I didn't," Amy said.

"Right. Except if you would have shut that door we'd be in the hospital with Earl," Broker said.

They clinked glasses.

A message was waiting on J.T.'s voice mail from a Washington County deputy who was checking around about missing ostriches. Amy returned the call and explained that the owner was gone and she was house-sitting, and she confirmed that a large male was missing from his pen.

Broker crossed his fingers. The more he thought about it, he worried that a county cop would overhear somebody at Timberry Trails Hospital talking about an ostrich-kick casualty. It was the kind of loose grounder that John E. would run out. He was on the verge of calling the sheriff's office and personally confessing when the phone rang.

The deputy again; they'd found Popeye kicking an abandoned horse barn apart in Dellwood and they had darted him with a tran-quilizer gun. Could someone come pick him up?

Amy said her trailer was in Iowa. The deputy said give him a few minutes. He called back and said they'd found a local farmer who'd cart Popeye for one hundred dollars. Coached by Broker, Amy gave the deputy J.T.'s address, fire number, and directions.

An hour later, a Dodge Ram pickup pulled into the yard. Popeye, groggy and twitching, lay in the bed. They backed into the barn, up to the stall, and lowered the tailgate. Broker and Amy helped the driver drag the bird over it. Popeye weakly raised his head, blinked, and resumed his nap. The amused driver took his fee and left.

Walking back to the house Broker and Amy stopped, jolted by a sudden temperature drop of twenty to thirty degrees. Broker hunched his shoulders and squinted into the bitter northwest wind. "Weather Channel," he said.

Inside, rubbing their red hands, they studied the televised Dopler map. The cold front bulging down from North Dakota and Saskatchewan had purple edges and a bone-white heart.

"Jesus, it's already ten below in International Falls," Amy pointed at the map.

There was no snow in the forecast, just polar cold.

Unloading Popeye left them exhausted after their jag of a day. They went into the kitchen and couldn't face the rest of the ostrich chili in the refrigerator. So they ordered a deluxe pizza. When it arrived they split the bottle of Pepsi, settled down in front of the TV, and raided J.T.'s movie library. They were arguing about whether to watch *Erin Brockovich* or *Contact* with Jodie Foster when the phone rang.

Chapter Thirty-nine

Jolene savored Broker's brief phone message as she ate a quick Healthy Choice microwave dinner. Earl had been moved on down the line. A broken arm. She'd skip the flowers.

Monday, Hank would go to the nursing home, and the vigils, hanging on his every breath, would finally end. Which left the question of Hank's extended care.

She remembered Allen's unsaid promise. *If it comes to that, I can help.*

God, she couldn't bring herself to think about it directly—but she so wanted to be free of them all.

So she paced in the kitchen and fantasized that her hair was long again and that she was reclining in a salon with other women waiting on her, doing her hair and her fingernails and her toes.

Things were moving ahead, so why was she so edgy? Why did she have this gummy metal taste stuck to the roof of her mouth? Her thoughts felt flimsy, like puzzle pieces jumbled in her skull.

Nervously, she analyzed the sensations and concluded that all the tension and sleeplessness had made her thirsty. She wanted a drink. The dry colors in her head would swell up, go fluid, and run together. Smooth and easy.

So she kept busy. Another trick she'd learned from Hank. She checked all the baby monitors in the house to make sure they were working. Then, in a frantic lurch of mood, she craved a cigarette.

For half an hour she rummaged through the house—drawers, cupboards, the pockets of Hank's clothes still hanging in the closets. Nothing. Not even one of Hank's stale Camels. Back in the kitchen, she paced and got weaker. Get in the Accord, drive to the Cenex store up on 95. It would take about seven minutes. She'd have a pack of cigarettes. Twenty diversions.

A cigarette would be bad but it would blunt the deeper urge.

Or would it just lower her resistence so it would be easier to take that first drink? Dammit. She needed more willpower.

But you weren't supposed to use willpower, you were supposed to work the program, which was basically learning to delay gratification through talking a lot to other people. You were supposed to displace. Because willpower was an idea that got you off alone in your head and . . .

Whack! Jolene kicked the Kenmore refrigerator.

Bullshit.

It wasn't drinking that had her shook up. Goddamit. *Hank had turned the TV on and off.*

He was *in there* watching them.

She stared at the circular stairway leading down to the lower level and Hank's room. She had to go down there and feed him, change him, stay ahead of the bedsores.

He'd turned on the TV for her.

But not for Allen and Garf.

Really spooked now, she had this image of her nerves like pink toothpaste all squirted out of the tube. Like her life now, after Earl and Stovall. No way could she put it back the way it was.

Well, screw this. Hank would have to fly solo for fifteen minutes. She grabbed her car keys and headed for the garage. Ten minutes later, she was sitting in the parking area of a Cenex station inhaling a Marlboro Light.

Nicotine turned cartwheels in her clean blood. It helped.

But not much.

She drove back to the house, parked, walked out of the garage, and shivered in a gust of suddenly cold wind. On the porch, finishing her cigarette, she amazed herself. On one hand, she was losing her mind. On the other, she was turning into a suburban ditz who didn't want her house to smell like cigarette smoke.

Her house. Stay with that.

She went in, brushed her teeth, swished with Scope. In the middle of this task she realized she really was alone in the house. No music in the basement. No Earl.

Now, with things getting tricky, she suddenly missed him.

No, she missed his function in her life.

But Jolene's whole idea was not to depend on men anymore. Right?

So, you're going to figure this out on your own.

Your house.

Your money.

Your life.

No men allowed.

All you have to do is hang on through the weekend. Milt will come to the rescue. This time next week you'll be visiting Hank in a safe, secure nursing home.

It's going to be all right.

He had receded far into himself and his vision turned black at the edges, tunneled, like looking the wrong way through two telescopes. The enthusiasms of simply tapping the TV controls on and off a few times had left him mentally drained, and now his fingers were like cold batteries, dead. It was a revelation. He'd had nothing to use to measure his strength before. Now he realized how little energy he had left.

And he saw it as a finite amount, nonrenewable.

And he saw something else. Something approaching with a calm, unhurried tread. A blur of color flickering into the edge of his vision. His heart and lungs were strong but his brain was flaming out.

Dying.

Everything he did from now on had to count.

Jolene steeled herself and entered Hank's room, determined to be businesslike. Just do the work. She believed in holding up her end of the deal. The deal had been for better or for worse. She could handle two more days of worse.

First she cleaned excess saliva from his mouth with the suction wand. Then she changed his wet diaper. As she fed him through his tube and added water to the IV drip, she watched him carefully for signals. He seemed almost asleep, eyes barely open. Lazy, dreamy, tired.

Dutifully, she stripped off his gown, brought in a dishpan of hot water, and gave him a sponge bath. She checked the incision where his gastrostomy inserted for leakage or infection. Then she rubbed his wasting body down with baby oil, shaved him, and trimmed his hair. She clipped his fingernails and toenails, and swabbed his gums and teeth with a sponge dipped in mouthwash.

She talked to him as she put his diaper and clean gown back on, as she struggled turning him, to put on clean sheets half a bed at a time. Just practical little asides. "Now I'm going to roll you over. Now I'm pulling on your gown."

Then she swept around the bed, taking great care to get all the hair and clippings. When she was finished, she removed all the cleaning materials. She took the old sheets and clothes downstairs to the laundry room and put them in the washer. She armored herself with reassuring smells of hot water, Spic 'n' Span, and Tide.

Feeling stronger, she returned to the kitchen, poured another cup of coffee, and stood, studying the restaurant-style stove. It was a regular flame thrower—must have cost eight grand, but Hank had insisted on getting it. He'd spent another hundred grand remodeling this house. He'd bought the new Ford for himself and the Honda for her.

And didn't renew his fucking health insurance.

That's a drunk for you.

Jolene looked around at the new granite counters, the tile floor, the new cabinets, the river scene out the windows.

Hers someday. Hell, it was hers now. She shook her head. Nothing lasts, Hank used to say. But they'd barely had even the first part of nothing.

She put on her coat and took her coffee out on the deck and lit another cigarette and pictured a happy mob of nicotine assassins stabbing the air sacs in her lungs.

She inhaled, exhaled. Dropped her head on her chest.

She'd have to sign over a deed on the house to Milt, as security, until they got through probate court. She could live with that.

Then the wind came up so frigid it must have blown in from

North Dakota. Jolene hugged herself and her heart quaked in her chest like a dry leaf. She snubbed out her cigarette and hurried through the patio door into Hank's room to get warm. She sat on the edge of his bed.

"I never lied to you, Hank. I told you I'd make you happy for a while, which, you'll recall, I did. I also told you I'd probably take you for every cent you had."

Jolene held Hank's wooden right hand in both of hers and said, "You laughed at me when I said that. But you know what, honey? I guess that's exactly what I'm doing."

He knew he should hoard his reserves of strength; the effort to move his finger was like shoveling steel. Fire discipline, he told him-self, reaching back to his most primitive survival instincts.

But she was right there, her warm flesh on his, and he could smell her lily body wash and he couldn't resist.

So he tickled her damp palm with the tip of his right index fin-ger. A sly, unmistakable wiggle.

Electrocuted, Jolene did not actually scream this time; it was more like a long gasp as she jumped off the bed, ran from the studio, through her bedroom, and up the stairs into the kitchen. She leaned with both hands braced on the counter until she caught her breath. She stared at the phone. Allen? No, she'd called him before and Hank had stopped his tricks.

That meant something, maybe.

Besides, Allen was an overeducated nice guy and right now she needed a little more red meat.

She snatched a card down from the bulletin board—the one Phil Broker had given her—and reached for the phone.

Amy answered the phone next to the couch, thinking it might be the sheriff's department again. She thrust the receiver at Broker. "For you, and she's shook up." Too ladylike to smirk, Amy curled her lip slightly.

Broker took the phone. "Hello?"

"Broker, something really weird is going on," Jolene blurted.

"Calm down."

"It's Hank. He's . . . doing things."

"Hank's *doing things*?" Broker repeated and Amy caught his goose bumps.

"What things?" Amy asked, huddled at his shoulder, head-to-head, with her ear against the receiver.

Jolene said, "The night before last, Earl left the TV clicker in his hand, like a joke. And I heard the TV come on and I went in there and he turned it off and on twice."

"Jesus," Broker and Amy read off the same page, eyes locked.

". . . the thing is, I called Allen and he came over and I remembered the cat had been on Hank's lap, and Allen thought it was the cat, you know. Except it wasn't the damn cat because about three minutes ago I was holding his hand and he very deliberately tickled my palm."

"Tickled?" Broker wondered.

"Goddammit, *tickled*. The way guys do. You know? Wanna fuck, like that? Tickled!"

"Let's get over there fast," Amy said, her face absolutely electric.

"You sure?" Broker said.

"What's going on?" Jolene yelled.

"Hold tight, we're on the way," Broker said.

Chapter Forty

Broker was speeding down the back roads again. "Remember, Allen Falken has a way of showing up over there," he said. "I'm thinking about the lawsuit? If he sees you around Hank, you could lose your license."

Amy brushed aside his concern. Her eyes focused straight ahead into a vortex of streaming leaves. "What if he's coming out of a coma?" she wondered.

"Can that happen?"

"*Anything* can happen." She threw up her arms; pumped, she bounced on the seat. "When you're dealing with the human brain we're like cavemen hanging our toes over the edge of deep space. Nobody really knows," her voice raced. "The proofs the neurologists use to diagnose persistent vegetative states are medieval. Visual pursuit? Whether the eyes focus on and follow an object? C'mon. There's a case history of patients who have been misdiagnosed, who are locked in."

"Locked in?"

"Right. They've lost voluntary control of their muscles. But they're still mentating?"

"Mentating?"

"Thinking. Feeling. And what if they get some muscle capacity

back? Or have some that's been overlooked. They can communicate. And that could be a basis for therapy that could restore function."

Her enthusiasm was infectious and Broker stepped on the gas.
He found himself at the threshold of a miraculous wish that Hank
Sommer could rise from his bed, fully recovered.

Amy squeezed his arm. "Everybody gave up on him but you.
You couldn't leave it alone."

"Easy, Amy. I don't buy the death of his accountant . . ."

"No, you never accepted what happened. You fought against it."

Perhaps. But Broker's core skepticism warned him to curb his
wishful thinking. Go slow, he told himself ironically as he raced
under clotted black clouds.

"Let's just calm down and take it one step at a time," Broker
said as he swerved down the dead-end road that led to Hank's house
and then eased down the twisting drive and parked in front of the
garage. The sky shut over them and it was almost night in the dense
white pines. They hurried up the steps.

Jolene opened the door and was on the verge of embracing Broker
when she saw Amy. The two women looked each other up and down
with an elaborate suspicion that cranked the urgency up a notch.

"Jolene, this is Amy. Amy's a nurse," Broker said.

Jolene and Amy did not shake hands.

"She is," Jolene said slowly.

"Hennepin County Emergency room, three years," Amy said.
Which was valid, Broker observed, but not necessarily accurate,
under the circumstances.

"This way," Jolene said.

*Okay, who's coming now. Hank could hear the scurry of several
pairs of feet coming through the bedroom. Jolene, Broker, and . . .
he saw the white-blond hair and the sassy gray eyes and the
freckles . . .*

The lynx.

*He instantly recognized Amy, the nurse from Ely. Her face had
been his last pleasant conscious memory.*

Amy, whom Allen smugly let take the blame for his willful mis-

take. And the moment Amy entered the room and saw him, her eyes glistened, filled with tears.

She thinks she did this to me.

Seeing the full burden of his condition projected on her face, he felt his own eyes flood with moisture.

Seeing the bright rush of tears come to Hank's eyes, Jolene, Broker, and Amy froze.

Amy said, "Jesus, he's looking right at me."

She reacted swiftly by focusing both eyes down toward the floor. Hank imitated the eye movement. She rotated her eyes up toward the ceiling. Hank matched her. She went left and right. So did he.

"Jesus."

Amy looked around the study, walked to the desk, took a piece of paper, picked up a pen, and wrote something. Then, with the paper behind her back she approached the bed.

"Hank, if you can hear and understand me, I want you to blink twice for yes, once for no." She held up the piece of paper on which she had written YES and NO.

She pointed to YES.

Hank was initially distracted by the salty taste of his tears which trickled down his cheeks and pooled on his lips.

Okay. This is it.

He had to go with Broker and Amy. It was game time. But how much time did he have? How many thoughts did he have left. How many words remained in him? He had wanted to be a writer, to make his mark with words. Now he was down to his last words and, like hoarded bullets, he had to aim them very carefully. He blinked twice and was shocked at the effort it took.

Amy immediately sat at the desk and printed blocky letters on a fresh sheet of paper.

"What?" Broker asked as Jolene hung on his arm, wide-eyed.

"Alphabet board, a crude one, but it'll work," Amy said without looking up. She was all business, totally focused on arranging the letters of the alphabet into five groups:

A B C D E

F G H I J

K L M N O

P Q R S T

U V W X Y Z

"Okay," Amy said, flushed, eyes bright. "I point to a group until he blinks twice, then I tap each letter in the selected group until he blinks again. We write that letter down. Then we start over until we get a word. I'll tell him to shut his eyes for three seconds to indicate a new word."

Jolene studied Amy through a rippling curtain of shock. An expression was forming on her face that groped toward a question: *Who is this woman and what is she doing in my house?*

"You mean he can *talk* to us?" she asked, disbelieving.

"Yes," Amy said, getting up and returning to Hank's bedside.

Jolene followed her, getting the distinct feeling that she was the spare wheel, that Broker and this Amy were some kind of *team*. She looked to Broker for reassurance but his attention was riveted to Amy and her attempt to communicate with Hank.

Amy was speaking to Hank now, patiently explaining the sheet of paper in her hand. When she finished, she asked him. "Do you understand?"

Too many things mobbed his thoughts—everything that had happened recently and in his entire life, all the people he'd known.

It was not the time to overwrite.

Time to pick the first right word.

What's the most important thing he had to tell them?

Amy was waiting for his response. Okay.

He blinked twice.

"Here we go," Amy said. Her finger pointed to the first letter group. No response. She moved to the second. Again, nothing. Number three.

Hank blinked twice. Her hand moved to the first letter in the group. He blinked twice.

"K," Amy said. Her finger moved back to the first group and they started over. Nothing on the first group. Then two blinks on the second and two more on the fourth letter in the group.

"I," Amy said. She did not start over at the top but went to the next group down and got a response on the second letter. But Hank blinked four times.

"L," said Amy. She turned to Broker and Jolene. "Four blinks, what do you think?" she asked.

Jolene felt the bottom start to fall out but she was good at puzzles, so she said, "He means twice."

"Could be," Broker said.

"L," Amy said. She and Broker locked eyes. The letters materialized like a cold draft coming off of Hank and they raised the short hairs on Broker's forearm. He realized he was holding his breath.

Amy went down through the groups getting no response and went back to the top and got a hit. Scanning across, Hank's eyes selected the fifth letter:

"E," Amy said.

They could hear each other breathing as Amy worked through the groups. The next stop was on the third letter of the fourth group.

"R," Amy said.

Broker put his hand to his forehead, and his palm came away damp with sweat. He and Amy locked eyes again.

Seeing the two of them react, Jolene started backing away from the bed.

"Keep going, he hasn't shut his eyes," Broker said.

"Right," Amy said. She pointed through the last group, returned to the top, worked her way down, and Hank blinked the fourth group again. Fourth letter.

"S," whispered Amy as Hank shut his eyes. She printed KILLERS on the bottom of the sheet of paper.

Broker counted under his breath—one, two, three. Hank's eyes popped open.

"New word," Amy's voice rasped. Their eyes met, glanced away. Life and Death Charades.

"N," Amy said.

"O"

"T"

Hank shut his eyes. And Jolene felt like Hank, Amy, and Broker were slowly forming her firing squad. Fucking Earl. Should have never . . .

"A"

"M"

"Y" Amy's voice was barely audible. The hot yellow eyes clamped shut.

"What?" blurted Jolene, "Amy? *Her?*"

"Shhh, new word," Broker said.

"F"

"A"

"U"

"L"

"T"

Hank shut his eyes. Sweat popped on his forehead, pooled in the wrinkles under his eyes, and dripped down his cheeks.

"What are you two doing? Leave him alone," Jolene said, moving forward, as she picked up a towel from the bedside table and mopped his face and chin. "He's exhausted." She threw down the towel, spun, and confronted Amy. "He means *you?*"

Amy nodded.

"How does he know your name? Just who the fuck are you?" The question was directed at Amy but Jolene's eyes were suspiciously fixed on Broker.

Gently, Broker took Jolene by the shoulders and moved her aside. "New word," he said softly.

"N," Amy said.

His concentration was shattered and he lost track of the letters, but he knew what he wanted to say. Not Amy and not the other nurse. Allen, he wanted to say. And Earl for Stovall. Fatigue was centrifugal, dragging his eyes back into loopy orbits. He had to fight it. Had to keep going. Where was he? Amy's finger had moved to the last group.

"U," Amy said.

Broker watched Hank's eyes tremble, yielding to spasm. He reached out and to steady Hank's shoulder and felt the loose, wasted muscles and wished he could infuse strength through his own arm.

"R," Amy said.

"S"

"E"

He was lost, utterly spent and lost. He tried to blink sweat from his eyes and his lids stuck together, and when his eyes opened he was back on the Wild Mouse, *his eyeballs rolling and lurching in their sockets. Then oblivion.*

Jolene stood back, her arms folded, her mind winding out. Hank could blink-talk. Wonderful. And all these days they'd been talking in front of him. He'd obviously overheard Earl and her arguing about what happened to Stovall. So he thought she was in on it. It would sure look that way. She'd needed the money and Earl went to try and get it for her.

Killers, he'd said.

Plural.

Two killers.

If this blink business continued, he was going to implicate her, along with Earl, in a murder. And she thought fervidly, *Hank, honey; I'm really trying to do it your way, I really am—but if you keep this up I'll never get the chance.*

Jolene was so absorbed that she momentarily forgot the Amy-Broker show going on at the foot of Hank's bed. They huddled over the brief message printed at the bottom of the sheet of printer paper. *KILLERS—NOT AMY FAULT—NURSE,* it said.

"Nurse? Nancy Ward's the only other nurse . . ." Amy puzzled.

Broker tried to remember the tired, dark-haired recovery-room nurse in Ely. "Could he mean . . . ?"

Amy squinted at Broker, heaved her shoulders. "Killers? I don't know."

"Is he trying to say . . . the other nurse somehow . . . ?" Broker said.

"Deliberately?" Amy whispered. "She's still working. I took some leave. But she needs the money." Amy paused, Broker caught her hesitation, and they both looked up.

Jolene regarded them through wary eyes, arms still crossed. "What's the deal, guys? I feel kind of left out."

Broker said, "We were just thinking: what if there's a possibility what happened to Hank wasn't an accident."

"We," Jolene said, pointing first to Broker, then to Amy. "Who the fuck *is* she?"

Amy stepped forward and Broker held up a cautioning hand. But Amy waved him off and squared her shoulders. "Mrs. Sommer—Jolene—I'm Amy Skoda. I was the anesthetist who attended Hank during and after surgery in Ely."

"Uh-huh," Jolene unfolded her arms, recrossed them, and folded them tighter. "Let me get this straight, honey. I'm suing you, right?"

Amy bit her lower lip, nodded.

"Okay," Jolene said, swinging her eyes to Broker. "And you two know each other from up north?"

"That's right," Broker said.

"And you came down together?"

"Yeah," Broker said.

"In Hank's truck?"

"Right again."

"And you've been staying together at the ostrich farm, huh?"

Amy spoke up quickly. "It's not like that."

"Of course it isn't," Jolene's eyes briefly thrashed Broker, moved back to Amy. "So what's this *deliberate* stuff about?"

Broker shrugged. "What if the nurse in the recovery room acted with intent when she turned off the monitor. Hank might have seen her do or say something . . ."

Hope gripped Jolene and untied the knot of her crossed arms. Freed, they floated up; her hands opened, questioning: "But he said 'killers,' like more than one?"

"He's not exactly dotting all his i's, is he?" Amy said.

Jolene speculated on this new option for a few beats. She smiled sweetly at Broker. "You're a regular Crusader Rabbit. First you send Earl packing. Now you're trying to clear her?"

"Hey, Jolene, c'mon," Broker protested.

"No, this is good. So, what happens if I pick up the phone and call my lawyer."

"I'm in a *lot* of trouble," Amy said.

"Let me think a minute," Jolene said.

Arms folded across her chest again, she paced across the room; the room in the big house that wouldn't be hers anymore if Hank got down to serious testifying.

Okay, what Jolene knew was this: The legal system in America was based on the presumption of innocence. And the American criminal system was based on the principle that if you don't have a witness you don't have a crime.

So. This Amy was gaga with authorship; she had "discovered" Hank. And she and Broker were cooking up a theory about a nurse in Ely.

When the idea hit Jolene, it was better than the movies. First, she needed time. She needed to get Hank and these two isolated from cops and lawyers until she figured out how to put Hank out of commission. Keep him breathing but not blinking. And for that she needed Earl, broken arm and all. And since Broker and his natural pale blonde were getting off on playing detective so much—why not rev them up?

"This nurse," Jolene said. "Are you sure she's up there working?"

"Pretty sure," Amy said.

Jolene pointed to the phone on the desk. "Find out."

Amy looked to Broker, who shrugged—*sure*—so she went to the phone and punched in a number. "Judy? Yeah, Amy. How's it going. Nah, I'm down in the Cities, doing some shopping. Is Nancy working tomorrow? She is. Just curious how she's holding up. Yeah, there's a lot of that going around. I'll probably see you guys, Monday. Yeah. Bye." Amy put down the phone.

They all took a few beats to absorb Amy's phone conversation. Then Jolene gauged their eyes and said, "So, let's take a drive and test your theory."

"What do you mean?" Broker asked.

"I mean, I'll put off calling Milt and give you one chance to prove it. Twenty-four hours. We take Hank on a car trip." She walked to the phone on the bed stand and placed her hand on the receiver. "Take it or leave it."

"Up north, in his condition?" Amy asked.

"To Ely," Jolene nodded.

"I don't think so, unless he's in an ambulance," Amy said.

"You know what an ambulance *costs?*" Jolene set her jaw.

Amy looked to Broker who said, "Jolene, it's pretty risky."

Jolene picked up the phone. "They said I couldn't bring him home from the hospital. But I did. So how's it more risky than her—" she pointed the phone at Amy—"coming over here and inviting all kinds of legal hell? Look, Hank's beat, he'll sleep for eight hours. It's cold but the roads are dry. The only thing is, Earl took the Ford. His van's here but I don't have the keys. And my Accord isn't big enough. How reliable is the Jeep."

"The Jeep's okay," Broker said.

Jolene returned the phone to the cradle. "So? We have a cell phone, we have a nurse. What do you say?"

"Four hours, maybe we could do it," Amy said.

"He'd just be asleep?" Broker said.

Jolene nodded. "We'll be on main roads. Hell, with you guys along, he'll be in better company than alone here with me. So c'mon, let's load him in your car, drive up to Ely to your lodge. Rest up, and first thing in the morning, let's confront this nurse. If you're right, Amy's off the hook, you get to be a hero, and I've got a stronger case."

Jolene's straight-ahead energy was infectious. Broker looked at Amy who held up the paper with the alphabet blocks. "It would really be something," she said.

"C'mon," Jolene encouraged, "a little adventure, for Christ's sake."

Broker studied Hank, asleep in a blue gown. "He can't travel like that."

"No problem," Jolene said. "I'll put him in a fleece sweat suit. We'll build up the back of the Jeep with blankets and pillows so he can recline, like in his bed. One of us will have to ride in back with him and move him from side to side."

"We'll trade off," Amy said and her eyes swung hopefully to Broker.

"See," Jolene said. "We can pull it off."

Broker thought about it. He thought about how guys like J.T. were always telling him all he could do was entrap people; how he never *solved* anything. "Okay, let's do it; show me where the blankets are."

"We'll bring the blankets, and pack a diaper bag, with some

Ensure for his tube; you go out through the garage, open the door, and back the Jeep in." Jolene bristled with efficiency.

Broker went to move the Jeep. Amy helped Jolene pack a travel bag from the bed table. Hank was fast asleep.

"So, how's an upright lady like you wind up with a rough-trade guy like Broker?" Jolene asked casually when they were alone.

"Oh, he's not really like that, that's just an act," Amy said.

"Convinced me," Jolene said dryly. "So, you suspected this other nurse or what? Is that why you came down?"

"No, no. That was Broker, he was suspicious about the timing of your accountant's death so close after Hank's accident. But he checked it out with the Washington County sheriff's department . . ."

Jolene stiffened up. "He did?"

"Actually, J.T. did. He's the guy we're staying with. He's a retired homicide detective. They were all rookies together in St. Paul; J.T., Broker, and John Eisenhower, the Washington County sheriff. And Wash-Co said there was no foul play involved with Stovall. Just that he had some pretty weird hang-ups and they got out of control. Broker is having trouble accepting that. He hates being wrong."

"Rookies?" Jolene wondered. "You mean, like cops?"

"Well, Broker was never a proper cop. He worked lots of undercover for the state Bureau of Criminal Apprehension."

Jolene smiled, big and easy. Slowly, she reached out and raised a wave of Amy's hair on her palm. "This is really thick. Have you ever thought of wearing it up?"

"Usually I just put it in a ponytail," Amy said.

"Sure, I can see that." Jolene smiled again. "Look, will you excuse me for a minute. I need a quick cigarette to take the edge off and collect myself." As she turned to leave the room, she switched off the baby monitor on the bed table because, as Earl had pointed out, baby monitors pick up and broadcast cell phone conversations.

Chapter Forty-one

Allen had been kneed in the stomach once, coming down from a rebound in high school ball. He'd sprawled on the gym floor for five minutes, gasping, convinced he'd never catch his breath again.

Right now Allen was having trouble catching his emotional breath. Seeing Broker and the nurse, he briefly lost his bearings and contracted a sudden fatigue. His thoughts turned a tired yellow, the color of nicotine stains on the fingers of a smoker.

The color of Hank's fingers.

He'd looked out the window of an examining room and watched Broker and the nurse as they left the hospital and got into a dilapidated red Jeep. It was about Hank, of course. Why else would they be together, here?

On automatic pilot, he had changed into his street clothes, gotten in his car, and driven home. He flirted with denial and resolved to shake it off. So he pulled on his wind suit and shoes and went outside and tried to run. He got no farther than the row of box elders that lined the common area of his town house. He stood in place and watched the trees lose their leaves— showers of rounded, yellow, fat triangles, whipping back and forth across his shoes. The trees were going dormant, parts of them dying.

Coming apart.

It was all coming apart.

Should he call Milt? And what? Gossip? Milt didn't know any-thing.

He went back inside, and instead of showering and shaving he paced back and forth in his living room. He rubbed the stubble on his chin and encountered his reflection in a hall mirror. What had been a liberating gesture this morning now made him look seedy. He saw the movie box on the coffee table and remembered the clown's sad, watchful eyes.

He had to know. He had to go to Hank's and ask Jolene if Bro-ker had brought a nurse around.

Back in his car, he drove through revolving doors of icy wind and leaves. It was dark when he arrived at Hank's. Halfway down the driveway his low beams picked up a dirty glare of orange on red and he put on the brakes. He slowed and crept forward. It was the rusty Jeep he'd seen Broker and Amy get into.

His fatigue vanished as sudden excitement flushed his veins.

Fight or flight had always been a concept. Now it was a primi-tive tug-of-war clawing inside his chest.

Allen parked, got out, and saw that the front door was ajar. Crouching, eyes and ears pitched to high alert, he slipped into the house and made his way through the familiar rooms to the kitchen, where a disembodied voice stopped him cold.

"What?" said Broker's voice. Like a challenge.

Allen froze, swiveling, looking for—and then his eyes fixed on the baby monitor sitting on the kitchen counter.

"Alphabet board," said a second voice that Allen recognized as Amy's.

"Okay," Amy continued, "I point to a group until he blinks twice, then I tap each letter in the selected group until he blinks again. We write that letter down. Then we start over until we get a word. I'll tell him to shut his eyes for three seconds to indicate a new word."

"You mean he can talk to us?" Jolene's voice.

"Yes." Amy.

Then the sound of paper rustling. Amy again. "Do you under-stand?"

Allen put his hand out on the counter to steady himself.

This was not happening.

But it was, because Amy said, "Here we go."

After a moment.

"K," Amy said.

"I," Amy said.

"L," Amy said. "Four blinks, what do you think?" she asked.

"He means twice." And that was Jolene.

"Could be," Broker said.

"L," Amy said.

"E," Amy said.

Even through the cheap monitor Allen could hear them breathing.

"R," Amy said.

Then came some words that Allen couldn't hear because of static. His cheek was practically on the counter, his ear pressed to the white plastic speaker.

"Keep going," Broker said. "He hasn't shut his eyes."

"Right," Amy said.

Allen's hair prickled like needles in his scalp. Hank was *communicating*.

"S," Amy whispered.

Allen held his breath.

"New word."

Amy's voice rasped in the monitor and Allen jumped at the sound.

"N," Amy said.

"O," Amy said.

"T."

. . .

"A," Amy said.

"M"

"Y," barely audible.

"What?" Jolene blurted. "WHAT?"

Static.

"Shhh, new word," Broker said.

"F," Amy said.

"A," Amy said.

"U," Amy said.

"L," Amy said.

"T," Amy said.

Each letter drove a stake into Allen's chest.

More static. Garbled sounds.

"New word," Broker said.

Hyperventilating now, Allen listened to the next word, fully expecting to hear his name. Instead he heard: "Nurse," which didn't make sense. Nor did the conversation that followed. But then it did make a kind of sense. They seemed to have reached an impasse. Hank was spent, asleep.

This was more information than Allen could process.

His chest churned from the tug-of-war, from the stomp of fear that shouted *run away*. But something else, too, a bright spur of anger.

Fight them and survive.

Think. They're not that smart.

Run.

He did run, but just to move his car up to the road, where he tucked it out of sight on the shoulder. Heart pounding, he dashed into the pines, then came to a halt. He was making too much noise. He looked around, amazed at how ordinary things—trees and leaves and pine needles—had acquired hard, glowing edges; danger did that, etched this new world in sharp relief.

So be stealthy.

Quietly he stalked around the garage. It was suicidal, but he was compelled to face the thing that was coming to destroy him. All he had to do was get up on the deck, peek in the window.

The reflection of clouds in the patio door jiggled. The door opened. Allen ducked beneath the edge of the deck as he heard footsteps walk out onto the deck. A second later he smelled igniting tobacco and saw a nervous cloud of smoke jet above him. He snooped up and saw Jolene smoking a cigarette. Her face was etched, almost metal with resolve. She held a cell phone to her ear. She was pacing, agitated.

And then he heard the phone ring and the urgency in her. "Earl," she asked firmly. "Can you drive?"

Allen carefully listened to the entire phone conversation. By the time Jolene finished he knew his life had changed and that his entire education and training had prepared him for this particular crisis. To know how to read the signs and act decisively.

He mounted the stairs and watched Jolene leave the studio.
Broker and Amy were in the house. He didn't know where. But, for
the moment, Hank was unattended. It was time to take another
chance.

He found himself in a totally new place that was also very familiar. Sometimes surgeons were called upon to make fast decisions
about who lived and who died.

Triage.

*Hank fluttered awake as Jolene walked past his bed and disap-
peared into her bedroom. He smelled an after-scent of tobacco and
that made his throat ache. Then he felt a gust of cold air on his face.
His lurching eyes caught motion in the windows. Leaves. Branches
heaving. He tried to focus his eyes. Wasn't going to happen, he was
too tired.*

Then, wait, a person; slipping in through the door.

Broker?

No, not Broker.

Hank recognized the blue wind shell the man was wearing.

Christ, it was Allen.

*Silent and grim, Allen moved swiftly to the bed, pulled a pillow
from under Hank's head. No parting thoughts, hardly even eye contact. All business, Allen lowered the pillow, blocked out light and
plugged Hank's mouth and nose with clean cotton.*

Death smelled like Tide.

. . .

*Then the pillow pressure released and Allen stuffed it back
under Hank's head, bounded to the patio door, and was gone. Hank
panted, regaining his breath.*

Footsteps.

Chased Allen away.

Amy and Broker.

Amy smiled, seeing Hank's eyes flutter once and then close tight.
"Okay, Hank, we're going for a ride; we've got a real comfortable
bed made up for you."

Allen! Look out for Allen! He knows!

· · ·

"He's beat, look at his eyes," Broker said.

"You just take a nap, Hank; you're going to be fine," Amy said.

As Hank sank deeper into a stupor of fatigue they eased him up, bent him in the proper places, and lowered him into the wheelchair he'd come home from the hospital in.

Allen was here! He tried to kill me!
Listen!
But he was too damn tired to even open his eyes.

Chapter Forty-two

Earl had just lost an argument with a nurse about trading his Percocet prescription up to morphine when his cell phone rang on the stand next to the bed. He just stared at it with fogged eyes because it could only be one person. So he let it ring. Fuck her.

Five hours out of the recovery room, his left cheek, chin, eye, and ear had turned deep black and blue. His neck was stiff. They said they were concerned about concussion. In the meantime, the staff kept popping in to *view* him: Earl Garf, the ostrich-kick novelty.

His left upper arm was now held together by a thirty-four-millimeter titanium rod. The surgeon had accessed the ball of the left humerus through an incision in the shoulder. Then he'd inserted the rod down the bone channel and, working under an X-ray machine to get his alignment, had joined the rod and broken bone in place with two screws. Then he sutured the gashes in Earl's biceps, lightly casted the whole business, and folded it into a hanging traction sling.

The pain was nonspecific at this point, more like just everywhere. The fingers of his left hand peeked from the sling and were starting to resemble Oscar Meyer wieners, plump and brown-gray. But he could move them.

Because his neck was stiff, he had to rotate his whole upper body to turn his head. Percocet was not doing it. He needed morphine. He began to marshal his case to present to a doctor.

But then, after the phone stopped ringing his pager buzzed on the table. With difficulty, he swung his right arm across his chest and pressed the call button.

6666666.

The devil, the end of the world; the code he and Jolene used for a major emergency. Now what?

Again, with difficulty, he reached over to the table and manipulated his cell phone in his good hand. He punched Jolene's wireless number.

She answered immediately except it wasn't an answer, it was, "Earl, can you drive?"

"Hey, fuck you. I'm off the island, remember? I got a broken arm because of you. I may never bench-press again."

"Listen, Earl, things just got serious," Jolene said.

"Which part of 'fuck you' don't you understand?"

"I mean serious, Earl; NoDak serious."

More personal code. NoDak meant the convenience store in North Dakota. It meant life and death. "Okay. I'm listening," he said.

"Good, because Hank's talking."

That brought him up sharp; the Percocet haze wavered and dimmed as a cold streak of sweat shot down the inside of his stitched broken arm. He tried to focus on the voice in the phone. "Hank is *talking*?" he repeated, incredulous.

"He's not *word*-talking with his mouth, he's *blink*-talking with his eyes. The point is—he's communicating. You may remember certain conversations we had in front of him about you taking Stovall into the woods and leaving him to die nailed to a fucking tree?"

Kicked by an ostrich and now this. Unbelievable. "So what's he saying?"

"What happened was, this afternoon he tickled my hand with his finger. I didn't call Allen or you because you guys laughed at me the other night. So I called Broker."

"Sure, fine; makes *perfect sense.*" Earl was having trouble controlling his voice.

"Any rate, Broker comes over with this nurse . . ."

"Like real light blond?"

"Right. And we're all excited and I'm not tracking—like, who is this chick? But she knows her stuff, she makes this alphabet board thing and gets him to wink to select letters to make words. Guess what his first word was?"

Earl gritted his teeth, heaved up, and swung his feet over the side of the bed. Funny how the idea of Hank talking put his pain in perspective. He eyed his clothes which hung on hooks in the small bathroom alcove. "What?"

"Killers."

Earl started hyperventilating and struggled to get his breathing under control. "Did he name anybody?"

"Not exactly, he blinked out the words: 'Not Amy fault.' "

"Who's Amy?"

"The nurse Broker brought."

"I don't get it." Earl discovered he had more than partial use of the fingers of his left hand, limited range; but he could painfully grasp and hold. Maybe he *could* drive. Thankfully his van was an automatic. He managed to pull on his jeans. He held the phone wedged to his ear with his good shoulder.

"She was the anesthetist in Ely. She's one of the nurses we're suing for Hank's accident. She came down with Broker. They're working together."

"I still don't . . ." But he had a bad feeling.

"Broker didn't arrive just to deliver Hank's truck, he used that as an excuse because he'd read about Stovall in the paper and he was suspicious. Then he tried to get close to me."

"Try, shit. There was no daylight between you."

"Well, that's what he's good at, see; the nurse got real excited about Hank. A regular babbling fucking brook. She was telling me how Broker was an undercover cop. BCA."

Earl started hyperventilating again.

"Earl? You there?"

"Jesus. Fucking. Shit. We are—"

"Yeah, how do you think I feel. I said *was*—he's retired. But he knows all these cops."

"Shit!"

"We have one thing going for us. The last word Hank blinked was: 'nurse.' Then he was exhausted, or something; and he fell asleep. I have no idea what he's getting at, but Broker and this Amy start making like detectives and think he meant the other nurse up there in the recovery room tried to kill him. So, I'm playing for time and I suggested we pack up Hank, drive up to Ely, and try his blinking routine on the nurse."

"The old killer-nurse theory," Earl said.

"It buys time. Maybe twenty-four hours." She paused and Earl heard her exhale. "You sure can get offered some fucked choices in life," she said.

"Amen," Earl said.

"So, can you get a cab back here, pick up your van, and meet me up there?"

"Like you say, it's a fucked choice, but I'm with you." Despite his pain, Earl smiled because it felt like old times.

"Okay, we're going to Broker's uncle's place. It's called Uncle Billie's Lodge, on Lake One. They say it's just outside Ely. Any gas station can direct you. Nobody is there this time of year. You with me so far?"

"I'm still here. Uncle Billie's Lodge on Lake One in Ely, Minnesota. Then what?"

"Page me with sixes when you get in position, like outside the front door. I'll lure Broker out. Then I'll try to distract him so you—"

"I get the picture."

She paused, then said, "So you better bring *it*."

"I thought we weren't like that anymore," Earl said, clicking his teeth.

"I don't see any other way," Jolene said.

She clicked off the phone, flicked her cigarette, and watched it spiral out, sparks in the gloom. She straightened up her shoulders and raked her fingers through her short hair.

She reminded herself that *she* didn't kill that guy in North Dakota.

And she wasn't going to kill Amy and Broker, either.

Chapter Forty-three

They'd folded down the rear seat and put in a futon mattress and blankets. Broker lashed Hank's wheelchair to the rack on the roof. Hank slept on his side with a pillow between his knees. Amy was stretched out next to him. Jolene rode shotgun. They had good tires and a full tank of gas. The heater worked just fine.

"I don't want to talk to anyone until he gets a full night's rest. And he's fed. And he's comfortable with his new surroundings," Jolene said.

"Understood," said Broker, who was feeling very agreeable. The day had taken on an irresistible momentum. Hope rode with them. Broker wondered if the brief exercise with the alphabet system could foreshadow some kind of recovery.

He settled in and focused his attention on the cold, empty pavement unreeled in the Jeep's high beams. Interstate 35 going north was almost deserted, as if the plunging temperature and the wind had swept away the cars.

Earl heaved out of the cab with his trench coat slipping off his shoulders. He was only able to get his good arm in a sleeve. The shredded left sleeve hung empty. Cursing at his clumsiness, he paid the cabbie and fumbled one-handed in his jeans pockets for his keys.

Just as Jolene had said, the house was deserted and his van was in the garage. Goddamn chickenshit Rodney still had the Ford.

He lurched going through the door and slammed his sling against the doorjamb.

"GODDAMN SONOFABITCH!"

The curses echoed in the empty house. They'd left for up north: Jolene, Hank, Broker, and the smarty-pants nurse with the alphabet board. Now he had to follow them. And he didn't want to think about what was going to happen.

Shit.

He was still wearing his hospital gown under his coat. A nurse had knotted the belt around his waist as he rushed through processing. He wasn't wearing undershorts. Or socks.

His shoes weren't tied.

All that was too hard, bending with his cast and sling and the swollen fingers.

And he was hungry, but he didn't have time for that, either.

Plus, he hurt, but he couldn't afford to take any more of the pills because he was heading into a four-hour drive. Muttering, he went down the stairs and stooped to the file cabinet next to his computer and opened the bottom drawer. In the back, behind some folders, he located the small canvas zipper case. With difficulty, using his numb left fingers to wedge the case against his hip, he unzipped the case. He removed the heavy Colt automatic and the two loaded magazines—fat, stumpy bullets in a staggered row. They looked like spring-loaded teeth from a small tyrannosaurus rex. Earl shook his head. The pistol was a fossil from another era.

He tried to remember the last time he'd cleaned the .45.

Hell, he hadn't even fired the thing for years. Stovall hadn't known that, though.

Goddamn Jolene. This off-and-on roller coaster had to cease. When this is done, we're going to take the money and go someplace warm. An island, maybe, full of people who speak a different language to limit her ability to get into messes.

He inserted the magazine, pulled the slide with difficulty. Snicker-snack, the mechanism loaded a round in the chamber. Okay. He set the safety. Then he put the other magazine in his jacket pocket, grabbed at a fleece sweater, some socks, gloves, a hat. He stuffed them in the first thing that came to hand—a plastic bag from CompUSA. Funny, he hadn't been to CompUSA lately.

It'd be cold up north.

Which forced him to think in practical terms. The ground would be permafrost, impossible to dig; and he couldn't anyway with his arm. So hopefully the lakes wouldn't be frozen, because that's where they'd have to put Broker and the nurse.

And what about Hank?

He was in the middle of this thought, coming up the steps into the kitchen, headed for the refrigerator, hoping to find something to eat real quick—

When the needles raked his bare ankle.

Goddamn fucking cat!

Everything that had happened and now this. It blew his stopper. He yanked the Colt from his pocket with his good right hand, flicked the safety, and—

BLAAM!

He blasted a round at the ball of gray fur and scrambling claws and punched a ricochet notch in the floor tile that sent shards of terra-cotta flying all over, pinging off the walls and windows.

The empty casing flipped over in a plume of cordite and tinkled in the heavy burner grates on the stove.

Fucking cat was still booking through the living room.

BLAAM!

Missed again, hit the far wall, and the impact knocked two pictures down.

"I'll get you when I come back," Earl shouted, his ears stinging from the violence of the shots. He shook his head. Cat crossing his path, a bad sign at the beginning of a bad project.

Swinging his gun hand to clear the blur of cordite in the air, he opened the refrigerator, found nothing easy to carry except four cans of Diet Pepsi linked by a web of white plastic. He put his gun back in his pocket, took the soda and a box of day-old glazed doughnuts from the cupboard, and went to the garage and got in his van.

Ten minutes later he was driving west on Highway 36 heading for the junction of I-35. He had three-quarters of a tank of gas, and he was on his second doughnut and was halfway through a Pepsi.

Steppenwolf was playing on KQRS. Which was a good sign. It canceled out the cat. He rubbed the head of the *War Wolf* action figure taped to the dashboard, then reached down and turned the volume up all the way, gobbled the rest of the sugar dough, and rocked behind the wheel.

Heavy metal thunder . . .

For better or worse, that's me, he thought.

Here I come.

Allen sprinted through the pines, crashed through some underbrush, and jumped in his car. Their fault, not mine, he thought as he sped away, shifting through the gears.

I could have stopped it right there. Hank dies peacefully in his sleep. The End. But no, they had to come back. Now more people will have to pay.

Interesting the way the logic worked in this new world. Clearly they were bringing this on themselves. Almost with a mind of its own, the Saab raced toward the Timberry Trails Hospital. He visualized the procedure he must perform; he knew exactly what he had to do next and what he needed to do it.

He'd be reversing his skill-set, operating outside the OR.

The opposite of fixing.

He put his chances at one in three of getting out of this.

"One in three," he said out loud.

But, if he correctly understood Jolene's phone conversation with Garf, he had some leverage. He now recalled the odd talk he'd had with Garf about crucifixion, just after Hank came home from Regions, after they discovered his health insurance had lapsed. And after they'd discovered that Hank's wacko accountant had put all Hank's funds in a trust where Jolene couldn't get to it.

And then the accountant was found frozen, nailed to a tree, taking masochistic body piercing to a new height. Everyone at the hospital had talked about it. Preoccupied with his own dilemma, he had not put Garf's questions, and his own precise advice about the placement of the nail, together with Stovall's death. Clearly Garf was trying to reclaim Hank's money for Jolene. Clearly Garf was much more dangerous than previously thought.

And so was Jolene.

And so was he.

Congratulations, Allen. You finally made it to the bigs.

Timberry Trails Hospital appeared below him on its own cloverleaf; compact, red brick, it could have been a small bible college.

Allen had leapfrogged the tango. He imagined he was wearing spurs, that they jingled. He parked and took his doctor's bag and walked through the icy dusk toward the main entrance. The parking lot was almost empty. A slow end to the day. The OR would be practically deserted unless they got emergency business. Or they brought a woman down from Maternity who needed a C-section.

There'd just be a bored anesthetist on call, probably watching television in the anesthesia office.

He let himself in the side door and slipped down a stairwell and came out in the hall near the pre op desk.

Just as he expected, the corridors on either side of the red line were deserted. And the sounds of college football came from the only office door that was open.

Allen removed his watch from his left hand and put it in his pocket. Then he poked his head in the door. A lean young man dressed in blue scrubs and bonnet looked up, then came alert.

"Hey, Allen, what are you doing here? Is there something scheduled I don't know about?"

"Nah, Jerry; I just need a favor."

"What's up?"

Allen held up his left hand and pointed to his bare wrist. "I left my watch somewhere in here. The last place I was before I left today was the anesthesia workroom, talking to Jeannie. Toss me the keys for a sec."

Jerry reached in his pocket and flipped a key ring. Allen caught it and paused, feigning interest in the TV. "Who do you like?" he asked.

"Notre Dame."

"I'll be right back."

The anesthesia workroom was just three doors down the corridor. Allen found the key and opened the door. He hit the light switch and went in. The room was designed like a long, gray closet lined with cabinets and shelves. The center of the room was jammed with anesthesia carts from the day's surgery.

Off to the side, Allen saw what he was looking for: an anesthesia tray that hadn't been cracked for a cart and had been set aside to be returned to the pharmacy.

He snapped open his bag, unsealed the tray, and took several ampules and stopper bottles of narcotics. He selected some needles, closed the tray, and returned it to the counter on the far side of the room. He found an elastic tourniquet in one of the open carts. From the cabinets along the wall, he took a couple of IV bags, some IV tubing, and another bottle filled with white liquid. He snapped his bag shut.

Time elapsed, less than two minutes. He slipped his watch back on his wrist, turned off the lights, closed the door, and went back down the hall.

"Bingo," he said to Jerry, holding up his hand that now sported his Rolex. "Right next to the sink where I thought it was."

Jerry, deep in his game, just held up his open palm. Allen dropped the keys into it and hurried from the hospital. Going to his car he ignored the frigid air that ice-picked his eyes. It was time to focus. To visualize the task ahead. He drove toward the Interstate on deserted asphalt starched with frost.

The procedure would be easy. The people would be the problem. He thought of Jolene and Garf as patients on a mission, propelled by crude ideas and armed with cruder implements. There would be complications.

Allen took a deep breath, calculated—no, he was wagering now, betting. Gambling.

He flipped open his cell phone and pressed some plastic, keying in the letters: GA. The Caller ID function searched his queue. Because Garf was assisting in Hank's home care, Allen had logged his cell and pager numbers.

Garf's name, followed by his number, popped up on the screen. Now it all depended on Garf having his cell phone and pager close at hand. His car ran smoothly and he was gaining ground. Perhaps the fierce cold pressing on the windshield helped concentrate his mind. His reflexes were functioning perfectly. He had never believed in luck.

Until now.

He punched in Garf's cell number.

One ring, two, three. Patience, Garf had the broken arm.

"What now?" answered a surly voice after ring four.

"I wouldn't stop in Ely and ask directions to Uncle Billie's Lodge if I were you. Especially wearing a cast and considering what you and Jolene are planning for Broker and the nurse."

Long pause. Then: "Who the hell is this?"

"Professor Rath." Allen smiled.

"What a minute," Garf said through the road noise. Then. "Okay. I know who you are. Give me a reason why I should continue this conversation."

"Because it turns out we have a lot in common. Where are you right now?" Allen asked.

"Heading north. I just passed Cambridge."

"Stop at Tobie's when you get to Hinckley," Allen said. Tobie's restaurant was the traditional halfway pit stop to Duluth. "What are you driving?"

"I'm in the van. Freezing my ass."

"Park in the lot, stay in the van. I'll find you." Allen switched off the phone and stepped on the accelerator. It was an amazing sensation. His life was rolling like dice.

Chapter Forty-four

He was moving in the back of a car and it was all black outside the boxy windows. Not far away he sensed terrific cold. But here, inside, bundled in his bedding, the sensation of motion was enjoyable. Especially enjoyable considering the last thing he remembered was Allen coming in through the patio door to suffocate him with a pillow.

Now he was just inches from a snoozing Amy Skoda, whose hair tickled his cheek and smelled like herbal shampoo. She reclined beside him. They were like Roman lovers at a feast.

Maybe he had dreamed the scene with Allen.

Maybe he was dreaming now.

In the front seat Broker and Jolene discussed procedure. If it turned out that Hank could make a case that Nancy Ward, the recovery-room nurse, had acted with malicious intent, Broker insisted on calling the St. Louis County sheriff's office.

Jolene thought Milt should be in on the decision. But she understood Amy's status and was willing to hold off on Milt until the next round of communication with Hank.

Broker shook his head. "We don't know how much energy he's got left, how long this can go on. I want someone else around to verify what we're doing."

Jolene worried her lower lip between her teeth, squinted at the luminous numerals on her digital watch, and looked out the window.

"Okay," she said. "But we wait for the morning. I want him to get a full night's rest."

Broker nodded. "How we doing back there?" he asked, calling over his shoulder.

There was no answer. Jolene twisted in her seat. "They're both asleep." She turned back around and gave the silence between them enough time to go from informal to personal. Then she inclined her head. "You and me; we're water under the bridge, right?"

Broker did not answer so she extended her hand and poked a finger in his right thigh. "So you were a cop?"

"Who says?"

Jolene tossed her head toward Amy in back. "Miss Goody Two-shoes told me."

"It was a long time ago," Broker minimized.

"You should have told me, you really should have," Jolene said.

Broker shrugged.

"An undercover cop?"

"I worked some time undercover."

"Is that where the police record came from, made up for working undercover."

"Yeah."

"What about drugs? Did you work around drugs?" Jolene asked.

"Some. I didn't like working drugs. Mostly I went after illegal gun traffic," Broker said. He braked slightly as the loneliest, coldest, eight-point buck in Northern Minnesota trotted stiffly across the frost-bleached highway.

"Really? I thought cops were big into busting people for drugs," Jolene said.

"They are. It's their buffalo, the resource that supports their way of life. We should legalize them, like booze."

"That's radical for a cop."

"Ex-cop."

"Okay, ex-cop." Jolene nodded respectfully.

Broker returned the nod. "People can learn how to quit getting high. You'd agree with that."

"I'd agree with that," Jolene said.

"Yeah, well, try to learn how to quit being dead after you've been shot five times in the chest with a Tec Nine converted to full auto."

"And the drugs are the reason a lot of people are shooting each other," Jolene said.

"There you go," Broker said.

"Sort of like what Hank used to call a worldview, with the buffalo and everything," Jolene said with a wry smile. Then she turned away and stared out the window. The dashboard lights created a transparent mirror effect in the glass, and she saw her face superimposed on the darkness.

Of the many hard parts to this thing, the hardest was that she still liked him a lot.

No one wanted to turn off their cars in this weather. An inferno of auto exhaust clouded the air and made the vehicles in the parking lot of Tobie's look like they were on fire. Allen, always prepared, popped his trunk, opened his winter survival bag, and pulled out a fleece sweater and his Goretex parka, put them on along with a warmer hat and gloves. Then he closed the trunk, picked up his medical bag, walked over to the green Chevy van, knocked, and then opened the door.

Garf's hair was askew and silver-tipped with ice. His face looking like raw Polish sausage. He sat behind the wheel with his bare chest peeking between the askew hospital robe that he wore under his coat. His empty left sleeve stuck out akimbo, his left hand was in a sling and poked from the coat and rested on the steering wheel. He looked demented, Shakespearean, in that getup.

There was this big pistol sitting in his lap.

Allen, getting in, sitting down, had learned about guns working his way backward from wound ballistics at Regions, back when it was Ramsey County Emergency. He identified the weapon as an old, 1911 military-model .45. It made a big hole and had been designed specifically to knock a man down with one shot.

"Okay," Garf said, sliding his right hand over the handle of the pistol and pointing it at Allen. "The next thirty seconds are the most important of your life. Talk."

Allen stared into the muzzle of the pistol and took a moment to anesthetize the stammer of panic he felt swelling up in his gums and teeth and tongue. Then he smiled tightly and peppered Earl with concise sentences: "You talked to Hank, I talked to Hank. You told him what happened to Stovall. I told him how I accidently gave him the wrong medication in the recovery room up there. He can hang both our asses." Allen checked his watch. "Ten seconds. Anything else you want to know?"

Garf stared at Allen for a long time.

Allen, reassured, continued in a more relaxed tone. "I saw Broker and Amy bring you into the ER early this afternoon. I went to the house and was in the kitchen when they were in the studio with Hank. When they did the alphabet-board bit. I heard them on the baby monitor. Then I went around the back of the house and hid under the deck when Jolene came out and called you. I tried to get in and do it quietly with a pillow but they came back and I had to leave. Sorry."

Garf had to laugh. "The fucking baby monitor?" Then he narrowed his eyes. "A pillow? What happened to, you know, the Hippocratic Oath?"

Allen smiled. "What'd Jolene mean when she said this is NoDak serious?"

Garf lowered his eyes and scratched the pattern on the wooden handle of the pistol with a fingernail. It made a distinct sound. Maybe the hinge of fate.

Allen continued. "I get the impression you and she have been here before."

Garf's eyes came up. Allen thought they might have been very nice eyes once and had been filled with many possibilities. Garf said, almost tenderly, "And this is your first time."

Allen, all business, brushed the comment aside. "So how are you going to find the place? Ask everybody in town?"

Garf took a deep breath, winced; mistake, his ribs.

"I remember how to get there," Allen said. "And what were you going to do with them after you shot them full of great big holes? There's ballistics to worry about. And messy body fluids. And what about Hank. He has to stick around, you know. There's millions of dollars at risk."

Garf shifted his feet, turned away, and stared at the frost crystals gnawing through the window glass.

Allen opened his medical bag, scooped up a bag of lactated ringers along with glossy bends of IV tubing. "Now, listen to me," he said. "If you and Jolene do it my way, we can get out of this."

Machines quit when it got this cold. They were damn near the only thing traveling on wheels.

"Maybe this wasn't such a smart idea," Broker said as he took an exit just past Virginia and pulled into an Amoco station. It was a different kind of storm, invisible, like J.T.'s vampire in a mirror. They couldn't see it because it didn't snow.

It didn't snow because the cold had killed anything that tried to move, including the wind.

He got out to pump the gas and Amy and Jolene sprinted for the john, and they were all stunned almost dumb by the temperature. Road salt bleached a gritty borax-white on the metal skin of the Jeep. They could almost hear the steel molecules shriek as they hugged tight.

"Jesus," Jolene said, hoofing back from the can, hands over her bare ears. Her breath made a cloud thick enough for the children of Israel to follow through the wilderness.

"Twenty-seven below," Broker said, coming back from paying for the gas. "If the wind comes up, the windchill will be fatal. End of story." He handed out Styrofoam cups of coffee from a cardboard tray, candy bars, and snacks of beef jerky.

Jolene, who wasn't wearing her hat, shook her head. "It makes you crazy."

"Grease up," Broker said, offering her a jerky.

The cold was bad enough on the deserted Interstate. When they creaked through the empty streets of Ely, they left the blacktop and the comfort of artificial light behind and crunched onto the gravel. The high beams converted the trees and swamp grass into sinister patterns at the side of the road, and the cold became lunar, utterly foreign to warm flesh.

And J.T. was right about his Jeep. It didn't look like much on the outside but everybody in the Chrysler plant in Detroit must have been having a good day when they made it, because the car had heart and kept pulling through the cold.

They turned at a frost-shriven sign—UNCLE BILLIE'S RESORT—and drove down the wooded drive. Broker stopped the Jeep in front of the lodge and got out and looked up at the ice-pick stars.

He left them in the Jeep with the heater running while he dashed inside, turned up the furnace, started a fire in the fireplace, and folded out the sleeper couch for Hank.

Then he came back and he and Amy each took one side and lifted Hank from the back of the Jeep and hauled him in a two-man fireman's carry. Scurrying beside them, Jolene hesitated when she heard an eerie, twanging, hollow sound.

"What's that?"

"Ice forming on the lake," Broker said.

Jolene went inside and balked at the moose head with its horns spread out from over the mantel. She shook her head. "Men are really pretty weird, you know?"

Then she and Amy made Hank comfortable on the rolled-out couch. They folded blankets to insert under his knees and calves to elevate his feet. Broker brought them pillows and quilts to prop up his back and sides.

Jolene changed Hank's diaper and administered a water drip to his gastro tube. Amy shook her head in amazement.

"This guy may have a tricky airway but he has an incredible set of lungs."

"There's no justice," Jolene said. "Two packs of Camel straights a day all his life."

Hank continued to sleep.

Broker squatted by the fire and watched the two women work side by side and couldn't help comparing them—the way they moved, the way they wore their jeans. Amy filled hers to the brim while Jolene's seemed to follow along with her. Amy's naturally freckled aura and her trim lines were maintained by constant patrols of exercise and denial. He suspected that if her discipline faltered she would put on weight.

They moved between the kitchen stove and the fireplace, trying to convince themselves they were warm. Amy made a pot of hot tea.

Broker listened to the roof timbers creak as he fought mild disorientation. They really hadn't been out in it; but just the idea of temperatures this cold got inside their brains and slowed their thoughts.

His and Amy's, anyway, because they became drowsy, lazing near the fire. Jolene reacted in the opposite direction, nervous, pacing; she explored the lodge, she fretted over Hank's minute-by-minute condition. She kept looking at her wristwatch, fingering the pager clipped to her belt.

Amy opened and heated cans of soup; found the ingredients for toasted cheese sandwiches. As they ate, Broker mentioned contacting Deputy Dave Iker. You know, like let's get this show on the road.

Jolene reacted testily, accused him of reneging on the deal.

After the meal, she continued her pacing. She switched on the satellite TV, tore through the channels, turned it off.

Broker figured these nervous tics were all the stuff she'd been keeping in, the strain from looking after Hank for the last week. Now, with Hank showing signs of stirring from his coma, she was dropping her guard, getting a little spacy, letting it out.

She started and her right hand went to her pager, which must have vibrated against her hip because she pressed the button and focused on the number on the viewer. Immediately her head came up and she looked gravely, directly into his eyes.

"What is it?" he asked.

"Nothing, some wrong number," she said.

It was a look he remembered from somewhere. He had to stop himself and think back. Maybe that night just before they went to bed.

"I'm going out for a smoke," Jolene said abruptly, her face suddenly stiff, her words jerking. But she pulled a box of Marlboro Lights from her jacket pocket and opened it. The first cigarette snapped and broke apart in her fingers. She ignored it and selected another one. Put it in her mouth.

Broker didn't know that she was a closet smoker. But it made sense, given the AA background, the stress of dealing with Hank.

Jolene pulled on her coat, hat, and gloves and said, "I won't be long."

As she went out the door, Broker joined Amy in front of the fire. "What do you think?" he asked, nodding at Hank.

"I keep pinching myself."

"Yeah," Broker grinned. "I know what you mean. It's kind of profound."

"You read about things like this once in a while. A patient wakes up from a coma." She bit her lip and her eyes rolled up hopefully. "I don't want to jinx it by wishing it comes true."

He stooped to add more kindling to the fire and fiddled with the poker. A lot had changed in the last few days since he'd left his sickbed in this room and traveled south to the Cities.

Thinking about how he'd nailed Earl, he smiled, remembering the T-shirt: OLD AGE AND TREACHERY WILL ALWAYS WIN OUT OVER YOUTH AND STRENGTH. It took the edge off the paranoia about his wife hanging out with younger men.

Another thing. He felt even with Amy now. Hank really had cleared the air between them.

Mainly he felt confident again. More like his old self.

Broker felt an icy draft and the front door opened and Jolene stuck her head in. "Hey, Broker. There's something out here you should check out."

He heaved to his feet, hung the poker back on its stand, and walked toward the door. "What is it?"

"I'm not sure. It's by the woods."

"Probably a deer," Broker said, stepping through the door.

Jolene took him by the wrist and the elbow and tugged him toward the steps. "Over here . . ." Suddenly she clamped down on his wrist and gasped. "Jesus Christ, what's *he* doing here?"

Broker spun.

The rush he felt didn't come from outside. The pine branches in the yard light were still as statues. It came from inside his chest and speeded up his eyes.

"Trick or treat, motherfucker!"

The voice hissed behind his back. Galvanized, Broker yanked against Jolene, who clung to him. So he had to fling her aside and spin, raking back his left elbow, cocking his right fist.

His elbow swept empty space and he thought he glimpsed a grotesque smile on Earl Garf's bruise-streaked face.

He heard Amy scream, turned to find her, which was a mistake, because Earl clubbed the butt of the .45 down behind his left ear and it all went black.

Chapter Forty-five

Amy had screamed, "Look out," but the man had already stepped across the doorway and struck Broker from behind. Broker's knees gave out and he crumpled to the porch. Coming forward, she recognized the belted black leather trench coat Earl had worn in the barn earlier today, except now it had an empty sleeve and Earl Garf had his left arm in a sling.

Earl sneered and commenced to kick at Broker who was trying to push himself up off the porch. When kicking didn't satisfy him, he bent over and swung the pistol again, and the steel hitting Broker's skull sent a sickening slap into the dark. Broker fell forward and lay still.

Jolene grabbed Earl's good arm and screamed, "What's he doing here?" Seeing Jolene moving to intervene, Amy had the racing contextual thought that this was more of the same from earlier—the hostility between the two men carried to absurd lengths.

And Earl looked crazy right now, with his bare chest red with cold against a torn hospital patient's robe under the heavy coat. When he aimed a kick at Broker she saw his bare ankle between the cuff of his jeans and his Nikes.

"Hey, wait a minute," Jolene yelled, pushing forward.

Earl swung the pistol at Jolene, backed her off, and yelled, "Just shut up and do what I say." Then he lunged across the porch, his eyes burning up with cold, and she saw what Jolene had seen. There was someone else out there.

Suddenly, Amy knew she was next.

Immediately she set her feet to bound back into the lodge. She'd been raised up here. She'd played in this building as a child. She knew where Uncle Billie kept his guns—in the closet in his bedroom—and she knew there'd be a twelve-gauge pump and she knew how to use it.

But Earl pointed the pistol at her face and her feet wouldn't move fast enough, which gave him time to snake out a foot and trip her. Then, as she tried to regain her balance, he shoved her roughly against the doorjamb and forced her to her knees.

And in that moment, with her face smarting like a red pincushion and the air all freezing needles, she saw the other person heave into the light.

"What the hell," Jolene blurted.

"It's cool," Earl reassured her.

Allen Falken stood over Amy with a syringe in his hand. In the other he held a black medical bag. In an open space between two sliding plates of panic, Amy noticed he was wearing latex gloves and he needed a shave.

"How're we doing?" Allen asked conversationally as he stepped over Broker. Then, as he knelt, he said, "Earl, take hold of Amy, would you; I want her absolutely still."

Through another window of shock, Amy recognized the calm authority of a surgeon greeting his team as he entered the OR.

She scrambled to escape, which prompted Earl to grab her around the waist with his good arm. Earl smelled like spoiled meat and disinfectant.

"Hello, Amy," Allen said. "This will sting a little but then you'll find it quite pleasant. Five hundred milligrams of Ketamine will produce a hypnotic effect. But you know all about that." He jabbed her in the thigh, right through her jeans.

Amy's panic immediately lost its jerky gallop and she rolled out and up with the graceful thrust, and she was alone and poised in a slow-motion dive into a wide pool of peace. A beautiful vertical entry. No splash. A perfect 10.

. . .

Allen quickly drew another shot from a stopper bottle and injected it in Broker's thigh. Then he addressed the shock on Jolene's face as he took out a box of rubber gloves. "Put these on, please."

"Wait a fucking minute here," Jolene said, looking to Earl.

Allen smiled at her. "How's Hank? Has he been blink-talking any more? Giving away any more family secrets?"

"How do you . . . ?"

"In a minute," Allen said. "Right now, let's drag her inside and shut the door. It's cold out here."

He and Earl manhandled Amy through the doorway and laid her on the wooden-plank floor near the fireplace.

"Earl? What's going on here?" Jolene demanded.

"There's three of us now," Earl said. "He's got the plan and I've got the gun and you better have the smarts to go along."

"That's clear as mud," Jolene said.

Allen continued to smile patiently. "We're going to put Hank back to where he was before he started this blinking business."

"He hasn't *stopped* blinking that I know of," Jolene almost shouted.

"I'll get to that later. First we have to deal with her," he pointed to Amy, "and him." He jerked his head toward the door.

"Deal?" Jolene said.

"Kill, okay?" Earl said. "Only Allen is going to do it nice, not sloppy like you had in mind."

Jolene slumped her shoulders. "Jesus, how'd we wind up *here*?"

"We arrived one step at a time," Allen said. He pointed at Earl. "Him." Then he pointed at Jolene. "You." Finally he tapped his own chest. "Me."

Jolene shook her head.

Earl tried to explain. "Jolene, he knows everything. He saw Broker and Amy together when they took me to the hospital, so he went to the house and heard you three guys doing the alphabet thing on the baby monitor, then he went in back and heard you on the cell phone calling me." He turned to Allen. "Just tell her straight-out. Trust me, it works better that way with her," Earl said.

Allen nodded, then gently explained. "Killers, plural, remember. Earl is one killer and I'm the other." Allen spoke in the factual tone he used when discussing a patient's case with family members. "In the hospital, when Hank was in the recovery room, I gave him the wrong medication when I found him unattended. No one saw me, and when I realized what I'd done I assumed it would look like a respiratory arrest caused by a sloppy nurse-anesthetist and a lazy nurse. So I turned off the alarm on the monitor and left the room."

Why, you fucker, Jolene was careful not to say.

"See, nothing but cool," Earl did say.

"At first I thought it was a mistake, that I was confused from fatigue. But the more I thought about it I realized I don't make mistakes of that magnitude. So, on some level, I must have been acting deliberately. The crude explanation is that I allowed my personal feelings to intrude on my relationship with a patient. It's always been obvious I've been very attracted to you, Jolene. And I saw how Hank didn't appreciate you. And it's been hard, watching you go through this ordeal."

"Wow," Earl said, starting to grin again.

"You did that to Hank?" Jolene balled her fists.

Allen went on in his patient voice. "And Earl did that to Stovall and you were ready to do it to Amy and Broker. And here we all are."

"Jolene, listen," Earl said, "he's got this really cool idea. We hide the bodies in plain sight."

"And the Ketamine only gives me ten to fifteen minutes to set it up," Allen again offered them the box of Latex gloves.

"Set what up?" Jolene asked.

"Her suicide. See, she feels so bad about what she did to Hank, she just can't live with it. Allen will stage it with drugs and stuff to make it look exactly the way an anesthetist would do it," Earl said.

Allen, less patient, now shook the box of gloves.

Jolene and Earl exchanged questioning glances.

"Fingerprints," Allen said. "You have to wipe this place down while we take care of Broker. Anything you touched."

Jolene and Earl pulled on the tight rubber gloves. A knot of birch popped in the fireplace, showering the hearth with sparks, and they jumped. Allen, focused and calm, did not.

"Broker," Jolene said.

"We were thinking, so we stopped at a liquor store," Earl said. He pulled a brown paper bag from his trench-coat pocket with his good hand and removed a fifth of Johnny Walker Red Label scotch. "We prime him with this stuff, we dress him less than perfect for the weather, and put him in his truck, take him in the woods, stage a crash, and leave him for the cold."

"And Hank?" Jolene almost whispered.

Allen was taking items out of his bag and arranging them on a rough coffee table. "When we finish here, and get Hank back to town, I'll inject his eyelids with something that will numb them so he can't blink." The drug was Botox—botulism toxin. It was commonly used in cosmetic surgery to smooth out wrinkles. Allen would inject it in the levator muscles to immobilize the eyelids.

Jolene stared at him. "Something?"

Allen smiled. "I could have brought it along and done it here but then you wouldn't need me anymore, and maybe Earl would shoot me and dump me in the woods because I know too much."

"Not bad," Jolene said.

"Now," **Allen said. "Amy** was an anesthesia provider, so she'd have some sophisticated ideas about getting high. I'm going to give her a long run for a short slide." He and Earl each took one of Amy's arms and lifted her to the fold-out couch. They dropped her next to Hank and their shoulders touched. Her weight shifted and her long hair drifted across her face.

"Wait a minute," Jolene said, touching her own short hair nervously. For the first time she noticed that Amy had taken off her sweater and was wearing a kind of neat print blouse, with a blue-patterned cave painting of stick figures on gray and gold. Her fingernails were painted this deep purple. "You're going to leave her there?"

Allen and Earl stared at her.

Jolene said, "I mean, if I have to clean up, I don't want to watch while she . . ."

"Okay, let's put her in a bedroom," Allen said. They struggled through the kitchen and down a hall. Arms folded across her chest, Jolene followed them.

The bedroom was cold and musty; there was just an antique mahogany four-poster bed and matching dresser. There were used prescription pill bottles on the dresser and a World War II picture. A tube of Ben Gay lay on the night table. It was the kind of room where an old guy lived alone.

Allen and Earl hoisted Amy to the bed and arranged her with pillows behind her back, to make her appear comfortable. Allen went back for his bag.

Earl said, "So, we thought—if they're traveling together, they could be romantically involved."

"That'd be my guess," Jolene said dryly.

"Then what if the lodge is found in some disarray, evidence of drugs scattered around in the wake of Amy's suicide. And some booze. It might look like Broker was distraught over Amy. He finds her dead, he gets high, drinks too much, and takes off on a fuck-the-world drive too fast; he goes off the road, knocks himself out, shatters the windshield . . ." Earl grinned.

Allen's calm voice continued behind her, in the doorway. "Then we clean up after ourselves, go back home, and no one knows we were here. We read about them in the newspapers. North-woods lovers claimed by suicide and grief." He paused. "What do you think?"

"You're the doctor," Jolene said.

Chapter Forty-six

Jolene had remained mostly quiet. Now she turned and studied Allen's face, which looked haggard, with a day's growth of beard.

Anticipating her question, Allen said, "Someday, when this is over, when the money is in the bank, when Hank is in the ground, and you and Earl have worked out the terms of your relationship—perhaps we could see each other."

Earl snickered. "C'mon, you guys, let's keep it clean."

They were gone, out of his range of vision, somewhere else in the house to where they'd taken Amy. It was just about over. For Amy, for Broker, for him. It infuriated him that Allen, Jolene, and Earl were going to win.

Hank's thoughts were just embers, but the thing that was coming for him was clearer now. Almost distinct.

But at this moment he was riveted to the story unfolding in front of him.

Allen's patient courtship of Jolene was based on bad math. Allen had factored in three deaths: Amy's, Broker's, and, eventually, Hank's.

The expression on Earl's face corrected the arithmetic. When the time was right, Earl would add Allen to the total.

And Jolene was the catalyst, the fire, thought Hank, that we have all swarmed to. And being a drunk, she would always back-slide to Earl in moments of crisis.

Hank had heard everything since they came inside. He could not see Amy and Broker, but he understood the play. He had glimpsed Allen, Earl, and Jolene through lidded eyes as they caucused in front of the fire at the foot of his bed.

Allen was very thorough on details and methods, but he should have stayed with working inside immobile, drugged bodies. The outsides of alert moving bodies were still beyond his aptitude. Allen wasn't ten words into his brilliant plan when Hank realized that Earl was going to kill him. Earl, who knew a good thing, would assist Allen in staging Amy's suicide and leaving Broker out in the cold. He'd watch approvingly while Allen destroyed Hank's eyelids. He'd wait until Allen had outlived his usefulness, presumably after the malpractice case was resolved, and after Allen had quietly finished the job of murdering Hank in a medically plausible way.

Then Earl would make Allen disappear.

And at the every end, Jolene would figure out a way to pension off Earl and seize the last, highest grip on the situation—eagle claws.

Too bad. Jolene, Earl, and Allen held great potential as characters if only he could script them before Allen came at his eyes with the needle.

Of the three, the only one he held any hopes of redemption for was Jolene. Of course, he was biased.

Allen came back from the bathroom down the hall where he'd emptied two square lactated plastic ringer bags. After he passed them through the fingers of Amy's right hand to acquire her fingerprints, he hung the bags from a handy tine on the left antler of a European-mounted twelve-point white-tail deer rack on the wall over the bed.

He took two long, glistening lengths of plastic tubing from his bag. Again the trick with the fingers, like she was handling them. They were jointed and each had a blue clip with a white wheel. Then he did something with needles, hooking one tube to the other at a joint.

"The hard thing is starting your own IV," Allen said. He took out a strip of rubber tourniquet and he tied it around her arm above the elbow. Then he turned Amy's left hand, evaluating the network of now-plump blue veins feeding between her knuckles. As her fingers spread open a tightly folded piece of paper fell on her lap.

Allen paused to unfold it.

"It's the alphabet thing," Jolene said.

"Crude," Allen said, smoothing the paper on Amy's jeans. "All wrong. The letters shouldn't be arranged in normal sequence. They should be grouped according to priority of which letters are most frequently used in speech."

"Well, it worked good enough," Jolene said.

Allen folded the paper and slipped it in his pocket.

Agitated, Jolene said, "Allen, for Christ's sake, she's waking up."

Amy moaned softly, her eyes revolved as Allen placed his needle, checked his blood back-flash into the IV, removed the actual needle, left the IV stent in place, and hooked it to the tubing.

"She's semiconscious, she won't really be aware. Because—" he opened a bottle containing a white liquid and poured it into the bag on the left—"she's about to really relax with five hundred cc's of Propofal in a slow drip."

The white stuff dripped down the tubing and Allen raised Amy's right hand and used her fingers to thumb the wheel on the blue roller clamp.

Amy sighed and rolled her eyes up into her forehead. Allen pursed his lips and patted her leg. In a remote voice, he said, "You won't feel a thing. I couldn't let them shoot you, could I?"

Then he held up a glass ampule full of clear liquid and swiftly cracked it open between the two red lines on its nozzle and deposited the contents in the bag on the right.

Jolene, watching his nimble fingers, was reminded of someone who was adept at assembling things that came in boxes, good at reading instructions.

"Now, this is one hundred cc's of Fentanyl, a very potent narcotic and the anesthetist's drug of choice. They're famous for abusing it and miscalculating their highs, so a lot of them OD on the stuff," Allen said. "We leave the clamp closed on this drip for right now, let her loll around in the induction agent, then I'll open this clamp all the way, it'll feed through the port into the other IV tube, and in a minute she'll be apneic."

"Apneic?" Jolene said.

"Stop breathing."

They left the bedroom, put on their coats, and joined Earl on the front porch. Earl had rummaged around in Broker's travel bag and replaced Broker's boots with tennis shoes. He found a light fall jacket on the coat rack by the door and pulled it loosely over Broker's shoulders. Broker was turned over on his back and he kept instinctively cringing into a fetal position in an effort to keep warm.

Seeing that, Jolene looked away.

"I managed to get a third of the bottle into him," Earl said. "But I think the drug is wearing off. What if he wakes up?"

"We don't want him totally overdosed. He's got to drive, remember?" Allen said. "Now, go bring our cars down here, transfer Hank's bedding to the van, and then put Broker in the Jeep. You can drive him," he said to Earl. "I'll follow in my car." He tossed his car keys to Earl, who handed them to Jolene.

Broker flopped back and forth on the porch, Ketamine going out, the scotch coming in.

"See," Allen said. "It's like he's drunk. You can probably coax him to his feet and walk him to the car."

This last idea genuinely excited Earl, who began to address Broker in a deeply sympathetic tone. "Come on, buddy. Time to get up. We gotta go feed the ostriches."

"Cut the shit," Jolene said.

"Aw, why? I kinda like the idea of him walking to his reward. Better'n me having to carry the sucker."

The two of them managed to get Broker to his feet and walked him down the steps. Allen watched them stagger off toward the Jeep. Then he went back inside and stood for a moment, warming his hands at the fire. He turned and found himself staring directly in Hank's very open, alert, angry eyes.

"Well, hello," Allen said, curious.

Very deliberately, Hank cocked his left eye at Allen and winked.

Chapter Forty-seven

Hank was resolved to go out on his kind of play; he'd bet it all on one gesture. Either he'd get the needle or a response.

Allen was startled and his hands began to shake—from excitement, he told himself. This *was* exciting. So he smiled stiffly and studied Hank. "So you really are in there? Have you been eavesdropping again?" He couldn't help giving in to a twitch of clinical fascination.

Hank blinked twice.

"Two means yes," Allen said. "Okay. Just a minute then." He dug Amy's famous crumpled alphabet paper out of his pocket, smoothed it out, and held it up. Hank's sneering eyes fixed on it and Allen granted their hot wish. "You want to talk?"

Two blinks.

Allen let his finger rove the groups and Hank began to blink.

"P"

"U"

"S"

"S"

"Y"

Hank shut his eyes.

"Bravo, Hank; crude to the end," Allen said, but a film of

sweat started to form across his forehead and on his upper lip. After everything he'd accomplished he was back where he'd started; the object of Hank's offhand contempt. Allen felt an impulse to plunge his thumbs into those eyes and squash them like grapes.

Hank's eyes popped open. Now he was sweating, too. They glared at each other.

"I win; you lose. Top that," Allen smiled kindly and then he swept his upturned hand to the letter groups like a waiter indicating the way to a table.

"D"

"U"

"M"

"Who? Me? Really. I'd think the opposite was true."

"T"

"H"

"E"

"Y"

. . .

"U"

"S"

"E"

. . .

"U"

. . .

"K"

"I"

"L"

. . .

"U"

"You mean Earl?" Allen's voice quavered a bit. He heard car motors turn off. Doors slam. A drop of his sweat fell on the paper, blurring some of Amy's letters.

Two blinks.

". . . And Jolene?" Allen's voice turned dry and he swallowed a stammer; the novelty was wearing off, this pointing and blinking.

Two blinks.

The door opened and Allen dropped the paper. His hurried gesture held Earl and Jolene's attention for a beat.

"What's going on?" Earl asked.

"Nothing," Allen said.

Earl eyed him for another moment, then said, "We have him in the Jeep. Now what?"

"Like I said, you drive the Jeep, I'll follow in my car. We find a spot for him to go off the road. Jolene, you start wiping the place down. Anywhere you touched before we got here. We come back, do a walk-through, load Hank, and that's it."

Then Allen walked back to the bedroom and thumbed the white plastic gauge open to the bottom of the roller clamp and the Fentanyl started to flow into Amy's IV.

Jolene watched him do it.

Efficient, practical; he could have been turning off the lights.

She watched the narcotic streamline into Amy's blood. Her hips raised into a wanton arch on the bed, her head thrust back, her eyes revolving up. The euphoric spasm collapsed as Allen and Earl went out the front door and she watched Amy writhe, chin on chest, tongue protruding, drool starting to flow down her chin into a curl of thick, white-blond hair trapped beneath her cheek.

Jolene turned away and resented them for leaving her alone with *this*. And she shut her eyes and saw cops and lawyers and judges. She saw matrons forcing her to strip and sticking their fingers in her and making her put on prison cottons.

And *THAT* was the future if she didn't do *THIS*.

Goddamn Broker shouldn't have lied to me, she told herself.

But she couldn't take her eyes off Amy, couldn't stop watching her breaths getting shallow and coming further and further apart.

Never hurt anybody when I was sober before.

She spun and stalked into the living room, fished in her coat pocket, took out her cigarettes, lit up, and paced in front of the fireplace. About three drags into her Marlboro she darted a glance at Hank.

Hank looked back.

Great, she thought, now he's awake and watching. Maybe he'd been listening all along.

Maybe he knew Amy was in the next room with a slack, stoned grin on her face, dying; that they were parking Broker in the woods where he'd freeze to death; that Allen was going to kill Hank's eyes.

"This isn't me," she told Hank. "Uh-uh."

Hank continued to stare at her so she amended her wishful declaration: "This isn't me most of the time. It certainly isn't who I want to be."

Shaking now, she went back into the bedroom and studied the IV hook up.

"Fuck," she said.

Fuck, fuck, fuck.

What if?

Experimentally, her Latex-clad finger curled around the back of the blue clamp, her thumb caressed the small white plastic wheel. She listened to Amy's thready breathing.

Why would she paint her fingernails a dumb color like that?

Her thumb debated, moving the wheel up and down. She saw how simply it worked. Flattening the tubing and cutting off the flow. All comes down to this cheap plastic piece of shit, probably cost eighty-nine cents, probably some nine-year-old kid made it in Singapore or China.

Fuck.

She thumbed the wheel up the track and then down the track. Up, down. She pulled away, nervously puffing on her cigarette, and left the white wheel at the top of the clamp. Off.

For now.

It'll give me a little time to think.

She went back in the living room and paced in front of the fireplace.

Allen was such a mixture of innocent lamb and cold, efficient operator. And Earl was all smiles, like a big cat who was lying back for the moment, sort of amazed by the machinations of this dazzling killer mouse who'd danced onto the scene. Who was trying to impress her.

And she knew what Earl was thinking: Allen was another loose end, a tricky one, for sure; but he'd have to be dealt with. She turned and saw Hank still watching her like an old billy goat.

"What?" she shouted at Hank's relentless eyes.

Two blinks.

"Oh Christ, when is this going to stop?"

Two more blinks.

She sat on the edge of the fold-out couch and toyed with the wrinkled sheet of paper that Allen had dropped. This insistent new sound whistled from Hank's mouth. A jerky panting sound.

Everyone else had; why not me? She started smoothing out the sheet of paper. Amy had this tall, bold way of printing; strong letters, upright, nothing weak about them. She was like Broker, probably—never sick, no flaws.

She could imagine them walking around in the fucking woods, being healthy together.

"Okay, okay," she said and let her finger linger on the alphabet game. Hank's eyes snapped from group to group and line to line.

"H"

"I"

"T"

"Hit?" she puzzled. Then she saw the longing in his eyes, shining through the clay of his flesh. Hank always could put a lot into a glance. And she wasn't so bad when it came to fast reading of a pair of eyes. She inhaled and exhaled in a very exaggerated manner.

Two blinks.

"You want a hit?"

Two blinks.

"Aw, God." She slid across the blankets, turned, and reclined next to Hank. She wished she could shake out her hair the way he liked. Yeah, well, she wished a lot of things.

"You and me, honey; like in *Casablanca*, remember, when smoking was sexier than sex."

She leaned over and, as she kissed Hank on his motionless lips, she felt his breath mingle with hers. Then, she turned her hand so the cigarette fit between his lips and sealed her cupped fingers over his mouth.

Bogey one last time.

Hank sucked in and the nicotine mushroomed in his lungs, invaded the air sacks, and pillaged through his blood, and he could feel his entire circulation system brighten up like a mile of Christmas lights strung through a bombed, blacked-out city. It made the sperm dust jump.

This was the tough lady he'd fallen in love with the moment he saw her walk into that church basement. He'd thought to soak in her like the proverbial fountain, but she was no fountain; she was a Raymond Carver short story when he met her, up to her neck in low-rent heartbreak, with the tatters of her alcoholism not quite tucked all the way in. Now here she was with her growing pains, stranded in a North Woods *Crime and Punishment.*

His heart began to beat faster. There wasn't much time left. And she was the only legacy he had.

Jolene lowered her head to Hank's shoulder and could have cried. But if she were the crying type she couldn't come out of this on top. Which she fully intended to do, one way or the other. So she appreciated the last hand Hank was playing, having his last smoke before they put on the blindfold. And now he was blinking again.

She removed the cigarette from his lips, flipped it into the fireplace, and held up the paper.

"A"

"L"

. . .

"K"

"I"

"L"

"L"

. . .

"E"

"R"

"L"

. . .

"W"

"A"

"R"

"N"

"What am I supposed to do? This isn't exactly an ideal situation."

"G"

"E"

"T"

. . .

"T"

"O"

. . .

"F"

"I"

"G"

"H"

"T"

. . .

"U"

. . .

"W"

"I"

"N"

*Oh, shit. Hank felt the control slipping away as a flutter of color
blotted his concentration. Coming to smother him. He blinked wildly.*

"What?" Jolene yelled. The paper was starting to come apart,
damp from her sweaty hands.

"S"

"A"

"V"

"E"

. . .

"T"

"H"

"E"

"M"

"Easy for you to say," Jolene said, and then she saw his eyes revert to their loopy aimlessness. She shook his shoulder. "C'mon, Hank, don't go away now. Christ!"

She got up and hugged herself in front of the fire. Looked past the kitchen, at the hall to the bedroom where she'd paused Amy's slow-motion Fentanyl toboggan.

Save them. How? Allen had the plan. Earl had the gun.

But Hank was right, it wouldn't be that hard to get them going at each other.

But Allen was the only one who could fix Hank's eyes and keep all the secrets safe.

But what if Allen didn't disable Hank's eyes. What would Hank say then? See, that was the rough part—she didn't know.

Staring at the flames, she imagined the opposite of fire. And that's what was going on out there in the dark. Broker's body was slowly filling up with ice-cold. The diving-seal syndrome. His fingers and toes would go first, freeze white and hard as piano keys as the blood drained from his extremities and pooled around his heart and lungs. It would abandon his brain and would make a last-ditch stand in the engine room.

Gee, all the neat stuff I've learned.

He lied to me.

The bottle of scotch they'd used to marinate Broker shimmered in the firelight, on the desk next to the fireplace. With his fingerprints on it.

She stared at the rubber gloves on her hands. They made her feel removed from life. A ghost. Not really here.

Johnny Walker Red Label.

Festive.

She'd never liked scotch. She'd liked invisible alcohol that didn't overpower your breath. She'd been a vodka drinker. Sneaky. Vodka Seven. Gimlets. Fruity tastes.

Story of your life with Earl. Sneaky.

The whole idea with Hank was to get away from that.

Look at it, two-thirds full. A color somewhere between piss and raw gold.

How long is it now, Jolene? Fourteen months?

I came to believe that a higher power could restore me to sanity.

A sane, safe little sheep, following Allen and Earl to the chunk of change at the end of the rainbow. She'd get her wish, she'd be a rich wire mother.

Jolene shuddered.

The warm part of her, the cloth mother trapped in the bottle, called out to her. She peeled off the rubber gloves and reached out her hand.

Chapter Forty-eight

Jesus, what a night for cold-blooded murder.

Allen and Earl stood talking about how they were going to do it. Their freezing breath mingling with car exhaust in the crossed high beams of the Cherokee and the Saab. Broker was slumped in the passenger side of the Jeep, his cheek flattened against the windshield.

The Fentanyl for Amy was clean, almost like extreme medicine; but this was killing a man.

And Allen, who had Hank's cryptic message streaming with a coldness all its own inside his mind, was very aware that once the killing started there were no rules governing Earl and Jolene, beyond sheer self-interest and the reach of their arms and what they held in their hands.

And Earl had the gun.

Such was the flavor of Allen's thinking as he discussed how Broker would die.

"So, how exactly are we going to do this?" Earl standing there, no hat, with his blond hair frizzed out wild; he looked like a lame Nazi rock star in the outlandish, one-armed black leather trench coat.

Allen kept staring at Earl's sternum, bare; the young, healthy skin fogged with red chilblain under the clumsy coat. Back in the lodge, in his medical bag, Allen had a scalpel. Easy in under the sternum and up, prick the heart. He'd bleed out internally. Less mess.

Which left the problem of disposal. Allen shook his head; he was becoming disoriented by the cold. One thing at a time.

"We have to make it look like he lost control and went off the road."

"The road we came in on?" Earl asked.

"I think a secondary road in the woods would be better. We don't want him found right away. Something less traveled. With a sharp turn."

"Okay. What we can do is put him behind the wheel, wedge his foot on the gas, and hold down the clutch and put the Jeep in gear. Then we get back out of the way, use something—a stick—to pop the clutch, and off he goes into a tree."

"We just have to make sure it hits hard enough to shatter the windshield," Allen said.

"What if he wakes up?"

"With everything he's got on board? Plus, hypothermia tends to put you to sleep." Allen shook his head.

Earl grinned. "For a long fucking time."

"Let's get going," Allen said. *Lights*, he thought. *Music.*

A mile of back road from the lodge, Allen turned down a logging trail that was cushioned with frozen pine needles and leaves that crunched like cornflakes. He followed it along a swamp or the edge of a lake until it curved back into the woods. He slowed, and then crawled around a tight left turn and a down a short slope. At the bottom of the incline the road turned left again in front of a stack of pulpwood logs.

Six feet high, twelve feet long. Which was perfect—denser than a single tree, more mass targets to hit. And the frozen ground was virtually free of snow, just a few leftover clots like dirty melted marshmallows.

He stabbed his brake lights to alert Earl behind him. Earl stopped, cranked down the window, and leaned out. Allen had his window down too and yelled back, "This is it. Back up to the top of the hill. I'll go to the bottom, turn around, and put my lights on the pile of logs."

The Jeep backed slowly up the hill. Allen continued on, positioned his car clear of the turn, and left it running, lights on, so his high beams illuminated the target. Then he yanked six logs out in the top tier, so they extended and drooped like tusks toward the road. One of them was bound to come through the windshield and hopefully brain the driver. Then he jogged up the slope.

Earl had parked the Jeep just above the lip of the short hill, pointed toward the logs. He tried to pull Broker over behind the wheel. But his sling made it too awkward.

"You got to help me with this," Earl said.

Allen nodded and swiftly positioned Broker. Earl said, "I got it in neutral, so jam his right foot between the floor mat and the accelerator."

Allen accomplished this with some difficulty; it was a tight working space, it was dark, and the cold was dazing.

The engine raced.

"Okay," Earl said. "It's a nineteen-ninety model, so no air bag to worry about. Now we need a stick." So they hunted for a branch, discarded several, and finally a slightly bowed six-footer met Earl's approval.

"This is the tricky part. I'm going to push in the clutch with this stick and you have to shift into first and get back out of the way when I release the clutch. You ready?"

"Ready."

Their voices were magnified by the desolation and the cold. Allen could see sweat freezing on Earl's chin stubble and glisten on his abdominal muscles. How was he doing this without a shirt?

The Jeep's engine whined, being wound tighter and tighter.

And Broker was slumped forward in the harness of the seat belt. Allen could not see his face. Allen felt a nuance of remorse. Broker was the innocent bystander sentenced to die by the rules of triage.

"Here we go," Earl yelled. He eased up on the stick so the engine wouldn't stall, and, as the Jeep lurched forward, he yanked the stick altogether.

The Jeep rumbled forward, picked up speed, and plowed down the slope. Allen and Earl were already running downhill when it smashed diagonally into the pulp logs with a hollow thud of metal, frigid plastic, and shattering glass. The engine whined once and then quit.

Silent. A slight smell of burning electric circuits and one headlight still on, making a fractured pool of illumination.

"The light is good, lets the battery run out," Earl said.

Two of the logs Allen had pulled out ripped a long gaping hole in the windshield. Even better, one of them had struck Broker a glancing blow to the head and Allen had seen him jerk on his seat belt tether like a crash-test dummy. The driver's-side door sprung out, stuck open on its broken hinge.

Panting huge white clouds, Allen and Earl inspected the results. The ground beneath their feet was hard as brown, rippled iron and left no tracks. Broker now had blunt trauma to the skull going for him in addition to being drugged and gavaged with scotch. A thick curd of blood and torn scalp matted his left temple and eyebrow. A fast dribble broke out of the mess, streaked down his left cheek, and dripped from his chin. His dark sodden hair was spangled with flat, translucent pebbles of windshield glass. His breath made a trickle of steam. Allen wanted to be sure Broker was dying, so they stood for long minutes, stamping their feet and hugging themselves in the insane cold, watching Broker's life leak away.

"Look," Earl said, "his blood is freezing solid off his chin."

"Okay, let's go," Allen said.

They rode back side by side in the Saab, happy for the powerful heater, the comfortable upholstery, the solid performance that kept the wheels turning.

"There's something we have to talk about," Allen said.

"Oh, yeah?" Earl asked.

"It's about Jolene. When the insurance company sees that the anesthetist they're defending has committed suicide, they'll probably be in a mood to write a check. That will be tempting after what she's been through. You have to convince her to hold out. After tonight, Milt will be more determined to go for a jury trial."

"Which means a lot more money," Earl said.

"Which means a lot a more money," repeated Allen. "But there's a catch."

"Always is," Earl said.

"You have to move out of the house."

"So you can move in?" Earl laughed. "Look, I've already been through this. I understand, I'm out, okay?"

"Good. That way Milt will think he's easing Jolene away from your influence and under his own."

"Uh-huh. Somebody should tell him that Jolene is always under her own influence. Except when she was drinking. And if she hasn't reached for a bottle after what happened today, she never will again."

"But you see what I'm getting at?" Allen asked.

"Yeah, you and Milt want me out of the picture."

Allen laughed politely.

And Earl joined him, ha-ha. But then Earl surprised him with his answer. "I hear you. No bullshit, Allen, this is a class magic trick you put together tonight. You got us off the hook. And I won't fuck it up. But let me tell you one thing about Jolene. She's loyal. She and I have been on and off for years, but we always took care of each other. And we'll keep doing that. The question is, what are you going to do?"

"I'm doing it," Allen said.

"I mean, are you going to get moral qualms if the boy-girl thing with you and Jolene doesn't work out the way you want it to, which, count on it—with her—it won't."

"It's not like I want to marry her," Allen said.

"I hear you, look what happened to the last guy who did," Earl said with a straight face.

Allen attempted to control the mirth welling up on his face and then decided, no, it was spontaneous, and that was part of the reason he was in this. So he let the laughter come out.

Earl joined him and soon they were both caught in a laughing fit.

"I don't know if this is appropriate," Allen said, struggling to get his composure back.

"Why not, we're going to win it all. No need to be greedy, there's enough to go around," Earl said.

Allen drove the last mile back to the lodge trying to feel less paranoid about Earl. They got out and tramped up the steps.

"Okay, we clean up, bundle Hank back in the van, and go home."

"Sounds good," Earl said, twisting the doorknob.

Earl balked and spun around. "It's locked." In a sudden fit of anger he pounded his fist on the door. "C'mon, Jolene, open the fucking door. It's cold out here." Then he turned and smashed at the door with his good elbow.

Nothing.

Allen reached to restrain him. "Don't, you're leaving marks on the door, we don't want it to look . . ."

Earl flung Allen off. "Get your fucking hands off me."

"We can't afford complications," Allen shouted. "Stop trying to break in the door, it makes it look like somebody was here. It'll ruin everything we've done. What if there's an alarm?"

A thought briefly crowded the anger from Earl's eyes. Then he narrowed them. "There's no alarm out here. So what's going on?"

"I don't know. She locked the door."

They stood for a moment, shivering. Allen, stamping his feet, said, "Let's go back to the car and sit a minute; maybe she'll open the door. She had to hear you beating on the door."

They got back in the Saab and Earl turned on the radio and got some college station out of Duluth and he made an attempt to listen to a discussion of gay, lesbian, and cross-gender issues on campus. Rankled, he banged off the station.

"Jesus Fucking Christ, can you believe this shit? You know Bob Dylan came from up here? Now this?" He kicked Allen's dashboard. "Like fucking Iraq," he muttered cryptically.

Several minutes of very awkward silence went by.

"What do you think?" Allen asked.

"She's up to something," Earl said.

Allen said, "There's always an open window. My dad used to say that; let's try the windows."

They heaved out of the car, hunched their shoulders, and immediately began to shiver violently. "We have to take it easy, the cold is making us a little nuts," Allen said as diplomatically as he could. "You go around that way, I'll go the . . ."

"Uh-uh," Earl disagreed, and pulled the pistol out of his pocket for emphasis. "We go together."

Seeing the gun, Allen felt a deep tremor of fear start in his chest, and the wellspring of the stammer that had tormented the first sixteen years of his life started up. The procedure was starting to unravel into human-system failure. He nodded. "Right, let's go together."

Methodically, they began working their way around the lodge and found it to be a very well-built, one-story structure of cedar planks with tightly fastened combination storm windows. And all the curtains were drawn and the lights were out. There was a mud porch but the backdoor was locked.

Furious, Earl kicked at this rear door and screamed, "Jolene, quit fucking around. Open the door." He stepped back, squared his shoulders, and shook his head. "This is bullshit."

Allen watched it rear up, the thing he feared above cancer cells and hidden arterial bleeders—human irrationality—as Earl swung the pistol and shattered a pane of glass on the back door. He pushed the gun hand through the broken pane and twisted the doorknob.

"There, we're in."

"You cut yourself," Allen said in a dull voice, pointing to the red smear on the Earl's rubber glove.

"Just a nick," Earl said, moving into the a darkened room, feeling for a light switch.

"Don't touch anything. Let me bandage the hand and clean up the blood. It's evidence. Think."

Being in from the cold improved Earl's mood slightly but he still growled, "I'll think after I find what Jolene's up to." He eyed Allen suspiciously, as if to say: *What are you and Jolene up to?*

"Your hand," Allen repeated.

"Okay, let's fix it up." Earl had stopped calling for Jolene. Now they proceeded cautiously, turning on lights as they went. They moved from the rear of the lodge down a central hallway, past the door to the room into which they'd moved Amy.

Allen noted that the door was closed. As he went by he tested the knob. It rotated half a turn and stopped.

Locked.

But by then Earl was in the main room and had turned on the lights. "What the fuck?" he blurted.

Hank was gone from the daybed.

"The bedroom door is locked," Allen said.

"Jolene, goddammit!" Earl roared and moved his gun from the weak fingers of his left-hand sling, which had been carrying it, so he could hold the cut on his right hand close against his chest, to stop blood dripping on the floor. Heedless of the blood trail, now he transferred the pistol to his bloody right hand.

Allen, still stunned by the cold, struggled to recover his concentration. Flashes of personal terror helped. He had to think. He had fallen in among the patients and his plan had collapsed for want of qualified help.

He moved swiftly to his bag, knelt, and forced his stiff fingers to function. He took out sterile gauze pads and a roll of adhesive tape. Earl watched him intensely; but not so intensely that he saw Allen slip the scalpel, handle down—a number-ten blade in a number-three holder—up the cuff of his jacket.

But then Earl held up his hand in a less hostile, moderating gesture. Allen came up from a crouch, balanced on his toes, with bandages and tape in his left hand; the haft of the slender stainless steel knife rested out of sight, just above his right palm. He steadied his eyes on the red skin just below the notch of Earl's sternum.

"Wait a minute, wait a minute," Earl said, his eyes swelling.

"What?" Allen asked.

"The scotch. It was right there," Earl pointed to the desk next to the fireplace. His face was pained.

"So?"

Earl shook his head. "Aw, Christ, *Jolene*? What a time to fall off the fucking wagon."

Chapter Forty-nine

There was this sleep-ocean and he was sinking to the bottom, down in the dark where he bumped into fish without eyes, who were blind dreams.

The whiskey on his tongue tasted like cold kerosene. Dingleberries of frozen blood stuck to strands of his hair. Then, a dream with eyes swallowed him and he was surrounded by an empty playhouse where he was the only one in the audience, while up on the stage a cast went through the wooden motions.

And, ah shit, man, I've seen this one before.

Amy, Jolene, poor Hank blinking, Popeye the ostrich, and Earl Garf emerging out of the shadows with his hand upraised.

A bad play. Not quite real life. Real life came down to a question of altitude. Vaguely, Broker understood that he'd spent the last two years on his knees in a world that was three feet high.

No real life without kids in it.

No way.

Poor Amy. Poor Jolene. No kids.

Tried to live in their play. Fun for a while. Flirting. Sex. Some rough stuff.

But not real life. Uh-uh.

Real life was the sound of his daughter's voice; and the way it worked, just when you thought you were going to get a good night's sleep—every time . . .

Daddy, I need you, said three-year-old Kit.

Broker thought she might be calling out to him from the other side of the world.

And he just had to get up.

Broker unglued his eyes in a fit of uncontrollable trembling and wondered how the hell he got hair in his mouth, with clumps of frozen blood on it. His hair was too short . . .

Okay. So it was a nightmare, after all. A nightmare in which a flap of his scalp had ripped off and dangled down the side of his face, and that's how the hair got in his mouth.

And now he made out the faint twinkle of stars, but they were inches away, right in front of his eyes, and that had to be a bad sign. They should be up higher, over the black horizon with the other stars and the sickle moon behind the spidery branches of the trees.

With an extra-deep shudder he saw what an empty witch-tit woods it was; bleak enough to give a druid insomnia. Then he saw he was surrounded by shattered glass and the pulpwood log that had almost taken his head off projected through the windshield. Some twinkles of this glass fell from his hair, and he saw it was the worst kind of nightmare.

Your basic North Woods nightmare about freezing to death in a car wreck on the coldest night in history.

A tiny voice way down at the base of his brain hissed: *Move, dummy.*

Right.

He lurched against the seat belt, raised his hands, and found them frozen. Well, not quite; but definitely unresponsive. The individual fingers did not work and had joined together into a mitten-like flipper. His thumb refused to move. He raised his right hand and slammed it palm up against the steering wheel and felt excruciating, shark-bite pain. Good. Still some circulation left.

He moved the hand to the seat-belt buckle and . . . nothing happened. The opposed thumb, which separated him from other mammals, was no longer an option. He had a paw. In a few more minutes it would turn into a hoof.

He tried to picture Earl and the sequence of events that delivered him here, and immediately rejected the notion as a waste of time and heat. All he knew was now: shock, head wound bleeding, probably broken ribs, whiplash. And the biggie—hypothermia.

He was minutes—less—from passing out for good.

It was up to the lizard to save the human.

All he had was reflexes.

And a few old Indian tricks.

If somebody's going to kill me in the woods, give me a city-boy mouse-clicker every time.

Earl, you fucking dummy, you should have checked my truck. Broker shoved his petrified right hand into the back and levered up the rear-seat backrest. His numb fingers pawed on the stock of the Mossberg twelve-gauge that he'd loaded and prepositioned within easy reach, because—always go with your gut—he was worried about Earl.

He herded, perhaps paddled, the shotgun forward and pawed it across his lap. Then he reached back, hooked a strap of the survival pack on his thumb, and yanked it out. Panting jerky clouds of breath, he pawed the bag to his chest and used his teeth to open the snap, fumbled inside, and found the haft of a Buck sheath knife. Using both palms and his teeth, he tore the knife from the scabbard. Then, with the knife awkwardly positioned between two hands frozen in an attitude of prayer, he sawed though the seat belt.

Faintly in the slender moonlight, he saw blood on the blade. Didn't feel the slash he put in his thigh.

Onward.

Tipping sideways, Broker fell through the open driver's-side door holding the knife, the shotgun, and the bag in his cramped arms, and crunched down on the icy ground. His insides milled around, confused; having fallen, he found it impossible to get up.

So here's the deal, which his dad had beat into him, and the Airborne sergeants at Benning had refined: *After* you die, *then* you get to quit.

Yeah. Yeah. Broker lurched up on elbows, blundered to his knees, and fumbled in the pack. There was a heavy fleece sweater, mittens, a space blanket; but he was too far gone for that. What he needed was . . . a flare.

He held the beautiful red cardboard tube between his palms—sulfur, wax, sawdust, potassium chlorate—and strontium nitrate for its own internal oxidation. This fucker would burn at 3,600 degrees Fahrenheit underwater.

Yes.

Urgent now, he left the flare with the shotgun and lurched forward on his knees because his feet wouldn't work, his ankles ended in wooden blocks. He'd adjusted to horror as normal working conditions for this night, so he didn't waste time being surprised when he saw that Earl had exchanged his warm boots for running shoes.

He tottered on his knees and fell against the crumpled front fender of the Jeep where one headlight still burned weakly. Thus illuminated, he knee-crawled past the pile of pulpwood logs to where the loggers had heaped the pile of slash.

He filled his arms with branches and knee-crawled back and heaved the thicker branches under the gas tank. Going back and forth in this fashion, his head was briefly occupied with warm hallucinations from his childhood. Hot chocolate. Toasted marshmallows.

Now he moved to the front of the Jeep and kneed and elbowed himself up between the stack of logs and the crumpled hood. Clamping his forearms and elbows, he hauled at the pulpwood. One by one, he yanked the tiers of logs forward, piled them on the hood and through the shattered windshield.

He rolled over, fell off the Jeep, and, as he studied his makeshift pyre, he entertained more childhood memories. "To Build a Fire," one of the first stories he'd ever read, by Jack London. Except that guy fucked up.

Not me.

His knees buckled and he toppled over and crawled on his belly, a crab shape shifting to a snake. He wormed his way to the pack.

Holding the flare and the shotgun between his palms, he kneed his way back to the pile of wood under the gas tank. It was too dark to read the instructions printed on the flare, but he knew they said, among other things: ALWAYS POINT FUSE AWAY FROM FACE AND BODY WHILE IGNITING

Just have to ignore that little bit of advice for now.

Broker couldn't use his hands for fine gripping, so he had to clamp his teeth on the strip of black tape on the side of the flare and yank it to expose the cap. Then, carefully, he bit down on the metal cap and pulled it off.

To ignite the torch he had to strike the friction surface on the top of the cap against the fuse end he'd uncovered. But right now, the friction surface was between his teeth, pointing down his throat. When he used his knuckles and his teeth to revolve it around so it faced out, the cap promptly froze tight to his lips and tongue.

But it was generally in the right direction.

Immediately, he gripped the flare between his palms and struck it like a fat red match across the cap in his mouth. The sulfurous whoosh charred his cheek and shot a fiery spout in the night. Broker dropped the flare in the wood under the gas tank, thrashed the frozen cap from his lips, and scuttled back with the shotgun.

Cradling the Mossberg in his elbows, he crawled away from the flames sputtering under the Jeep—six feet, seven, eight. Enough.

The flare might do the trick by itself. But the wood was really cold and the gas tank far away from the flame. He didn't have the time to wait and find out. So he rolled over, pawed the safety latch, and set the gun to fire.

Squirming now, he came around with the shotgun still cradled in one elbow and jammed his blunt fingers into the trigger guard.

All his life he'd lectured people about not riding around with loaded guns in their cars. And because he was basically a lizard right now, his memory was faulty. Had he jacked a round in the chamber in J.T.'s Quonset hut? Because if he didn't, there was no way, with these hands, he could work the slide and load one now.

Broker aimed the muzzle at the gas tank and poked at the trigger.

The gun kicked back and out of his elbow. But a streak of flame shot from the barrel and tore into the under side of the Jeep. For a split second the muzzle flash illuminated the piled logs and brush. A gasoline mist curtsied with the flare's chemistry. Then the gas tank erupted.

The explosion filled the woods with fire, rolled Broker over, popped his eardrums, and blistered his face.

He came up grinning.

Now *that's* how you build a fire, Jack.

But it was way too toasty, so he scrambled away from the blaze that now reached up twenty feet into the air, snapping and sparking through overhead birch branches.

He was in agony, of course, smashed between freezing and

roasting. He might lose fingers and toes. But he was back in the game. He thanked the lizard, proceeded up his brain stem, and tried to marshal conscious thought.

Earl. Somehow followed them.

If Earl did this then Amy and Jolene were in danger.

And Hank.

These thoughts, though dire, grabbed no traction on his shivering. More immediately he struggled to stand and tried to stamp circulation back into his feet. He managed one pirouette in front of the bonfire and toppled over. The blood in his hands and feet had turned to broken glass and needles.

Getting up, he noticed the reflection of the flames glitter beyond the trees. Lake ice.

And then Broker saw more lights appear across the lake. Squares of electric lights popping on. Windows.

Stamping, falling, getting up, he hugged himself and tried to flex blood back into his stinging fingers. Using his teeth, he managed to pull on woolen mittens from his pack. After working up the courage to explore the gash on his scalp, he pulled off a mitten and touched his fingers to his face. Nothing. Feeling ended at his wrists. He licked at the numbness next to his mouth and tasted blood Popsicles. Burnt steak from the flare.

His concern for Amy, Jolene, and Hank was still relative and dreamy, far removed from the local question of his own survival.

Then, a pair of lights beyond the trees caught his attention. They moved with purpose, slowly getting larger. A vehicle. But was it attracted by the fire?

Broker stamped and staggered and fell down and got up and waited as the headlights poked and lurched through the woods and materialized in the form of a Ford pickup. He hobbled to it as the driver got out and peered at him. They recognized each other.

It was Billie's neighbor, Annie Lunder, which meant that Earl hadn't hauled him very far from the lodge. In her late sixties, swaddled in wool and fleece, Annie had not changed one bit and was still edgy and mean as a doubled-bladed axe. She and his Uncle Billie had fallen out of love and hated each other since the Korean War— something about a property-line dispute and Billie marrying her sister, Aunt Marcy, now departed.

Annie winced, seeing his torn face in the firelight. "Philip Broker, you feral child; I swear you were raised by wolves. Look at you out here in tennis shoes in this weather. And playing with matches. What the hell are you trying to do? Burn down my woods?"

"Phone," Broker croaked. "Life and death."

"What's that?" she squinted, cupping one gloved hand to the side of her hat.

"Nine one one. Billie's lodge."

Chapter Fifty

She had grabbed Hank's legs and hauled him unceremoniously off the daybed, through the kitchen, and bumping down the hall into the bedroom. She positioned him with a pillow at his back, tilted against a closet door so he could clearly see her go to Amy on the bed.

"Okay, get a good look. Now you can be happy because we're all going to die when they get back." Jolene yanked the IV from Amy's hand. Christ, his eyes were rolling again. She didn't even know if he saw it.

Then, not even rolling. Shut. He now lay on the floor truly looking like a corpse. A few feet above him, Amy nodded on the bed, her breathing shallow and labored. A single tendril of blood marked her left wrist where the IV had been inserted. The plastic stent now dangled along her shoulder.

Jolene stood at bay, between them.

She held the scotch bottle in one hand and a shotgun she'd found in the bedroom closet in the other. Except the goddamn gun wasn't loaded because she couldn't find any goddamn shells for it. And the room was a shambles from her desperate search.

Fucking gun safety for you.

And looking for those shells may have been a fatal diversion, because she'd neglected to get her cell phone from the living room, and there was no phone in the bedroom and now they were in the house. She'd heard the glass break at the backdoor and heard the shuffle of their footsteps and their voices. Then she saw the door-knob twist. And the voices moved on, into the main room where they'd discover she had moved Hank.

Then they would be back.

Okay, she had to do it.

She raised the bottle, took a drink, and the whiskey surged in her throat, teared in her eyes, and caused her to cough. She set the bottle down on the floor and studied the door which was secured only by an old-fashioned hand slip lock. She picked up a straight-backed chair from next to the dresser and stockaded it at an angle, the backrest wedged under the knob. That would stop Earl for maybe half a second.

There was the window. Nothing but thermal glass and storms. She didn't see them trying to break in through the window on a night like this.

"Okay, now what?" she said to Hank's prone form. He'd apparently passed out from fatigue, so he wasn't even there to witness her one big moment.

"Just like a fucking man, build me all up and then—pfsst—go limp on me."

He'd never explained how there were no rules for this hero stuff; you kind of made it up as you went along. Being scared shit-less was the main thrill so far.

She appreciated the irony; how she had quit drinking to change her life. Now she was drinking to get the courage to really change it.

No, she was drinking because Earl would understand the behav-ior under stress. And when she drank she always went to him for help. God, if only there was a phone in here.

Get . . . them . . . fight.

"Okay, baby," she said under her breath. "I'm working on it."

It meant she'd have to open the door enough to show the gun and let Earl smell her breath. Oh, Christ. It all came down to that. Here we go. Bottom of the ninth, two outs and two strikes, and one pitch to decide the World Series.

She reached for the Johnny Walker and took another slug, a big one that flooded her with warmth. And the footsteps were coming back down the hall, no longer cautious shuffling, striding. Angry.

A fist pounded the door.

Earl.

All her adult life she'd had to anticipate and avoid Earl's anger. She had never manipulated it. Now it was the only way out of this mess.

"Jolene, goddammit, I know you're in there."

Earl. Real mad but, judging by his voice, trying to control it.

Good.

She put down the bottle and wracked the slide on the shotgun like they do in the movies because it sounds cool except, Earl always said, if you're in the shit it's kind of dumb not to have one in the chamber already and telegraph your position.

Silence after the mechanism. Like they heard.

Jolene blurted, "Earl, I got a gun in here. A shotgun was in the closet. I've been thinking, and no way I'm coming out if Allen is there." The slight slur and wavering control in her voice was real, not faked. Thank you, Johnny Walker.

"Open the door," Earl said.

"I don't trust him and the more you're around him I don't trust you," she shouted.

"Open the door, now!"

Jolene took a deep breath, removed the chair, shoved the lock latch, and cracked the door.

The big .45 came up smoothly at the full extension of Earl's right arm so the business end of the barrel made a cool circle against Allen's forehead.

Under his breath, Earl said, "Sorry, but you got to go along until I get her calmed down. Jolene management is an art I have spent a lifetime acquiring."

Allen stared at the door, at the sounds of the chair moving, the latch freeing up. He was not reassured. They were getting tricky on him. They were deviating from his plan, and now there was the wild card of Jolene's drinking on the play.

The door opened an inch, just enough to see one of Jolene's eyes over the huge tube of a shotgun that poked out at them. The sour musk of alcohol was unmistakable on her breath.

"Okay, Jolene, see?" Earl wagged the pistol in Allen's face.

"I'll only talk to you if we're alone," Jolene said.

Allen spoke up. "Jolene, put down the gun. Where's Hank?"

"Shut up," hissed Earl.

Jolene's voice was quick to capitalize on the edge of anger and frustration in Earl's: "Don't you see what he's doing?"

The pistol pressed against his forehead was a steel tether that held Allen motionless. The shotgun sticking out the door was pointed at his chest. They were ganging up on him. Allen felt a rivulet of nervous sweat streak down between the scalpel handle and the hollow of his right wrist.

So this is what it's like to be a patient. This was street surgery. He was on their level, which was the level of desperation and anger and drunken decision-making. He had lost control of the situation and was smack at the bottom of the behavioral ladder with the two classic caveman options: he could try to run or he could fight. Not fight conceptually, like with the Fentanyl. This time it was fight with his hands.

"Earl, honey," Jolene blurted. "I was so worried when you went off with him that you wouldn't come back." Her voice teetered on an alcohol crutch and was beautifully nuanced with fear, need, and tiny tugs of long-dormant affection.

"You and me," Earl said.

"There it is," Jolene said.

"For Christ's sake, you two," Allen's voice cracked with distress.

The hammer on the big Colt clicked back. "Hands on your head. Now slowly turn around." As Allen turned, the pistol left his forehead and returned as an insistent prod at the base of his neck. "Outside, Allen. Move," Earl ordered.

This numbing awkwardness must be shock, thought Allen. In disbelief, he raised his hands carefully, so as not to dislodge the scalpel. "I don't get it; I came all this way to show you a way out of this mess."

"Shut up. Now, real easy, get out your car keys."

"My car keys?" Allen gulped, uncertain.

They were into the main room now, heading for the door. Then they were outside where the cold clamped down, solid, crushing.

"Get out your keys and open the trunk of your car," Earl said.

Allen's teeth chattered as hysterical laughter almost took him, because he couldn't tell if his shaking jaw was the stammers or the temperature. He flashed on the image of his car in long-term parking at the St. Paul Minneapolis International Airport. A ripe smell would seep from the trunk around spring thaw.

"It doesn't have to be this way," Allen said.

Earl's reasonable tone was at odds with the impossible temperature, with his misshaped posture and attire, bare-chested in the heavy coat, the humped sling.

"Allen, listen carefully. She's got a gun and she's boozed up. And she's got Hank in there. She won't come out as long as you're walking around free. So I'm going to tuck you away for a while, disarm her, talk her down, and get us all back on the same page. We still need you to fix his eyes, right?"

"Why do I have to get in the trunk?" Allen protested.

"What would you prefer? More fresh air? How about I nail you to a fucking tree. C'mon—get in the trunk."

Allen stared at his car. He was certain that if he climbed into that trunk he would never get out alive. His eyes darted left and right. There was enough moonlight to make out a lattice of birch trees against the star-blistered sky. A dull glare of ice glimmered on the lake. A few feet away were bristles of frost-coated, weathered white planks. A sturdy boat dock extended twenty yards into the lake.

But the boat dock led nowhere. There was no place to run. Earl had the gun.

Carefully he lowered his right hand to his right jacket pocket and began to work out his key ring. As he did he let the handle of the scalpel slide down into his palm.

Allen had only a second to decide. He pulled out the keys, letting them jingle; then as he thumbed through the keys, searching for the right one, he fumbled, then dropped the key ring.

For a beat Earl's eyes followed the keys. Then he said, "How come you don't have your gloves on?"

In that fraction of a second, Allen let the scalpel drop from his sleeve. His fingers caught the familiar curved handle, twirled the knife, and, in one smooth decisive movement, he wheeled and struck upward at the notch where Earl's ribs joined over his diaphragm.

. . .

The moment that Earl marched Allen away from the door, Jolene slipped out of the room and shadowed them down the hall. As they went out the front door she tore through the main room, going through drawers, checking shelves, looking for a box of shotgun shells.

Nothing.

So this was making amends to people we have harmed.

With an empty shotgun. Right.

And all she had was part of the truth to go with. Even if it damned her. She grabbed at the phone on the desk, which was hard-wired so the emergency dispatcher could trace the call. Strangely, as she punched in the numbers, she was not thinking of Amy, or Hank, or Broker out there in the dark; she was thinking of that poor, dumbass NoDak store clerk.

"Nine one one," the operator said. "Is this a life-and-death situation?"

"They're going to kill us next," Jolene shouted.

"Who's trying to kill you?"

"One of them's a doctor. He gave the nurse an overdose of narcotics to make it look like suicide, and the guy who lives here—he drugged him and put him out in the cold to die. He's in a red Jeep. An old one. Please send me some help."

"Calm down, where are you now? What kind of narcotics?"

"Uncle Billie's on Lake One outside of Ely." Jolene held up the empty glass ampule. She wasn't sure how to pronounce it, so she sounded it out: "Fentanel, I think it says. Goddammit, hurry; we need cops and an ambulance."

The gunshot rearranged the flimsy architecture of her resolve and she screamed, "They're shooting."

Jolene dropped the phone, seized the shotgun like a club, and yanked open the door. There were witnesses and there were witnesses and, goddammit, it was time to pick and choose.

The problem was that when Allen spun to strike, so did Earl.

"Hey," Earl shouted, irritated. Swatting at Allen's face with the big pistol. He did not see the tiny wafer of the world's sharpest steel streak up.

But Allen was not used to sticking scalpels into moving targets. He attempted to adjust the angle of his thrust to compensate for Earl's sidestep. Earl grunted when the blade went in.

Shit.

Allen could tell by the tension on the tip that he'd missed the heart and hit the sternum and tangled into muscle.

Then the Colt exploded right in front of his face. Not aimed; reflex on the trigger.

Blam! And the cold shattered with the explosion because Allen's ears stung and needles of cordite pincushioned his nose and cheeks.

Blood was all over, slippery black, coursing over his hand, steaming and freezing on his face. He must have nicked an artery. Reassured, he withdrew the knife. Earl staggered back, his knees wobbling, but he swung the gun.

Allen ducked, dodged, and sprinted to the dock, the only way open to him. His hope was that Earl couldn't manage to turn, aim, and stay on his feet. And he was right, because Earl toppled over, falling heavily on his broken arm.

As Earl bellowed in pain, Allen's shoes pounded a creaky tattoo down the frosted decking. Left and right, moonlight reflected on glassy planes of ice. Would it hold him? Skim across that ice, double back to shore, hide in the trees until Earl lost consciousness.

Blam!

Ha. Missed.

The second time, Allen didn't hear the shot; he felt it rip into the back hollow of his left knee and tear out the side of the kneecap. In an air pocket of shock, he could clearly visualize the shattered bone, tendon, and torn muscle. Then the icy planks rushed up and smashed his face. He rolled over and saw Earl trying to get up. But Earl was so far away and Allen lost the sound. Time and space elongated. He didn't know how long he coiled there, watching Earl rise in slow stages like a drunken elephant.

But finally, Earl did stagger to his feet and lumber forward, waving the pistol uncertainly in front of him.

Then a glare of headlights blinded Earl and threw his shadow huge against the trees. Somewhere in that glaring light, Allen heard Earl shout, "Fucker, you cut me."

Allen giggled. Shock and now hysteria. Earl had fallen down again. *Bleed out, bleed out.* He marveled at the anesthetic virtues of physical shock; he felt no pain yet. So he scrambled crablike on two arms and one leg down the icy dock.

The lights went out. People were yelling. The dock planks shook under oncoming, trudging footsteps that were overtaking him.

"Okay, you," Earl suddenly loomed over Allen, blocking out the stars. Somewhere in that black mass Earl was pointing the pistol.

Allen kicked frantically with his good leg, hooking one of Earl's unsteady feet, and the gunshot jerked away. As Earl lost his balance, Allen kicked wildly again and slashed up with the scalpel, drove it into Earl's inner thigh and butchered through denim and muscle for the femoral artery.

Thick arterial blood sprayed his face and as he lurched back he saw another shape racing toward him. A familiar lily scent came through the bloody taste of sticky copper pennies.

"Jolene?"

But she raised the clubbed stock of a shotgun and smashed it at Allen's bloody face and knocked him into a whole new universe of suffering. Even as he reeled in pain, an airtight, rational pocket of his mind protested: *Jolene, I-I lov-ve you, this-s isn't fair. Look at all I-va-va da-done. I saved you. I set you up for life.*

Earl had collapsed on him, drenching him with blood, but something else. Allen's last kick had glanced up off Earl's chest and passed under his armpit and tangled in the sling, and now that Earl had toppled over double, the tightly knotted trench-coat belt had twisted with the sling and trapped Allen's leg and—oh, shit—the big klutz was falling off the dock.

"Jolene, help," he shouted.

Earl's dead weight was slipping toward the ice like entrails sliding from a gutted carcass. And he was pulling Allen with him.

"Jolene?"

She hit him again with the gun stock. No. Not hit. She figured out what was going on. She was pushing him with the gun, shoving him over the side. Prying him. Her eyeballs were focused tight-white neon.

"Bitch," Allen screamed.

It was a long way to the ice. Earl's body was heaped, facedown, piling up accordion-like three feet below the level of the dock. Allen's hips were hung on the edge. He seized a steel pipe that served as a piling with his left hand, and he raised the knife in his right hand to menace Jolene.

They both paused to gather their strength, eyes inches apart, the thick clouds of their breath mingling.

Then, Allen heard a crash and bubbly wallowing sound. Earl's weight cracked the thin ice and began to sink. Jolene swung the gun butt at Allen's hand on the piling. Unsteady, her first stroke missed. Allen's slashed back at her with his knife.

And he missed, too.

As she moved in to strike again, Allen instinctively let go of the piling and grabbed at her, clamped his fingers into the waistband of her jeans, jerking her forward, down on her knees.

They teetered on the edge of the dock, Jolene flailing with the shotgun, but feebly, in too close to do any damage.

Allen still had the dexterity in his hand to reverse the direction of the slim knife, twirling it daggerlike. He made a fist and swung overhand, throwing all his remaining strength in a powerful hay-maker. She shoved the gun at his face, blinding him momentarily. Amid a confusing lurch of movement, he felt the blade plunge deep, through muscle. He wrenched it free and struck again, overhand, and felt it sink past the muscle into bone.

Chapter Fifty-one

The closest phone was at the lodge.

Annie's truck headlights streaked down the driveway and he barely heard the shot through the ringing in his ears as they turned into the parking lot. That's when he saw Jolene bolt from the porch holding something in both hands. Trailing ragged jets of breath, she sprinted toward a hulking shape, and that was Earl staggering down the boat dock.

Broker couldn't open the door handle with his frozen paws. All he felt was a numb jarring back up his arm.

"Help," he yelled to Annie. "Open the open. OPEN THE DOOR!"

The truck was still moving as Annie leaned over and jerked the door handle. Broker rolled out and immediately collapsed as his numb feet failed. He yelled, "Get outa here. Somebody's got a gun."

He looked around. Where's Amy?

Then—shit. He picked up motion at the end of the dock. Someone crawling. Earl was after her, had to be her. So that's where Broker headed, following Jolene, but, Christ, his hands and feet were solid cubes and he toppled forward. He struggled up and tried to run on the wooden blocks. Fell again.

Get up. Save Amy.

BLAAM! Another gunshot whistled in the dark. He turned to Annie in the truck and shouted, "Annie, get out of here. Do it. *Now*."

She didn't need a second prodding. She floored it and reversed up the drive. And now he was alone and somebody had a gun.

Wonderful. He staggered on his square feet.

Voices now. But underwater voices. Slow, garbled.

Not just slow, frozen slow. Even more sluggish because ice cubes had replaced his brain. Each step required all his concentration.

Then he saw them outlined in silver moonlight, and the violent white smoke of their breath. Amy wasn't there. Now Earl was down and Jolene and Allen Falken were fighting on the end of the dock.

Allen? What the fuck . . . ?

Earl was tangled up with Allen somehow. Make that Earl's body, because it looked like Earl didn't live there anymore. His body had slumped over and was dragging them both off the dock. Jolene was swinging a shotgun at Allen. Allen was swinging back.

Broker kept lurching down the dock, dragging his frozen feet like Boris Karloff.

Then Earl's dead weight jerked Allen over the edge, which caused Allen to yank Jolene down in turn. Broker kept coming, slipping now in a lather of icy blood. When he saw the twinkle in Allen's fist, reflex took over and he dived as the knife streaked overhand.

Broker flung out both his arms to block and cover Jolene, and collided with the squirming bodies. A hot wire stung deep into his left shoulder, withdrew and struck again, going deep into his left arm above the elbow joint. This time it stayed put.

Pain was abstract; there was so much going around that this new arrival had to stand in line. Amy had said cold sequesters sedation. It sequestered pain, too. Or, maybe, after the last hour or so, pain had just become his natural habitat.

Allen's bloody hand slipped off the skinny haft and, desperate for purchase, he grabbed Jolene's shotgun with both hands. Jolene immediately released the gun and Allen slipped farther down, let go of the gun, and clawed at her clothing. Her shirt tore and her stomach trembled slick, fish-belly white. Her knees pumped, churning ice water in Allen's face.

"Please," Allen screamed as his weight, anchored to Earl, pulled Jolene farther over the edge, which jerked Broker over, belly down on the planks. Broker's right arm pawed for a grip, and, anchored around a piling, his left arm was extended across Jolene's chest and hooked under her chin. Jolene thrashed, hip deep in the water, and grabbed the arm with both hands. Her hold broke the flex of his elbow and she slid deeper into the water, and Broker pitched over with her.

He knew the water at the end of the dock was deep, perhaps twelve feet, and the ice, while thin enough to break under a falling body, was strong enough to hold somebody down who became trapped beneath it. If she went into the hole after Earl and Allen, she'd be gone forever.

Glacier water stung Broker's forearm and they all jabbered—wild—the North Atlantic protest-dialect of the drowning freezing. In the hoarse bedlam, Allen's face contorted in a forest fire of white breath, level with Jolene's squirming hips, splashing up to his neck in the black lake water and broken ice, trying to avoid Jolene's fierce kicks.

"Please!"

Jolene writhed on Broker's bad arm, going after Allen, kicking and kicking until his last scream ended in a thrashing garble of bubbles. Allen Falken's eyes bulged in disbelief as the water blinded him, and the weight of Earl's body slowly towed him down.

Utterly focused, Jolene kicked at the top of his head and deliberately held him under. It was dead, silent work punctuated only by the hysterical rasp of her breath and a stream of fading bubbles.

Then there was just Broker and Jolene and the vast silence that dwarfed simple words like *help*. And the burning stars. And then the urgent panic of their breathing resumed.

Allen's last drowning spasm broke her grip on Broker's arm. For a frantic beat Jolene turned and threw out her hands, trying to grab and climb Broker's hooked arm, but her hands slid off his icy sleeves.

When the water reached her lips she shouted, "No, goddammit!" She surged up reaching, and the pain exploded full red and grinding in Broker's left elbow, as Jolene's right hand caught behind the haft of the scalpel. She anchored her left hand across her right wrist and held on.

Then Broker felt a buoyant lift to the pain. Nothing was pulling her down anymore. She'd floated free from Allen's dead weight.

He tried to lift her, but his shoulder was stiffening and he couldn't move. If he released his hold on the piling they would both go in and under the ice.

Teeth chattering, they stared at each other.

He was back where he began, at the mercy of the glacier water, and he had lost his strength and she was dying by inches and degrees. Within his grasp.

"Try to climb my arm," he croaked.

She responded with a spasm of shaking. Then she gritted her teeth, let go with her left hand, and tried to reach past him for the dock, but it was too far and the effort almost cost her her grip on the knife imbedded in his elbow. She locked her left hand back on her right wrist. He saw she had no strength left.

"Hold on." His voice rasped like a frigid ignition trying to turn over. Hers wasn't much better.

She shuddered. "I'm good, I had a toddy." But he could see she was losing it, slipping into the water.

The stars were their sequined shroud. And dancing among them, Broker saw the blue shimmer of the aurora. Now red. Then red and blue together slapping the dark trees, rippling on the ice.

He had wanted so much to save her and here she was dying in his arms, starting to sag lower in the water as the scalpel blade began to work free. He should say something. He should . . .

The stark blank verse of police radio traffic intruded on his grave-side sermon. And he turned his face and saw that the light show was earthbound, financed by St. Louis County and originating from the rotating flashers on two cruisers, two ambulances, and a fire truck.

Many men's voices, now, shouting, breathless. Stabbing flash-light beams. Then the clump of pounding feet. The dock shuddered as several figures in tan and gray St. Louis County parkas belly-flopped on the planks next to Broker. Arms shot out, someone—maybe Dave Iker—clamped a hand into Jolene's short, icy hair, couldn't get a grip, and then grabbed her by the scruff of the neck and lifted her bodily.

As Jolene was hoisted from the water there was a moment when she and Broker were face-to-face. Her lips jerked, cramping her features into a horrible grin.

"Jesus, Broker; you look like shit."

More hands pulled them in, swaddled them with blankets. Broker rasped, "Jolene, what happened?"

"I called nine one one," she croaked back.

"But what happened?" he repeated.

She raised her face past him to the stars and, this time, all her facial muscles fired on cue and she did smile.

Broker held it together long enough to tell the cops to look for two bodies under the ice. Then they loaded him into an ambulance and the shock, the intense cold, and his wounds finally hit him. He stared at Hank, who lay asleep or unconscious on an adjoining stretcher, thought for a moment, and muttered, "We have to feed the birds."

A paramedic applied pressure bandages to Broker's head and arm, ran an IV, and, in the course of calming him down, gathered that Broker was referring to J.T. Merryweather's abandoned ostriches.

In the other ambulance, Jolene lay under blankets on her own stretcher and listened to the medics work on Amy right next to her. When they had stabilized Amy's vital signs, one of the paramedics turned to Jolene and asked her how she was doing.

And Jolene said, "I want to talk to my lawyer."

Chapter Fifty-two

Broker heaved on soft morphine waves. Eddies. He was reminded of the movie *Midnight Cowboy*—everybody talking at him, can't hear most of what they're saying.

"Well, it's about two weeks till deer opener," Dave Iker said, "and I figure, if all else fails, we can wire a stick to your stump in place of a trigger finger. You might have luck with that arrangement."

"Or," Sam, the giant deputy, said, "since you're now qualified on the car bomb, maybe we could find where the deer congregate and pursue that technique."

The jokes were getting old by his second day in a room at Ely Miner Hospital. He contributed drugged smiles and an occasional wiggle of his head. Otherwise they had him immobilized on the bed.

Amy was recovering in another room from the Narcan cocktail that reversed her Fentanyl overdose. Once Jolene walked by his bed with Milt Dane. Someone said the St. Louis County attorney had set up shop down the hall in another hospital room and Hank was blinking out a statement.

Two grand juries were in the works—one up here and another down in Washington County.

It was said that the wife's role in everything was murky.

In moments of lucid pain between morphine doses, Broker

recalled Jolene calling him out into the night and her shocked yell, "What's he doing here?" just before Garf hit him on the head.

Had she been clinging to his arm in fear or trapping his arm so he couldn't fight back?

Broker lay on his back with his arms and legs extended and elevated on cushions. A bald patch of his scalp was held in place by fifteen stitches. It felt like someone had launched a rocket off his charred left cheek.

The stab wounds in his shoulder and upper arm had been cleaned and lightly bandaged. Sterile gauze separated his fingers and toes, which were flushed a vivid pink and were bulbous with blisters.

The local cops had a pool going, betting on how many fingers and toes Broker would lose. Shari Swatosh, the paramedic, had signed up for the long-shot wager, opting for all twenty fingers and toes, plus his winky.

Dr. Boris Brecht had spent four years as an army doctor, most of them in Alaska with ski troops of the mountain division. He thought the pool was very funny. He wore a stethoscope around his neck, and a blue denim shirt with a Mickey Mouse decal embroidered on the chest pocket. He wagged his finger to reassure Broker. "Blisters that go all the way down to the tips of fingers and toes are good. Pink is good."

As he inspected Broker's bubblegum toes, he was mainly concerned about infection. Yesterday, when they'd brought Broker, Amy, and Jolene into Emergency, Brecht had immediately suspended Broker's hands and feet in a huge sitz bathtub. He'd kept the water temperature between 100 and 108 degrees. He'd cleaned and stitched Broker's wounds as he sat in the tub.

Through thick goggles of shock, Broker had watched his pallid fingers and toes slowly change from ivory to blush and start to sting as the blood crept back.

"Reaction to extreme cold varies from person to person," Brecht had explained. "Certain groups are more susceptible than others. Blacks are three to six times more susceptible than whites. People born down South are four times more vulnerable than people born up north. Genetically, people with type O blood are more predisposed to cold trauma than type A or B.

"Basically, you weren't out that long. And you'd ingested a lot of alcohol, and alcohol tends to dilate blood vessels. That's *not* a recommendation to drink in the woods.

"You might loose some fingernails and toenails but, as long as infection doesn't set in, you should recover full function. There'll be some minor nerve damage and your extremities will be more vulnerable in the future. Probably you should work on your coping skills when it comes to cold weather."

"Like Florida," Sam counseled.

Broker went out with the morphine tide.

He woke in the darkened room and heard a studied hush of machine-made beeps and sighs circulate in the corridor. Blue ghosts in white shoes drifted silently up and down the hall, passing his open door. One of them paused, looked in, and treaded soundlessly toward him.

Just a shadow at first, backlit by the hall lights. Then, as she emerged from shadow, he saw it was a lean woman, hatchet-faced, with her dark hair in a bun. And she held something in her upraised hand. Broker's heart began to beat faster when he saw it was a syringe and nurse Nancy Ward was coming right at him.

Sequestered, Amy's word again. It felt like his fears and his facts were suspended in morphine free fall. But then Nancy smiled warmly and push the shot into his IV and he felt the latest gentle wave lift and cradle him.

"You know what I think," Nancy said, as she checked his dressings, his blisters, took his temperature, and checked his pulse. "He just thought he was so damn smart and we were a bunch of hicks up here. Doctor Mister Allen Falken. Well, you and Amy showed him, didn't you? Turns out he was just another dip-shit swampy."

Broker smiled, a nodding idiot smile he'd mainly seen on people he had busted.

Nancy adjusted and fluffed his pillows. "The word is the reporters are going to start showing up tomorrow, but it's pretty much over; Mr. Sommer, I mean. He did his blinking for the prosecutor and now he's slipped into a coma for real."

In the Temple of Morphine, there is no bad news. Broker continued to smile.

"You just lie back and take it easy, because you have a visitor," Nancy said.

Then Nancy disappeared and another slender blue figure took her place. Amy's hair looked out of place and her face was pale, like the Roto-Rooter had been through her entire circulation system. She had a plastic bracelet on her wrist and an IV in her arm, just like he did, except her IV bag was on a stand that rolled on casters beside her.

"We have to stop meeting in this place," Amy said.

Broker grinned.

"God, look at you. I'll bet you haven't smiled this much ever. Listen, I talked to Boris and he says your hands and feet—don't worry, you're going to be fine."

She paused, picked up a sippy cup with a flexible straw from the bedside table, and held it to his lips. Broker, cotton-mouthed, gratefully sucked the ginger ale. "Have to keep your fluids up," Amy said, then she put down the cup.

"One of the paramedics told Dave Iker you were babbling about ostriches, so Dave came to me and I explained about the farm. So Dave called down to Washington County and your friend, the sheriff, had a deputy go around to J.T.'s neighbors and find a guy who knew how to watch the place. The birds are all right."

Broker continued to grin.

Amy cocked her head. "Jolene told me it was the baby monitors."

As Amy talked, Broker tried to fit his mind around the story according to Hank. The whole thing about Allen giving the wrong meds. Garf and Stovall.

Broker tried to listen from behind his soft morphine window. Maybe this was what it was like for Hank. People talking at him.

"The St. Louis County prosecutor asked the questions with an alphabet board. Hank blinked back the answers." Amy clicked her teeth. "They were pretty short answers. How Jolene got Allen and Earl fighting each other. But there were these gaps . . ."

Broker couldn't stop grinning.

"Like, how did they control Jolene? Or was she playing along for time? I guess we'll never know because her lawyer cut an immunity deal for her to testify before the grand jury."

Amy held up her hand and rotated her palm. It didn't mean anything to Broker. Amy shook her head. "I forgot, you're drunk. My fingernails. She came by to check on me earlier this evening. She brought polish remover and new polish. She painted my fingernails red . . ."—her non-IV hand floated up—"and she put up my hair."

Broker grinning, long-glide. Hair?

"Jolene and I don't have a lot in common; she didn't exactly graduate from Women's Studies, did she? All I know is, she saved my life."

At some point, she went away and left him alone to ponder simple things; Jolene saved Amy and he saved Jolene. And nobody saved him, this time, except himself, and that's the way it should be.

In the morning the morphine tide went out and Broker was beached on dry pain. Pain brought the virtue of clarity. And the scent of lilies.

When he opened his eyes she was standing looking down at him. She seemed to have grown an inch and maybe it was her posture, like she'd laid down something heavy. Maybe it was him being flat on his back.

Milt Dane stood in the doorway; floated was more like it. He wore recent events strapped to his back like a jet pack, and he tended to zoom around a few inches off the floor. A layered legal situation was taking shape in which he represented Amy, Nancy Ward, and Jolene against Allen Falken's insurance underwriters.

Probably it was just the residual morphine, punching up the edges and textures, that made Jolene look like a page out of the kind of glossy magazine that he never read. He'd heard about Madison Avenue sneaking tiny, subliminal death heads into images of invincible beauty. But he didn't see any grinning skulls in her green eyes.

Milt must have brought some of her clothes because she wore perfect-fitting Levi's, a white T-shirt, and a short leather jacket. Her face glowed, baptized in glacier water and born again clean. They stared at each other for a long time and his eyes were full of questions. Her eyes brimmed, but not with answers for him.

"So what do you think?" she said.

Broker thought about it. "I think you were more implicated in what happened than Amy or myself could testify to." Her lawyer was present. Broker didn't really expect a reply. So he summed it up. "I'll never know if you did the right thing or just the smart thing."

Jolene smiled, and all Broker learned from her smile was that she was deep enough for mystery. She patted his cheek. "Hank used to say, 'I didn't make the world.' Well, I didn't make the world, either, but I'm sure as hell going to live in it the best way I can from here on out."

She bent forward and kissed his forehead. "Another thing, be patient. I think your wife's going to call. A smart woman doesn't leave a guy like you loose for long."

Probably she was right. Then she turned, and it was clear from her expression that she was busy and had places to go. When she left the room, Milt came over to Broker's bed and gently touched his undamaged shoulder.

"You're not such a bad guy for an ambulance chaser," Broker said, "but the next time you want to take a canoe trip, tell you what—don't call me."

Milt squeezed the shoulder. "Thanks," he said. His eyes drifted to the doorway where Jolene had disappeared. "Without you, we would have lost her."

Broker nodded and for a moment he absorbed the low-key, leaving-on-a-jet-plane vibrations Jolene and Milt put out. Then he asked, "Hank?"

Milt looked away, shook his head.

Broker nodded again. Then he inclined his head and his eyes toward the doorway. "Like I said, watch yourself when you get in among those rocks."

The exhausting ordeal with the letters had ended. He'd done his best and then his mind had just turned to sand. Whatever happened now, it would happen without Allen and Earl. And without him.

Jolene had taken her first steps and would just have to take her chances. Just like he'd have to take his chances with whatever came next.

He had come full circle. Milt and Jolene tucked him in and hov-

ered for a moment over his bed. Then, slowly, they backed away and turned out the lights.

So he waited in the dark. Beside a trail he knew it would come down.

At first it was just a color—yellow—and then, as it moved closer, it assumed the shape of a man. He understood this was merely manifestation; the way he chose to experience it.

So he made himself tidy inside and remembered the first time he'd seen it coming, calm, like this. All the other times it grazed him with a lurid action beat: shock, fear, pain, adrenaline hemorrhaging, and the brimstone reek of cordite.

It had been on a late morning when the air was the color of steaming tea. This yellow blur floating against the ferrous-red dirt and all the green God ever made. It was hot that day. The sky was the blue heart of a Bunsen burner. They were sweaty and dirty and dressed, as usual, to kill. They were sprawled along the path, taking a break next to baked, fallow fields that were cracked and choked with weeds.

And Hank and his squad were kin to the weeds: poisonous, itchy, and bristling with stickers. They had all gotten so dirty they would never be clean again. And then they saw the yellow come floating, a man in saffron robes and bare feet.

Gook in the open.

Reflex rifles came up, the solitary figure filled a few peep sights.

Hey, man, check this dude out, someone yelled, the way he walks.

It's cool. Just one of those monks, walking.

The peeps moved off.

And he came on with his shaved head and his bare feet and his saffron robe swaying and his sturdy brown arms swinging. A man who moved like a clean, upright flame. His clear brown eyes focused right through and beyond them, like they were mud from somewhere else that had gotten out of control and had acquired guns and airline tickets to his country. And Hank had remembered absolutely recognizing how this guy knew exactly what he was doing. He was walking one hundred percent present in the moment and every one of them watching were wishing like hell they were someplace else.

Absolutely perfect goddamn walking.

Just look at the way he placed his foot in the dust, the way his heel came down and then his instep, and the ball and then the toes. This guy could teach the world to walk.

They'd watched him come on, one step at a time, and by the time he passed them they were all up on their mud feet.

Eyes right.

Hank was a grown man the day he learned to walk. And he never forgot the presence of that moment and how it had a one-pointed heft and carry to it; simple, like a country song about a hanging in the morning.

Tried to live his life that way.

Maybe he'd managed a few gestures that came close.

And now he just had to put one foot in front of the other.

So . . .

When you walk, walk.

And when you fight, fight.

And when you live, live.

And when you die . . .

Acknowledgments

This story happened because many people took the time to explain and show me what they do every day. Herbert Ward, M.D., chief cardiothoracic surgeon at the V.A. Medical Center, Minneapolis, and Lori Harris, CRNA, helped assemble the starter materials.

Dave Akerson, former St. Louis County deputy, and Pat Loe, a pilot at the U.S. Forest Service Seaplane Base in Ely, Minnesota, talked me through the ropes of wilderness rescue procedures.

John Camp, Craig Borck, and Chris Niskanen were good company on a long, wet, cold moose hunt in the Boundary Waters Canoe Area.

Ronald E. Cranford, M.D., assistant chief, Department of Neurology, Hennepin County Medical Center, took me on rounds. Marsha Zimmerman, RN, also at Hennepin Country, explained general emergency room procedures.

Sheriff Jim Frank, Washington County, Minnesota, again patiently answered questions about law enforcement, and Washington County deputy Larry Zafft provided pointers about computer crime.

My neighbor, Don Schoff, walked me through his ostrich operation, Schoff Farms, in River Falls, Wisconsin, and reacquainted me with bringing in a hay crop over a long summer.

My cousin, Kenneth Merriman, M.D., A.B.O.S., A.A.O.S., at the Hastings Orthopedic Clinic, Hastings, Michigan, fielded medical questions as did Boris Beckert, M.D., of the Stillwater Medical Group, Stillwater, Minnesota, and Brian Engdahl, consulting psychologist at the V.A. Medical Center, Minneapolis.

Special thanks to Kevin J. Bjork, M.D., general surgeon at the Stillwater Medical Group, for taking me along on a surgeon's day in the OR; and to Jeff Reichel, CRNA, for tips on anesthesia and for troubleshooting a draft of the manuscript.

Bill Tilton continued as a rock of support and critical reader.

Literary snipers Kim Yeager and Jean Pieri ruthlessly flushed out and liquidated macho overwriting.

Larry Miller contributed the title on short notice.

Sloan Harris at ICM and Dan Conaway at HarperCollins made sure I got my exercise and taught me that a writer can pass through the eye of a needle.